the trouble with christmas

the trouble with christmas

AMY

USA TODAY BESTSELLING AUTHOR

ANDREWS

Entangled Publishing, LLC
2614 South Timberline Road
Suite 105, PMB 159
Fort Collins, CO 80525
rights@entangledpublishing.com
Visit our website at www.entangledpublishing.com.

Amara is an imprint of Entangled Publishing, LLC.

Edited by Liz Pelletier
Cover design by Bree Archer
Model Photographer: Wander Aguiar
Cover images by
rcreitmeyer/Depositphotos
bluejayphoto/Getty
Metallic Citizen/shutterstock
karandaev/Depositphotos
Interior design by Toni Kerr

Print ISBN 978-1-64063-819-8
ebook ISBN 978-1-64063-820-4

Manufactured in the United States of America

First Edition October 2019

ALSO BY AMY ANDREWS

This book is dedicated to all the Christmas freaks out there. You are my kind of people.

CHAPTER ONE

Joshua Grady—Grady to all who knew him—didn't want much out of life. Just this ranch, Sunday night football, and to be left the hell alone. At thirty-five, with twelve years in the military, including a tour of Iraq and two of Afghanistan, he figured he'd earned the right.

He was a goddamn war hero. He even had a shiny medal and a fancy piece of paper from the government to prove it.

Unfortunately his uncle, who owned the ranch, had other ideas.

New tenant incoming.

Grady scowled at the text. Then scowled at the plume of dust advancing in the distance as a vehicle made its way slowly down the rutted road leading to his cabin. Jamming his Stetson on his head, he strode out to the porch, his big hands curling around the circumference of the rough-hewn wood of the railing as he sucked in the frigid December air. His scowl deepened, and Grady shoved his hands on his hips as the car rounded the bend and appeared from the center of the dust.

He blinked twice at the beat-up old van with lurid green and pink panels emblazoned with huge yellow flowers. *Jesus.* It was the Mystery Machine. And about as out of place here in rural Colorado as a tractor on Fifth Avenue. The vehicle pulled to a halt and the engine cut, and Grady half expected Scooby and the gang to tumble out as the door opened.

They didn't.

A woman slid down from the cab. Grady had been expecting a woman—Susan something something, his uncle had informed him when he'd arrived to get the cottage ready yesterday—but it didn't mean he had to like it. Living outside Credence meant not having to be sociable with anyone, least of all a woman who filled out blue jeans in ways that made him remember how much he liked women in denim.

Grady had decided a long time ago on a solitary life and was *not*, consequently, settling-down material, despite his well-meaning uncle's assertions about the joys of holy matrimony. He'd sure as hell stayed away from Credence during the summer when a nationwide ad campaign had brought busloads of single women to the small eastern Colorado town, hoping a few might stay and make Credence their home—and some of the Credence bachelors their husbands.

A couple of dozen *had* stayed, but he wasn't interested in any of them. Or this woman, either. He'd told his uncle repeatedly the last couple of weeks that he didn't want the cottage rented to some artist, and it was hardly his fault accommodations were scarce due to the sudden spike in population.

That ridiculous ad campaign hadn't been his idea.

But the land—several thousand acres of it—including the cabin *and* the cottage belonged to his uncle, and Burl Grady had the final say. Not that Burl had ever played that card until now, but it was the first time in three years Grady had regretted knocking back his uncle's very generous offer to sign over the ranch to him forthwith rather than waiting for it to come to him in his uncle's will.

He had enough money to buy his own damn ranch but his uncle had wanted to retire, and taking over the reins had been the one way Grady could think of to repay his aunt and uncle for stepping up during the worst time of his life.

Except now he had to put up with Little Miss Blue Jeans for a month.

She didn't see him as she walked toward the white fence that partitioned off the field to the front of the cabin, but Grady couldn't look away. She was hard to ignore. Her hair was contained in a bright-green knitted hat, so he had no idea whether she was blond, brunette, or redhead, but her knee-high Ugg-type boots and her sweet rounded ass swinging in those jeans were way more fascinating anyway.

Neither short nor tall, she was amply proportioned, a fact emphasized by her leaning on the top rail of the fence, which pushed out her ass. Grady shut his eyes. He'd never gone for skinny—he liked fullness and curves and this woman needed a flashing neon sign attached to hers.

Opening his eyes, Grady diverted his gaze, concentrating instead on seeing the vista in front, a sight of which he never tired. A couple of his horses grazed in the field on the grass that was getting sparse now, given the onset of winter. He'd need to feed them later but, for a moment, he forgot his chores and the angst about his unwanted guest and sucked in the deep, clean air of eastern Colorado.

The sky was a brilliant cloudless blue, the winter sunshine more for show than effect, given it was a brisk forty-two, but they'd forecast snow for the next week, so he'd take the sunshine—weak or not. Too soon the sky would be bleak, tree branches would be a parched frozen gray, the fields blanketed in white.

Right now, there was still a tinge of green, and the sight of it filled him with a sense of belonging so profound it swept his breath away.

Even if there was a woman in blue jeans messing up the picture.

Blue jeans and no coat—just a thin-looking long-sleeve T-shirt. For God's sake, she was going to freeze to death out here.

As if she knew he was thinking about her, she moved back from the rail a pace or two and slowly turned in a circle, her face lifted to the sky, her arms outstretched. It was the kind of pose kids adopted when it was snowing, opening their mouths to catch some flakes. She wasn't opening her mouth, but she appeared to be trying to catch some sunshine.

There was nothing particularly remarkable about her face. She wasn't stunningly pretty or ethereally beautiful or even chipmunk cute. She was kind of average-looking. Not the sort of face that launched a thousand ships. More…girl next door.

That should have made him feel better. It didn't.

It was on her second turn that she spotted him standing with his hands on his hips, staring at her like some creeper, and she gave him a little wave. Grady didn't return it.

"God…sorry," she called. An easy grin spread over her face as she broke into a half jog.

"You must be Joshua." She pulled to a stop at the bottom of the four steps, her warm breath misting into the cool air.

Her cheeks were flushed and her nose was pink and there was absolutely nothing average about her eyes. They were lapis lazuli, and they looked at him with such frankness, like they were assessing him and not just physically but mentally, cataloging and memorizing every single detail, even the ones he didn't want anyone to see.

"Grady," he ground out, feeling exposed and pissed off that this woman who couldn't even *dress for the weather* and was driving a *cartoon car* was having such an effect on him. "People call me Grady."

If she'd picked up on his surliness, she ignored it, tramping up the stairs to stand beside him, holding out her hand to shake, which Grady took reluctantly. "I'm Suzanne St. Michelle."

She pronounced it *Su-sahn Saan Meeshell*, which sounded very posh and very French and made Grady think about French kissing and then just kissing in general. He dropped her hand.

What the ever-loving fuck?

"Man," she said, her accent 100 percent New York as she half turned to the view and inhaled deeply. "You're really living the dream out here, aren't you?"

Grady gave a ghost of a smile. He'd learned a long time ago that dreams were made of dynamite and horseshit. She didn't appear to need an answer, though, as she chatted on.

"It's so easy to forget in the city that there's all this space and land and sky. It's so flat, and there's nothing for miles except fields and cows and horses. They're such beautiful creatures, aren't they?"

Her question appeared to, again, be rhetorical, and she barely drew breath before leaping into a change of subject.

Christ. She was a talker…

"I bet the stars are magic out here, aren't they?" She paused to look at him this time but held his gaze only for a beat or two before she glanced back at the field and kept right on going. "Yep. No light pollution out here in the middle of nowhere. I bet it's dark as pitch in the middle of the night. It's the kind of sky that would have given van Gogh wet dreams."

She faltered slightly, barely a hiccup in time, just enough for her to frown slightly, like she knew she'd just said something a little inappropriate. But, flattening her hand against her belly, she forged on.

"And it's so quiet, no horns or traffic or blinking lights or sirens or crowds, or people for that matter. No background hum of chatter all around you. It's so…serene."

Yes. *Exactly.* Serenity. Something *Su-sahn Saan Meeshell* had pierced in about two seconds. Grady strapped on some mental Kevlar.

Suddenly, she turned back to face him with

those startling blue eyes, pulling her woolen hat from her head. Fine, almost white-blond hair cascaded around her shoulders like a flurry of snow.

Yep…there went his serenity.

"So…" She inspected his face before dropping her gaze to take in his plaid flannel shirt, his well-worn Levis, and his even more worn boots. "You're, like, a…cowboy? The real deal?"

Grady was silent for long moments. Was that another rhetorical question? When she continued to look at him expectantly, he answered. "I'm a rancher."

She wrinkled her nose in concentration. "What's the difference?"

"Ranchers ranch. Cowboys wrangle cows."

"Kinda like a shepherd?"

Grady blinked. "Sure." In the way a shark was kinda like a fish.

She was looking at him expectantly, those blue eyes trained on him as if she was waiting for him to elaborate, but Grady had just about surpassed his quota of words for the day.

"Okay then," she said after several awkward seconds of silence that she—*hallelujah*—didn't feel the need to fill up. "Your uncle said you'd show me the cottage?"

Grady nodded, grateful for something to do even if it did mean extending his time in Little Miss Chatty's company. He glanced at the van and tried not to wince. "Drive your…vehicle round back."

Thankfully she didn't talk anymore—no more questions or inane observations—she just took the two paces to the stairs and headed down. Maybe she'd used up her quota of words for the day, too? The thought cheered him as he followed behind her, his gaze looking anywhere but at the swing of her ass.

• • •

Van Gogh's wet dream? What the hell, Suzanne?

She cringed. But she'd always been the same when she was nervous, even as a kid. Filling silences with pointless chatter. And Cowboy Surly or *Rancher* Surly had gotten the full verbal-diarrhea treatment.

As soon as she was done unpacking, she was calling Winona to demand an explanation. Her friend, who'd come to Credence after the first single-women campaign had gone viral and decided to stay, had convinced Suzanne a change of scenery would be good for her muse and, god knew, a Christmas away from her parents' sterile, minimalist brownstone had been too good to pass up. Hell, she would have visited Winona on *Mars*. But her friend really should have warned her about Grady.

Suzanne wasn't used to speak-as-little-as-possible-while-looking-all-sexy-and-brooding men. Men in jeans with hats and big-ass belt buckles who had rough hands and looked like they knew how to chop down a tree, ride a bull, deliver a calf, light a fire, and build a rudimentary shelter.

All before breakfast.

Men with rugged faces and beautiful lips, who looked like they'd forgotten more things about the birds and the bees than she'd ever learned.

She was going to need a handbook for Grady, and hopefully Winona had a copy.

But Winona had been right about one thing. Her muse was definitely stirring. It had crept up on her as she'd stared out over the field at the grazing horses. That itch, that…compulsion to put the scene down on canvas. To memorialize it in oil. And it had positively *slammed* into her like a sledgehammer as her gaze had connected with Joshua Grady.

Everything, from the way his height and breadth had dominated the porch, to the squareness of his jaw, the worn leather of his boots, and that shiny belt buckle riding low between his hips, had been inspirational. Suzanne hadn't painted anything original in well over a decade, but those first few seconds she'd clapped eyes on Grady had been an epiphany.

Now *there* was a subject to paint.

It was as if the heavens had opened and glories had streamed down and a giant hand with an extended index finger had pointed at Grady and whispered, *"Him,"* in Suzanne's ear.

The prospect had been equal parts titillating and terrifying because landscapes were easy, portraits not so much, and she hadn't been able to decide whether to throw up or run away and hide.

The universe, however, had delivered verbal diarrhea.

Pulling her trusty old transport van up outside the cottage, Suzanne slipped out of the car as Grady was stomping his feet on the welcome mat and taking off his hat. Opening the door, he said,

"Ma'am," indicating that she should precede him.

Hot damn. He'd *ma'am*ed her. It wasn't the first time she'd been *ma'am*ed in her almost thirty years, but it had been the first time her clothes had almost fallen off at hearing it. There was something about the way this man *ma'am*ed that made Suzanne aware she had ovaries.

She walked into the cozy, open-plan cottage dominated on the far side by two large windows just as Winona had indicated. She knew instantly where she would set up her easel. Crossing to the windows — drawn as only an artist can be to light — she stared out over acres and acres of brittle winter pasture and, in the distance, a large section of wooded land.

"Bedroom's that way," he said from behind.

She turned to find him standing in the doorway, obviously not planning to enter. He pointed with the hand that held his hat to the left where she could see a bed through an open door.

"The heating" — he swiveled his head in the opposite direction, using his hat to again point to the far wall and the modern glass-fronted freestanding fireplace — "is gas." Switching his gaze to the kitchen area situated between the two windows, he said, "Kitchen should have everything you need. You have bags?"

Suzanne blinked at his obvious desire to be gone. It made her curious, and hell if it didn't make her want to paint him right now. From her vantage point, with the light behind him, he wasn't much more than a tall, dark shape taking up all the space in her doorway, but his presence was electric, looming.

But not in a threatening way. It was…spine-tingling, and her pulse skipped a beat, which made her feel like an idiot. She'd just met the guy. How freaking *embarrassing*.

"I…have so much stuff." Suzanne crossed to where he stood, determined to be businesslike to cover for her ridiculously juvenile response. "A couple of bags, a dozen canvases of varying sizes, about a zillion different paints, a box of books because there's nothing quite like the smell of a book, don't you think? My pod coffee machine because I'm such a caffeine junkie, and heaven help anyone who talks to me before my coffee every morning. Some CDs and a player, which I know is a little old-school, but Winona said the internet can be pretty spotty out here, and I *have* to paint to music because silence drives me nuts. Some groceries I picked up in Credence and—"

Suzanne stopped abruptly, aware suddenly by the ever-flattening line of his mouth that she was babbling. He was staring at her with an expression that left her in little doubt a simple "yes" or "no" would have sufficed.

He gave a brief nod and shoved his hat on his head. "I'll give you a hand." Then he turned on his heel and strode to her van.

It took the two of them fifteen minutes to unload everything. Fifteen long, silent minutes broken only by Suzanne occasionally directing him as to where to put something down. Sliding the van door shut with a muffled *whump*, he turned, his gaze settling on her face. The brim of his hat threw his face into shadow, which made him hard to read. But this close, she could see he had light-green eyes and some stubble. Short but enough to still feel rough.

"If that's all, ma'am, I'll be going?"

If that was all? Joshua Grady really *did not* want to stick around. Suzanne knew she was an average woman. Average height, average looks, average size fourteen who could probably stand to lose a few pounds from her ass and thighs—she was more pear than hourglass. Good teeth, nice smile, clear skin. She was…attractive at best. A six who could push herself to a seven, maybe an eight for a gallery opening or one of her mother's exhibitions.

She'd had boyfriends both casual and longer term—she was no blushing virgin—and she got along well with members of the opposite sex. But she wasn't the kind of woman to whom men *flocked*. She was pretty sure this was the first time she'd actually repelled one, though.

If only that turned off her muse. Unfortunately, *she* was a fickle little tramp and always had been. *And* she'd been MIA for a good ten years while Suzanne had reproduced other artists' works in the very lucrative field of museum and insurance-required reproductions.

Until today.

"Thanks so much, Joshua," Suzanne said. It would have taken her much longer to unpack the van without him, and it was appreciated. "May I call you Josh?"

The angle of his jaw tightened. "No."

Suzanne blinked at the blatant rebuttal and the

morphing of his face from craggy and interesting to bleak and forbidding. But even more intriguing were the mental shutters slamming down behind his pale-green eyes. Shooting him her best flirty smile, she attempted to make amends. She could flirt with the best of them if required, and she'd never met a man who didn't appreciate being the object of a little flirting. "Well…anyway…I'd like to make you dinner to thank you for everything. What are you doing tomorrow night?"

Grady clearly *did not* appreciate the flirting.

His brows beetled together, a deep *V* forming between them. "Look, lady." He paused and drew in a breath. "I know there was a whole single-women thing that happened here over the summer and that a lot of dudes around these parts are looking to get hitched, but I'm not one of them. I don't know what my uncle told you, but I am not in the market for a woman. Not for dinner or dating or a relationship or even a quick tumble in the sheets. I like peace and quiet. I like solitude. I've said more words today than I have all week. So you stay here"—he cocked his head at the cottage— "and I'll stay there"—he pointed at the back porch of his place—"and we'll get along just fine."

He drew a breath again, and Suzanne could do nothing but stare. It was the most animated his face had been since her arrival, and it was a thing to behold, his square jaw working, his eyes glinting with cold *steel*.

Suzanne blinked as realization cut through her artistic drive. Did he think she was here to… ingratiate herself with him? To…date him? Have *sex* with him? Did he think his uncle had pimped her out?

Did he think she was here to get herself *a husband*?

Jesus, what kind of Dark Ages bullshit was this? Sure, six months ago, the town may have been awash with single women looking for love, but Suzanne wasn't any part of that, and she most certainly wasn't here for a man.

A spike of indignation quickly flared into a slow, steady burn of anger. This dude's ego was as big as the whole damn ranch. And, flash of pain or no flash of pain, he could go and do something exceedingly sexual and anatomically impossible to himself. Suzanne narrowed her eyes, better to aim her death rays at him.

"Look, *mister*. This whole brooding cowboy act might work on some women, but I think I can *contain* myself around all your manly man bullshit, and here's a newsflash for you. I'm here to *paint* not *hook up* or trap some…*cowpoke* into putting a ring on it. All this *y'all* have"—she went deliberately *southern* as she gestured wildly around her—"is real charmin', but I'm a *New Yorker*. So yeah, you stay over there, and I'll try and resist the urge to leave love letters on your porch every morning."

She was breathing hard by the time she stopped, and her pulse was thumping like a jackhammer through her ears, but *man* was she ticked. He, on the other hand, appeared to be unaffected by her vitriol. Giving her a barely there nod, he pulled down on the brim of his hat.

"Ma'am," he said, then calmly walked away.

Suzanne watched him go, so damn pissed at him and his assumptions and how good his wide shoulders looked as he strode toward his cabin, she could barely see straight. Her muse, however, was popping champagne corks.

Which did not bode well.

Not for her *or* Joshua Grady.

CHAPTER TWO

Grady headed straight for his fridge and popped the tab on a Coors Light. He swallowed half the can before he drew breath, wiping his mouth with the back of his hand, irritation simmering through his blood. He walked out to the front porch and sat his ass down on the top step, staring out over the front field again.

A cowpoke? The woman had called him a *cowpoke*?! Okay, her word choice had been deliberate, but he *wasn't* some hillbilly cowboy.

And why on God's green earth did her opinion even matter?

So she had the kind of body that ticked all his *hell yeah* boxes. She had curves and thighs and hips his fingers itched to explore. She had eyes he could drown in. But he'd only just met her. *And* she drove the Scooby Mobile for fuck's sake!

How could anyone who drove a cartoon car be taken remotely seriously?

Yet his skin felt tight and itchy as he grappled to understand the clash of emotions battling like gladiators inside his chest. Half an hour in *Su-sahn Saan Meeshell*'s company and he was about as thrown as he'd been that time Valentine, his horse, had been spooked by a rattlesnake and tossed him on his ass.

And he didn't like it one little bit. Not from some mouthy blonde outsider who'd looked at him like he was a piece of chewing gum on her designer Uggs.

Okay, maybe he'd asked for the cowpoke crack. He had pretty much accused her of husband hunting and had all but pulled out his dick and pissed around his house to mark his territory, but that look in her eyes just before she'd asked him what he was doing tomorrow night had scared the bejesus out of him. Her incredible eyes had lightened and gone all teasing and, on the heels of calling him Joshua, calling him *Josh*, he'd panicked.

Gone on the attack.

His mother had called him Joshua. And Bethany, his high school sweetheart, had been the last woman—girl, really—to call him Josh. And they'd both died, along with his father, in a horrific interstate pileup in terrible conditions more than seventeen years ago. *December*, seventeen years ago.

Yeah. Merry *fucking* Christma*s*.

His cell vibrated in his back pocket, and he grabbed it, grateful for the distraction. It was another text from his uncle.

Suzanne settling in okay?

Grady gave a soft snort. She had looked very at home standing in front of the huge picture window of the cottage, the flat, brittle landscape behind framing her curves. He, on the other hand, was seriously fucking disturbed.

He tapped *yes* and sent it.

Burl's reply was instantaneous. *What's she like?*

Grady grimaced. Unprepared. Annoying. *Disturbing.* And his kind of hot. But Grady settled on something more neutral to send his uncle.

Chatty.

A crying tears of laughter emoji appeared on the screen. Burl may have been sixty-five, but he'd always been a gadget man. New tech had never fazed him. Grady would bet his last nickel his uncle was probably at Annie's at this time of day, enjoying his *retirement* from the ranch, eating pie and laughing his ass off, huddled over his screen.

Do you good to use your words. You're going to turn mute out there by yourself.

Grady rolled his eyes at his uncle's exaggeration. He shot off a quick reply. *People talk too damn much.*

Three little dots appeared on the screen as his uncle composed his reply. They wavered for long seconds as if Burl was writing a tome, but when the words appeared long moments later, there were only two. *Be nice.*

Grady didn't want to be nice. He wanted to get through this month like he did every December— as quickly as possible. Not entertaining some artist chick from New York City who used the words *wet dream* in casual sentences with people she'd only just met and had the most freakishly unsettling eyes.

I'll be civil.

Thanks to his military training, Grady had never promised things he couldn't deliver, and he'd already been not very nice. He'd accused her of something he had no basis for and besmirched Burl's character in the process. His uncle was a good, decent, honorable guy who'd brought Grady to the ranch to live after his parents' tragic deaths and given him a way to channel his grief and anger that was productive instead of destructive.

He probably should apologize to both of them. But he wouldn't.

Burl sent a gif of Judge Judy rolling her eyes and, despite the situation, Grady cracked a smile as he shoved his phone back in his pocket. Somewhere behind him, he heard the sound of a car engine firing to life with a couple of sickly splutters and, a few seconds later, he was watching the dust kicked up by Suzanne's god-awful van as she left the property.

Grady perked up at the thought that maybe she'd decided her temporary landlord was too much of an asshole and to get out while the going was good. But he dismissed it quickly.

He'd never been that lucky.

• • •

Suzanne grimaced at the strong, bitter coffee a woman called Annie had just poured. It wasn't the sort she was used to; in fact, Suzanne probably hadn't ever ingested drip-filter coffee. Annie grinned and said, "Good for the digestion."

Winona introduced the women, and Suzanne blushed as her friend raved to Annie about Suzanne's talent with a paintbrush. "A painter, huh?" Annie glanced around at the beige walls that boasted some food advertising posters that looked as if they'd been there for a couple of decades and some framed black and white photographs of what she presumed was Credence town center back in the day.

"I'd always had a hankering for paintings on my walls. Just never got around to it."

"You've got a lot of places to hang art here," Suzanne said as she took note of the wall space. In her opinion, there wasn't a wall in existence that couldn't be improved by adding art.

Annie nodded absently. "You take commissions?"

"I do, but…" She doubted Annie could afford her fee. "I do reproduction stuff, nothing original." Hopefully that would all change during her time in Credence. "But I can definitely recommend someone to you if you'd like?"

"Ain't got a lot of money."

"That's fine. I know where all the bargains are to be had, too."

Annie beamed. "Thanks, I might just take you up on that. Pie's on the house," she added and shuffled off to her next customer.

Winona quirked an eyebrow at Suzanne. "Look at you go, babe. Already fitting in here."

Suzanne laughed and rolled her eyes before taking another sip of coffee and remembering she wasn't in New York anymore. "This stuff'll put hairs on your chest." Her voice cracked a little as the coffee coated her vocal cords on the way down.

Winona grinned across at her. "There's better coffee at Déjà Brew—that's Jenny Carter's new place down a bit farther. But the pie makes up for it."

Oh *hell yes* it did. This pecan pie was one of the

best things she'd ever put in her mouth—just as Winona had promised. Suzanne shut her eyes and moaned as the warm savory ooze of melted butter mixed with the sweet hint of maple syrup and the crunch of nuts slid over her tongue. Actually freaking *moaned*. She'd never tasted pecan pie like this, certainly never had it served with melted butter puddling on top of it, but *holy taste buds, Batman*, it was divine.

She was coming to Annie's every day for a slice of this artery-clogging heaven. Well worth the heart attack.

"So…how are you finding the cottage? Didn't I tell you those windows are perfect?"

The windows were amazing and the view spectacular. But… "I wish you'd raved less about the light and spent some more time giving me the lowdown on Grady."

Winona shoved a hand through her dark curls, scrunching her nose a little. "Burl's nephew?"

Suzanne nodded, absently wishing she had a mass of lush curls instead of fine, dead-straight fluff. She'd always envied Winona's looks and confidence and her ball-breaking attitude, refusing to be dismissed by people who were quick to disparage her for writing erotic romance fiction for a living.

"I don't really know him," she continued. "Burl was the one who showed me the cottage. I think Grady was in the barn or something. Why? Is he a pain in the ass?"

He was *something* all right. He'd sure made an impact for a guy who hadn't said a whole lot. Suzanne pursed her lips. "Let's just say for a man of few words, he managed to convey his displeasure over me being at the cottage loud and clear."

Winona raised an arched brow. "That doesn't sound very neighborly of him."

Suzanne almost laughed. "I don't think Grady does neighborly." Try as she might, she just couldn't summon an image of him knocking on her door with a smile and a basket of home-cooked muffins.

On the back of a horse in fringed chaps twirling a lasso above his head? *Yes.* In a field fixing a fence, his hat pulled low? *Yes.* Driving a tractor or some other big-ass bit of machinery with no shirt on? *Yes.*

Stretched out buck-naked on her bed with the light flooding in through the windows as he watched her paint? *Yes, yes, hell freaking yes.*

"You want me to talk to Burl?"

Suzanne shook her head and opened her mouth to deny the request, but a deep voice got in before she could say a word. "Talk to Burl about what?"

Winona smiled and stood. "Burl."

She hugged the older man, who was big and rangy, his frame still strong despite his gray hair. He had Grady's green eyes and a nice smile. "You must be Suzanne." He held out a weathered hand, and Suzanne shook it. "My nephew giving you grief?"

Suzanne chose her words carefully. "I...get the feeling he...prefers his own company." Burl *was* Grady's uncle, and he'd been good enough to rent the cottage to her, so it would have been rude to trash talk his nephew. Plus, this wasn't high school.

Burl nodded. "Yeah. He's a bit of a loner, I'm afraid."

The opening strains of The Eagles' "Desperado" played in Suzanne's head as she thought about Grady, a lone figure on horseback riding fences for the next three or four decades. It made her kinda sad.

"Will that be a problem?" Winona asked. "Is he…"

Her voice trailed off, but there was no doubt what she meant. Burl clearly took her meaning with no offense. "No. He's fine. It's just a tough time of year for him is all, and he likes his space after twelve years in the military." He nodded thoughtfully at Suzanne, his astute old gaze running over her as if she were a prize mare. "Do him good to have some company for a change."

Suzanne wasn't as confident about that as good old Uncle Burl. Grady had made it clear he didn't want anything to do with her, but she smiled and said, "Why don't you join us?"

"I'd love to, but my wife's the jealous sort." He cracked himself up, which left Suzanne in zero doubt his wife was the exact opposite. "I gotta keep going. Just came in to pick up some of Annie's cobbler. Best in the county."

"Best in the state, Burl," Annie quipped in a crotchety voice from over at the counter where she was taking someone's order.

"Yes, ma'am," Burl agreed, winking at Suzanne and Winona before bidding them goodbye.

Suzanne watched Burl head for the counter, aware of the weight of Winona's gaze settling on her profile. "Are you sure you're going to be all right out there, babe?"

Dragging her gaze off Burl to face Winona, she smiled. "Of course. I'm not worried for my safety." If anything, Suzanne felt safe as houses with Grady's brooding presence just down the way. There was something about the man that screamed protector. Probably those twelve years in the military. "I just wish he wasn't so…"

"Un-neighborly?"

Suzanne shook her head. Rugged. Capable. *Cowboy.* "Interesting."

Winona leaned forward, her curls following as a light switched on behind her eyes. "Bug-under-a-microscope interesting? Or hot-piece-of-ass interesting?"

Taking another mouthful of heaven allowed Suzanne to stall and forget for a moment about Grady's ass walking away from her earlier, cupped to perfection in a faded pair of Wranglers.

"He's very…manly." Which was a gross under-statement. Suzanne was sure he could probably impregnate the entire female population of the United States with just one of those long, silent looks.

"Ah. *Manly.*" Winona's lips twitched as the glint became a full-on blaze. "So a manly, surly military type? Sounds like an erotic author's wet dream to me."

Suzanne cringed at her friend's word choice, reminding her how badly she'd run her mouth. He probably thought she was a ditz. Or some sexually depraved *artiste* from the city who painted abstract shapes of a vaguely sexual nature. Like her mother. But his brooding silence had made her feel too awkward to stay quiet.

"Maybe you should take my bed at the board-inghouse," Winona continued, her voice light and teasing. "And I'll go live at the cottage."

No. The word reverberated around her skull, her muse jerking at the suggestion. She had no barometer for sarcasm. "I think I want to…paint him."

Even now, Suzanne's muse twitched restlessly, like a tempest beneath her skin. Images and colors, light and shadow, flow and symmetry swirled through her mind in a kaleidoscope of sensation that was dizzying.

That got Winona's attention. "Oh *really*?"

Suzanne nodded. "Yeah."

"That's great, babe," Winona enthused, her hands covering Suzanne's.

Winona, who had seen some of Suzanne's aimless doodlings one day, had always championed Suzanne's talent, convinced she was more than capable of being an artist in her own right. But Suzanne had been told a long time ago that she didn't have the raw gift her mother possessed, and she'd known it was true.

Sure, Suzanne could paint, she had *talent*, but a true artist needed more. Those mad scribblings she did late at night didn't count; hell, they weren't even *art*. They were just…exercise. All talent needed to be exercised. But her true calling was reproduction. Give her another artist's painting, and she could study the colors and the brushwork and the techniques and reproduce it perfectly.

Rembrandt. Gauguin. Turner. Monet. Kahlo.

Van Gogh. Cassat. Picasso. She'd done them all and more and been paid very nicely both from private collectors as well as publicly funded museums, art galleries, and other places that displayed priceless paintings.

Or copies of them anyway.

And she loved it. She loved her job. Who'd have thought art forgery could ever be a legitimate profession?

"I don't know." Suzanne withdrew her hands nervously. She didn't want to get too far ahead of herself. It had been so long since she'd painted anything original, she didn't know if she was even capable. And portraits were…tricky. It was best to stick to the landscape for now. "We'll see. Don't hold your breath."

Winona nodded, but she did an excited little squiggle in her chair anyway, and Suzanne laughed, grateful for the day they'd been introduced at one of her mother's art exhibitions in Chicago a few years ago. Suzanne had been instantly drawn to the older woman, who was loud and irreverent and spoke her mind. Winona was the real deal, and for someone who dealt in fakes for a living, it had been a refreshing change.

Suzanne usually headed to Chicago, to Winona's, in between commissions to clear her head. And this time, at Winona's urging, she'd come to Credence.

"So…" Suzanne shoveled more pie into her mouth as she glanced out the window at the afternoon shadows lengthening down the main street. "You're really going to stay here?"

Winona smiled and nodded. "I really am."

"It seems so…"

"So?"

"So *not you*. You've always been so…*Chicago*."

Winona grinned. "I *love* it here. I didn't expect to—I only came because I thought a bunch of bachelorettes coming to the ass-end of nowhere to hook up with a farmer would make a great plot for a book. But…" She shook her head. "It really crept up on me, and you should see the land I've bought at the lake. It's…everything I never knew I wanted."

Suzanne returned the grin. How could she not? Winona's was so infectious. "How long until the house is finished?"

"Benji was hoping to get it done by Christmas and before the first snow of the season, but…there are disadvantages to living in a rural area." She shrugged. "We're aiming for spring."

"And you can write in the boardinghouse?"

Winona had told her that several of the women who had chosen to make Credence home were still living at the boardinghouse that had been made available for them. "Mostly. Sometimes I go out to the lake and sit on the end of the pier if there's no one there." Her gaze drifted to the door, and Winona's expression changed. "Oh hello, here's trouble."

Suzanne frowned, turning to find a police officer—a seriously hot police officer—entering Annie's, taking off his *Top Gun* sunglasses to scan the diner. He removed his hat to reveal a buzz cut mostly black aside from the scattering of salt coming through the spikes of pepper. He had sharp cheekbones, and the fuzz on his head was mirrored by a five-o'clock shadow along the hard cut of his jaw as his gaze flicked over Suzanne, then zeroed in.

It was the kind of gaze that compelled confession.

He was tall and broad, his stride long and determined if just ever so slightly uneven as he headed in their direction. *Holy RoboCop, Batman.* "Who is that?" she asked, turning back to face Winona.

"That is Arlo Pike."

Suzanne heard the tightness in her friend's voice. "He an asshole?"

"Nah. Just a stickler for the rules, which makes him a little too uptight for my liking." Winona was more free love and artistic expression than laws and boundaries. She grinned suddenly. "And extra-special fun to rile."

"Something tells me he's not a man who's easily riled."

Winona shrugged. "That's what makes it so much fun."

Suzanne suppressed a smile. Winona liked to toy with men, mostly because she did not suffer fools gladly and too many guys made sleazy assumptions about what she did or tried to denigrate it or both. "He's a hottie."

Winona gave a brief nod, not bothering to deny the undisputable fact. "And he knows it." She plastered a beguiling smile on her face and said, "Officer Pike," as he stopped beside their booth.

He nodded stiffly and, in a no-nonsense voice,

said, "Winona." He clearly had no desire to tangle with her today. He turned his attention to Suzanne. "Excuse me, ma'am, I'm assuming, as you're the only person in here who's *not* a local, that the lurid green…vehicle in the back parking lot belongs to you?"

Suzanne bit down on a laugh at his clear distaste for her van. "Ethel? Yep, she's mine."

The officer blinked. "You named your vehicle *Ethel*?"

"Sure." She shrugged. "Doesn't she look like an Ethel to you?"

"No, ma'am." He looked like naming cars was a damn fool idea.

"Last I checked, Officer," Winona chimed in, "it isn't against the law to give your car a name, is it?"

"Nope, not illegal." Although his tone left neither of them in any doubt he considered it stupid.

"So this is a social call, then?"

Ignoring Winona's jibe, he met Suzanne's gaze again. "Your left passenger tire is flat."

"Oh." Suzanne sat up straighter. Shit… "I didn't notice anything. It didn't feel flat when I was driving."

"Might be a slow leak. If you give me your keys, I can change it for you and take it to the auto shop to be fixed."

If Suzanne's muse hadn't already fixated on a surly rancher, she might very well have swooned at this small-town hospitality. She couldn't imagine a cop in New York offering to change her tire.

"Slow day, Officer?" Winona dug some more.

"No bad guys to catch?"

He shot her a tight, aloof smile. "Bad guys fear me," he said with a confidence that bordered on arrogance but, Suzanne had to admit, was kinda hot. He held out his hand to her. "Keys, ma'am?"

"And what makes you think she can't change her own damn tire?" Winona inquired, arching her brow.

Suzanne had never changed a tire in her life. She definitely *did not* want to change this one, and she didn't care how un-feminist that made her. But Winona was on a roll, and Suzanne knew better than to interrupt.

"I don't know whether you got the memo or not, but women are perfectly capable of"—Winona lowered her voice and leaned closer to him— "looking after themselves."

"Yes. Thank you." The angle of his jaw went white as it tightened. "I've been on your website."

Winona's face lit up. "Really?" she purred.

"There was a pornography complaint." He smiled, obviously enjoying himself. "Just doing my job...ma'am."

Suzanne had never seen Winona speechless until now. For a second, her mouth just hung open before she laughed. "A pornography complaint? I hope you dismissed it."

"The Credence Police Department investigates all complaints thoroughly."

He sounded like a public service announcement, but Winona clearly had his measure. "I hope it was educational."

Suzanne swore she saw the faint twitch of Arlo's

lips before he turned back to her and the original reason for his stopping. "Keys, ma'am?"

Fishing around in her bag, Suzanne handed them over. "Thank you, Officer."

Arlo's hand closed around them. "Ma'am," he said and took his leave.

Suzanne watched him go. Officer Hottie's back view was as delectable as the front. So why was it Joshua Grady's ass and how soon she might be able to see it again, the only thing she was thinking about right now?

CHAPTER THREE

Suzanne woke the next morning from a night of disturbingly vivid dreams about her new neighbor and the compulsion to paint riding her hard. Normally her day didn't start until nine or ten and involved a lot of lazing with coffee and her favorite blueberry bagels, then a leisurely Uber to the loft studio her parents had bought for her in Greenwich. She painted until the light faded, then went home.

Next day the same. Rinse and repeat.

A commissioned piece of art could take her anywhere from a week to three months to complete, depending on the size and the purpose of the project, because Suzanne was damn good at what she did. She was careful and methodical, taking pride in every brushstroke, every color match, every subtle nuance of the original work.

Rushing wasn't an option. You rushed an artist, you got rotten art.

This was nothing like *that*. This was a wild frenzy in her blood. A jungle drum. A siren's call. She *had* to paint. Now. No lazing, no coffee, no bagels. No waiting for the sun to rise enough to create the perfect light conditions. She just had to put paint on brush, thanking God she'd decided to prep some canvases last night as she'd set the cottage up to her liking.

The subject? *Joshua Grady.*

Except Suzanne couldn't go there—she just

couldn't. He may be what her *muse* wanted Suzanne to paint, but her head and her heart did not. Could not. She'd come to Credence to tempt her muse with the kind of vastness she could see outside her windows. The faded wintery green of the grass in the field, the stark bare branches of the trees lining the drive, the lazy graze of animals, the arc of blue sky. The vista she'd been so enamored with yesterday as she'd slid out of Ethel.

She hadn't come to paint a...rancher. She certainly hadn't expected the whispers of a muse far more enamored with Grady than the starkly beautiful landscape. But she was the one in control here, damn it. She was in charge. And she would channel this sudden flush of creativity into bringing the landscape to life. Not Joshua Grady.

She *would* bend it to *her* will.

Because painting people—portraits—was difficult and, oddly, Suzanne felt like she had her training wheels on again. Sure, she'd *copied* portraits over the years, but that was easy—that was copying the artist's color palette and brushstrokes, not painting the subject. Because painting another person, re-creating their presence and their personality and that special *thing* that made them an individual was a real skill. One she didn't think she possessed anymore.

If she ever had.

One that required deep study of the subject. An intimacy that usually only grew from hours of sittings and close observation. She'd known Grady for less than a day. And just because he appeared to be imprinted on her retinas and her fevered nighttime imaginings were remarkably detailed didn't mean she was capable of doing him justice on canvas.

So she was *not* going to paint him. She was going to go back to basics. She was going to stand in front of this window, and she was going to paint what she saw. Landscapes were far easier to portray, and she was going to paint the hell out of one—paint until her fingers bled.

Her hand poised above the large canvas, Suzanne stopped. It was quiet. *Too damn quiet.* She crossed to the CD player and flicked through the offerings. Mostly she listened to different styles of classical music because her work usually involved pieces from a few hundred years ago, and the power and passion of Mozart or Rachmaninoff fit the times and the emotion of the works. Today she chose Gregorian chants because there was a freeness to the rhythms that was very reflective of the openness of the scenery outside the window. There was also a meditative quality that seemed to fit the majesty and mood of the landscape.

Suzanne cranked them up. It probably wasn't the kind of music people listened to at high decibel ranges, but as the chanting swelled around her and filled her head, it blocked out all the white noise of her doubts and insecurities and the furious whispers of her muse. It helped her find her center, to tap into the frenzy washing through her blood, to look out the window and let the frenzy guide her brush.

And, by the end of the day, whether it was good, bad, or indifferent, she'd have something that was *hers*. A Suzanne St. Michelle original.

She took a deep breath and dipped her brush into the paint.

• • •

Grady barely felt the chill as he stripped off his freezing, sodden shirt in the equally freezing concrete shell of the mudroom. The silence was distracting. Too distracting, and he could think of little else. The last three mornings, he'd gone about his chores serenaded by *chanting monks*. Which was strange but…whatever. It didn't bother him or the animals, and it gave his ranch hands something to laugh about.

Except now there was no music. And that *was* bothering him, because he suddenly realized he was thinking about her—something he'd been trying not to do. Had her power gone out? Was she sick? Had she fallen in the cottage and smacked her head on the stone floor? Had some kind of seizure? Was she unconscious? Had she decided to up and leave?

Yeah, right…he should be so lucky.

Grady shook his head, growling to himself as he flicked off the running faucet and plunged his hands into the steaming-hot sink of water, washing off the caked-on muck from his hands and arms and chest courtesy of a calf that had gotten itself bogged in a freezing quagmire caused by recent rain and melting almost-frozen ground.

He'd managed to rope it out with the help of two of his hands, its plaintive mooing and the distress of its mother keeping everyone focused on the job, but somehow, when they were almost there, he'd managed to lose his balance and fall into the frigid mud.

His hands had laughed their asses off as they'd dragged his out of the muck.

The hot water felt good on his chilled skin as he picked up the cake of soap and lathered his arms and chest and neck. He needed a real shower, of course, but he'd learned a long time ago to wash up before he went inside. The plumbing in the mudroom was way more forgiving than the more delicate pipes inside the cabin.

Thankfully his jeans weren't as mucky. Ordinarily he'd have stripped them off in the mudroom, too, and walked from the barn to the cabin in his underwear—isolated living did have its advantages—but he wasn't about to do that with *Suzanne St. Michelle* nearby.

And great…just great. He was thinking about her again.

He obviously wasn't getting laid enough. Just how long *had* it been since he'd been with a woman? Well over a year ago. Probably closer to two. Because that had to be it, that had to be the reason he couldn't stop thinking about the curvy New Yorker even though she'd stayed on her turf exactly as he had demanded.

Reaching with one hand for the fresh towel that hung over the hook above the sink, he pulled the plug with the other, then proceeded to towel dry. At least up until he heard a faint gasp and spun around to find the woman on his mind standing just inside the doorway, her curves hidden in a huge red coat, that green knitted cap pulled down low over her forehead and ears.

His hands paused mid drying the back of his neck. The room wasn't big, maybe five feet by five feet, which meant she was way closer to him than he was comfortable with, given his state of undress.

"Oh…I'm…sorry." Her breath misted into the frigid air as her voice faltered. "I didn't know you were in here."

Her eyes fell to his chest, zeroed in on the nickel-size scar just beneath his right collarbone courtesy of some shrapnel, before straying to his pecs and abs for what seemed like forever, the awkward silence stretching. Normally Grady wouldn't bother filling it because silences were where he felt most comfortable and the other person generally rushed in to fill them up. But Suzanne wasn't bothering, either.

At least not with her mouth anyway.

Her eyes were a different story. They were having an entire conversation as they roved all over his chest. She was looking at him like he was a slice of one of Annie's pies, and Christ if that wasn't like a bullet straight to his dick. The kind of friendly fire he could do without.

Fucking hell. He didn't want to be pie. Not *this* woman's. Not any woman's. He wanted to be…tofu. *Nobody* lusted after tofu.

"Had some trouble with a calf." Grady felt like an explanation might help the situation, but he still felt like an idiot making small talk.

"Was it being born?" She pulled her gaze from his abs to his eyes. "Did you have to stick your hand up inside and drag it out? I saw that on a documentary once and couldn't believe how messy it was. And how calm the mother was. I mean, I'm not sure I'd be okay to just stand there while someone stuck their entire arm up my hoo-ha, right?"

She hesitated for a moment like she'd done the first day they'd met, like she wasn't sure this was a topic for polite conversation. But her mouth had already committed, so she jutted her chin and went for it.

"I know it has to be done and, let's face it, a calf is much bigger than a man's arm—"

Her gaze dropped to his arms via the scar, his chest, and his belly button. She was looking at him like pie again. Annie's pecan pie with melted butter. Sweet and savory all at once. An orgasm for the tongue.

Not tofu. Plain, tasteless, *orgasmless* Tofu.

"Even yours," she continued, forcing her gaze back to his face, and it took Grady a moment to pick up the thread of her ramblings. She shuddered. "But no thank you. I mean, seriously, females of all species really do get a raw deal. I bet you if the males had to push out disproportionately bigger babies through the passage provided for the process, they'd have invented some kind of handy zipper system a long time ago. Some dude would have patented the bejesus out of it."

She stopped abruptly, snapping her lips closed as if her mouth had finally received the frantic *shut the fuck up* messages from her brain. Her cheeks looked pink, but then so did her nose, so it was probably just the nippy December weather.

Grady stared at her, not only at the amount of words she'd spoken but at the content of her monologue. "We…" He spoke because it felt like his turn, but he didn't even know what to do about cows with zippers. "We don't calve in winter."

"Oh, right." She nodded briskly, her cheeks definitely growing pinker now. "That makes sense. Who wants to be cold *and* in pain, right?"

She gave a funny little half smile that ended quickly and awkwardly. Then they just stood and stared at each other for several beats longer than was normal or even comfortable, their warm breaths misting into the air.

Tucking her hands into the pockets of her red coat, she said, "I hope it's okay to have a look around?"

Grady gave a brief, terse nod. "Just don't go too far or go near the animals." Last thing he needed was to rescue some damn fool city slicker who'd wandered off and gotten herself lost.

She nodded absently as her gaze drifted again, licking over his chest, lingering on the scar. He should be freezing, half naked in a room that was little more than an icebox, but with her looking at him like she was trying to commit every line and chest hair to memory, he only felt hot.

Really fucking hot. Melted butter on pecan pie hot.

"I hope—" Her voice sounded a little uneven, and she cleared her throat. "I hope my music hasn't been disturbing you the last few days."

He wasn't sure why she was making small talk—although it was preferable to incessant observations about cow hoo-has and zippers. Nor was he sure why he was standing ramrod straight in front of her, thinking about pie when he should be grabbing the spare shirt he kept in the cupboard above the washbasin and getting decent.

But up had been down since the moment she'd arrived.

"It's fine," he dismissed. It hadn't been the music that had been disturbing him, that was for sure.

She nodded again, glancing around the room briefly before settling her eyes back on his chest. "Well...I guess I'll..." She didn't finish the sentence as her gaze once again zeroed in on the scar, and her lips rolled together in contemplation. "Do you mind—?" She stepped forward and raised her hand tentatively.

When he didn't move because he was paralyzed by the realization she was actually going to touch him, she became bolder, stepping in closer again as her fingers made contact. She was so close now, he could smell her. Coffee and snickerdoodles? And something sharp, maybe chemical. Paint, he supposed.

"Is it a bullet wound?"

Grady flinched as she touched the scar, her fingers like icicles as they sunk into the small indentation. He closed his eyes as *heat* bloomed from the center, spreading like a ripple, burning like a furnace down the length of his body.

Blood pulsed hard and thick, *everywhere*. Damn it, she might as well be wrapping that cold hand around the throbbing hardness pressing into the zipper of his fly. It was probably forty degrees in this concrete box, but it felt like a sauna, and it was an easy 120 inside his boxers.

He swallowed. "It's from…shrapnel."

He had no idea why he wasn't stepping back. He should step back. He should have said, *Yes, I do mind*, told her it was *none of her business*. He should be finding a shirt.

Find a fucking shirt, idiot.

"Did it hurt?"

Surprised by the question, he glanced down to find the bulky knit of her hat a whisker away from brushing the underside of his chin. "Like a bastard."

She looked up and they were close—her *mouth* was close—her fingers a balm to the old wound that still made his shoulder ache on cold winter mornings. His heart thumped like a jungle drum and *god almighty*, it was hot enough in here to grow bananas.

"Was it bad? Did you bleed a lot?"

His throat was dry as the concrete beneath his feet. "It bled some." Then, finally getting his shit together, he took a step back, and her hand slid away.

If his distancing bothered her, she didn't show it, just simply said, "Thank you for your service."

Grady didn't know what to say. He *never* knew what to say to this standard platitude. He appreciated the sentiment, but he'd just been doing his job. So he nodded, his pulse reverberating like a dinner gong in his ears, as she slowly backed out of the room and disappeared from sight.

Reaching for the sink, Grady gripped the curved edge in both his hands and hunched over, dropping his head down between his shoulder blades and taking some deep steadying breaths.

January could not come soon enough.

• • •

Suzanne returned immediately to the cottage, her heart thumping as she tore off her hat and scarf and jacket with shaking hands. She *had* to paint Joshua Grady. She *needed* to paint him. *No more of the landscapes she'd been trying and failing to paint the last three days.* They'd been an exercise in frustration, so dull and lifeless, and she'd stopped and started so many canvases, it was demoralizing. She was beginning to think her mother had been right about original art not being Suzanne's strength.

But now... All she could think about, *could see*, was Grady stripped naked to the chest, an old shrapnel wound marring the taut perfection of his skin. He was a solid, silent presence in her head, beckoning her without even lifting a finger, both mirage and real all at once, and her muse was fully aroused.

Christ, she'd been totally deluded thinking she could control her, thinking *she* was in charge and not her muse. It was laughable that she'd ever believed she was at the helm of this creative imperative when she was actually at her mercy. The sight of Grady had been like rocket fuel to a muse that had been trying valiantly to take flight for the last three days.

Sweet, sweet Jesus, her muse was riding the kind of high people usually took drugs to achieve.

Suzanne crossed to the easel, putting up a brand-new five-foot canvas. Joshua Grady deserved a life-size canvas. Impatiently, she organized paints in the kind of frenzy that hampered productivity rather than enhancing it, but eventually she was ready to go. She just needed music.

Country music. It could be nothing else. Which was a problem because *Suzanne St. Michelle* did not own any country. Thankfully, the internet behaved, and she found a public playlist dedicated to country rock and she turned it up, the music amplified through her Bluetooth speaker. The roar of an opening guitar riff filled the cottage with a dirty kind of earthiness that reminded her exactly of Grady, and as a band called Rascal Flatts belted out about life being a highway, she made her first brushstroke against the canvas.

Suzanne didn't put away her brushes until one in the morning. She hit stop on the music, and it cut out as abruptly as it had started, leaving her alone in the stark silence of a rural Colorado night. She couldn't believe she'd painted all day. Suzanne had always just put her brush down as soon as the light faded and stopped for the day, easily separating from her work.

Even these past three days with her creativity running amok, she'd been able to stop.

She *never* got this way. Like a *real* artist. She knew people who did—her mother always sculpted obsessively when she was working on a piece—and she had friends who talked about the phenomenon, but she'd never experienced it firsthand.

Until today. Today she'd been *possessed*.

Her eyes were gritty, she was thirsty and hungry—she'd only eaten some Oreos dunked in milk all day—and she desperately needed to pee. Her jeans and knit top were streaked with paint, as were her hands and her hair and no doubt also her face. And now that the fervor had ebbed, she became aware of the chill inside the cottage, having not turned on the heating.

Her feet were sore, her legs ached, her temple throbbed, and there was a mild cramp in her wrist and an annoying twinge in her lower back. She was cold and hungry and aching. Put succinctly, she was abso-*freaking*-lutely wrecked. The kind of deep-down weary that invaded her bone marrow.

But she was *exhilarated*.

Her pulse was flying, and she was breathing hard as her gaze roamed over the canvas, over her first original work since college more than a decade ago. Her hands trembled a little at the thought. She'd done it. She'd *really* done it.

And it wasn't flat or lifeless. Joshua Grady *glowered* from the large canvas in all his glory, his eyes blazing with the same intensity of the day they'd met when he'd accused her of plotting to trap him into marriage.

Or whatever ridiculousness had been in his mind at the time.

The way she'd captured that look, that flare of *hell no* in his expression, sang to her. It was as if she was back outside with him, watching it happen all over again, and she shivered.

She breathed in and out with measured breaths as her bleary eyes roved over the intricate details of his face.

It could have *been* him, standing there, staring at her.

Or his head anyway. The body wasn't his. Her muse, inspired by the mudroom, had demanded she paint him as she'd found him—half-naked. But Suzanne had flat-out refused. As inspiring as she'd found Grady stripped to the waist, it didn't feel right to paint him *any* kind of naked. He *had* to be clothed. But her muse was a determined little vixen, and they'd waged an internal war for hours as Suzanne had worked.

In the end, Suzanne had been so damn mad with that persistent little voice, she'd deliberately attached Grady's head to Michelangelo's *David*— the big marble dude with the tiny weenie in the Galleria dell'Accademia in Florence.

She wanted naked? She could have naked.

And Suzanne had painted enough replicas of the statue over the last decade to make it an easy job. She'd been faithful to the statue, too, much to her muse's chagrin. Except for one addition—a knot of raised scar tissue just under the right collarbone.

Suzanne's breath went all funny remembering that moment. Remembering how still Grady had been, his face impassive as her fingers had explored the soft ragged pucker of the wound. Remembering how she'd been *compelled* to map it, to know its dimensions, its depths, and its boundaries.

Her pulse had skipped madly at her wrist and temples and washed through her ears at her daring. She'd felt jittery and short of breath, and her hand had shaken a little, but she'd not been able to stop the impulse. She'd half expected him to spring away at her tentative touch, but he hadn't. Not at first anyway. He'd just stood and let her explore, heat pouring off him despite the arctic feel of his skin.

Seeing that wound had made her hot and cold all over. The implications had rocked her to the core. What if it had been lower or to the left side of his chest? Or higher, getting his neck? Or his head? What if it had sliced through a vessel or ricocheted off bone?

She had to breathe in and out deeply and slowly to quash the spurt of anxiety.

Forcing her thoughts back to the painting—to her *baby*—she assessed it critically. For damn sure it wasn't *art*. Her mother would not be impressed. Simone St. Michelle had very definite ideas about what constituted art and what did not, and she'd waste no time pointing out that Suzanne's portrait was more…caricature than anything else.

But none of that mattered right now because, to Suzanne, this portrait was 100 percent Grady and very, very real.

And with the joy of that accomplishment swelling in her chest, she flicked out the lights, padded to her bedroom, stripped out of her paint-stained clothes, and collapsed on her unmade bed, burrowing her chilled body beneath the down duvet and falling headlong into sleep.

CHAPTER FOUR

If Suzanne thought she was one and done with committing Joshua Grady to canvas and that she'd be able to move on to something clsc, shc was sorely mistaken.

She'd woken with the same dire urge to paint thrumming in her blood and propelling her out of bed, but she'd had zero intention of painting Grady again. He and that epic battle with her muse were yesterday, and she was keen to move on.

But with Brooks and Dunn blaring from the speaker, it didn't take her long to realize it was Grady's eyes emerging from the canvas again. *What the hell? No.*

No. No. No.

But her muse giggled with excitement. She *freaking* giggled. *And* she had her way.

It was a strange conundrum. Suzanne feeling compelled to paint Grady again by her little internal dictator but not liking it, not one bit, pushing back as much as she could within the confines of the compulsion. Because it was impossible to have a career painting only this damn rancher, and she would not paint him without clothes no matter how much her muse begged.

By the time she was done, it had been another long day, pushing into the night as the music pumped around the cottage. Her body ached again, and her eyes felt like peeled grapes, but this portrait was even better than the last. Her chest expanded painfully as her gaze flowed over the granite stillness of Grady's expression. Yesterday's image had been the fiery Grady, annoyed at her presence. Today's was the gruff, tight-lipped cowboy.

The *rancher*.

Just to teach that interfering little hussy of hers a lesson, she'd attached Grady's head to a reproduction of *Vitruvian Man*—the iconic Leonardo da Vinci drawing of a naked man in two superimposed positions inside a circle. Grady's surly, silent expression and the shrapnel wound were perfect for the deep, dead-eyed stare of Leonardo's four-armed, four-legged man.

Not to mention probably being a little more accurate in the junk department.

But still, she sent a tiny prayer to the heavens for the gods of artistic pursuit to forgive her for both today's and yesterday's transgressions against *art*; then she cleaned up the paints *and* herself before heading to her bed and oblivion.

• • •

On the third morning, Suzanne was determined not to paint Grady. No matter how much it itched beneath her skin and her muse demanded it. She'd been determined to try her hand at the landscape outside her window again, and those first brushstrokes had been encouraging. But without her even knowing it, the strong ridge of his throat took form and shape before her and she was halfway done with his face before she'd even realized it was him.

Man…she was *pissed* now.

But Suzanne had the last laugh, flipping her muse off by placing Grady's head on a Botticelli-style cherub flying through a blue sky and puffy clouds, a bow and arrow poised to strike. The body was all cute and soft, in stark contrast to the hard planes and angles of the adult face and the brutality of that shrapnel scar. She'd even gone overboard and painted the slightest uptilt to his beautiful lips.

If her muse insisted on this repetitive farce, then two could play that game.

The next day, Suzanne didn't even try to resist the wild internal urgings to yet again paint the man whose face she was coming to know intimately. She just prayed at some stage that cold, hard bitch inside her would be satisfied, and then they could both move on. Until then, she'd continue waving the middle finger at her by refusing to succumb to her muse's pleadings to paint Grady's body.

So it was a no-brainer to turn back to Michelangelo, capturing the superlative magnificence of what was, by all accounts, his most famous fresco on the ceiling of the Sistine Chapel—*The Creation of Adam*. Suzanne was thrilled at how she'd nailed both the expression on Grady's face and the detailed musculature of Adam's reclining body as she replicated on canvas one half of probably the most iconic art image in the world—the touching of two outstretched fingers.

Except for the addition of that wound just

below the midpoint of the right clavicle, it was an exact replica.

Adam but not Adam. *Grady*. And it was perfect.

The day after, Joshua Grady's face got the Atlas treatment. The second-century Roman marble version currently residing in a museum in Naples—not the one standing outside the Rockefeller center.

Because, in this bizarre protracted arm wrestle with her muse, why the freak not?

She didn't do the flowing old-man beard, but the head was all Grady. Grady from the mudroom, his face rigidly impassive as he'd stood there and *endured* her touch just as Atlas endured *his* burden, knees bent, back bowed by the weight of it all.

When she was done, she congratulated herself on her choice, the stoicism of Atlas an appropriate match for Rancher Surly. And then there was Grady's scar, faithfully replicated as she'd done on all the others. It was a fascinating piece of anatomical precision that made the paintings feel more personal.

More Grady.

Her muse was unimpressed but hell, she'd made her bed. If she would just let Suzanne paint something else, anything else—*anybody* else—things might be different.

Placing her brushes in the sink, Suzanne wandered over to the other four paintings resting against the far wall, evenly spaced apart. Walking up and down the line, several times she eyeballed the art as Keith Urban belted out a ballad. From *David* to *Vitruvian Man* and the cute winged cherub to Adam and now Atlas, she didn't know how to feel about any of them.

This hadn't been her flexing her artistic wings—it had been some ridiculous power struggle with her muse. There wasn't much original here, just more replicating other people's work.

But...they didn't feel like reproductions—they felt fresh and new.

Because of Grady. Because of his eyes and his mouth and his cheekbones, the granite set to his jaw, the surly calmness of his expression.

And...the shrapnel wound.

"Enough now," she said out loud to the room. "Enough." Please, for the love of all that was holy, let it be enough.

Stretching her arms, Suzanne dropped her head from side to side to ease the kinks from her neck and shoulders. Standing in one spot for hours, her arm outstretched, was not good for the human skeleton. It caused all kinds of muscular aches and posture problems and, back home, she had a weekly massage session.

Suzanne doubted there'd be a masseuse in Credence. Maybe, if she kept up this pace of output, she could drive to Denver every week and get one?

But for now, most of all, she needed sleep.

Picking up the brushes she'd used over the course of the day, she cleaned them thoroughly and packed everything away, ready for whatever demands her muse would make in the morning. Inserting the plug into the kitchen sink, she poured olive oil over her hands and proceeded to remove the caked-on paint. It was much kinder on the skin and far less toxic than chemical removers. No doubt she had paint in her hair and probably on her face, as was often the case, but she'd save them for the shower.

Absently turning on the faucet to wash away the oil, Suzanne waited for the water to spill out and fill the bottom of the sink. And waited.

She got nothing.

Hmm. Trying again, she turned it off and then on again. *Still nothing.* One more time for the win didn't change the outcome, either, as she pushed her face close to the faucet, waiting for that first drip, trying to peer up to see if it was planning on arriving any time soon or if there was some kind of weird blockage. There didn't seem to be a blockage, and not even turning the faucet all the way on managed to produce a single trickle.

"No, please no." She swore under her breath. She needed a freaking shower, damn it. *Please don't let the water be off.*

Grady hadn't mentioned sudden cessation of water supply as a possibility. She knew they were out in the middle of nowhere, but still, this kind of thing didn't happen in New York. Not without warning anyway.

Damn the man.

Did he think his only responsibility as her landlord was to stand there all tall and brooding? With or without his shirt? *"Shit."* She thumped her hand against the metal of the drainer in frustration.

Heading to her bedroom, she sent up a swift prayer to the patron saint of plumbers—*was there a patron saint of plumbers?*—to please, please, please let it just be the sink. Not the shower.

Please, Saint…Cistern? *Not the shower*.

Striding into her bathroom, Suzanne opened the shower screen and reached in to turn on the faucet. Nothing. Freaking *nada*. She turned both hot and cold faucets on all the way, hoping it would make a difference. Still nothing.

"Double shit."

Turning them off with an annoyed twist, she reached for her phone in the pocket of her smock. Almost eleven thirty. Grimacing at the time, she sighed. She couldn't wake Grady now and demand he come and fix it. It was too late, and didn't cowboys get up at the crack of dawn to do all the macho cow stuff? He probably went to bed at sundown.

And what did cowboys wear to bed, anyway? Plaid? Fringed chaps? Woody from *Toy Story* onesies?

Nothing?

Suzanne blinked at the bizarre thoughts coming at her from left field. What the hell? She was obviously *way* more tired than she thought.

Or had breathed in a little too much paint thinner.

Go to bed, Suzanne. She looked longingly at the shower and sighed. It wasn't the first time she'd gone to bed without a shower. Hell, it wasn't even the first time *at this cottage*. But the water had better be back on by morning or she'd be hunting Joshua Grady down even if it meant saddling up a horse and going all cowgirl on his ass.

• • •

The water was back on the next morning, a fact that became immediately evident as a bleary-eyed Suzanne padded from her bedroom at just after six thirty, making a beeline for her coffee machine. About the same time she registered her feet were wet, the noise from the running faucet over the kitchen sink pierced her consciousness.

Suzanne glanced down, spying the water that was almost lapping her bedroom door, realizing that the entire flagstone central living area was one huge puddle.

Oh no, dear God no. What the fuck, Saint Cistern?

Galvanized into action, Suzanne dashed to the sink, splashing through a half inch of water. Making a dive for the faucet, she turned it off hard and pulled the plug. She must not have turned it off last night in her frantic on/off twisting as she'd pleaded silently to the universe to deliver water.

Shit. Damn. *Fuck.*

The water drained out of the sink with a final insulting gurgle, and Suzanne turned slowly to survey the damage. She wasn't sure when the water had come back on, but the puddle was widespread, making its way almost into her bedroom and all the way to the front door, soaking into the big old rug decorating the flagstone and…

Jesus Christ! Her paintings!

"*No*. Oh no, no, no," she whispered as she splashed through more water, her heart racing, bile rising in her throat. "Please don't be ruined."

Shit! Maybe this was some kind of divine retribution? Had the Gods of Art sent a flood to destroy her work? The sick feeling in her gut intensified the closer she got. She might have been conflicted over how she felt about the paintings but right now, they meant *everything*.

A bitter tang of relief swept her system as Suzanne realized the puddle hadn't yet encroached on her paintings. In another fifteen minutes, it'd have been a different story.

Snatching them up from where they were leaning against the wall, she lay two on the long kitchen countertop and the other two propped on the worn leather couches, little islands of high ground in the sea of water that had pretty much covered most of the massive living area.

Atlas Grady, enjoying the elevation of the easel, was obviously safe.

Suzanne took a second to let relief wash through her. Her legs shook, and she sat on the arm of one of the couches for a moment as the adrenaline ebbed.

That was the kind of near miss she could do without.

A sudden spike of irritation at Grady followed close on the heels of her relief. Yes, it was her fault for leaving the faucet on. And the plug in the sink. But damn it—why had the water gone off in the first place?

What kind of rental was this?

And how in the hell was she supposed to clean up so much water with the one lousy mop in the cottage? She didn't know, but she bet Grady did, and this was his cottage, so he could damn well help.

With the residual slick of adrenaline settling into her bones, she stalked to the door, splashing all the way. Yanking it open, she yelled, "Grady! *Grady!*" too irrationally annoyed to even feel the slap of frigid air on her bare legs.

Suzanne didn't need a mirror to know that her neck veins were probably sticking out. Hell, she wouldn't be surprised if she suddenly turned green and burst out of her T-shirt. Her mother would be horrified by her lack of decorum. She didn't care. Her paintings had almost been ruined, she wanted someone to rant at, and Joshua Grady was it.

"Get your ass over here now," she hollered.

She had no idea if he was at the house or the barn or out pulling some other calf out of a bog somewhere, but she was pretty sure he'd be able to hear her even if he was at the ass-end of the ranch.

Leaving the door open, she spun away from it as she surveyed the situation. Hell…where did she even start? The decision was clarified as her gaze fell on Atlas.

With the paintings, dear Suzanne, dear Suzanne, dear Suzanne.

The paintings!!

Shit, Grady *could not* see these paintings! He wouldn't understand. Hell, *she* didn't understand.

Hearing the slam of a distant door, the adrenaline rapidly reformed, hitting her system like a charge from a cattle prod, and Suzanne leaped into action, sweeping the paintings up one by one, sloshing through water as she carried them into her bedroom and propped them against the walls. She swore she heard booted feet on the flagstones outside as she whisked Atlas off the easel and made the last dash to her room.

• • •

Grady squared his shoulders as he glared at the open cottage door, bracing himself for entry. Not because he was worried or scared of whatever it was the damn fool woman was screaming her lungs out over. It was probably some poor spider she'd already scared half to death by her hollering. No, he was bracing himself for impact. He hadn't been able to stop thinking about the other day in the mudroom—or dreaming about it, for that matter—and, after another restless night, he was tired and irritated and not feeling too disposed toward Suzanne *fucking* St. Michelle right now.

Hell, if she'd yelled fifteen minutes from now, he'd have been gone for the day, and she'd have had to deal with her own damn spider.

But she hadn't.

Dropping his head from side to side, Grady stretched out his traps, psyching himself up for the encounter. Deep breath...*here goes nothing*.

Stepping through the doorway, Grady noticed two things. The enveloping warmth of the cottage that almost made him sigh in relief after even a brief sojourn out in the frigid air.

And the splash of water.

Puzzled, he glanced down at his boots and the puddle of water surrounding them. Puddle?

Glancing farther afield, he realized it was more than a puddle—a fact confirmed by the watery gray sunlight illuminating the large window opposite where an empty easel stood. Light reflected off the watery surface, and Grady realized it was *everywhere*.

What the ever-loving fuck?

A noise to his left drew his gaze as Suzanne appeared from the bedroom, pulling the door shut. Her face was flushed, and there was a smudge of blue paint on her forehead that was distracting as all fuck. He almost missed the mix of emotions playing across her face and reflecting in her blue eyes. Panic, distress, irritation, and, if he wasn't very much mistaken, guilt.

What had she done?

But that thought barely got out of the starting gates as his gaze widened to encompass all of her and any sense of rational thought fled. Her hair was in disarray all round her head, and he was pretty sure she had some streaks of paint in that, too. Even more distracting was her T-shirt boasting a Columbia University logo and *no bra*.

Yep—blue paint? What blue paint?

Grady didn't like to brag, but he'd been a champion no-bra detector in high school. It wasn't exactly something he'd put on his résumé now, but what could he say? He'd been fifteen and horny and obsessed with boobs.

Ascertaining whether or not a woman was wearing a bra at one glance had been his superpower. And Suzanne was very much *not*.

She was also sans pants, her legs bare, her

T-shirt just skimming the tops of her thighs, which were full and lush, following on from the curvy line of her hips.

Like one of those old fashioned pinup girls.

Christ. He swallowed. It was like the universe had decided this was to be his Christmas of temptation, peered inside his head, and produced a woman to his exact specifications.

Merry fucking Christmas, dude.

"You should have warned me I was going to need rain boots," he said.

Grady blinked. He had no idea where that had come from. What he should have said was, *What the ever-loving fuck, lady—you flooded my cottage.* It was what he'd planned on saying when he'd opened his mouth. But apparently you didn't have to be a horny teenager for no-bra to make you stupid.

She blinked, too, apparently as taken aback as he was. Fuck. *Get it together, doofus.*

"What in the hell happened?" he demanded. Better. *Much better.* Finally his testicles had dropped.

"The water went out."

Grady raised an eyebrow. "Doesn't look like it."

"Last night," she said, her voice testy, her lips pursed as she folded her arms crankily.

Oh, Jesus *have mercy, woman. Do not fold your arms like that.* Grady forced himself to keep his gaze trained steadily on Suzanne's face.

"When I was washing out my paints after eleven, there was no water."

"I had water at nine. It must have gone out after that." Grady shrugged. "It happens sometimes out here."

He felt the need to add that because she was glaring at him like the water going out and the subsequent flood at their feet was somehow his fault. They lived in a rural area—services sometimes went on the blink. No biggie.

"Still doesn't explain why half the water in Colorado is on my cottage floor."

She sucked in a breath. That was both bad and good. Bad because it emphasized how naked she was under her T-shirt. Like he needed a reminder. Good because it meant she was angry, and he'd rather she looked at him like he was everything wrong with the males of the species than look at him like he was pie.

Pecan pie with puddles of warm butter. Which brought him back to the puddle of water at his feet.

"I'd been trying to fill the sink to wash up. I thought I'd turned off the faucet."

"Clearly you didn't."

"Yes, thank you," she snapped with a mutinous glow in her eyes. "I can see that."

Grady shoved his hands on his hips as he glanced around, assessing the situation—anything to keep his mind off a pair of legs he suddenly wanted to feel wrapped around his waist. "Well… there's no real harm done."

She blinked. "Are you always this cool in the midst of…disaster?"

"This is a disaster?" In the realm of disasters, he'd take it over a tornado, the bottom falling out of the beef market, or a dose of mad cow disease.

"The cottage is flooded." She said it kinda slowly, taking care to emphasize each word like maybe she was talking to the village idiot.

Jesus, she was a drama queen. It was hardly Old Testament stuff. Which reminded him it was Sunday and that he should be in church being delivered from temptation. Instead of staring it down.

But he wasn't much of a churchgoer.

He mentally braced himself to return his attention to her person—her face. Not her legs. Not her no-bra T-shirt. Her face. And that streak of blue paint.

"The floor's waterproof. It hasn't reached the walls." If he was mimicking her slow, village-idiot cadence, it was her own fault. *She started it.*

"The furniture has wet feet and the rug's soaked through."

He shrugged. "They'll dry."

"Oh… Well…" She looked around like she didn't quite believe him. "Okay, then."

"Why don't you go and put on some clothes?" Grady held every muscle he owned in hard lock, his fingers biting into his hips as he fought the urge to drop his gaze. His jaw ached from clenching his teeth. "I'll get the wet vac. It shouldn't take long."

She looked down at herself, an expression of surprise flitting across her features as if she was only just realizing her state of undress. He suppressed the urge to roll his eyes.

"Oh yes, right." She glanced at him then, and there was a pinkness to her cheeks as she nervously pushed a hand through her flyaway hair, making things move interestingly beneath her shirt.

She was going to be the death of him. He'd

known her for a week, and she was already leading him around by his dick.

He gave her a brusque nod, turned on his heel, and left.

• • •

Grady was back ten minutes later with the industrial-size wet vac he used in the barn from time to time. It wasn't the cleanest piece of machinery he owned, but it'd suck up the water in the cottage, lickety-split. He also had a stack of clean towels to dry the floor thoroughly because on a freezing gray morning with the sun hidden behind clouds, it was going to need some help.

Thankfully, Suzanne was fully clothed in track pants and a hoodie. The pants were loose, not clingy, and she'd rolled them up to the knees. The hoodie was pushed up to the elbows and decorated with paint stains. Her hair had been pulled back in some kind of haphazard knotty thing at the back of her head, held in place by what looked to be a very fine paintbrush speared through the center. Already some strands had worked loose, brushing her face.

She'd also put on a bra. Thank fucking Christ.

"I'll suck up the excess water," he informed her, refusing to give himself any more time to ogle the woman. He pointed at the towels he'd tossed on the couch. "Follow behind me and dry off the floor."

He didn't give her a chance to reply or object or suggest another strategy because she was insulted about his gender role assumption. He liked big, loud machinery and he'd used it before. He just started up the vac and got underway, pleased that its noise obliterated any chance for conversation. He wanted to get this done and get out of here.

He had a ranch to run, goddamn it.

Grady's job was much quicker than hers. The industrial-strength machine easily sucked up the water, making short work of it. He was also able to stand erect while Suzanne chose to do her bit on her hands and knees rather than bending over or squatting.

He resolutely decided not to think about *that* as he steadily sucked up water, and, between the two of them, they got the job done.

Grady was on the last section near the wall that separated Suzanne's bedroom—*the* bedroom; it wasn't *hers*, for fuck's sake—from the living area. The water had almost made it to the wall and didn't appear to have spread into the bedroom, but it was better to be safe than sorry. Flagstones were notoriously uneven, which could cause little gutters, allowing some water to flow under the door.

It didn't occur to him *not* to check the room. Grady didn't half-ass anything, and it made sense to confirm all was well in the bedroom while he was here. There was a rug just inside the entrance that might easily soak up a lot of water before being symptomatic of a problem. So he thought nothing of opening her door. He did look around to tell her he was going in, but he couldn't see her, so he assumed she was kneeling in the kitchen hidden behind the counter and the noise was prohibitive to calling out.

Turning the knob, Grady stepped inside. There was no immediate squelching of the rug, which he trod over back and forth to be sure as he assessed both it and the nearby flagstones for signs of water encroachment. Satisfied all was well, he turned to exit when his gaze fell on several canvases leaning against the wall.

Curious as to just what kind of painter Suzanne St. Michelle was, he paused to give them more of his attention. Grady blinked. *Nudes*, apparently. He recognized the famous figures on the canvases at first glance, and it took only a few moments for him to realize that Suzanne had talent.

Grady may not have had an artistic bone in his body—he couldn't even draw a straight line with a ruler—but clearly the woman could paint. It was on second glance, however, he realized something startling.

Something *outrageously* startling.

His face staring out from each of the five canvases. Not his body but most definitely *his face*.

What. The. Fuck.

CHAPTER FIVE

Grady blinked and blinked again. Shaking his head, he grappled with what he was seeing, trying to make sense of the images that were familiar but not. His thoughts were spinning like a tumble dryer, and he couldn't concentrate with the vac rumbling like a goddamn jackhammer in his brain. Switching it off, he dropped the head of the apparatus on the rug and moved closer to the paintings.

She'd…superimposed his head on famous works like *David* and that dude with the four arms and four legs that da Vinci—or maybe it was somebody else?—had done. The reproduction of the subjects was very good but, with his head substituted for theirs, the paintings looked surreal. Like those big boards with people's bodies printed on them and a cutout where their faces should be so other people could stick their heads in for a funny photo opportunity.

Grady did not think they were funny.

Maybe she was just a frustrated classical artist hiding behind silly doodles, and she was here to try her hand at *serious* art. And failing. Giving up at the last hurdle and…painting *his* face instead.

It was very definitely him. She'd captured with startling accuracy the hardened loner who stared back at him from the mirror every morning. There was nothing caricature-like about the detail of his face or that haunted kind of look in his eyes. And then there was that circular puckered wound placed beneath the right clavicle on every painting.

The bodies may have been different but she was, he was sure of it, painting him.

What. The. *Actual.* Fuck.

Heat flushed through his system, building rapidly to a simmer and then a boil. The flow of his blood washed loudly through his ears. Why on God's green earth was she painting him? Why? And, also, *fuck that stalker shit.* He planted his hands on his hips, becoming more and more incredulous at her audacity. He hadn't given her permission to paint him.

She couldn't just...*do* that, could she?

"Grady?" His name coming from a distance barely disrupted the red mist fogging his brain. The second time pierced it like a bloody great anvil. *"Graaaady!"*

It sounded like she was in motion, and he was sure he could hear her feet on the flagstones getting closer, and then she burst through the door, skidding to a halt on the rug, her gaze taking in his closeness to the paintings and, if she had two functioning eyes in her head, the rigid set of his jaw and the expression of absolute fury on his face.

"Grady." She took a couple of steps closer, but his gaze flashed over her in a beam of hot rage and she pulled to a halt. "I can explain."

Oh, she could, could she? Well...he'd like to hear that. "Explain why you've been over here all this time *painting me* like some stalker." His knuckles whitened as he dug his fingers almost painfully into his hips and stared at her, waiting for her explanation.

Her eyes darted to the paintings and back. "To be fair…I haven't really been painting you."

Heat crept up Grady's neck. She was going to *equivocate* now? "Yeah," he insisted, his jaw throbbing from how hard he was clenching it, "you have."

She shook her head, her blue eyes large in her face. "No…I've been painting *David* and *The Creation of Adam* and *Atlas*—"

Grady stabbed his finger at the nearest painting, pointing to his face peering out from beneath the golden curls of a cherub. "Me."

"The faces, sure," she said, hastening forward but stopping abruptly again at his glare. "But the bodies aren't."

That was true. And really fucking true for *certain* parts. A less educated, less secure man might have felt emasculated looking at nude paintings of micro-dicked men that were *not* him. But Grady had been to an art gallery or two; he knew tiny weenies were *a thing*.

Also, he wore size fourteen boots. *How about them apples.*

Grady stabbed another finger at the paintings, pointing directly at the bullet wound on Adam. "Me," he repeated, his voice as deep and earthy as dirt.

Her cheeks, which were already flushed, seemed to get even rosier, but she stared him straight in the eye and jutted out her chin like the day she'd arrived when she'd called him a cowpoke. "This is none of your business."

"The hell it's not, lady." He didn't raise his voice, choosing instead to inject it with a high level of do-not-fuck-with-me. It was the voice he only ever used in war zones. Or on recalcitrant bulls. "You can't paint me without my permission."

"Actually—" Her forehead wrinkled into blue lines of consternation. "I hate to get all technical on you, but I can. As long as I don't sell it or exhibit it for profit, I can paint whatever I want. Whoever I want. From the president of the United States to the queen of England and everyone in between, and I can certainly fill every spare inch of this cottage with paintings of you if I wanted to, and there's nothing you can do about it."

Grady had thought his anger had reached its peak. Turned out, he had hidden peaks. And that the universe hadn't stopped fucking with his life just because he was hiding from it out here in bumfuck eastern Colorado. It was *still* trying to screw him.

And not the good kind of happy-ending screwing.

"Lady, you have *acres* of land out there." He didn't even try to keep the exasperation out of his voice as he jabbed a finger at the window. "There are trees and fields. There are cows and horses and barns. It's called nature, and it's quite popular hereabouts. Maybe you should try painting that?"

"Well, I'm sorry, but it turns out your trees and cows just aren't that inspiring. Trust me: I have several shit landscapes shut away in that closet over there because I can't even stand to look at them and, as far as I'm aware, only one of us here studied fine art at Columbia, so if you don't mind, I won't take any art advice from the person who—"

Her lip curled like she was going to say *who herds cows for a living*, but it wasn't what slipped from her mouth.

"*—didn't,*" she ended.

Grady ground his teeth together. He couldn't give a rat's ass what she thought of him and how he earned his money. The opinion of some woman he'd only just met who had a streak of blue paint on her forehead and was destined to be a pain in his ass was less than zero in his estimation. So he cut to the chase.

"I want them. All of them."

Which wasn't strictly true. It wasn't like he was going to hang any of it. But he sure as hell wanted to see how well they'd burn. Maybe roast some marshmallows over the flames.

Her eyes grew large at his command, and she moved, dodging around him to put herself between him and her paintings, her legs planted wide, her arms akimbo, as if she could block any attempt he made at getting to them.

Right. Her and which army?

"Back off," she said, shaking her head vehemently. "They're mine, I painted them, they belong to me. And you can't have them."

Despite another uptick in Grady's temper, he almost laughed at her as she swayed slightly, back and forth on her feet, her hands out in front as if she was about to karate chop him. He figured this was her ninja stance, but those curves and that streak of blue paint on her forehead ruined the badass.

"They're *of* me," he reiterated.

She shook her head again. "That's not the way

copyright works, Grady. I painted them. They belong to me."

Grady shoved his hands on his hips. "Hand them over."

"You want them?" Her eyes narrowed as she squatted a little lower. "You're going to have to take them from me."

Grady blinked, taken aback by the challenge and the almost zeal-like quality in her gaze. She was dead serious. These…*bizarre* paintings obviously meant something to her. They meant something to him as well, but if she thought he was going to *wrestle* her for them, then she was mistaken. Grady had spent far too long in the military witnessing force to be a party to it in his civilian life.

Plus, Burl would probably kick his ass. When he put his mind to it, his uncle had a look that made Grady feel seventeen all over again.

"I think you're being a little melodramatic now, don't you?"

"Art is serious stuff."

"You painted my *head* on a cherub," he said incredulously.

"It's a *Botticelli*," she snapped.

"I don't care if it was painted by a chorus of *actual* angels."

She crouched a little lower. "I'm not handing over my paintings."

Grady did laugh this time as Suzanne eyed him like she was going to spring into bloodcurdling action at any moment. "Relax, crouching tiger," he said with a wave of his hand, his voice low and grim. "I'm not going to *take* them from you. I'll *buy* them off you."

The last thing Grady wanted was to fork out hard-earned cash for a bunch of paintings he was just going to torch. But if that was what it took…

Suzanne pulled abruptly out of her ninja stance, her arms dropping to her sides. "Wh-what?"

Oh yeah…that did it. She had no interest in *giving* them away, but with some cash in the offing, suddenly she was interested. "How much?" he demanded.

She was frowning, looking at him like he'd grown another head. "They're not for sale."

Grady cocked an eyebrow. "Honey…*everything's* for sale."

"These aren't." She folded her arms.

Hmm…okay. It was going to be like that, huh? Suzanne St. Michelle wasn't going to be some pushover. He should have known that from day one when she'd yelled at him and called him on his bullshit.

"I'll give you a hundred bucks."

Her whole face contorted into an expression of surprise followed swiftly by a twist to her lips that reflected her degree of insult. Her face clearly said, *You have got to be kidding me*, and he hurried to clarify.

"Each."

Six hundred bucks was a ridiculous amount of money for art that belonged on the sidewalks of Montmartre or in the local high school art competition. But he was good for it.

She blinked several times, her expression morphing quickly as she broke into laughter. *Laughter.* She was *laughing* at him. "A hundred bucks? *Each?*"

More laughter, her hand going to her stomach like it was actually hurting to laugh so goddamn hard. Despite his irritation, Grady had to admit, she had a great laugh—light and musical, a woman's laugh. It'd been a long time since he'd made a woman laugh, even if it was sarcastically.

"Clients pay me tens of thousands of dollars for my paintings," she said when her laughter had faded enough to communicate.

It was Grady's turn to blink. He glanced at the canvases. *What the fuck?* Sure, she could obviously paint, but that was *preposterous*. Although, to be fair, he hadn't been able to see the artistic merit in the many pieces he'd seen hanging in famous galleries, either. "I'm assuming what you do for your clients is a little more…highbrow?"

Surely people only paid big bucks for capital-A art, and Grady seriously doubted there was a thriving rich people's market for caricatures.

She cocked an eyebrow. "Well, at least I know where to come if I ever want a backhanded compliment."

"I'm sorry. I didn't mean…" Grady shook his head, no idea why he was apologizing. "I'm not really the guy you come to for compliments of any kind."

She snort-laughed this time. "Ya think?"

Grady felt the tug of a smile at the corners of his mouth but suppressed it. He was trying to negotiate a deal here, not get distracted. "Okay, so… How much do you want? For the paintings."

And just how much was he prepared to pay?

"Remembering that I'm just a simple rancher with a long, hard winter ahead of me." He injected some John Wayne into his voice. *That's* how badly he wanted those paintings.

She ignored the eyelid batting. "You could offer me a million dollars for each of them and I still wouldn't sell. These paintings are…priceless to me and not for sale."

Priceless? Who in the hell did she think she was, and what size checks was her ego writing to make her think those five…*caricatures* more at home next to Garfield or in the pages of *Mad Magazine* were priceless?

Grady's jaw muscle ticked as his patience wore thin. "I must insist."

That mutinous look he was beginning to know so well hardened her gaze to chips of blue ice. "I'm sure women don't tell you *no* very much, Joshua Grady, but read my lips. N. O." She spelled it out for him just in case he was an idiot of the highest order. *"No."*

Pain flared along his jaw, warning Grady he'd better ease up or he might shatter it completely. The problem was, they were at an impasse and, short of physically stealing them off her, there wasn't a lot he could do if the deluded woman wasn't smart enough to make a quick buck.

But that didn't mean he'd give up. He'd just execute a strategic withdrawal—for now.

"*You* read my lips, *Su-sahn Saan Meeshell.* If I ever see one of these paintings"—he stabbed his finger at them again—"out on display somewhere, there will be hell to pay. By the time my lawyer is done with you, you won't even be able to get a gig painting a cinder-block restroom facility in the Alaskan wilderness."

Grady didn't have a lawyer. His uncle had one in Denver, but his office was run out of a strip club, and Grady was pretty sure he spent more time getting lap dances than winning cases. But Suzanne didn't have to know that.

She gave him a horrified look like the mere suggestion of showing them was preposterous. "Oh, you can rest assured, these are *not* for public consumption."

Grady frowned. It sounded like she was... ashamed of them. These so-called *priceless* paintings she'd painted. Yet she wasn't going to give them up or sell them to him. Which made them what? For...private consumption? Her own viewing pleasure?

Man...*do not go there.* Do not put pleasure and Suzanne St. Michelle in the same sentence. Just go. Get out—now!

"I'll hold you to that." Tipping his chin at the vac, he said, "Leave it outside when you're done. I'll pick it up later."

And with that, he turned on his heel and strode out of the cottage straight for the barn and the ATV and a herd of cattle that needed hay and were about as far away from Suzanne and her paintings and her curves and that fucking blue paint on her forehead as he could get.

•••

Suzanne sat on the end of her bed as the door to the cottage slammed shut. *Shit.* That had *not* gone well. She stared at her paintings, a sick kind of dread sinking in her stomach as Grady's face times five stared back at her.

"What are you looking at?" she said waspishly to the figures that all seemed faintly accusing now. Or maybe that was her guilty conscience talking.

But she'd just…panicked. When she'd emerged from behind the kitchen counter, she'd suddenly noticed the vac had fallen silent, and then she'd seen her bedroom door open and she'd *freaked out.* Not as much as she had when she'd thought he was going to forcibly remove the paintings from the cottage, though.

It was in that moment she realized what they'd come to mean to her.

Sure, looking at them, they were just more of the same for her—art reproductions. But it was what they *represented* that was important. She hadn't had this urge, this driving need to paint in such a long time. Maybe not ever. Growing up in the shadow of a famous artist, it'd been hard to find her own way, her own style—her own *voice.* Especially when everyone expected her to be a chip off the old block.

That kind of pressure had been almost paralyzing.

It'd been easier to pour her creativity into mimicking. Into copying. And, for the first time, instead of criticism for her artistic choices, she'd been praised. And when she'd started to earn a legitimate living out of it, she'd grabbed it with both hands.

It had been the final nail in her artistic coffin for her muse, though. Or so she'd thought. But it must have only been in a deep freeze, because her muse was a living, breathing pulse in her breast, and it was because of Grady and those paintings. The thought of him taking them away had been too much to bear.

She may have battled with her muse these past five days, deliberately trying to curtail her, but she was back, and Suzanne was very much afraid that if she handed these paintings over, her muse would go away again. Because what if they were the key to this artistic rush? This flow had been so new, too new to know how tenuous it might be, and if the paintings were gone, would her inspiration go with them?

What if she couldn't paint again? She felt like she was fighting for her artistic life here.

Having this body of work to look at gave her courage that she *could* do it. That this wasn't a flash in the pan. That she could find her own voice. Yes, her muse needed to stop being such a tyrant and let Suzanne stretch her wings. And Suzanne needed to stop playing it safe by falling back onto the crutch of other people's art. But right now she was painting again, and she needed to trust that this was all part of the process and that she'd find her true artistic self in there somewhere.

So yeah, these paintings *were* priceless. To her. Grady might not be a fan, her mother certainly wouldn't be, but how did she put a price on getting her mojo back?

She had these paintings to thank for that. And Joshua Grady.

• • •

Grady walked into The Lumberjack, or Jack's, as it was known, about three in the afternoon. He was still ticked off from his encounter with Suzanne, despite trying to exorcise his anger through hard physical labor. Jack's was at least a distraction. Grady usually drank alone, so it was a measure of how desperate he was right now that he was seeking out company.

"Hey, Grady."

Tucker Daniels greeted him. He'd taken over running Jack's from his daddy quite a few years back, before Grady had returned to Credence, and was the kind of bartender who could tell when a customer wanted to talk and when they wanted to be left the hell alone.

Grady usually always wanted to be left alone. Not today.

"Tucker." Grady nodded. "I'll get a Bud Light, please."

Tucker grabbed the requested bottle of Bud and opened it, setting it on the bar. When Grady sat his ass on a stool, Tucker cocked an eyebrow. Grady normally took his beer to a booth and drank it, because he didn't do chitchat.

Sometimes Burl, who was *king* of fucking chitchat, joined him. His uncle was Grady's self-appointed are-you-okay person, appearing regularly for welfare checks and always seeming to know just where to find him.

"Business looks good." The whole single-women

thing from the summer had definitely helped out Jack's customer base.

Tucker shot a puzzled look in Grady's direction before glancing around at the mostly full booths and the group of women crowding around the jukebox. "Yup."

Grady took another swig of his beer as the Backstreet Boys sang about wanting it that way. He winced as he placed his beer down. "Shit music, though."

"It's an acquired taste," Tucker agreed with a laugh.

"Thought it was illegal to play anything but country in Credence?"

"I'm being inclusive."

Grady barked out a laugh. "Boy bands?" As far as he was concerned, boy bands had always been a bad idea and should definitely have stayed in the nineties.

"Sure, why not?" Tucker shrugged, then grinned as he indicated the women by the jukebox with a lift of his chin. "Frankly, if they'd asked me to load up hardcore thrash metal, I'd have done it. Don't worry, you can still find Dolly and Waylon. Come back next week and the Christmas songs will be loaded."

Christmas. *Shit*. Schmaltzy Christmas music. Grady made a mental note to avoid Jack's until the New Year. Still, he forced himself to be polite and conversational because that's what people did when sitting in bars. "Any holiday plans?"

Tucker's eyes narrowed. He leaned forward slightly and clicked his fingers in front of Grady's face. "Hello, are you in there, Grady? Blink twice if you've been abducted by aliens."

Grady shook his head. "You're hilarious."

"Seriously." Tucker flicked the dishcloth in his hand over his shoulder, resting it there for easy access. "Who are you?"

"What? I can't sit at a bar and talk?"

"No offense, dude, but you're not a shoot-the-breeze kind of guy."

Grady had probably spoken less than fifty words since he'd sat his ass down. "This is being chatty?"

"For you it is."

Lifting his beer, Grady took another swallow, neither confirming nor denying alien abduction but seriously contemplating it as a reason for his irrational attraction to Suzanne St. Michelle. Surely only something *woo-woo* could explain that?

"Ah." Tucker nodded sagely as Grady's silence stretched. "It's a woman thing."

Grady placed the Bud on the bar. *Say what now?* "A woman thing?"

"You have that *I don't know what just happened to me* expression that, in my experience, usually involves a woman."

"You're full of shit."

Tucker laughed. "God's truth," he said, hand on heart. "You want to talk about it? I've been doing this bartender thing for a while; I'm practically a social worker."

"Nope." Grady would rather be gored by one of his bulls.

"C'mon, dude," Tucker cajoled. "Try me. First session's free." He grabbed a cardboard drink coaster out from under the empty beer a little farther down the bar. "Tell me what you see in the wet spot."

"Think I'm going to need a couch if we're talking wet spots."

"The couch will cost you."

Draining the remainder of his beer, Grady said, "It's not a woman thing." Then he handed over his empty bottle and nodded to indicate he wanted another.

"And how does that make you feel?" Tucker asked as he grabbed another Bud.

Grady was about to tell Tucker to shove his barstool psychology, but a woman's voice from somewhere behind him entered the conversation. "What's not a woman thing?" she asked.

Turning slightly, Grady found a curly-haired Amazon sliding onto the stool beside him. He recognized her instantly as Winona Crane, Suzanne's friend. She was building a house out near the lake. Burl had pointed her out once when she'd been in Annie's at the same time and gleefully told Grady all about the erotic romance author who had arrived in Credence with the influx of women over the summer.

"Grady's come in here looking like a slapped ass and pretending it's not a woman thing."

Winona took one look at him and nodded. "Yep," she said, turning back to Tucker. "It's a woman thing." And then she frowned and said, "Wait... Grady? You're *Joshua* Grady."

Grady also frowned. The woman flat-out ogled him, putting Grady on high alert. What was it with the women in town suddenly? "Yes, ma'am," he confirmed and swallowed half his beer in one go.

"Ohhhhh," she said, all breathy and speculative. "I see."

See? What did she see? "Ma'am?"

She didn't answer him, turning back to face Tucker instead. "It's definitely a woman thing."

Grady blinked. *What?*

Tucker grinned. "Okay now, Miss Winona, what do you know?"

"You remember me telling you my friend from New York was coming to stay for a little while over the holidays?"

Tucker nodded. "Sure. She's an artist."

"Yes." Winona nodded enthusiastically. "A painter. Well…" She tipped her head sideways to indicate Grady. "She's staying in his cottage."

"Ah." Tucker's gaze returned to meet Grady's. So did Winona's. He was beginning to understand how one of those bugs pinned to a board felt. "That *does* explain it." He glanced at Winona again. "What's she like?"

"She's awesome. She forges art—*legally*—for a living. Her work is amazing, so accurate, and museums and galleries and private collectors pay her boatloads of money for it."

A *legal* art forger? That was a thing? He couldn't even wrap his head around that one. But at least it explained the accuracy and the professionalism of those paintings. Apart from one or two major deviations, of course…

"But she's grown up in the shadow of her very famous mother, who's probably the country's most prominent sculptor. Between the pressure of that and her job of reproducing other people's art, she's lost her way a little. I've been telling her for months she should take a break and come to Credence for some inspiration."

"And has she found it?" Tucker asked.

Winona glanced in Grady's direction, a little gleam in her eyes. "I think she has."

Tucker's gaze also swung over him, and Grady felt hot and then cold all over. "You know I'm right here, yeah?"

This was why he lived alone and drank alone. He didn't have time for high school bullshit in his life. And he didn't want to be anyone's *inspiration*.

The music changed to Justin Bieber, and Grady figured that was a sign.

"Well…" He threw back the rest of his beer, placed the bottle on the bar, and slid off the stool. "That's my cue to leave."

He should have stayed at home. People could be a distraction, but they could also be pains in the ass. He forgot that sometimes when he was away from them for a while. These two were a classic example. He didn't need to spend his Sunday afternoon being tag-teamed by the psychological equivalent of Laurel and Hardy.

"Methinks he doth protest too much," Winona said to Tucker.

Christ, they were breaking out the Shakespeare—definitely time to leave. Grady shot them both a grim smile as he threw a ten dollar bill on the bar. "Parting is such sweet sorrow," he said as he turned and walked away.

CHAPTER SIX

Suzanne woke late the next day *not* in a lather of excitement about what she was going to paint but with a lump of dread feeling like a cement block tied to her feet. Her muse was nowhere to be found. Just as she had been nowhere yesterday after Grady had slammed out of the cottage.

His disapproval had hung like a big storm cloud over her head, sapping all her creative energy. After her five-day burst of productivity, it felt like *death*.

So she'd gone back to bed—the cold, dull weather perfect for such denial—crawled under the covers, and binge-watched the last season of *Portrait Artist of The Year*, a British television show to which she was addicted. She followed it up with reruns of *Antiques Roadshow* because some of the art that people brought along was amazing.

Her favorite had been a young woman whose grandmother had recently died and left her a painting she'd bought in a garage sale for ten dollars more than twenty-five years ago. Everybody who'd ever seen the painting had hated it except for the woman and her granny. It turned out to be an early Gainsborough worth several hundred thousand dollars.

Suzanne had almost peed her panties, she'd been so excited.

Glancing down the bed, over her body and the

jut of her toes, the paintings of Grady stared back at her. The sum total of her work. *Her* work. Five lousy paintings. What if this was all she had? What if this feeling she had today persisted, and she only ever had this one week of creative magic?

Suzanne shut her eyes against a wave of emotion that felt very much like loss, which was absurd. How could she mourn something that had only been fleeting?

Dragging the covers over her head, she pulled her knees to her chest and lay in a fetal ball for several minutes. It was cocoon-like but empty, which was how it felt inside her body at the moment—a big black hole, a yawning empty well.

Her cell rang, and Suzanne didn't even bother emerging from the covers, just groped for the phone on the bedside table and pulled it under the covers with her. She didn't look at the display as she hit the Answer button. She knew it would be Winona, who'd called several times last night.

"Hello."

"Suzanne, darling…is that you? Are you sick?"

Suzanne blinked at her mother's cultured accent, the shock of hearing her voice profound. Her mother had not been impressed about Suzanne up and leaving for Credence. And when her mother was annoyed, she tended to freeze people out for a while.

Displacing the covers, Suzanne sat bolt upright. "Mom?"

"You sound all muffled and stuffy. I told you that you'd catch something going all the way out to eastern Colorado. It *blizzards* there."

Suzanne was too speechless to ask bigger questions at the moment. "It blizzards in New York, too, Mom."

"Yes, but at least there's a Duane Reade on every corner, darling. Do you have tea? I'll make sure there's plenty for when you come home next week."

There followed a thirty-second monologue on the merits of different kinds of tea, but it took Suzanne only five seconds to zero in on the most salient part of the conversation thus far.

When you come home next week. Yeah…about that…

She *had* told her parents she'd come home for a few days over Christmas. They'd been so set against her going to Credence it had been a concession she'd been willing to make to get them off her back about her Colorado plans. Not that she needed their approval or permission to leave—she was a grown-ass woman who left home regularly for painting gigs all around the country.

She'd just been tired of the constant *conversations* they'd had about it, and frankly, Suzanne wasn't the kind of person who liked to cause her parents angst. She'd been primed from a young age that it wasn't good for her mom's creative process.

But, even as she'd made the concession, she'd had absolutely no intention of following through with it. Part of the reason she'd chosen to travel to Credence when she had was so she didn't have to spend another soulless Christmas with her parents. She loved them dearly, but they just didn't *do* Christmas.

Not the way she'd always yearned for. Not the way all her friends' parents had, the way the rest of the country seemed to, the way Winona had promised she would. Not in that big, fat Hallmark way with miles of garland and tinsel and mistletoe and a huge fuck-off tree bursting with baubles and lights and looking so damn pretty, a person couldn't help but sigh every time they gazed upon its glory.

Simone St. Michelle's idea of a tree was a minimalist structure from the latest name in the art world made out of bent wire coat hangers she'd bought at a gallery twenty years ago. It had a single ice-blue light at the top, twisted within the wire like it was in some kind of *prison*. Apparently, it was a statement about the commercialization of the season.

There wasn't a piece of holly, a single candy cane, or a carol to be heard at the brownstone.

Suzanne had complained bitterly about her parents' lack of Christmas cheer over the years to no avail. She'd been so jealous of school friends' houses that had glowed—inside *and out*—with seasonal joy. One of her favorite things to do in December was to go with her friends to check out the window displays at Bloomingdale's and Barneys and Saks Fifth Avenue, then finish up at Rockefeller Center to ice skate beneath the massive Christmas tree.

That ice rink was her Christmas happy place and made it bearable going home to a wire tree with a solitary blue light. And this year, her happy place was with Winona. It wasn't at Winona's house on the lake as they'd hoped, but the boardinghouse in town was going the full Christmas with garlands and a real tree and carols and homemade eggnog.

And Suzanne wasn't going to trade that for a wire tree and a posh restaurant that specialized in *deconstructed* festive menus. Seriously, who did that? Wasn't that a sin against *Jesus*?

Unfortunately, she hadn't yet thought of an excuse to give to her parents for not returning to New York. Frankly, she'd been hoping the Colorado weather would come to the party and she could use unsafe travel conditions as a valid excuse. With snow predicted next week, her chances had been looking up but, apparently, this conversation was happening now.

Suzanne took a steadying breath and bit the bullet. "Mom...I'm not coming home for Christmas."

There was a long pause down the line. "What? But...we've never spent a Christmas apart."

The quietness of her mother's voice was more effective than any other tone she could have adopted. If she'd yelled or scolded or even cried, Suzanne could have rallied against it, but her mother's *disappointed* voice was the hardest to take.

Suzanne just didn't disappoint her parents.

Shit. How did a person tell her *mother* she didn't want to see her at *Christmas* without being disappointing? Winona's mother had passed away three years ago, and Suzanne knew that Winona would give anything to have one more Christmas with her mom. And here Suzanne was trying to weasel out of *this* one with her mom.

It was ridiculous; her parents didn't even *believe* in Christmas. Not like other people did anyway. Why was it so important that she be there? Sure, it would be the first time in twenty-nine years they had Christmas apart, but…it had to happen sooner or later.

Casting frantically around in her brain for a suitable excuse—something compelling—she grabbed hold of the first thing that sprang forth. "I've met someone. I'm spending Christmas with him."

Suzanne wasn't sure who was more stunned at the blurted admission—her mother or herself. Met someone? *That's* what she'd chosen? That was a degree of stupid she hadn't even realized existed until now. An image of Grady stripped to his chest in the mudroom appeared unbidden, and she quashed it.

Shit.

"But, darling…you've not even been gone for two weeks."

"No…I met him before that. Through Winona. We've been keeping in touch online."

And just like that, she was off to the races… building this lie instead of trying to walk it back, which made her feel lower than a snake's belly. But despite her initial panic, it *was* a good ruse. Her mother had always fretted about Suzanne's lack of romantic entanglements.

Artists need to love, darling.

"He lives in *Credence*?" Her mother said *Credence* in much the same way she said *street art*.

"Yes, here, at the ranch. He's a…rancher." She

swallowed as she dug the hole a little deeper. But if Suzanne was going to successfully pull off this lie, she was going to have to be convincing, and at least she could talk about Grady with conviction.

It wasn't like he was ever going to know. She'd be back in New York in a few weeks with their *relationship* over and neither he nor her parents need ever know the truth.

"The…rancher?"

"Yes." Suzanne crossed her fingers behind her back.

"So you're staying at his place? There's not a cottage?"

Suzanne thunked her forehead against her drawn-up knees and shut her eyes as the hole deepened. "There is a cottage." The most convincing lies always held as much truth as possible, right? "I was in the cottage. But I'm…not now, no."

She needed her mother to believe it was serious. Serious enough to not come home for Christmas. Suzanne shacking up with a *rancher* in *rural Colorado* ought to do it.

"Oh…well…that's… Why didn't you tell us you were going to be with a man, Suzanne?"

Good question, Suzanne, why didn't you? "It's… still new, and I didn't want to jinx it." *Dig. Dig. Dig.* Crap…she was digging herself all the way to hell.

A long pause followed, and Suzanne was happy to let it stretch. At least while they weren't talking, she wasn't lying. "Well…okay, then," her mother finally said. "That's fine…we'll come to you."

Suzanne's head snapped up, her eyes goggling wide open. *What the?* If somebody had put a gun to her head and asked Suzanne to guess what her mother would say next, *Fine, we'll come to you* wouldn't even have been in her top one hundred choices.

Her mom and dad coming to Credence? For Christmas? Ah…no.

Big. Fat. No.

And not just because her mom thought she had a rancher boyfriend now, which she *very obviously did not*, but because she didn't want them ruining her first-ever real Christmas with all their bah humbug ways. But even more than that was the issue of her paintings. If her mother came, she'd want to see what Suzanne was working on, and Suzanne wasn't ready for that. Not yet. Not when *she* didn't even know where it was going yet.

Her mother's tutelage over the years had been the kind of stuff that art students could only dream of, and it had been formative but also…stultifying. Criticism may well have been insightful and well meaning but also unhelpful for the creative process. What Suzanne was creating now was too new for any kind of critical eye.

Grady's had been bad enough.

"But…but…it blizzards here." Suzanne honestly did not know what else to say. Her brain had temporarily flatlined.

"Let's keep our fingers crossed it doesn't."

Dear god, if Suzanne didn't come up with a way to stop this, her parents would really make the trek. Her pulse tapped wildly at her temples. She couldn't let it happen. "There's no accommodation in Credence," she said, panic begetting inspiration.

The reason she was out here at the ranch in the first place was lack of paying places to stay.

Thank you, all the single ladies!

"But…we could just stay in the cottage, couldn't we, as you're not staying there anymore."

Crap. *The cottage.* Damn it, the universe was already punishing her over the fake rancher boyfriend thing. Karma really was a bitch.

"It's a ways out of town, Mom."

"I'm sure we'll cope."

Yes, but would *she*? Suzanne's pulse kicked up as she racked her brain for a suitable reason for them *not* to make the trip. Something that would put her mother off the idea of coming within a hundred miles of Credence.

Something worse than blizzards.

And then a light bulb flashed on over her head. "Trust me, Mom, you really wouldn't like it here at all. Grady is a Christmas freak. Honestly, there's enough tinsel strung about the cabin to go twice around Credence. It's like…the North Pole exploded overhead. Grady just *adores* this time of year, and when he knew I was coming, he spent a week getting everything all tinseled up for me. He's like whatever the opposite is of the Grinch. He's… the Christmas fairy."

Suzanne didn't have to know much about Grady to know *adoration* was not in his range of emotions and fairies weren't in his vocabulary, Christmas or otherwise.

"That sounds…" For a moment, Suzanne was sure her mom was going to say *horribly redneck.* "Lovely."

Which roughly translated to *horribly redneck* in Simone St. Michelle speak. Suzanne seized on what might be a chink in her mother's plans to travel to Credence.

"Did I mention the mistletoe? So. Much. Mistletoe. Grady says it's so that wherever I am in the cabin, he can kiss me. Doesn't that make you just want to swoon?" Her mother hated public displays of affection more than public displays of Christmas. "And boy, does he keep his promises, if you know what I mean. He's so demonstrative, Mom, I'm just dizzy with it all."

Suzanne forced out what she hoped was a deliriously happy sigh, feeling super lousy for her deception. God...she was a *terrible person*. But she couldn't just roll over and let her parents ruin yet another Christmas. Was it so wrong to want to do her own thing just this once *and* protect her mother's feelings?

"That's...*lovely*."

Suzanne almost laughed, but instead she said, "I really don't think you and Dad will enjoy yourselves here. It's not the kind of Christmas you're used to, Mom. I'm sure you can do without me this once, and I'll be back in New York to watch the ball drop with you both."

"But...I was looking forward to meeting your rancher."

Her mother sounded quiet again. A little...hurt, even, but also like she was reconsidering. Suzanne ignored the hot lash of alarm at the thought of her mom and Grady coming face-to-face and concentrated on soothing her mother's worries.

"You will, Mom."

On the twelfth of never. They would certainly be *over* when she returned to New York.

God…Grady would probably murder her and bury her out in one of his fields if he knew what she was telling her mother right now.

"Please, Suzanne." Her mom's voice wobbled a little, and she cleared it.

Suzanne frowned, tuning in suddenly to the pleading uncertainty in her mother's voice. Her mother never sounded unsure, and a prickle fanned up her nape. *Please?* Please what?

And she knew with sudden conviction that something was wrong.

Terribly wrong.

"Mom?" Suzanne sat a little straighter. "What's the matter?"

"Your father and I… Things aren't so good between us and…I just want one last Christmas where we're all together."

Things aren't so good between us? One last Christmas? What in the hell was her mom trying to say? That their marriage was in trouble? Since when had her parents' marriage been in trouble? They might not be the most demonstrative of couples—they'd slept in separate bedrooms for as long as Suzanne could remember. But that was because her mom kept odd hours, particularly when she was working on a piece, and her father was a very light sleeper. There was still enormous affection and common interests binding them together.

They were a good team, the toast of the New

York art world.

Albie, her father, was an agent and, along with a select list of New York's elite artists, he had represented Simone for four decades. In fact, he had *discovered* her, and they had this perfect symbiosis between professional and personal that was the envy of the art world.

They *got* each other.

Sure, they fought. Her mother had an artistic temperament and often neglected everything in the midst of a project. But they'd always made up.

"What do you mean, *aren't so good*?"

"I just…don't know if we'll be together next Christmas."

Suzanne sucked in a breath. "Mom…no." The thought that her parents might split up was… shocking. She knew it was none of her business. She wasn't a kid any longer, and her parents were allowed to do what they wanted with their lives, but…separation?

"You've always been the glue that held us to-gether, darling. I'm very much afraid we can't do it without you, and I can't bear the thought of hav-ing to sit opposite your father on Christmas morning and not know what to say."

Suzanne blinked. What the hell? *She'd* been the glue? That couldn't be true, surely. But her mother sounded so…empty, so…lost, it was like a knife twisting in her heart. Whatever nonsense was going on with her parents, it wasn't just some flash in the pan.

It was serious.

"Mom…" Suzanne didn't know want to say. Her

mother was always so authoritative, she wasn't used to her sounding so small and helpless. "I'll come home for Christmas." Even as Suzanne said it, a ball of disappointment pulled tight in her gut. She'd been so looking forward to spending the day with Winona and the others at the boardinghouse. But there'd be other Christmases. "I'll see what flights are available and call you back."

"No." Her mother's voice went from soft to stridently vehement. "Absolutely not, darling. Of course you must spend your first Christmas with your rancher boyfriend. I absolutely insist."

"Mom…" Suzanne sighed. "It's fine. I'm sure he"—*my fake rancher boyfriend*—"can do without me for a few days." Suzanne was pretty damn sure Joshua Grady would throw a party the day she left. "I'll spend next Christmas with him."

"I insist," her mother continued. "Besides, I think it'll do your father and me good to get out of our old routine, out of our comfort zone. I am set in my ways over certain things, and I think that's starting to frustrate your dad, so we need a shake-up. While I wish Winona had decided to go to the Caribbean, eastern Colorado will do just fine. A change of scenery and some time away from New York is just what we need right now."

Suzanne knew her mother was making sense. It was the kind of couple's therapy a shrink might suggest, and had she not just fabricated a whole life here that didn't exist, Suzanne would be all for it.

But she had. She now had a *rancher boyfriend* she was *living with* in what she'd pretty much painted as *Santa's freaking grotto*.

"Mom, I don't think—"

"Please, Suzanne," her mother cut in, her voice equal parts urgent and desperate. "I promise I won't disparage the way your rancher chooses to celebrate Christmas. I would never embarrass you like that, darling. Whatever he wants to do, I'll be fully involved. I'm willing to try anything because we need this, and I…don't know what else to do."

God… Suzanne swallowed. How was she supposed to say no to that? This was her mom, who never asked her for anything. Her *parents*. Who loved each other. Were good for each other. Who belonged together.

It wasn't her mother's fault that Suzanne had dug herself a great big hole that couldn't be refilled without getting a lot of mud in her face. *Crap*… There was no way she could say no to her mother when the stakes were so high. "Of course," she said on a loud exhale of air. "Grady and I would love to have you." Then she shut her eyes and waited for a lightning bolt to blast through the roof and fry her to a pulp.

None was forthcoming.

Her mother gave a little, rather undignified (for her) whoop, and Suzanne blinked. "I'll book flights now and text you the details."

The phone cut off in her ear, and Suzanne flopped back against the mattress, pulling the covers over her head again as she curled her legs into her chest and disappeared into her cocoon of what-the-fuckery to contemplate all the ways Grady could kill her out here where no one could hear her scream.

• • •

At just after five o'clock that night, Suzanne walked along the path that connected the cottage to the cabin. It was dark already, the sun having finally slipped below the horizon a half hour ago, and the air was frigid, a constant puff of steam misting into the air from her mouth. Thankfully it was lit enough by the moon to navigate the path without assistance from a flashlight.

In one hand, Suzanne carried a bottle of red wine—a nice one she'd brought with her from New York—in the other, a bowl containing the warm pasta dish she'd cooked earlier. Just because she mostly lived on two-minute noodles and Oreos when she was painting didn't mean Suzanne couldn't cook. In fact, she very much enjoyed the process as long as she had time on her hands, because cooking was a kind of art, too, and all art should be lingered over.

But today, with her muse rocking in a corner somewhere, she'd had plenty of time *and* the ingredients to make her penne arrabbiata or, as she'd coined it, Suzanne's Ass-kissing Pasta. It was quick and simple and smelled delicious with the handfuls of basil leaves she'd thrown in, and her stomach grumbled as she stood on Grady's back porch and knocked on the door.

She only hoped it worked, because there was some serious ass-kissing to do if she hoped to convince Grady to be her fake rancher boyfriend. Grady, who had already made it plain he was not a

fan of her or her work and was probably still—
rightly—pissed about the paintings. But, *man*, was
Suzanne grateful to have those paintings in her
possession now. She had a feeling she was going to
need the leverage.

When she'd been in the throes of creating
them, they'd flowed from the purest place inside
her, and the thought of sullying them with what
was essentially bribery didn't exactly thrill
Suzanne. But surely he'd be able to see her cause
was noble even if he'd never met her parents?

Didn't cowboys go for all that noble shit? Wasn't
that part of their code?

Suzanne knocked again as the chilly air seeped
in through clothes not suitable for a freezing
December night in eastern Colorado. Because it
was only a short walk, Suzanne hadn't bothered to
bundle up, wearing just her jeans, a light sweater,
and her knee-high Uggs. She'd figured she'd only
be out in the air for less than a minute, and it'd
save her having to unravel in Grady's cabin because taking clothes off near him reminded her of
him stripped down to the waist, and she was still
trying really hard to forget that incident.

But apparently, he was going to make her wait.
Probably hoping she'd turn into a Popsicle on his
doorstep.

Was he *that* mad? Yeah. Suzanne gave a mental
nod. *He was that mad.*

Annoyed, she lifted her hand to knock a third
time—she knew he was in there; she'd watched him
go inside an hour ago just as the deep purple chill
of twilight had descended. The door opened before

her knuckles had a chance to connect, and Suzanne had to tense her quads to stop from stumbling forward.

He frowned at her. *Just for something different...* "What did you break now?" he asked as delicious warmth from his cabin made her very aware of her fripples high-beaming him.

Suzanne was torn between the urge to brain him with the bottle of red—it wasn't *that* nice—and full-on ogling his body. If she thought Grady in Levis, plaid shirt, boots, and hat, smelling like hay and hard work, was something, then Grady in sweats and an old T-shirt was something else. There was a faded logo on the front, and he smelled like soap and toothpaste. His hair was damp around his head and, if she had to guess, she'd say he wasn't long out of the shower.

She suppressed the ridiculous urge to take a step forward and lean in, to bury her face in his shirt and revel in the kind of soft that hinted at a thousand washes. She locked her quads tighter instead and gritted her teeth for a beat before consciously *un*gritting them and plastering a smile on her face.

"I come in peace." She thrust the bottle of wine at him and offered him the bowl of pasta. "Truce?"

His frown morphed to a scowl as he eyed the pasta like she'd laced it with strychnine. "Why?"

Suzanne kept smiling. "Because we're neighbors, because we're a long way from anywhere, and because it's the festive season."

He shifted warily, and Suzanne's gaze dropped to his feet, bare against the wooden boards, and her belly did a cartwheel. Why she found his feet sexy—apart from their obvious *size*—she had no idea. Basically, this man and her body's response to him were a complete and utter mystery.

She was blaming long-term exposure to paint thinners.

"I thought we'd agreed you were going to stay over there, and I was going to stay over here?"

"It's the festive season," Suzanne repeated, resisting the urge to grit her teeth again.

Grady pointed to his face. "Does this look like a face that gives a rat's ass about that?"

Nope, it did not. His face was *not* lit with the festive spirit. Burl had said this was a tough time of year for Grady, and there was that shrapnel wound. Had something tragic happened when he'd been on tour one Christmas?

Whatever his problem with the season, Suzanne realized as he stood stubbornly in his doorway making no move to admit her, she was going to have to give him an acceptable reason for him to admit her, because *neighborly* wasn't going to work.

"I have a…proposal I think you'll be interested in."

His eyebrows rose fleetingly before he was frowning again. "I already told you, I'm not in the market for a wife. Or a bed warmer."

The outrage she'd felt that first day they'd met surged again, heating her blood. The man really had an ego the size of Colorado. "It's not *that* kind of proposal. Nor is it a *proposition*."

He folded his arms like she was trying his

patience, but it didn't stop the funny hitch in her breath as the T-shirt stretched very nicely across his biceps. "Fine…why don't you enlighten me?"

Suzanne looked over his shoulder, where she could see high ceiling beams and the flicker of a flame in a fireplace. It looked cozy and inviting. Shame Rancher Surly was guarding it. "Could we maybe talk inside like two reasonable adults?"

"Nope."

She bugged her eyes at him. Jesus, he really didn't quit, did he? "You like being a hard-ass?" The fact that he was going to make her state her business while freezing her butt off on his doorstep was not endearing her to him.

A nerve ticked in his jaw. "What do you want, Suzanne?" His voice was hard, but there was a degree of weariness to it. Or maybe that was exasperation.

"I need a favor." She cleared her throat.

"No."

He went to shut the door, but Suzanne stopped it with her hand holding the wine bottle. For crying out loud, anyone would think she was about to ask him for a kidney.

"Please," she said as their eyes met and locked, his the stormy green of an approaching tornado. "If you help me, I'll hand over the paintings."

He eyed her for long moments, his face a mask, his eyes unreadable. Then he pulled the door open. "You have five minutes."

CHAPTER SEVEN

The cabin was magnificent. It wasn't luxurious, but it was *big*, with exposed rafters and a huge rustic chandelier made from an old wagon wheel and suspended by chains from a large beam. It hung directly over the fat leather couches positioned in front of the massive stone fireplace, where huge chunks of wood glowed orange and the roaring flames spread tentacles of glorious warmth.

In front of the hearth and bordered on three sides by the couches was a big rug that looked Turkish in origin. More rugs decorated the acres of wide honey floorboards in the open-plan living areas, similar to her cottage. Against the far wall to her left sat a cabinet made from dark wood, and next to that was what looked like a fish tank. It was large and only half full of water, but she could see plants and a filter bubbling away, so she presumed something lived in it. A few feet from the tank, an archway opened into what appeared to be a hallway leading to, Suzanne presumed, the bedrooms.

The living space flowed into the kitchen area, which was separated by a long bench topped with black marble. Two large windows, although not floor-to-ceiling like hers, flanked the open kitchen area and looked out over the front porch and the field where Suzanne had first seen Grady's horses grazing. A smaller window, situated above the sink, had a similar view.

Suzanne placed the bowl and the wine bottle down on the bench. "Wow," she said as she craned her neck, her eyes taking another tour of the magnificent ceiling before lowering her gaze to his. "This is amazing."

He lifted an eyebrow. "What did you expect?"

Not this. She hadn't expected the cabin to be so…polished. Like a woman had designed, decorated, *and regularly cleaned* the space. She'd expected it to be more…male. More…Wild West saloon.

Minus the hookers.

Aware of his gaze on her, waiting for her to qualify, Suzanne said, "A lair." Much to her surprise, one side of Grady's mouth kicked up and, before she could think better of it, she said, "Careful there, Grady, you almost ruined all that grumpiness you've got going on."

Suzanne regretted it immediately as he stiffened and folded his arms again. *Way to go, Suzanne.* Bring out the ogre just before you ask him to be your fake rancher boyfriend and go all National Lampoon on his home.

"All right, then," he said, his voice gruff and businesslike. "Let's hear it."

She swallowed, nervous again. "Do you mind?" She pointed to the wine. Grady looked like he minded very much, but Suzanne needed some alcoholic fortification for what she was about to ask. "Trust me, we're both going to need a glass after I get through what I need to say."

"That bad, huh?"

"I don't think you're going to like it." Suzanne

sure as shit didn't.

"Color me surprised," he said, his voice laced with sarcasm as he crossed to the kitchen, pulled out two glasses from a high cupboard, and poured the rich ruby wine.

Suzanne grabbed hers and took an immediate fortifying gulp.

"Christ," he said from the other side of the kitchen bench, picking his up but not taking a sip. "Just say it already."

Placing her glass down, Suzanne tried to find her center through the slow wash of her pulse in her ears and the sudden thickness in her throat.

Right… Just. Say. It.

"I didn't picture you as a pet fish kinda guy." Yeah, okay…she totally chickened out. But she just needed a little more time to gather her nerves. It was tougher than she'd thought standing in front of him, asking him to be her fake rancher boyfriend.

"I'm not," he said, with a dismissive shake of his head as if tough guy ranchers didn't own fish. "It's a turtle."

Suzanne glanced at him. A turtle? Like a *turtle* was somehow a manlier pet to have than a fish? "*You* have a pet turtle?" She supposed it suited him—nothing soft and cuddly for Grady. Hell, she was surprised it wasn't a porcupine.

"Yes."

She blinked. He said it so matter-of-factly. "O… kay."

"What kind of pet should I have?"

"I don't know…a dog? Don't ranch dudes have dogs?"

"I've had dogs. Turtles live longer."

His lips were tight and his face was closed and forbidding in a way she hadn't seen before, leaving Suzanne in no doubt she'd just stirred some Old Yeller memory when she was supposed to be getting him on her side. *Fabulous.* "Does it have a name?" she asked, trying to shift the focus from deceased pets to living ones.

He sighed. "Zoom."

The laugh that spilled from her lips was completely involuntary. She'd expected him to say something like Rex or Rambo. Zoom was just too damn…cutesy. Nothing about Grady said cutesy. "*You* have a pet turtle named *Zoom*?"

He didn't bother to reconfirm, just shoved his hands on his hips, his patience clearly at its end. "Quit stalling."

Suzanne dropped her gaze to the bench—damn it, he had her number. Okay, fine. Sucking in a quick, deep breath, she ripped the Band-Aid straight off. "My parents, who are coming to visit, may be under the impression that you and I are romantically involved and living in sin in this cabin and that you are wild about Christmas, so much so that the place looks like something out of a Hallmark movie with enough tinsel and lights to be seen from *space*, and there's mistletoe everywhere because you can't keep your hands or lips off me."

Grady stood perfectly still. Suzanne knew this because she snuck a peek at him from among the fluffy strands of her hair that had fallen forward. Then slowly, very slowly, he lowered his glass to the bench. It made a slight muffled *tink* as it met marble, which clanged as loud as a ringing bell inside her head.

She'd have rather he'd banged it down and splashed wine everywhere than this controlled kind of calm.

"You told them *what*?"

"I'm sorry, Grady," she said, daring to meet his gaze now, hoping she'd be able to convince him it'd been a tiny white lie that had escalated out of control. His green eyes sliced into hers like razor blades. "I'd told my mom I wasn't coming home for Christmas, and then she said *fine, we'll come to you*." She beseeched him with her eyes, trying to impress upon Grady how much that idea sucked. "So I panicked and told a little white lie about me coming to Credence to be with you because I *can't* take another minimalist Christmas, Grady, I just *can't*, and I thought telling them I was shacked up with a guy who goes the full Griswold wouldn't just stop them from coming but send them screaming in the other direction..."

Drawing breath, Suzanne picked up her glass and swigged another gulp of wine. She was aware of every beat of her heart reverberating against her pulse points.

"But it didn't," Grady supplied, his face like stone—hard and unmoving except for the tick of a nerve at the angle of his jaw.

She nodded. "It didn't. They're still coming."

"So...*un*tell them."

It was a low, measured, reasonable demand, but Suzanne had dug herself too big a hole now. She'd totally fucked it up, and unfucking it without making herself look like some deranged chick who was so desperate for a man that she was fabricating a relationship was impossible. Self-preservation was a sucky reason to be hiding behind her lie, but she didn't want her parents to start wondering about the state of her relationships—or her mind, for that matter—when they had enough to be worrying about with their own relationship.

And who knew, maybe being around a newly *in love* couple would help her parents to find their own magic again? The focus *had* to be on her parents now, so it was just easier to go through with the farce than walk it back. *If* he agreed. If he didn't, she'd have to fess up and wear the consequences, but seriously…how hard could it be?

She glanced at Grady's forbidding face. *Impossible* by the looks of it.

"Or…" she said, her voice wobbling, betraying just how much was riding on his agreeing to the fake relationship. "And, just hear me out here…we could *pretend* that it's true."

His jaw did that clenching and unclenching thing again. "And why in the hell would I do that?"

"Because it's Christmas, and neighbors help each other out, especially at Christmas."

Grady bugged his eyes disbelievingly. "You want your drive shoveled? I'm your guy. You want a cup of sugar? Sure thing. You want me to play fake kissy-kissy under the mistletoe in front of your folks?" He shook his head. "Hell no."

But then his gaze dropped to her mouth and lingered hungrily, and the same breath-stealing tension she'd felt in the mudroom tightened her lungs. A wave of heat rolled between them, and the air sizzled as Suzanne's insides did a slow loop the loop.

"Please, Grady. I'll give you the paintings at the end if you help me out with this."

He dragged his gaze off her mouth and raked it over her face, the hunger replaced with twin lasers of doom, hot and piercing. If he was taken aback by her offer, he didn't show it as his mouth settled into a grim line. "Nope."

A moment of panic set in at Grady's definitive answer. Shit...what now? The last thing she'd expected was for him to walk away. She'd felt sure the paintings gave her rock-solid leverage. But then a truly inspired thought took form in her brain.

It seemed *panic* was the mother of invention for Suzanne. Or of snap decisions anyway.

"Fine, then, I'll give them all to Annie to hang in the diner. She's after some art for her walls. It's win-win."

Grady's pale-green eyes changed from indifferent to frosty in one blink. "You can't do that."

Suzanne shrugged. "They're my paintings. I can give them to whomever I like."

"They're. Of. *Me.*"

Grady enunciated each word with the kind of menace that had probably stopped many a bull in its tracks. But as ticked as he was now and as untouchable as he liked to come across, he *had* stared at her mouth before. And there *had* been hunger. That had been real. She'd *felt* it.

She'd felt it in her breasts and her belly and the backs of her thighs.

"As long as I don't sell them, I can do whatever the hell I want with them."

The angle of Grady's jaw blanched so white, Suzanne worried for a second that it might shatter. "They're of me," he repeated, his voice quieter this time but no less commanding.

Suzanne gave a casual shrug. "Maybe people won't notice."

"*I'll* notice," he ground out.

"So…help me." She placed the wineglass down and leaned forward. "Please," she added huskily, begging him with her eyes, appealing to his better nature.

Surely there *was* one underneath all that gruffness?

He stared back, his gaze hard, and the three feet of bench between them somehow felt like the Rio freaking Grande.

"Look…Grady. If you think I want this, that it's some kind of master plan to get myself a husband, you're full of it. I don't." She'd rather kiss up to a rattlesnake. "And I'm sorry I lied to my mother. More sorry than you'll ever know, but I did that as a favor to you—"

His loud snort interrupted her flow. "Jesus, Suzanne, stop doing me favors."

"To keep them away from the ranch," she continued, ignoring his interjection. "To put them off coming. And it backfired, and I really am sorry. But…my parents' marriage is in trouble, Grady. They're talking divorce. And my mom…she sounded so lost and devastated, and she isn't any of those things. Ever. They need a circuit breaker, a change of scenery to get things back on track, so if you won't do it for the paintings, maybe you can dig deep and do it for two people who just need a little hand in finding their way back to each other. They're my *parents*, Joshua, and trust me when I say this: I wouldn't ask if I weren't desperate."

The angle of his jaw worked some more, clenching and unclenching, as he stared at her for a long time, his face unreadable. "For how long?"

A flood of relief swamped Suzanne's body, but she quelled it quickly. He hadn't said yes yet. "Two weeks."

"What?" His brows raised in alarm. "*Two* weeks?"

"I know…" She held up her hands in a placating manner. "I'm sorry. It's longer than I expected."

Her mother had texted twenty minutes after she'd hung up with the flight details, and Suzanne had read it several times over, thinking surely her mom had made a mistake. But no, her mother had confirmed via text they'd *decided to have a nice long break*.

Two weeks. They were staying for two weeks, leaving a few days after Christmas.

It was fine, though, because Suzanne had a plan. "It's okay—I have a plan."

Grady stared at her incredulously. "Because the last one worked out so well?"

"Operation Hokiest Christmas Ever," Suzanne said, ignoring his sarcasm.

He didn't say anything this time, just picked up his glass and swallowed half his wine in one hit.

"I'm going to work my ass off these next two weeks getting my parents' marriage back on track while surrounding them in the tackiest, schmaltziest Christmas crap in the country, so they don't feel inclined to stay too long after they've realized they're meant to be together."

To say Grady looked unimpressed by her plan was a gigantic understatement.

"You don't have to do anything," she added. "I'll arrange all the schmaltzy stuff."

Given her lack of experience in seasonal schmaltz, Suzanne was going to have to do some research on that, but for someone who had craved it for as long as she could remember, it wasn't going to be any hardship.

"You can still go about your...ranching," she hastened to assure. Whatever the hell that involved. "We won't interfere with that, and I'll do all the heavy lifting with my parents, I promise. I'll keep them busy and run interference so they're not hassling you. Plus, when you come home from...the range every day, there'll be a hot meal"—she gestured to the pasta—"waiting for you."

"Home from the *range*?"

"Yeah, you know. Where the deer and the antelope play?"

He gaped at her, then muttered "Christ on a cracker" under his breath.

"All you have to do is smile," Suzanne said, ignoring his mutterings, eyeing him speculatively. "You do know how to smile, right?"

He met the question with a grim kind of blankness before lifting his lips into a smile that looked more menacing than festive. *Freaking hell.* They were doomed.

"Okay, well…" She nodded. "We can work on that." She smiled, trying to pass the criticism off as a joke, but his face remained implacable. "If you wouldn't mind faking some Christmas cheer, too, that'd help."

"*And* share my house. *And* stare at you with goo-goo eyes. *And* pretend I can't keep my hands off you."

Suzanne swallowed, getting a little weak down below at the thought of goo-goo eyes and those big hands of his. On her. "Right."

"I don't like lying." His voice was steely with disapproval.

"Yeah, well, you can get in line."

"You know no good will come of this, right?"

Suzanne nodded. Yeah, she was sure karma would bite her hard on the ass at some point for this deception.

He regarded her for a long moment. "Can you define what your expectations are around me not being able to keep my hands off you?"

Waves of hot prickles marched up her arms at his causal inquiry into the level of intimacy to be expected. Suzanne felt like she was seeing the soldier now—preparing, strategizing. She, on the other hand, was more of a fly-by-the-seat-of-your-pants kinda person. "You know…" Suzanne cleared her throat. "Putting your arm around me, holding my hand, hugging. That kind of thing."

"Kissing?"

Suzanne blinked at his frankness. Discussing

their deception like this in such a clinical way made her feel worse. "Well…there will be mistletoe."

His gaze dropped briefly to her mouth again like it had earlier. "So just under the mistletoe, then?"

"Not necessarily." Jesus, if he had to plan out ahead of time the moments he was going to kiss her, then this didn't bode well. "Just…wherever it feels natural." He gave her a look that left her in no doubt that kissing her wouldn't feel remotely natural.

He sure knew how to make a woman feel attractive.

"I don't know… Just follow my lead, I guess."

His jaw did that ticking thing again. "I like to lead."

Suzanne almost laughed out loud but caught it before it erupted from her mouth. "No shit."

"Twice a day—max."

She blinked at the clinical thrust of the words. Like he was negotiating the price of cattle or a discount on a new truck. "Sure, you want to set up some times in advance? Say eighteen hundred hours and twenty-two hundred?"

If he detected her sarcasm, it was impossible to tell. This man was the living end.

"Grady…I'm not sure we should be so prescriptive. I think we should aim for more spontaneity, depending on the situation."

"Twice a day," he repeated.

She stuck out her chin. If this was a negotiation, then two could play at that game. She was used to haggling her commission price. "Five."

"Three. And nothing in town. Only here on the ranch. This *relationship* stays on the ranch."

Wow. He really did *not* want to kiss her. "You care what people in town will think?" She'd have thought Grady cared diddly what *anyone* thought.

"Nope. But I've got to live here after you leave, and my private life is nobody's business."

Suzanne supposed there was some logic in that. Grady didn't strike her as the kind of guy who enjoyed public sympathy.

He folded his arms as if it was his final offer. "Take it or leave it."

"On the mouth."

Her parents were supposed to think she and Grady were an item—three chaste pecks on the cheek weren't going to cut it. He hesitated for a moment, then nodded.

"Fine," she acquiesced. "I'll take it."

"Fine."

"So…that's a yes? You'll help me with Operation Hokiest Christmas Ever?"

"It is. But I want a painting now. As a down payment."

Suzanne blinked. *What the?* "You think I'm going to renege on the deal?" Giving him those paintings was a necessary evil, a means to an end that would probably kill her, but she'd never go back on her word. She just hoped she wasn't giving him a piece of her muse, too.

"Consider it a sign of good faith."

"Oh yeah, and what's *your* sign of good faith? For all I know, you'll be lousy at faking it."

He regarded her for long moments before

picking up his wine, downing the other half, and striding around to her side of the bench. Suzanne's breath quickened as he got closer and closer, his sweats hiding none of the power of those quads, his gaze on her mouth utterly intent. She backed up a couple of steps as he closed the gap between them, her heart beating a wild tango.

Suzanne placed a hand on his chest as he stepped into her space. She meant to hold him back—she honestly did—but that T-shirt really was as soft as it looked, and the same hungry gleam she'd seen in his eyes earlier basked her in heat. An answering heat unfurled inside her as she curled her fist in his shirt.

"Grady?" she whispered, her pulse loud in her ears.

He grabbed her by the shoulders, as if unsure where to put his hands, and she knew, with sudden clarity, he was going to kiss her. And she panicked.

"That's not necces—"

The swift lowering of his mouth cut her off, and her eyes rounded as she looked at him, disconcerted to find him watching her, too. His lips were stiff and mostly closed and completely immobile, like he was out of practice. Or really sucked at it. And Suzanne held herself still and awkward in his arms and waited for it to be over.

But then, bit by bit, the timber of the kiss changed. His lips softened, his body relaxed, and he breathed out a little roughly; then his eyes fluttered closed and a strangled kind of groan came from somewhere deep inside his throat. The kind of groan that made her think maybe he didn't suck after all.

It was the groan that was Suzanne's undoing.

It opened up her senses, tapping into the taste and the smell and the touch of him. Wood smoke and red wine and the buzz of electricity just beneath her skin morphed her response from awkward to tentative, and she closed her eyes as his hands slid to her hips, pulling her up onto her toes, hitching her closer, and hers slid around his neck.

Their chests bumped together, their hips bumped together, and suddenly his mouth was all the right kinds of hard and soft, deep and wet, and when his tongue dipped inside her mouth and stroked along hers, it was Suzanne's turn to make some nonsensical noise in the back of her throat, somewhere between a moan and a whimper.

The kiss escalated. Grady's hands tightened on her hips as she shoved her fingers into the hair at his nape, the damp silky strands a sensual delight. He bent her back a little as he deepened the kiss, his mouth harder and wetter, demanding more. Suzanne gave it, returning fire, giving more, reveling in the hard press of him—his chest, his arms, his thighs.

Then, as suddenly as he'd swooped, he was gone, breaking away, stepping back, leaving them staring at each other, their chests heaving, the rough pants of their breathing loud in the charged space between them. His mouth was wet and swollen. She'd never seen Cowboy Surly look so damn undone.

God alone knew what she must look like.

"Well?" he demanded, his voice a low burr. "Will that do?"

Suzanne blinked as his tongue swiped at the moisture on his bottom lip. Will that *do*? She doubted she'd ever been kissed that well in her life. Sure, she'd had some great kisses, but this one? This one was like the Van freaking Gogh of kisses. Pulling herself back from the wackiness of *that* thought, she tried to get back on track. What had they been talking about? Oh yes, that's right, *faking it*.

If that was Grady faking it, she'd like to be the lucky woman who got the real deal.

She stared at him, her thoughts still in disarray, her pulse still booming so loud in her ears, she couldn't even hear herself think. Her brain was scrambled, her ovaries were cooked, and thank god for the bench or she'd have slid boneless to the floor.

Still too stupefied for conversation or any kind of deep analysis, Suzanne simply said, "Which one do you want?"

"The cherub."

Suzanne frowned at his quick-fire response. She expected him to not care or tell her to just grab the one that was closest, but he'd been very sure about his choice. "What's wrong with the cherub?"

"You painted my head on a *baby*. With *wings*."

"Okay." *Whatever*. It didn't really matter, she supposed as her brain started to power up again and the endgame came back into sight. "Fine. I'll bring it over in the morning. I'll be in and out of here the next couple of days decorating."

He winced. "When you say decorating, what do you mean exactly?"

"I pretty much made my mother believe your cabin is where they film all Hallmark movies."

"Great." His wince deepened. "Just how schmaltzy is it going to be?"

Suzanne didn't happen to think there was anything wrong with some cheesy seasonal exuberance—it was Christmas, for crying out loud. "The full schmaltz. We make it extra schmaltzy here with hardly anything at the cottage. The more we Christmas it up here, the more likely they are to want to spend time away from it. In the cottage. Where there's only one bed."

He sighed. "Fine."

"Do you have a spare key so I can get in and out?"

She couldn't quite believe they were casually talking about the logistics of her parental marriage intervention like that kiss hadn't occurred. She could still taste him, still smell the wood smoke caught in his hair, still feel the wild skip in her pulse, and yet she was talking tree trimming and keys.

Was he as poleaxed as her behind that inscrutable expression? Was his body still thrumming with the out-of-control mix of heat and happy hormones despite the return of his surly facade?

He glanced at her hand. "You're not in New York, Dorothy. We're in bumfuck Egypt. Nobody locks their doors."

"Oh…right…" She glanced at her wine, at the pasta, at the turtle tank, at the door. Anywhere but

Grady and his thoroughly kissed mouth. "I guess I'll be going." He didn't say anything, just stood there, his gaze intense. Putting on her big-girl panties, she lifted her gaze to meet his, forcing herself to smile and act normal. "Thanks again. For doing this."

"Don't thank me yet."

• • •

"Okay…let me get this straight," Winona said, her warm breath misting into the cold air inside Ethel because the van's heating was on the fritz. She was bundled up in her winter coat, scarf, gloves, and hat, as was Suzanne. "We're going to Denver to buy up the tackiest, most over-the-top Christmas stuff possible and then decorating Grady's place with it so your parents, whose marriage is on the rocks and are arriving the day after tomorrow, think you're in a relationship with a cowboy from Credence."

"In a nutshell."

"And I thought I had an active imagination." Winona shook her head. "I couldn't make this shit up."

"It's bad, right?" Suzanne glanced briefly across to her friend. "I'm going to hell."

"In the grand scheme of things that get you into hell, lying to your parents and bribing Grady are probably low down on the scale."

"Right?" Her friend's statement was buoying. "I mean, I'm not selling cigarettes to kids in the third world or jacking up the price of a lifesaving drug by five thousand percent overnight."

"Exactly."

Which didn't actually make Suzanne feel better. Lying and bribery were still shitty things to do.

"Stop at the next gas station; I'll get us coffee so we don't turn into Popsicles."

It was a lousy day for Ethel's ancient heating system to become recalcitrant. Suzanne knew she should just buy a new van—she could afford it—but Ethel had been with her from the beginning, from her very first commission. And paint stains and the reek of thinners really ruined that new-car magic.

Still, heat would be nice.

They stopped twice along the way before Suzanne pulled Ethel into the parking lot of a Christmas shop on the outskirts of Denver she'd found when Googling last night, because there wasn't enough tinsel and garland in Credence for Suzanne's needs. Hell, there wasn't enough in all of eastern Colorado. She'd made a comprehensive list of all the things she'd needed to turn the house into Santa's grotto, and she ticked through them mentally now.

It was that or think about the kiss—again.

So the guy could kiss. That should hardly be surprising, given how competently he did everything else in his life. Except *competently* wasn't the right word. *Competently* was thoroughly inadequate. *Masterfully* was much better. For a kiss that had started out like Grady hadn't ever graduated from the kissing-your-forearm school of tutoring, he had *owned* her by the time he'd pulled away.

She'd been left in no doubt that he could pull

off their fake relationship. She just needed to remind herself that it was *fake*. An act. It would be easy to forget if subjected to too many kisses of that caliber.

"Holy cow!" Winona's astonished exclamation pulled Suzanne out of the seductive web of last night's kiss. "I have no words," she said as they both stared at the twenty-foot-tall inflatable Santa Claus tied down to the roof of the shop. In his hands he held a sign that said, *Happy Birthday, Jesus.*

If anyone was going to hell, it was the makers of that abomination.

CHAPTER EIGHT

By four thirty, Suzanne and Winona were sitting in front of the fire as they indulged in a celebratory glass of red wine. The one from last night, which Grady had left on the bench top. They were laughing at the sweater Suzanne was wearing with dancing elves on a red background and Jingle My Bells knitted in cursive white print at the bottom.

She'd come across an entire aisle full of tacky clothing and gone a little overboard buying five pairs of sweaters in matching his-and-her styles. They were perfectly, kitschily awful. As were the T-shirts she'd bought, including sizes and styles for her parents, too.

Suzanne didn't even hear Grady arrive until the door swung open and both she and Winona turned with a start to see his very distinct silhouette in the doorway right beneath a terrible plastic sprig of mistletoe. Suzanne's fingers tightened around the wineglass. *Do* not *think about kissing Grady under that Mistletoe.*

Oops. Too late.

"Why is my cabin lit up like the Fourth of July?" he demanded, with barely a nod at Winona and absolutely no preamble.

"It's not that bad," Winona dismissed as Grady shut the door behind him.

All the windows had been frosted in fake snow and outlined with pink and green globes. The front porch railing and uprights were wrapped in lights, and a fringe of multicolored icicle lights draped off the gutters. They twinkled on and off in no particular sequence, and occasionally all flashed in unison.

"You want to hope Santa's not an epileptic," he grouched.

"I doubt he'd have a sleigh license if he was," Winona quipped.

She seemed completely unfazed by Grady's mood, and Suzanne wished she could be half as cool and confident. But then Grady stripped off his heavy coat and hat, hanging both on a hook near the door, and Suzanne was just grateful for the ability to make words at all.

He didn't bother to ruffle out his hair, which was suffering somewhat from being confined in his hat, because Grady didn't appear to give a shit what his hair looked like.

"How did you get them on the cabin without breaking your damn fool necks?"

Had Suzanne been in her right mind, she'd have told him women could do all kinds of stuff, including finding and climbing ladders and using tools like hammers, and very few broke necks or nails doing it. But the way his plaid shirt and jeans fit his body sapped all her fight.

"Burl helped us."

Grady grunted. "Of course he did."

They'd run into Burl in Credence when they'd stopped at the feed store to check out the Christmas trees in the lot that was apparently used for this purpose every year. Burl, knowing Grady would be out all day, had offered to help transport the tree they'd purchased and, when Suzanne had said she was decorating the cabin as a surprise for Grady, he'd stayed on and helped with the myriad lights. Suzanne was damn pleased they'd taken him up on his offer. The lights alone had taken Burl a few hours of pottering to complete, which had freed up her and Winona to complete the indoor decorations.

Suddenly, as if becoming aware of his surroundings, Grady's eyes skimmed the room. They landed on everything. Acres of garland and tinsel hung from every surface possible. From the exposed beams of the ceiling to the edge of the mantelpiece to the kitchen bench and the coffee tables. His gaze took in all the tinsel and holly and mistletoe, his eyes widening as he saw the lurid paper chain of butt-ugly fish in elf hats fringing the bottom of Zoom's tank.

Ornaments graced almost every flat surface. And not classy, elegant ornaments like her mother might choose if she ever slipped and hit her head and decided Christmas was worth celebrating. These were cheap, made-in-China imports, all plastic and tacky. Suzanne's favorite was fat Elvis in his worst kind of Vegas gear, including cape *and* a Santa hat, riding a reindeer. That one was in pride of place on the mantelpiece and actually played "Blue Christmas." Her next favorite was a snow globe with a Dunkin Donuts shop in it.

"Oh dear god," Grady said, his gaze growing ever wider as he pivoted slowly around. When there were very few surfaces not touched by Christmas, it was a lot to take in.

"Isn't it perfectly, horribly wonderful?" Winona enthused. "Just needs the tree decorated now, and it'll be complete."

The eight-foot tree had been left bare — Suzanne was keeping that as a family affair. Her mother would love that. *Not.*

"It looks like the Christmas fairy threw up in here."

"Good." Winona sighed. "Our work here is done." She stood, leaving a half glass of wine untouched. "Well, I better get going. I have a date with Bob and Ray at the old folks' home tonight."

"I'll be off, too," Suzanne said, also standing, seeing her opportunity to escape.

She wasn't sure she wanted to watch the differing shades of horror constantly shifting over Grady's face as he spotted some new insult to Christmas. And she really didn't want to be here when he discovered that she'd switched his toilet seat out for a special festive one. Nuts and holly and red berries were encapsulated in the clear plastic ring, along with Santa in a laden sleigh being pulled by reindeer.

And then there was the super kitschy snowman toilet lid cover and mat. The lid cover was the snowman's head, complete with a pipe for a nose, and the mat on the floor that sat snug around the pedestal was the snowman's body. Maybe worst of all was the three-foot inflatable Santa that currently sat in the Adirondack chair on the front porch, some green tinsel tied jauntily around his neck. She definitely didn't want to be here when he spotted it.

Or when he discovered the cherub painting propped against the wall in his bedroom.

Grady didn't say anything as they left; in fact, Suzanne wasn't sure he even noticed as he turned in slow circles, taking in the full festive purgatory of it all. It was probably best to just slip out anyway—he needed time to get used to his new surroundings, and she'd be here with him soon enough…

• • •

The next evening, washing up in the mudroom, Grady winced at the lights twinkling from the cabin. They'd greeted him from a mile away like Santa's fucking lighthouse as he'd driven in from the eastern boundary. But the normal house lights were on, too, which could only mean that Suzanne was inside.

Probably committing god knew what sin against Christmas in his cabin.

He'd been worried that having all those decorations in his place would bring back memories of long-ago Christmases. Ones he'd locked in a box inside his head marked *do not open*. He needn't have worried. Suzanne's unholy Christmas horror show was more the stuff of nightmares than fond memories.

And he was right in the middle of it all.

This morning, after lifting the snowman lid on his toilet, he'd had to literally sit on Santa's face to take a dump—a fact he would take to his grave. And this time tomorrow night, he'd be meeting her parents. Who thought he and Suzanne were shacked up and doing the wild thing.

Jesus. He must be getting soft in his old age. He was still pissed about the paintings but somehow, he'd agreed to a fake relationship. And it wasn't because of the paintings—although seeing the cherub waiting for him in his room last night had been surprisingly gratifying—it'd been the way she'd said, *They're my parents, Joshua.*

That right there had stuck a claw in his gut and twisted. He'd give anything to still have his parents alive and, had they been, he'd have wanted them to still be together, too.

Unwittingly, Suzanne St. Michelle had found his Achilles' heel.

Fuck. Why did it have to be *Christmas*? Any other time, he could have had some degree of separation from the emotion in her appeal, but this season always stirred up some pretty fucked-up memories. Which was why he hadn't wanted her here in the first place and why he was certain it wasn't going to end well.

Ever since Suzanne had pulled up in her ridiculous Mystery Van—not even two weeks ago—he'd felt like a bomb had been thrown into his very neat and ordered existence, and it made his skin itch just thinking about it. Grady knew all about explosions—real and metaphorical. In one way or another, they'd defined his life. It'd just taken him to the grand old age of thirty-five to realize that explosions could be made from sugar and spice and all things nice.

They could be made from green woolen hats

and red coats. From ridiculously unsuitable Ugg boots and a smudge of blue paint on a forehead. From the soft press of breasts and the erotic push of fingers into the hair at his nape. From the trace of red wine on lips to the sound of breathy whimpers at the back of a throat.

Christ. That kiss had been completely unexpected. He had no clue what had come over him, other than his dumb male ego being goaded by her *lousy at faking it* quip and rising to the challenge. Grady wasn't lousy at anything he set his mind to, but a quick *I hear faking things is more your wheelhouse* would have been far preferable.

She faked for a living, for fuck's sake.

But he hadn't really engaged his brain at all— he'd just moved to a beat that had been several belt notches below higher thinking—and it hadn't been until he was sliding his hands onto her that his brain had caught up with his body. And by then it had been way too late: Kissing her had become some primitive kind of imperative.

Which made him feel like a knuckle-dragging caveman. *Fuck.* These two weeks could not go fast enough.

Staring out the doorway and girding his loins to face the clusterfuck of his cabin *and* Suzanne, Grady's gaze snagged on the god-awful sprig of fake mistletoe hanging from a hook in the mudroom doorway. When in the hell had she put that up? It hadn't been there last night.

No. *Hell no.* Over his dead body, *no.*

Snatching it off the hook, he tossed it in the trash can near the sink, barely suppressing the urge

to rip it into tiny little pieces. She might have hung
the stuff from every beam in his ceiling, but she
couldn't have the mudroom. The mudroom was for
manly shit. For filthy boots and machinery grease,
for clothes streaked in sweat and all kinds of muck
and crap—sometimes *literally*—from the ranch.

She didn't get the mudroom.

The wreath on his back door stopped Grady in his
tracks—it hadn't been there last night, either. It
was made of garishly gold tinsel with red pom-
poms placed randomly amid the fuzz. Were they
supposed to represent baubles or Rudolph's nose?
In the center of the wreath, where a person could
reasonably expect to find nothing, Santa's jolly,
rosy-cheeked face stared back at him.

Grady shuddered. Where in the hell had she
found all this shit? www.tackyChristmascrapfor-
blindpeoplc.com?

Wishing he could *un*see the wreath, he entered.
Warmth enveloped him instantly, as did the aroma
of something hot and garlicky. The cabin had
smelled like this when he'd been seventeen and
come in after a long day working the ranch with his
uncle. But the woman in the kitchen wearing some
kind of snug green V-necked sweater that looked
as fluffy as a newborn chick was not his aunt.

She was his fake girlfriend. As of tomorrow.

"Hey." She smiled at him.

"We're not officially on the clock yet," he said,
turning his back to her to hang his hat and coat on
the hook and catch his goddamn breath.

"And hello to you, too," she said, ignoring his

testy response, and even though his back was to her and there was twenty feet between them, fingers curled around his spine. "I cooked some chili. Also picked up some of Annie's peach cobbler because... well...you live here, so I'm sure I don't have to explain, right? That woman is a national freaking treasure."

Grady gathered himself and turned around. "Agreed."

"You want to shower?" she said, a bowl in each hand. "And I'll serve up?"

"Suzanne..." He frowned, trying to figure her the hell out. Why was she trying to play house like they were the real deal? "What are you doing? Why are you acting all Suzy Homemaker?"

She put the bowls down with exaggerated patience. "My parents will be here tomorrow. We need to at least look like we've spent some time in each other's company. Plus, the more I dig into this, the more I realize I don't really know how to *do* Christmas. Not a full-on big fat *Christmas* Christmas, you know? The hokey kind that I implied to my mom you were into."

Yeah, he really wished she hadn't done that. The only thing Grady really knew about Christmas was how to avoid it altogether. Sure, he'd had almost seventeen years of perfect family Christmases, but that was a long time ago.

"Don't look at me." He shrugged. "I don't know the first thing about it, either."

"Right. So I bought some Christmas movie DVDs at that place in Denver because, no offense, but you don't strike me as the kind of guy with a

Netflix account."

"I'm not." Grady watched football on TV and that was it.

She nodded, clearly unsurprised. "I was thinking we should watch them together to get an idea of some of the hokey stuff we should be doing, and I thought you might be hungry after a long day out in the cold and we both have to eat. So yeah, I thought it'd be *right neighborly* of me, even if that word's not in your vocabulary, and I'm sorry if it's too Suzy Homemaker for you."

She was pissed. Her eyes glowered at him; her chest rose and fell a little faster. He sighed. "No, I'm sorry…you're right." He held his hands up in a placatory manner. "Thank you, it smells very good, and I appreciate it. I'll be ten minutes."

"Fine." She nodded, barely mollified. "But I'm starting without you."

Fifteen minutes later, they were sitting on the two-seater couch in front of the television deciding on which movie to watch as they ate their chili. Unlike the fireplace area that had several different seating choices, the corner nook where the television resided only had the one couch option and not a very generous one at that. It was usually just him watching football, so it hadn't ever mattered. But sitting this close to Suzanne had him reassessing his furniture.

It didn't help that she was slouched down against the back of the couch, her knees bent, her bare feet anchored on the edge of the couch cushion to stop her sliding off, the almost empty bowl of chili balanced on her stomach and supported by her thighs. It was distracting to see her so casual and at ease in his home, sitting next to him with barely a hand span between them like they did it every night.

Like it was the most natural thing in the world.

The feeling was not reciprocated. Grady spent his entire life keeping a mental and physical distance from people. It was how he'd survived those weeks and months after his parents and Bethany had died without totally cracking up, and it had become a habit. Except everything was assup with Suzanne. His body was enjoying her nearness too much, noticing every squiggle and squirm, his senses on high alert.

So conscious of her was he, everything else took a back seat, including his chili. It could have been a bowl of sawdust for all Grady knew.

"So…which one?" she asked as she forked chili into her mouth and scooped up the two DVDs she'd purchased yesterday. Everything shifted beneath her shirt very nicely. She filled out that sweater far too well.

She examined the covers. "The one with the couple in the sleigh? *A Knight Before Christmas*? Or the one with the couple in front of a tree covered in candy canes? *The Candy Cane Christmas Wish*?" She glanced from one to the other before thrusting the candy cane one at him. "I think the schmaltz is stronger with this one."

Grady shrugged, trying to act nonchalant. He'd rather watch paint dry than either of them, so… "Ladies' choice."

She gave him a brief smile and said, "Okay, candy canes it is."

Unfolding herself from the couch, she walked around the coffee table to the television and inserted the disc. Her ass was right in front of him, and Grady couldn't help but stare. Other parts of him were far less passive. It was the kind of ass a man could grab a hold of—not bony, not a thousand-squats-a-day firm, but round and soft, just like the peaches Annie used in her cobbler, and good Christ, he wanted to lean forward and *bite* it.

Grady stood abruptly as she straightened, thankful he was in jeans tonight, not his sweats. Sweats were not great at camouflaging erections. "I'll just grab some cobbler," he said. "You want some for when you've finished your chili?"

He ferried his half-full bowl to the kitchen, putting as much space between them as possible. Suzanne St. Michelle was a very bad idea. He'd loved and lost once a very long time ago, and he wasn't interested in ever putting his heart on the line again. He didn't get involved with women. Certainly not New York artists slumming it in Middle America, who thought lack of Netflix was some kind of mental deficiency.

"It's starting," she called as Grady lingered over plating up the cobbler, trying to quell his erection through mind power alone and failing. Not even thinking about that ridiculous cherub painting was working. Adjusting himself, he prayed that ninety minutes of saccharine Christmas stuff would do the trick.

It did. Within the first five minutes.

Grady counted twenty jingling bells, a dozen *Merry Christmas* greetings, and three snowmen. By the end of the film, he doubted he'd ever be capable of an erection again. He'd lost count of the bells and snowmen and angelic little children with toothpaste smiles wishing everyone *Happy Holidays*. Hell, if there'd been a partridge in a pear tree in the main street of the small fictitious town where the movie was set, he'd have been unsurprised.

There'd been five gold rings—*yes, really*—in one scene, so why not?

Still, he heard a sniffle and glanced at Suzanne as she dashed at a tear. What the hell? "You're *crying*?"

She turned red-rimmed eyes on him. "What? It was sweet."

"Yeah. I know. I can already feel my teeth rotting."

"He was a doctor who didn't believe in Christmas anymore," she said, her gaze imploring. "But now he does because the heroine's sick child helped him to see that every day you have is worth living and that special days should be celebrated. It was…" She scrubbed at her face. "Lovely."

Grady's lungs felt too tight for his chest at that little wobble in her voice. *She* was lovely. All red-eyed and emotionally invested in the most ridiculously fluffy plot he'd ever seen. Maybe that was the artist in her? They were sensitive types, weren't they?

Unlike soldiers.

The urge to put his arm around her crept up on him. *What the fuck?* He beat it back with words.

"God. You're a crier, aren't you?"

But a memory surfaced then—his father teasing his mother about being a crier. About her soppiness over movies and love songs and baby animals. His mother saying with a smile, "Scott Grady, you married a sentimental woman."

Grady blinked. Christ...when had that escaped the box?

"Uh, *yeah*." She blinked at him through a watery smile. "Emotional, touchy-feely artsy type here, remember?" Reaching for the second DVD, she said, "Ready for *A Knight Before Christmas*?"

"God no." Grady wasn't sure he could put up with another ninety minutes of schmaltz. Or Suzanne being all soft and sentimental beside him, reminding him of his mom. "I think we've got enough to go on, don't you? Awful his-and-her matching Christmas sweaters, snowmen, cookie baking, ice sculptures, snow angels."

"It's always good to have comparison data, though. Hell—" She looked over her shoulder as she made her way to the television with the DVD. "It's practically scientific."

Grady shot her a lukewarm smile, not feeling remotely scientific with her ass once again distracting him. *Unless it's anatomy*. Part of him wanted to pull the plug here and now, but part of him was actually enjoying the company.

No, he didn't understand why.

He *was* happy with his solitary life; he didn't need *company*. But sitting next to Suzanne, sharing his evening with someone other than himself, had been...nice. The light lilt of her laugh had been easy on his ear, and she smelled like peach cobbler.

Which was seriously fucking addictive. Who needed crystal meth when there was Annie's peach cobbler?

The movie opened with a note down at the bottom of the screen letting viewers know that the set designer had hand made all the wreaths in the movie. "Uh-oh." Grady glanced sideways. "I have a bad feeling about this."

A feeling that was absolutely spot-on. Within the first three scenes, there'd been enough wreaths to put one on every front door in America. He'd given up counting them.

"Looks like we're going to need more wreaths," he said.

She slid a side glance at him. "It is a little over the top, isn't it?"

The shot cut to another scene on the front porch of the heroine's house, which had not one, not two, not three, not even four but five wreaths. *Five*. All arranged artfully together like Christmas and the Olympics had given birth.

"Jesus," he said. "Do you think the set designer was high?"

"I don't know. I bet she's suffering from irreparable carpal tunnel, though."

When the shot pulled back to reveal the entire street had the same configuration of wreaths on their doors, Grady had taken all he could bear without some alcoholic fortification.

"Okay…I'm going to need some hard liquor to get through the rest of this," he announced. Making his way to the teak cabinet he'd found in a bazaar in Turkey, he opened the chest-height doors. "I'm a bourbon guy. What's your poison?"

For a moment, she looked hesitant, like she was going to decline, but then she said, "I like bourbon."

Grady did not let himself dwell on the idea of adding bourbon to peach cobbler; he just grabbed two shot glasses and the half-empty bottle of Wild Turkey and returned to the couch. Placing the bottle and glasses on the coffee table, he sat on the edge of his seat and poured two shots. Half turning, he handed one to Suzanne before grabbing his and settling back into the couch cushions. "How about we put some fun into the movie?"

Feigning a shocked expression, she said, "You're not having fun?"

Grady chuckled, and she smiled back, and he realized he *was* having fun. "This is my fun face, can't you tell?" He didn't give her a chance to answer, though, before launching into his proposal. "I propose we take a shot of bourbon every time we see a wreath."

"I don't think there's enough bourbon in Colorado for that, is there?"

He grinned. "You could be right."

She shook her head, wisps of her blond hair fluttering like fairy dust around her face. "Plus we could both be dead of alcoholic poisoning by the end of the movie."

"Okay, so let's just see how long it takes us to finish this bottle?"

He should at least have enough of a buzz on by then to cope with the seasonal schmaltz on the television, the curvy blonde beside him, and the uncomfortable feeling he was missing out on life sitting like a fucking great elephant on his chest.

Suzanne didn't look convinced as she returned her attention to the movie. He followed suit, and they watched as the heroine went into a shop with a wreath on the door.

"Wreath," she said and, not looking in his direction, threw back her shot.

Grady grinned and threw back his own.

CHAPTER NINE

Twenty minutes later, Grady *did* have a nice buzz on. So did Suzanne, if he wasn't very much mistaken. Her cheeks were flushed, and there was an interesting glitter in her eyes. They'd both had five shots, and the bottle was empty.

Twenty minutes.

"Well—" She upended her empty shot glass on the coffee table. "That's that. And there's still thirty minutes to go."

Grady upended his glass beside hers. "I predict more wreaths and that they're going to live happily ever after."

She gave a half laugh, half snort, which made Grady laugh a little more as she said, "You don't believe in happily ever afters?"

Grady most definitely did not. But even five shots of bourbon down, he knew a woman who cried at schmaltzy movies probably did. Hell, she probably even believed in love at first sight. And it was *definitely* best to steer this conversation in another direction altogether.

"I think somebody with that many wreaths is compensating for something not conducive to relationship longevity. Now, for the love of god, can we switch this off?"

"Oh but…they haven't made any snow angels yet."

"There were three dozen in the last movie."

"There weren't that many. Stop being dramatic." She bumped him with her shoulder. "Besides, I love snow angels. My mom doesn't approve of them; she thinks they're a delivery device for pneumonia."

A delivery device for pneumonia? Jesus, they were snow angels, not the plague! "So...you've never done one?"

"No, I've done them. Dad would take me to Central Park every year after it had snowed, and we'd spend hours making them. He thinks they're art. My mom thinks if anybody can do it, it's not art. We definitely have to get her to do a snow angel while she's here. Even if we have to crash tackle her to the ground."

Grady laughed. "I think I'll leave the crash tackling to you." Their gazes met for a moment, and they smiled at each other, the movie forgotten. The fact she was bribing him to be her fake rancher boyfriend—also forgotten.

Slowly, her smile faded, and she half turned toward him, grabbing her right leg and tucking it up under her so she was looking right at him. "I guess we should probably spend some time getting our stories straight."

He mimicked her actions so he was also facing her, their bent knees about a foot apart, but somehow feeling closer now that he could look into her eyes without turning his head. "Our stories straight?"

"Yeah, you know. For when my parents ask you, *So, Grady, tell us how you met our daughter.*"

Okay. That made sense. "What have you told

them already?"

"Very little, actually, so that's something. They think Winona put us in touch and we've been talking online, but we didn't actually meet face-to-face until I came to Credence. We could probably work on embellishing it."

Considering he barely knew Winona and he didn't *talk* or do anything else online with women, he was thankful for the heads-up. He sure as shit didn't want to embellish it, though. "I think we should just stick to the basics."

Embellishing lies made it hard to keep stories straight and, as he planned on talking to her parents as little as possible anyway, there didn't seem to be much point. He wouldn't be rude, but the reality was he'd be gone most days on the ranch, and he wasn't exactly a night owl.

It was past his bedtime right now.

"Fine," she conceded. "But I should know stuff about you. Like, where you were born and do you have any siblings and what are your parents' names and…the name of your first dog and what you were like in school and about Burl and the ranch and a lot of other stuff."

"Like whether I prefer chocolate or peanut M&M's?" Grady said, deliberately keeping it light because he'd much rather talk candy than his family situation.

"Yes. And your credit card number," she added with a sugary sweet smile.

Grady laughed. He may have initially thought Suzanne was here to find herself a husband, but he didn't think she was after his money. "Maybe next time you get me drunk on bourbon, I'll tell you that."

He was far from drunk, because Grady didn't do that, either, but the tension he'd felt whenever she got close was blissfully absent, and it felt good to not be so damn alert.

"Well, I think you should be drunk on bourbon more often," she said. "I didn't think you knew this many words."

Grady hooted out a laugh, grabbing his chest as if she'd wounded him. "Did you just call me dumb, Suzanne St. Michelle?"

She gaped at him, her cheeks flushing bright red as it dawned on her how her observation sounded. "Oh no…I'm sorry. I didn't mean…" Her hands fluttered in the air in agitation. "Please don't think—"

"I know I'm just a plainspoken…cowpoke," Grady interrupted, faking his best yokel accent. "I know I don't got me much dictionary learnin' but—"

Pressing his lips together to stop from smiling worked for about two seconds before he cracked, laughing at the horror on her face. She glared at him as she slowly realized he'd been teasing her.

"How long were you going to watch me squirm?"

He shrugged. "I hadn't made up my mind."

"Yeah, well, this is the last time I drink bourbon with you."

"I'm sorry for poking fun." But it had been fun to see her a little flustered.

"You have to admit, Grady, you're a man of few words."

"True. But not because I have the vocabulary of an ant."

"Because you're the strong, silent type?"

He shrugged. "The less you talk, the more you learn."

She crossed her eyes at him, and it was so unexpected, Grady chuckled. "That what being a soldier taught you?" she asked.

"Yep." Being in the military had taught Grady a lot of things, including shutting up and listening, which had suited a guy who was tired of people always wanting to *talk*. He'd been over talking about the tragedy that had forever altered the direction of his life.

"Did you like being a soldier?"

"Yes." The familiar ache in his chest glowed warm and bright. Grady had *loved* it.

"You were deployed?"

"Yes."

"Okay, well, we're down to one-word answers again, so I guess that means I'm getting a little personal."

She was teasing, he could tell, but the muscles in his neck had cranked a notch or two tighter. "I don't really talk about it."

It was her turn to laugh. "No kidding? But don't you think it's something your girlfriend would probably know?"

Girlfriend. Right. *Jesus…* "Three tours," he said, trying to keep the gruffness out of his voice. "One in Iraq, two in Afghanistan."

Nodding slowly, she said, "That must have been…"

Grady swore he could see the shimmer of tears puddling in her baby blues before she blinked them away, and he shifted uncomfortably. "A long way from Seattle, yes," he said, then winced internally at the flippancy in his voice.

"That's where you grew up?"

"Yep." Until the car accident had brought him to Credence.

"Burl said this is a bad time of year for you. Did something happen while you were deployed?"

He suppressed a snort. Lots of shit happened while he was deployed. But that wasn't what Burl had meant, and he really wished his uncle hadn't said anything. Sure, it had been vague enough, but Grady didn't really like people up in his business. Too many people in Credence had known his business when he'd come here as an orphan at seventeen, and he'd vowed to never feel that exposed again.

A man had his pride, damn it.

Opening his mouth to answer, he halted as she leaned in a little, proving she was the touchy-feely type by sliding her hand onto his forearm. "Sorry, forget that—it's really none of my business."

Grady forced himself to concentrate on what she'd said as her hand slid away. She'd given him a get-out-of-jail-free card, and he'd take it. "What about you? Are you New York born and bred?"

"Yes, sir." She gave him a little mock salute that would have seen her do pushups all day in basic training, but it did funny things to his breathing. Made him think about her in nothing but one of his old khaki army T-shirts, saluting him as she rode his dick.

Fucking hell. *Not helping, Grady.*

"And you're an art forger," he said conversationally, like she wasn't still riding him somewhere in the recesses of his mind.

"Well, technically I'm a reproduction artist, but yeah…forging, faking, making copies of other people's art is what I do."

"And people actually pay you to do that?"

She smiled at him as she leaned closer in a conspiratorial fashion. "They do. They pay me a lot of money."

Yeah, he remembered her mentioning that, but he lost his train of thought for a second as the V-neck of her sweater gaped a little and the creamy curve of her cleavage flashed like a neon sign in his peripheral vision. Her peach-cobbler scent combined with the bourbon on her breath to become an unholy turn-on.

"And who are these people?" he asked, yanking his brain out of his pants. "And why? People who can't afford an original but like to pretend they can?"

"Sometimes. Some private collectors just want a reproduction to display as a talking point or a brag piece or to just be up close and personal with a revered piece of art even if it is a fake. But oftentimes it's because they have the originals and want to protect them, have a substitute while the priceless piece stays under lock and key. The same goes for galleries and museums."

"So it's not illegal?"

"It's illegal if I paint the *Mona Lisa* and sign it

Leonardo da Vinci and sell it to a person pretending it's a da Vinci original. That's fraud. If they
know they're getting a reproduction, it's perfectly
legal."

"And lucrative."

She smiled again. "Very."

Grady was fascinated despite himself. He didn't
want to find her fascinating, this woman who was
here for one month and had manipulated him into
helping her deceive her parents—even if it was for
a good cause. But he did.

"Do you like it? Your job."

"I do," she said, but her smile dimmed. "Or at
least I did, anyway."

He frowned. "Not anymore?"

"I've been feeling more and more creatively…
stymied."

Her forehead furrowed into lines, her eyes
clouded with uncertainty, her teeth dug into her
lower lip. Her eyes—her face—were so damn
expressive, and Grady was captivated. "And that
means what?"

"I don't know my own…style. I've been mimicking other people's for such a long time, I don't
know what kind of painter I am. I used to always
paint my own stuff, when I was first starting out.
But it was…never good enough—"

"Says who?" Grady may have disliked the fact
that his face stared back at him from her canvases,
but she could clearly paint. To a guy who couldn't
even draw a stick figure, her paintings seemed
pretty damn good.

"A lot of people," she said with a quick dismissive

shake of her head. "And they were right. You could give me a bowl of fruit or an eastern Colorado landscape and tell me to paint what I see, and I can reproduce it faithfully. But there's never any…life to it."

Grady's face screwed into a puzzled expression. "*Does* a bowl of fruit have life?"

She shot him a rueful smile. "Yes, actually, it does. It's supposed to look and feel three-dimensional, like you can almost see the sun rising in the sky reflected on the skin of the apple through the window in the background. Like you could reach over and pluck it out of the bowl." She mimicked the action. "So eventually I…stuck with what I was good at, and that's been fine—I love my job, and it pays much better than what a lot of my artist friends make. But then Winona suggested coming here, and I desperately needed a change of scene, needed to get away from the familiar to explore this growing need I had to be me, to see if I could find myself as an artist again. And then I got here and…"

Her gaze took on a distant look, as if she was trying to find the right words somewhere out there in the universe or maybe inside her head. She was still looking at him, but she'd gone somewhere else entirely.

"The landscape here is so vast and raw, and it stirred something inside me, and I knew I could paint here, that my fingers were itching to paint. I realized I used to have that feeling all the time. That…urge, that…*stimulus*." Her gaze came back from far away, her focus now entirely on him. "You know what I mean?"

Oh yeah. Grady knew what she meant. He was fairly certain Suzanne hadn't chosen those words to taunt him. But he *was* taunted. Since she'd come to Credence and ruined his peace of mind, he'd been really fucking stimulated. "I do."

She gave him a self-deprecating smile. "God… sorry, artsy bullshit. Ignore me."

Except Grady *wanted* to know more. Like why she hadn't painted the landscape. Why she'd painted *him* instead. And if that wasn't a big red flag, he didn't know what was. He didn't *need* to know any of this for his fake rancher boyfriend role. He had his own psychological bullcrap to deal with; he didn't need hers inside his head as well.

Ignoring was a very good suggestion.

"Let's just watch the rest of the movie."

She turned her head toward the television, as did Grady, just in time for the couple to indulge in a very, *very* hot kiss. Back-her-against-the-door-and-kiss-her hot, shirt-scrunching, ass-grabbing hot. *Fuck.* It was so hot, he barely even registered there was a wreath right near their heads.

"Okay," she said, turning toward him again. "Maybe not."

And they both laughed, but Grady could hear the nervous quality of her laughter, and he was pretty sure there was a husky catch in his. And while they may not be looking at the television anymore, Grady was still thinking about that ass-grabbing kiss.

And the one from last night.

"Um…" he said, searching around valiantly

inside his head for something to distract them that wasn't anything too deep. "What about distinguishing marks?"

She blinked at him. Grady blinked back. Yeah... that was *dumbass*. He could have asked her favorite color or her favorite ice cream flavor or, hell, the name of her grade school art teacher. But his brain had given him distinguishing marks.

Like he was some kind of perv. Or filling out a fucking police report.

"I...have a birthmark."

Oh fuck. *No, no, no*. He did *not* need to know this. But it was too late. *Why?* Why had he asked that? Now he knew she had a birthmark, he couldn't *un*know it. And all he could think about was what and where. And how a boyfriend *would* know those things.

He cleared his throat. "Where?"

"My right upper thigh."

Her hand traveled up her leg and pointed at the spot. Grady told himself not to look; it wasn't as if he could see through her jeans. But he looked, zeroing in on her finger resting on her inner thigh about an inch from where it met her groin.

Good Christ.

He didn't know if he was imagining it, but he swore he could hear the rough exhalation of air from her mouth and smell the intoxicating aroma of bourbon on her breath.

"It's light brown, about the size of a nickel, shaped a bit like Texas."

Grady let out a strangled laugh. Texas? *Fuck*. Now he really wanted to see it. But instead of going there, he nodded and said, "Check. Texas birthmark, right upper thigh."

"What about you?" she asked as her hand returned to her knee.

He dragged his gaze back to her face. "I have a tattoo on my left shoulder blade."

"What is it?"

"An American eagle with *This We'll Defend* underneath."

"Oooh. Can I see?"

Grady, who had barely yanked himself back from the tantalizing knowledge of that birthmark, sat back a little at her request. Now *that* he hadn't expected. Her eyes glowed with interest *not* of a sexual nature, but that didn't stop his heart *or* his dick from taking a sudden leap.

Maybe it was the bourbon loosening his inhibitions, because somehow he'd gone from keeping Suzanne St. Michelle at arm's length to practically cuddling up on a couch with her and playing drinking games. Drinking games that had led to this.

Her looking at him with those big blue eyes, wanting to see his tattoo. Him contemplating showing her. Contemplating stripping her out of those goddamn jeans to find her little map of Texas.

And Jesus if that didn't sound all kinds of dirty.

"God, sorry." She swatted her hand in front of her face as if she were batting her request away. "That was…weird. Forget it." Her cheeks went all rosy. "I don't know where that came from. It was… very personal and not at all appropriate. You totally need to tell me if I overstep any boundaries. And definitely don't ever give me bourbon again.

We artists are bad enough with the concept of personal space without alcohol in the mix."

Grady, realizing he wanted her up in his personal space *badly*, tuned out her words as his gaze zeroed in on her mouth, following the constant movement as she spoke, flashes of her tongue adding fuel to the fire building in his groin. She was doing that talking-through-her-embarrassment thing again, and Grady, who'd never thought he'd find words and talking so damn addictive, considering he did them as little as possible, had to admit she had a way with both.

"...my father said it took him years to realize that an exhibition at a gallery was like watching a mass artistic fornication without the sex or nudity—"

She stopped abruptly and clapped a hand over her mouth at the same time Grady realized it had been a bad time to tune back in again, because all he could think about now was fornicating.

God...if there was ever a word that sounded like what it actually was, it had to be *fornicate*.

"What did you put in that bourbon?" she demanded in a husky entreaty, her hand sliding from her mouth. *Her delicious-looking mouth*. "You really should tell me to shut up before I run off any more at the mouth."

A buzzing started under his skin, his blood pounded thick and slow through his veins, and he couldn't help but think her suggestion was excellent as his gaze zeroed in on her lips.

"Joshua?" she said, her voice all low and husky.

It was the Joshua that did it. That was the

tipping point. The way she said it like a…balm? He wanted to suck her up. Eat her up. Absorb her into his soul.

So he shut her up. Not with words but with one swift swoop of his mouth across the small distance separating them, his hand sliding onto her cheek, his lips slanting over hers as he overstepped about a hundred boundaries.

God…she was dizzying, his heart was racing, the air in his lungs was hot, and she tasted like bourbon and smelled like peaches and he deepened the kiss for more. Who needed fancy perfume when cobbler and hard liquor were such a lethal mix? But it wasn't enough. His hand slid up her leg to her hip, gripping it and un-gripping it as she moaned into his mouth. He tugged, needing her closer — so much closer.

Against him, above him, under him.

Then suddenly she was moving, rolling onto her knees, her hand gliding to his shoulder, her thigh sliding over his, and he straightened to accommodate the move, a hand on each of her hips as she straddled him, settling herself against the rampant hardness of his dick as she kissed him from above now, her hair falling all around them in a curtain, trapping them in a cocoon of heavy breathing, bourbon, and bad ideas.

But she was hot in his arms and her tongue was playing tag with his and she was moaning and rubbing herself against the bulge in his jeans and her name was the symphony in his blood, the surge in his groin, the ringing in his ears. Almost of their own volition, Grady's hands slid up under her fluffy sweater, inching it up as he went, his hands straying to the front, traversing her ribs—up, up, up—until his trembling fingers brushed against the smooth satin of her bra and the soft mounds of her breasts filled his palms.

She gasped against his mouth as he squeezed, and she made a strangled kind of noise in the back of her throat as his thumbs brushed over the taut points pressing into the satin, shuddering as he did again and again and again. He wanted to fuck her like this.

Her over him, above him like this. He wanted to bury himself deep inside her and kiss up every moan and breathy little pant.

God, her mouth…it was addictive and it was ruining him. He couldn't get enough. He was fast becoming obsessed. In fact, he was so hot for her mouth and the noises she was making that he didn't even know her hands had strayed lower until she fumbled with his buckle, pulled at his belt. He groaned as her fingers brushed his erection through the denim, and in seconds the button was gone and his zipper was down and her hand was inside his boxers wrapping around his thickness and Grady's eyes practically rolled back in his head it felt so fucking incredible.

For a beat or two, he gave himself up to the overwhelming sensation of her palming him and her lips devouring his and the way her breasts filled his hands and how it was perfect and how he wanted more, wanted it all.

But that was his body speaking. His head was telling him something different, a backbeat that had rumbled louder and louder. A backbeat he just couldn't ignore anymore.

Bad idea. Bad idea. Bad idea.

Such a bad idea.

She cried in movies; he'd been dry-eyed since seventeen. She was New York; he was bumfuck Colorado. She was touchy-feely; he was all do-not-enter. She was on vacation from her life. This *was* his life. And it was perfectly fine.

God fucking damn it.

Grady tore his mouth from hers, dropped his hands from her breasts, making a grab for her hand creating the kind of havoc that was hard to forgo. He caught her around the wrist, stilling her maddeningly erotic action.

"Stop," he said, his voice rough as he panted hard.

Blood throbbed through his temples and pounded through his chest and the large pulse in his abdomen. His head fell back against the couch as he tried to catch his breath, his heated gaze meeting her confused one.

Christ, he wanted to kiss that look away, kiss her until the heat came back.

She didn't move for a moment or two, just sat, staring at him, her chest rising and falling quickly, her breathing loud. Her gaze dropped to his lap, to where his hand circled her wrist, to where her hand circled his dick, and Grady watched as realization dawned.

He hated that look.

"Shit," she whispered as she pulled her hand away from his dick like it was a live wire. Given its state, it fucking felt like one right now, too.

She moved then, scrambling off his lap, trying to unwind limbs and get off him as fast as she could, stumbling a little in the process as she yanked her top down and walked away from the couch, shoving her hand through her hair.

Grady shut his eyes, opening them again on a sigh. Absently, he noticed that the movie was still going and that the hero and heroine were standing in the town square in a crowd all watching a giant Christmas wreath being mounted on the edifice of the town hall.

Of course.

Zipping his unimpressed erection back in his pants, Grady pushed to his feet on unsteady legs. He couldn't believe how quickly things had escalated. How they'd been talking one moment and making out like it was their last night on the planet in the next. How a handful of days ago he'd told Suzanne to stay the hell away and tonight he'd had her boobs in his hands.

Grady couldn't remember when he last made out with a woman. Probably with Bethany when he was seventeen. They'd spent hours fooling around and, after a year together, had been each other's firsts. Sexual experiences since her death had been more about the destination than the journey.

Which had been perfectly *fine* by him and the women involved.

Turning around, he located Suzanne standing in front of the fire, her back to him, her arms wrapped around her body like she was cold. But after what happened on the couch, he doubted that was possible.

She turned suddenly and pinned him with a composed expression, her chin jutting a little in defiance. Like she hadn't just had her hand wrapped around his dick. But her mouth couldn't lie—those swollen lips still looked very well kissed. "That can't happen again," she announced.

Grady nodded. "I know."

"I'm not interested in taking this from fake to real."

He opened his mouth to say *really?* Because she'd been very fucking interested a minute ago. So had he. And that's because, like it or not, he was attracted to her. He hadn't felt this kind of pull in a very long time, and he'd bet the ranch she was attracted to him.

Which was seriously fucking inconvenient.

So maybe denial *was* better. Because he didn't want a woman in his life—he didn't *need* one, goddamn it—especially not this one who'd turned his house into a Christmas nightmare and given him an even greater aversion to wreaths.

"Neither am I."

He may want to have sex with Suzanne St. Michelle more than any other woman he'd ever met, but that was the sum total of his interest in her, and he was an adult in control of his impulses. He was practically a monk as it was, and there was always his right hand.

She nodded stiffly. "Good. Let's not cross that line, okay? It's complicated enough."

"Agreed."

Clearing her throat, she said, "I'll move my stuff into your spare room tomorrow morning. My parents should be here about two in the afternoon. Is it possible for you to be here when they arrive?"

Grady wanted that about as much as he wanted her in his house. Right now he'd rather be buried under a pile of Christmas wreaths than be a party to either. "I'll try."

If it worked out—fine. But he wasn't going to neglect his ranching duties because Suzanne had gotten herself caught in a lie. Resentment flared anew at the predicament and warred with a body still clamoring to be back on the couch with her.

He had known she was going to be trouble. He just thought she'd be the kind of trouble he could resist. The universe, however, had other ideas.

"Thank you." She dropped her arms, her gaze darting to the door and back again. "Well…I'll see you tomorrow."

Grady nodded. She didn't wait to see if any words would follow the nod, just strode across the room and out the door. It clicked shut behind her, and Grady eased down onto the couch, cradling his head in his hands.

"*Fuck.*" What had he gotten himself into?

CHAPTER TEN

A roil of nausea undulated through Suzanne's stomach muscles as she watched her parents' rental car turn in from the road to the ranch and make its way down the long drive to the cabin. Two thirty—right on time.

Another nervous pang rolled through her system. She'd had a busy day ensuring everything was all set to go. She'd moved her stuff out of the cottage and into Grady's spare bedroom. All the bedrooms were situated through the archway and ran off a long hallway. Grady's room was at one end and beside what was a smaller room he used as an office. It had a desk—neat-freak tidy—a big black leather swivel chair, and a state-of-the-art computer. There were bookshelves on one wall containing mostly agricultural and animal husbandry books, a three-drawer filing cabinet, and a leather couch that looked as if it had been well used.

Also, to her surprise, was the cherub, propped against the wall. Suzanne had half expected him to have burned it already. Or stashed it in the barn. Yet it was in his office, facing out, where he could see it every day.

Best not to dwell on that particular quandary.

Next to the office was the bathroom then another bedroom and next to that—about as far away from Grady's room as was possible—was

Suzanne's room. Thankfully, it was big enough to be able to store her paintings, her easel, and her art supplies.

She'd thrown open the back and front doors to the cottage to air it in preparation for her parents' arrival. It had smelled a bit like her studio, and Suzanne didn't want her mom asking questions about what Suzanne was working on. Not yet anyway. She'd stripped and remade the bed with fresh sheets and cleaned the bathroom.

As part of the plan, she had deliberately not put any decorations in the cottage. She wanted it to be a haven for her parents to escape to when the cabin cheer became too much. She had put up a tree, however—the tackiest artificial tree she could find on her Denver expedition.

The branches were stiff bristles of garish pink, and it came complete with its own yellow-and-green pineapple baubles. The angel on top was a hula girl wearing a Santa hat.

It was a tropical Christmas abomination. But it still looked better than that coat hanger disaster in their brownstone.

The vehicle—some fancy, expensive-looking four-wheel drive—pulling to a stop in front of the cabin brought Suzanne back to the present. She waved and plastered a smile on her face. This was it—showtime. There was nothing more she could do.

The only thing missing was Grady.

But she wasn't thinking about that because, if she thought about that, then she'd think about last night, about kissing him and the other stuff they'd done. Heavy petting on the couch like a pair of horny teenagers, his hands shoved up her top, her hands shoved inside his pants.

And she couldn't think about that with her mother's car door opening.

Grady had said he'd try and be here and, for what it was worth, she'd believed him even though she couldn't blame him for wanting to avoid her for as long as possible.

Why did she have to be so sexually attracted to her fake rancher boyfriend?

"Darling."

Suzanne's chest filled with a rush of love as her mom emerged from the vehicle, the blunt edge of her signature silvery bob sitting, as always, perfectly square with her jaw. She may have wanted to get away from her parents this December, and she'd only been gone for twelve days, but knowing they were going through a rough patch, that they were hurting, intensified the love she felt for these two people who had shaped and formed and loved her all her life.

After running down the stairs, she jogged to her mom and gave her a huge hug, a lump as thick as her mother's puffy jacket lodged in her throat.

"I love you, Mom," she whispered.

"I love you, too," she whispered back.

Her father appeared around the side of the vehicle, pushing his wild curly hair now heavily streaked with silver back off his face. He was tall and slender with round wire-framed glasses that gave him the air of a college professor. "Hey, honey."

"Hey, Dad, how are you?"

He gave her a smile that didn't quite reach his eyes. "Same old, same old," he said in an almost resigned way that rocketed Suzanne's concerns way off the charts, and she hugged him probably a little too hard.

"This really is the middle of nowhere, isn't it?" her mom said as she scanned the winter fields, the barren tree branches adding to the starkness of the landscape. "How does anyone even live out here?"

"It's not like home, that's for sure," Suzanne said, fixing the smile back on her face. "But Grady loves it."

At least that wasn't a lie. It was clear he did love this ranch, and Suzanne was happy to utter the truth whenever she could to counterbalance the deception.

"So where is this mysterious rancher boyfriend you kept so quiet?" her father asked, slipping his arm around his daughter's shoulders.

"Yes, darling. I thought he'd be here?"

"He's not far away," Suzanne assured, although she had no idea if that was actually the case or not. "It's a full-time job managing the ranch, so he's usually gone all day."

At least that's what she assumed anyway. She'd met a couple of Grady's hands, and she'd seen their vehicles come and go, so she knew he had help, but he wasn't exactly idle, either.

"Come inside out of the cold, and I'll show you around, then take you across to the cottage so you can settle in."

And hopefully, Grady would make an appearance soon.

"I see what you mean about him being a Christmas freak," Simone said, her gaze finding the blow-up Santa with his tinsel scarf perched on the Adirondack chair on the porch. She was staring at it like it was roadkill.

Suzanne forced a bubbly laugh. "He's so goofy, right?" She faked a besotted expression. "Come on, this way."

She entered the cabin before them, stopping a foot inside and luring her parents to the doorway, then clapping and pointing above them. "Mistletoe!" she said with a grin. "Gotta kiss—it's the rule."

Her parents looked at each other awkwardly, and Suzanne's heart sat heavy as a stone in her chest as they exchanged an even more awkward peck on the cheek. *Jesus.* Had this been happening for years and Suzanne had been oblivious?

Waving them in, Suzanne did a quick tour. Being open plan, it was fairly obvious where everything was, so she just pointed in the direction of the archway and said, "Bedrooms are through there."

Suzanne had strategically placed some of her belongings around the living area. Her Uggs by the back door, her coat hung on the hook. One of Winona's books sat on the coffee table in front of the fireplace, and her favorite wrap was slung over the arm of the couch. A cooking magazine she'd bought in Credence yesterday when she'd picked up the ingredients for the eggnog sat on the kitchen bench.

Not that her parents noticed any of those details

as their gazes darted around the multitude of Christmas decorations that formed a wonderfully horrible Yuletide clash.

"Wow...this is..." Her mother turned slowly around and around in pretty much the same fashion Grady had when he'd first seen what she'd done to his place. It was rare for her mother to be speechless.

Her father didn't appear to have too many words, either.

"I know it's a little over-the-top, but Grady is just like a little kid when it comes to this stuff. And...I don't know...I kinda like it."

Simone St. Michelle looked at Suzanne like an intervention might be needed, but she didn't voice her opinion, which was quite controlled for her mother. "Mmm," she said instead. "At least the tree is...minimalist."

"Oh no." Suzanne shook her head as she took in the bare tree that Burl has set up for her. "Grady is just obsessed with trimming the tree. But he wanted to wait and have us all do it together tonight. Isn't that so thoughtful of him?"

"Oh, no, darling." She could see her mother already thinking ahead to what kind of horror show the tree trimming was going to be. "We don't want to intrude on something personal like that, what with this being your first Christmas together."

Suzanne shook her head. "Nonsense."

No way in hell was her mom inviting herself to the ranch on the promise she'd be fully involved in Grady's (nonexistent) seasonal fervor and then weaseling out right at the start. Her mom had messed up Suzanne's Christmas plans by practically begging her for this break away, for a chance to work on her marriage, and that started tonight with them both doing something they'd never done together.

Terrible ornaments or not, few things under-scored the sense of family more than all being gathered around a Christmas tree. Or so she'd been told.

"Grady will be terribly disappointed if you don't. He's been looking forward to it. He even made a playlist for it. This is what families do at Christmas, Mom."

Suzanne didn't say *and you promised*. She didn't need to; the emphasis in her voice made it obvious enough. Which probably made her a lousy daughter, but Suzanne was in a tough spot—albeit of her own making. She was trying to help her parents *and* get the Christmas she wanted all while operating within the parameters of her lie.

She felt like she was juggling boiling hot kettles.

"Of course we'll be here," her father said with a strained smile. "Won't we, Simone?"

"Yes." Her mother brightened. "We'd love to."

"Good."

Suzanne beamed at her parents like it was the best damn thing she'd ever heard. Man, this was exhausting. Her parents had better have this patched up sooner rather than later because this act she was putting on was bonkers.

"Now, come and see the cottage. You'll be pleased to know I stopped Grady from going overboard in there. He did insist on a tree, but it's only a couple of feet high and one of those fake ones you seem to like so much. Trust me, for him, it's understated."

Her parents exchanged a glance like they weren't sure Grady had *understated* in his vocabulary. Poor guy, she really owed him big-time. But then she remembered he was getting her paintings—her priceless paintings—so it was a fair trade.

"Excellent," her father said, gesturing toward the door. "Lead the way."

They'd completed the tour of the cottage— Suzanne had insisted her parents kiss in that doorway, too, which had been just as lackluster— and were stepping outside to grab the luggage from the car her father had brought around when Grady appeared. He strode toward them from the direction of the barn, his big coat buttoned up, his hat pulled low, and his boots eating up the ground. His shoulders were squared like their predicament was a problem he was tackling head-on and, even from a distance, his cool green gaze pinned her to the spot.

Suzanne's stomach gave a lurch. *Nerves. Just nerves.* Not the memory of what they'd done last night.

And just like that, she was back on that couch with him, making out, all that coiled heat and energy she could see in his gait right now unleashed on her body. On her mouth, on her pulse, on her brain. His strong fingers biting into her hips and tugging at her waist and grazing across her nipples.

"Oh, here he is," her mother said. "My...he

walks like he owns the world, doesn't he?"

Oh yeah. Suzanne couldn't have put it better herself. His stride was so damn sure. So damn *male*. It made her hot just watching him prowl ever closer, his Wranglers hugging his thighs in ways that were utterly indecent. Suzanne flattened her palms to her stomach, very much afraid her clothes were going to fall right off the closer he got.

He wasn't smiling. He was supposed to be smiling. But she doubted that anyone was obtuse enough not to see that intensity in his eyes and know exactly what it was.

Pure, unadulterated sexual interest.

Holy crap. Give the man an Oscar. "Babe," she said, plastering a smile on her face as he got within arm's reach.

Suzanne didn't wait for him to make the first move, not sure, despite the set of his jaw and his forward momentum, if he would or not. With her pulse tripping madly, she slid a hand up his arm to his shoulder, stepped into his space, rose on her tiptoes, and pressed her mouth to his.

She felt the jolt go through him, felt the brief edge of his resistance before he let it go and kissed her back, his hands sliding around her, pulling her closer. He didn't deepen the kiss, neither did she, but it smoldered, then it sparked, then it roared to life between them, the hardness of his body like fuel to the flame, the aromas of saddle leather and hay and soap adding to the inferno.

But as abruptly as he'd lit the fuse, he snuffed it out, pulling back, chuckling light and easy against her temple, saying, "Where are our manners, *babe*," before kissing near her ear and whispering, "that's one."

While Suzanne's body cried out against the sudden cessation of pleasure and her brain scrambled to compute what he'd whispered, he was holding out his hand to her father. "Hello, sir, I'm Grady. Nice to meet you."

Suzanne blinked as her father said, "Albie. Albie St. Michelle." Had Grady just been…keeping score? While she'd been swept away by the intensity of a *closed-mouth* kiss, had he been ticking off his fake rancher boyfriend checklist?

One kiss down, two to go?

That was *cold*. Really freaking cold. Note to self—her fake rancher boyfriend could switch it on and off at random.

Consider yourself warned, Suzanne.

"Simone," she vaguely heard her mother say and was peripherally aware of her and Grady also shaking hands as a full head of steam build inside her skull.

"Mom, Dad," Suzanne said, yanking herself back from the bubbling lava pit of her rage, "meet Joshua Grady. He prefers Grady. I prefer *Joshy*."

She gave a little laugh and slipped her arm around his waist as she smiled up at him, a whole lot of *take that, dipshit* in her eyes. He smiled back, his eyes glittering at her with a whole lot of *oh no you just didn't*.

"So nice to meet you," he said, turning a friendly face back to her parents. "Suzy has told me so much about you guys."

Her mother's eyebrows almost lifted right off

her face. *"Suzy?"*

Simone St. Michelle had resisted all attempts by her father, her friends, schools, acquaintances, and colleagues to bastardize her daughter's name. Sue, Suzy, Susie Q (her dad's favorite), Susan, Susannah had all been met with disapproval. She'd named her daughter after Suzanne Valadon, a French painter known for her female nudes, and it had never been anything else.

Until now.

"Joshy likes to tease," Suzanne said on a half laugh, giving his waist a hard squeeze.

"What?" he said playfully. "You don't think she looks like a Suzy?" When her mother said nothing, he gave a chuckle, slung an arm around her neck, pulling her closer and dropping a kiss on top of her head.

On. Top. Of. Her. Head. He might as well have patted her instead.

"She'll always be Suzy to me."

Suzanne knew without a doubt he was going to call her that from now on. Freaking fabulous… "Well anyway," Suzanne said, realizing it was a small price to pay for his help, "I was just going to help Mom and Dad with their bags."

"I'll do that," he said with a smile that was so charming, Suzanne blinked twice in case it was a figment of her imagination. Charming had, thus far, not been in his repertoire.

She was starting to think the man had taken some acting lessons. Hell, if she hadn't seen that shrapnel wound with her own eyes, she'd be tempted to suspect he'd spent twelve years in some acting troupe instead of the military.

"Thank you, *Joshy*."

"Anything for you, my love," he said, swooping in again, whispering *"Two,"* against her lips before he laid a quick, hard kiss on her mouth and pulled away again. "So, Albie," he said like he'd just kissed a plank of wood. "Let's get you guys unpacked."

• • •

At quarter to six, Suzanne stood outside Grady's door, taking a deep breath. Her parents would be at the cabin for the evening's festivities in fifteen minutes. They'd expressed the need for a rest after their tiring day of travel, and while Suzanne suspected what they actually needed was some time to adjust to the high-octane level of Christmas, she was more than okay with them spending alone time together in the cottage.

Good for their relationship and her sanity.

She and Grady hadn't spoken since he'd finished helping her father unpack the car. He'd disappeared back to the barn for a bit, only returning to the cabin as night drew in and even then had only spared her a brief, "I'll be in my office," before he disappeared again.

Knowing that had been awfully distracting. He was in his office. With the cherub. Did that mean he actually liked it?

Or was he just saving it up for a mass burial/ bonfire at the end?

But he wasn't in his office now—she'd looked in there to find it empty—and he hadn't slipped outside again because she would have seen him leave, so he had to be in his bedroom. And she really needed to talk to him before her parents arrived.

Lifting her hand, she knocked on his door. It was a little on the timid side, which might have something to do with the nature of her request. When there was no response, she knocked louder. Nothing. Was he ignoring her? For the love of Zeus…why was a guy in his mid-thirties hiding out in his bedroom like some kid?

Steeling herself, she cracked open the door, saying, "Grady?" as she pushed it all the way open and peered around the jamb. He was just stepping into his bedroom from what she assumed was the bathroom, given he had only a towel slung around his waist and his hair was damp.

For a moment, she was too stunned to move. Well…too stunned to move anything *other* than her eyes, which took a slow trip over his chest and abs, the narrowness of his hips and the bulge between.

Oh Jesus. How could one man look so damn good? This was bad. *Very bad*. "Oh…" She averted her eyes, then turned her back. "I'm sorry. I knocked but…"

"Oh come on now, *Suzy*, don't be so modest." The sarcasm dripped from his voice. "I'm more covered than the cherub is."

Yeah, well…he was also a helluva lot more freaking manly than the cherub. Definitely more endowed. Not to mention he was actually *real*. Flesh and blood and bone. And other more interesting anatomical bits she really wished she wasn't thinking about right now.

"You're seriously going to keep calling me Suzy?"

"Yep," he said, and she heard rustling, a clink of a buckle, like he was getting dressed. "Payback's a bitch." Another beat or two passed before he said, "I'm decent now."

Relief lulled Suzanne into a false sense of security, and she turned to find he'd pulled on a pair of jeans—that was it. *Nobody* in their right mind would have called Grady "decent" right now. From his belt flapping open to the top button of his fly still gaping, he was thoroughly *in*decent.

"You're seriously wearing that sweater?"

Suzanne, who had forgotten the very reason for entering his room in the first place, glanced down at her sweater uncomprehendingly for a moment because hell, at least she was *dressed.*

It was one of the handful of terrible Christmas sweaters she'd bought in Denver. It was black with a large elf body on the front. The elf was female, in a red dress with a green belt, green shoes, and stripy red-and-green stockings. There was no face— in fact, the neckline of the elf's dress melded with the neckline of the sweater, which made Suzanne's head the head of the elf.

It was awful and absolutely perfect for the hokiest Christmas ever, and she'd bought it without thinking twice. She'd also bought a matching male elf for Grady, which was why she was standing in his room. His *bed*room.

"Yes," she confirmed, grateful for the prompt

but distracted again as she looked at him. There was a hardness to Grady's physique that a man didn't get from pumping iron. There were slabs of muscle beneath the flesh of his pecs and abs, rather than that pillowed delineation so popular on Instagram these days.

"Is there something you wanted?" The movement of his mouth dragged her gaze to the light whiskery growth around his lips, along his jaw, and halfway down his neck. "Or did you just want to indiscriminately ogle me?"

Oh crap. *Busted.* Suzanne averted her gaze as she gave herself a mental shake. He was right. What in the hell was she doing? Standing there staring at him with her tongue practically hanging out like Scooby-goddamn-Doo.

"Oh yes…sorry." Her brain kicked into gear. The sweater. In her hand. The one she'd bought for Grady. "Could you wear this tonight?" Holding it by the shoulder seams, she flapped it out so he could see. This elf was wearing a green shirt and shorts with a red belt, red shoes, and red-and-green stripy socks.

Grady stared at it like it was something he'd worn in on his boot. He shook his head. "Oh *hell* no."

Suzanne's fingers tightened around the synthetic woolen fabric. She'd expected resistance. "Big fat *Christmas* Christmas, remember?" she reminded him, jiggling it a little.

"It's fucking awful."

"Yeah." Suzanne bugged her eyes at him. "That's the point."

He eyed the sweater with disgust. "And they say cowboys are hokey."

"So you'll wear it?" She took a step forward.

"Nope." His vehement headshake stopped her in her tracks. "I wouldn't be caught dead in that."

"No one's going to know, Grady."

"*I'll* know." He shoved his hands on his hips. "Who even makes this crap anyway?"

"Santa's little helpers?" she suggested, trying to be cute.

Clearly she failed if his unimpressed snort was any indication. "More like Satan's little helpers."

Suzanne shrugged. "Does it really matter?" In the short time she'd known him, Joshua Grady had made no bones about being a proud man. But surely he could cope with a few silly shirts. They weren't exactly family dishonor kind of stuff. "Seriously, Grady, are you telling me your ego is that precious, you can't wear some funny his-and-her matching shirts and sweaters for the next couple of weeks?"

His eyebrows shot up his forehead before his eyes narrowed. "You mean there's *more*?"

Well crap…she hadn't meant to break that bit of news to him tonight. "I…may or may not have bought a few more."

He folded his arms across his chest—his *naked* chest—his gaze roving over her face as if he was considering his options. The angle of his jaw ticked, his lips pressed together in a tight line.

"Look, I don't make up the rules about this stuff. Apparently his-and-her sweaters are what people who are really into Christmas do, remember? The heroine's parents in that first movie wore them everywhere. Also, added bonus, it's the kind of tacky Christmas shit my parents can't abide. It'll definitely send them back to their non-Christmas cottage for marriage-building time."

Waiting another beat or two, he said, "Fine. I'll wear whatever you want. But if wearing hideous Christmas sweaters is a part of the deal, then I'm going to need another painting."

Suzanne gaped at him. "Josh—" She faltered at calling him by his real name. She hadn't planned to, but it had just flowed off her tongue. "Are you *really* going to screw me out of a painting every time you don't want to do something?"

He shrugged. "Probably."

Suzanne's temper flared again. "I told you, I'd give them all to you at the end."

"Yeah." He nodded, suddenly not so pissed off. "But it's more fun this way."

She suppressed the urge to tell him *again* that the only reason they were in this mess was because she'd tried to keep her parents *away* from Credence for *him*. But that was bullshit—it wasn't his fault that she'd been called on her bluff. Nor was the hole she'd dug herself trying to weasel out of it.

"Fine." She huffed out a breath. "Which one?"

"*David*."

Once again, he hadn't even paused to give it any thought. It was like he had a mental list he was keeping numbered in importance from one to five. Suzanne opened her mouth to protest—*David* was special. *David* was the painting that had started it all. But ultimately she supposed it didn't really matter. In a couple of weeks, none of them would belong to her anymore.

Her muse, who'd been ignored ever since her mom had announced she was coming to Credence, curled up a little bit more inside.

Sad and hurt and frustrated at the prospect, she turned on her heel and stormed out of his room. Marching to the end of the hallway, she strode into her room, grabbed the canvas, and marched all the way back to Grady's. He'd used the time to pull on a shirt, but that barely registered as she propped the painting against the wall.

"Satisfied?"

He crossed to it, inspecting it for long moments. Suzanne couldn't look. It was like a knife through her soul, and she blinked hard to dispel the prick of tears as he said, "Thank you."

She thrust the article of clothing at him. "Put on the damn sweater."

Thankfully, he shoved it over his head without any further ado, and she didn't stick around for any more commentary, just headed for the door. "They'll be here any minute," she tossed over her shoulder.

He didn't reply, and she stopped in the doorway, turning to check that he'd heard to find him wincing down at the sweater. He lifted his head and grimaced in her direction. "Don't even think I'm wearing any of these into Credence, Suzy."

"What?" she said, injecting sweetness and sarcasm into her tone. "And pass up the opportunity to screw me out of another painting?"

He snorted. "You could offer me a blow job to wear this into town and the answer would still be no."

It was on the tip of her tongue to tell Grady that even if his life depended on her sucking poison out of it, she wouldn't put her mouth anywhere near his dick. But the truth was, she'd spent most of last night fantasizing about blowing him anyway and, as un-feminist as it was, performing a sexual act on him would probably take far less out of her soul than parting with her paintings.

"Your loss," she said with a shrug because he looked entirely too sure of himself right now, and she was damned if he was going to have the last word. "I give excellent blow jobs."

Then she slipped out of his room.

CHAPTER ELEVEN

Grady spent the next hour making polite conversation with Suzanne's parents as they dined, which was a welcome distraction from persistent thoughts of just how good their daughter apparently was at giving blow jobs. He figured she'd said it just to get a reaction and, well…mission accomplished. Damn if he could think of much else.

Albie and Simone seemed like nice people but very sophisticated, and Grady was pleased to have had a life outside of Credence for a lot of years. Had he been more cloistered, their talk about art shows in London and Madrid and Florence might have made him feel like a hillbilly. They weren't being deliberately intimidating, he knew that, but another man may have felt a little inadequate.

The good thing, though, about them living in their New York bubble was their propensity to talk about it and their life there, which he encouraged, peppering them with questions. Because while they were talking about New York, he didn't have to talk about himself. Or the fake relationship he was having with their daughter.

Or think about how good she was at giving blow jobs.

Fuck. Dude, stop it!

But it was almost impossible to keep his mind fully on the conversation, especially when she was so damn touchy-feely throughout the meal.

Nothing over-the-top, just *constant*. A hand on his forearm, her fingers straying to his and toying absently, leaning in close to nudge his shoulder with hers, her arm slung casually around the back of his chair.

Twice she'd slipped her hand under his arm, her knuckles grazing his ribs as she looped their arms together and smooshed her cheek against his shoulder. He'd actually dropped a kiss on her head the first time. He had no idea why he'd done it other than her parents were watching and it had felt natural.

Which was all kinds of fucked up.

"All righty, then." Suzanne stood, and Grady started a little as she scooped up the plates. "It's tree time." She was heading for the kitchen by the time he'd dragged his mind from the gutter. "Josh has bought so many lights; just wait till you see them."

Her parents' gazes flicked to his sweater, then back to him. "Fabulous," Simone said with a brightness that didn't quite reach her eyes.

"Who'd like some eggnog?" Suzanne called from the kitchen.

"I will," Simone called, her smile fixed. "Make it a large."

"Mine too," Albie added.

"Mine three," Grady joked.

Albie and Simone weren't the only ones who were going to need some help from eggs, rum, and nutmeg to get through this ordeal.

Five minutes later, with the crackling sound of the fire in the hearth being drowned out by the painful strains of the Chipmunks singing "All I Want For Christmas," everyone was gathered around the tree. Grady and Albie were dealing with the lights he'd apparently bought. Which was utterly ridiculous. Leaving aside the fact that he didn't do Christmas, if he *did*, there was no way, in normal circumstances, he'd wrap a highly flammable product like a tree in what probably added up to the electrical equivalent of a small substation.

But these weren't normal circumstances. They were pretty fucking unusual circumstances, and he was playing a role. A role apparently requiring a Christmas tree that could be seen in fucking Australia.

In fake-rancher-boyfriend world, Christmas wasn't Christmas unless people on the other side of the planet could admire your handiwork.

"I have to admit," Simone said as she sipped on her eggnog, "the smell of this tree is pretty incredible."

"I know, right?" Suzanne said. "I think you should get a real one next year. Ditch that terrible wire thing."

"Oh, but darling, the pine needles make such a mess."

Grady had always thought that was one of the dumbest reasons not to have a real tree. He couldn't believe there were people out there who were so precious about spotlessness that they couldn't cope with a week or two of needle drop. Every year his parents had driven out to a tree farm and bought a freshly cut tree, and the smell of it in the back of their car was one of the most visceral memories of his childhood.

Just standing here now, smelling the tree, took him back to those times.

Which was why he avoided Christmas. The memories. He braced himself for the familiar pinch of pain, grief, and regret. And the even more visceral well of anger. He'd been robbed of so many tree-trimming events. Surprisingly, nothing came, just a slight bittersweet twist of nostalgia.

"I figure that'll do it," Albie said as he placed the last string of lights. "Turn 'em on, Grady."

Half expecting to be electrocuted, Grady plugged in the power cord. He swore he heard a low hum as the lights flickered on in a sudden burst of color.

Simone took a step back, her eyed widening, her hand fluttering near her chest as she said, "Oh my, that is…well lit."

Albie nodded, looking a little dazzled himself. "Very…bright."

"It's…*beautiful*," Suzanne announced with a hushed kind of reverence.

Grady glanced at her, at the glow of color on her face as she stared at the tree with the kind of wonder usually reserved for kids. And, if he wasn't very much mistaken, tears shimmered in her eyes.

"Thank you, Josh," she said, placing her eggnog down and crossing to where he stood. Grady tensed as she slipped an arm around his waist, her side melting into his as a deeply contented sigh escaped her lips. "It's…perfect."

Grady's pulse kicked and his breath caught and for a moment, he held really still. He wasn't used to this…to being casually demonstrative with any woman. It wasn't natural for him to be openly affectionate, and yet, part of him yearned to give in to it, too.

"Suzanne." Her mother gave her an indulgent smile as she shook her head. "I don't know if you know this yet about our daughter, Grady, but she tends to be a little emotional."

Grady wasn't sure if Suzanne's mother was being intentionally critical or was clueless to how her words came across, but he felt offended on Suzanne's behalf. There were far worse failings in life than being emotional. He'd spent more than a decade of his life fighting against ideals that could have done with a lot more fucking empathy.

Hell, he'd have thought that was exactly the kind of things an artist needed in spades.

Suzanne had annoyed, harassed, and irritated him. She was too talkative and too…touchy-feely. She'd invaded his space and his privacy. She'd pleaded, cajoled, begged, then finally both bribed *and* blackmailed him into being her fake rancher boyfriend. But her reasons were altruistic. Her heart was in the right place. And nobody got to criticize her, particularly when it was wrapped up in some kind of affectionate silly-little-Suzy remark.

Not even her mother.

Slipping his arm around her, Grady pulled her in a little closer. "I know," he murmured, glancing down at her. She chose that moment to glance up, and she blinked as if she was surprised to find him watching her. Her lips parted, and his gaze was drawn to her mouth. "It's one of the many things I like about your daughter," he said and smiled.

"Reminds me of my mom."

Grady wasn't sure why he'd said that—it just slipped out. He wished in an instant he could take it back, but then she smiled at him like he'd just given her the biggest compliment, and his chest felt like it was being squeezed in a press—and he kissed her. He might have kept it brief had it not been for that soft little satisfied noise in the back of her throat compelling him to linger.

It wasn't like the kiss from earlier, the one where he'd come from the barn and seen her for the first time since they'd made out last night. That time, his whole body had flushed with awareness and edginess, and an unreasonable kind of need to rid himself of those disconcerting feelings, to pass them on, had driven his feet to where she stood.

This wasn't like that. Hell, he wasn't even keeping score with this one. It was coming from a different place, one he didn't want to examine too closely. But it wasn't any less cataclysmic on his system. He wanted to deepen the kiss, to cradle her face and push his fingers into her hair and kiss her in the kind of ways parents should never see.

So he pulled back. "Shall we hang the ornaments now?"

After a discussion initiated by Simone—to establish a plan for the tree that would look the most aesthetically pleasing—was loudly overridden by Suzanne, they got sucked into the trimming. Playing his part, Grady paid no attention to aesthetics or her mother's attempts to police the placement of ornaments, whacking them on wherever took his fancy.

The more Simone winced, the more he knew he was doing it right.

Not that he could blame her for the wincing. Somehow, somewhere, Suzanne had found cat baubles. Baubles with cat faces on them. And she'd bought out the entire fucking shop. They were the most un-Christmas things he'd ever seen. Add miles of *blue* tinsel and Grady's laissez-faire attitude toward ornament placement, and the tree looked like it'd been decorated by a crazy cat lady.

Not to mention how much of a fire hazard/death trap it was.

The pièce de résistance was the angel on top. Suzanne had truly outdone herself with the angel. Although *festive dominatrix Barbie* was probably a better title.

Who knew sex shops sold Christmas decorations?

Beneath her long red coat with vampy white fur trim, she wore tight black leather pants and a crop top. Her shoes were the kind of stilettos made for niche activities like walking all over a man's chest while he masturbated. She held a glittery star in one hand, which he supposed was meant to look symbolic but was more ninja warrior than religious.

The only thing angelic about her was the mass of blond hair and the halo positioned above her head. But even it was crooked.

She looked like she'd just come from her angel-of-no-mercy routine at the kink club.

But Suzanne had already proclaimed it to be Grady's job to place her on the tree, giving some bullshit story about how it had been his job ever since he was a boy, so he was holding it dutifully, waiting for her go-ahead to place it. He didn't need to confer with her to know she was drawing everything out for maximum effect.

"So, Grady," Simone said as she surreptitiously shifted a bauble to a more *aesthetically pleasing* spot, "you mentioned your mom? What does she do? Do your parents live in Credence?"

There was a sudden rush and a popping noise in his ears as all the air in Grady's lungs was expelled. He hadn't been expecting the question. He'd stupidly opened the door to it, but considering it hadn't come up earlier and he'd been able to avoid personal questions all night, he'd been lulled into a false sense of security. He could feel the heat of Suzanne's gaze flashing across his face like a lighthouse beacon.

"No, they don't," he said, trying not to sound tight-lipped and forbidding because it had been a friendly inquiry from his *girlfriend's* mother. Grady was so used to everyone in Credence knowing his backstory, knowing that he *didn't talk about his backstory*, he forgot that not everybody in the world knew.

It just felt like it sometimes.

But these were typical getting-to-know-you questions, and telling Simone St. Michelle to mind her own damn business would not go down very well. Three sets of eyes were looking at him expectantly for more, and he knew it would be both rude and strange not to elaborate. Still, he steeled himself for the incoming platitudes.

"Grady's from Seattle," Suzanne said, jumping in.

She sent him a small smile, and even in that stupid elf sweater with her cheeks flushed from the fire or maybe the eggnog, he was glad she was standing right there. He may be here talking about stuff he didn't want to talk about—he *never* talked about—*because* of her and her over-the-top lie, but she'd obviously sensed his hesitancy and was prepared to run interference.

"That's right," he said. And he could have changed the subject and left it at that. Have them think that his parents were still alive and kicking back *home*. But there were bound to be follow-up questions at some point like, *Will your family be joining us for Christmas?* So it was better to just get it out there now when it fitted naturally into the conversation.

And then change the subject.

"I'm from Seattle. But my parents were killed in a car accident when I was seventeen. That's when I came to Credence. To the ranch. To live with my aunt and uncle."

A soft gasp escaped Suzanne's mouth, and he looked at her as her blue eyes softened, went glassy, and her brow furrowed in consternation.

Christ, she'd be lousy at poker.

Simone looked from Suzanne to Grady and back to Suzanne again, frowning. "You didn't know?"

"She does," Grady covered. "She just knows I don't like to talk about it very much."

As if taking her cue from that, Suzanne moved three steps to close the distance between them. Her cheeks were pinker, and he knew it was from the sudden flush of emotion across her features. She held out her hand to him as she got closer, and Grady took it, a wave of goose bumps marching up his arm. She intertwined her fingers with his and sent him a smile that was part sad, part apology, part thank-you.

God, the woman was an open book. She practically vibrated with emotion.

"Grady's been through so much," she said, breaking eye contact as she glanced at her mom, and Grady felt lousy for not telling the full story. For not mentioning Bethany or the fact that the accident happened this time of year.

But these people were all going to be out of his life in a couple of weeks, damn it. He didn't owe them his story. Plus, Grady knew there was a fine line between empathy and pity, and it narrowed even further the bigger the tragedy. He was done being pitied; he'd been done a long time ago.

Yes, he'd been dealt a turd sandwich seventeen years ago, but plenty of people had been dealt those and gotten on with their lives.

"I'm very sorry for your loss, Joshua," Simone said gently and with sincerity.

He shrugged. "It was a long time ago now. It's in the past."

Suzanne squeezed his hand again, and there was a moment of awkward silence — there usually was when people found out — as three sets of eyes settled on him. But Grady was well used to moving things along, to changing the subject.

"This" — he held up the angel, tugging his hand from hers as he held the abomination above his head with both hands—"however, is very much in the present."

Albie laughed, breaking the tension, and Simone gave a little shudder that pretty much said she wished it was anywhere *but* the present.

"If we're done trimming the tree, I can put it up top."

"Yes." Suzanne almost bounced on her feet as her gaze devoured the tree. "Put her on."

Grady had to wonder about Suzanne's normal Christmases if dominatrix Barbie had her so excited. She said they had been minimalist, but surely they weren't as bad as *this*? Because she wasn't acting here. She wasn't kidding around, playing it up for her parents. Or at least, Grady didn't think so. Suzanne was *really* into this. Grady took a couple of paces to the tree. It was about eight feet and, at six foot three—a few inches taller than her father—Grady's reach was the longest. He placed the *angel* on the top branch with minimal stretch, then stepped back.

"It's pretty as a picture," Suzanne said on a happy sigh, her hands clasped together in front of her, fingers intertwined.

Grady gave a mental eye roll at the atrocity he'd just performed. But between his acute awareness of the part he was supposed to be playing and that goofy look on her face, Grady didn't have the heart to rain on her parade. "Best. Christmas. Ever," he agreed.

Her parents exchanged a look that seemed to communicate they thought both Grady and Suzanne had lost their minds. But they had drawn closer together, possibly the closest they'd been all night, which was something. He was sure Suzanne wouldn't mind if mutual horror was a unifying factor—he certainly didn't. Not if it meant them patching things up quickly and getting on their way.

Then things could get back to normal around here. Assuming that was at all possible. Maybe there were just some things a person couldn't come back from. Like cat baubles and his head painted on a cherub.

"Speaking of pictures, I meant to ask earlier, Suzanne: Have you been doing any painting, darling?"

Grady watched as Suzanne's smile stayed fixed but the light in her eyes dimmed a little. "No," she said, avoiding her mother's gaze.

No? The woman had practically painted herself into a fucking coma every night last week.

"I don't…" Suzanne faltered, her voice trailing away.

Grady didn't know what was going on, but it was obvious Suzanne didn't want her mother to know she'd been painting and, on a rush, he leaped in to fill the space her unfinished sentence had left. "I'm sorry," he said on a deprecating laugh. "That's been my fault. I've been a little selfish, I'm afraid."

She shot him a small, grateful smile. "He has been keeping me quite occupied," she admitted, then flushed beet red.

"Well, now, I think that's our cue to leave," Albie said on a half laugh. "Come on, Simone, let's leave these two lovebirds to their evening."

Grady blinked. Lovebirds? It was good to know

their public displays of affection had been convincing, but Grady still felt awkward as fuck being Suzanne's fake rancher boyfriend.

General goodbyes followed as all four walked toward the back door. "I'll take you into Credence tomorrow," Suzanne said. "And Grady mentioned he'd love to show you around the place sometime, so we might do that tomorrow afternoon." She glanced at him. "Is that okay?"

Grady faltered. What the fuck? He would rather shoot himself in the foot than play tour guide to two city slickers. *That was not part of the deal.* His hand tense on the knob, he opened the door, nodding politely as the frigid air rushed in. "Sure. As long as nothing pressing arises."

"Oh, that would be wonderful. I'd love to see around your farm."

Grady wasn't sure if Simone was being obtuse or clueless, but Suzanne was quick to correct her mother. "Mom," she said with an eye roll in her voice. "It's a ranch."

"Sorry." She apologized with a rueful smile. "Your ranch."

"We look forward to it," Albie said with a nod, ushering Simone out the door, then, pointing above their heads to the doorframe, said, "Mistletoe."

They both looked up at the plastic plant. Suzanne laughed as she slid her arm around his waist. "Grady does like to increase his chances." Then she rose on her tippy-toes to kiss his cheek at the same time Grady turned his head, and her lips connected with his mouth.

Sort of.

It should have felt clumsy, but even this slight off-kilter kiss infused with rum and nutmeg managed to knock him on his metaphorical ass. It deepened, and the world around them faded for a moment as he forgot about the winter air and a tour he didn't want to give and the fact that this kiss was number four and he'd been very fucking specific about three being his maximum.

Grady dragged himself out of the kiss, staring at Suzanne for long moments, surprised to find they'd been so preoccupied, they hadn't even noticed her parents leave. Glancing away, he stepped inside, and she followed as he shut the door behind them, shutting out the cold night. He only wished he could shut out the smell of nutmeg and the taste of rum-infused lips.

He didn't like feeling this flummoxed, and right now it seemed vital to take back that control. "We didn't agree to me being a tour guide," he said, his voice gravelly as he moved to the central kitchen bench and grabbed for the docked phone, switching off the playlist.

He could only hear "I Saw Mommy Kissing Santa Claus" so many times without wanting to shove a pair of Aunty Cora's size-eight knitting needles into his ears.

"I'm sorry," she apologized, moving to the tree and standing in front of it so she was in profile to him, her arms wrapped around her waist. "I thought it'd be nice for them to have a look around and to have something to do."

Grady leaned his ass against the central island bench, watching as her gaze roved over every inch of the tree, a small smile lifting the corners of her mouth.

The mouth that had been on his a minute ago.

"I'd like to see it as well," she said absently, still staring at the tree. "I'd like to know where you go and what you do when you leave here in the morning. But it's fine," she said as she dragged her eyes away and turned to face him. Her blond hair was backlit by the blaze of lights so that she seemed to glow with Christmas. "I can make an excuse."

I'd like to see it as well. Seven little words that reached deep inside him. Grady didn't invite people to visit or *look around.* He was polite with his neighbors and loaned a hand if needed, but he never asked for one in return because he didn't want anyone nosing through his business. His lack of privacy after his parents had died had been indelibly imprinted on his psyche, and privacy in the armed forces wasn't exactly at a premium.

So he hoarded his privacy now. He had his few trusted hands who had been with him the last three years, and he had his aunt and uncle. His circle was wide enough.

It didn't need to go any wider.

Or so he'd thought anyway, but Suzanne taking an interest in the ranch, in what he did, wasn't causing alarm. Wasn't sending him in retreat or throwing up mental shutters. If she'd made that request the day she'd arrived, he'd have shut it down in the blink of an eye, but it didn't raise any red flags now.

"It's fine," he said, his voice deep as pitch. "I

don't mind." And he didn't.

"What?" She quirked an eyebrow. "You're not going to ask for a painting?"

Grady chuckled at her amused sarcasm. "You shouldn't go putting ideas in my head." God knew he had plenty enough of them right now. She smiled back, and Grady's lungs felt too big for his chest.

"Too late." She hugged her arms around her body again. "No returns." Then she turned away, gazing once more at the fire hazard in the corner. But within seconds, she was facing him again, her expression screwed into a serious little frown. "I'm sorry. About your parents. I…didn't know."

"It's fine." Grady shrugged. "You're not from around here."

"Did it happen at Christmas? Is that what Burl meant when he said this was a hard time of year for you? Not the military?"

Grady fought against the natural urge to retreat, to tell her to mind her own damn business. He'd hoped Suzanne wouldn't pry any further and he really wished she hadn't, but she looked so… earnest. So honest in her inquiry. Not fishing for the gory details, just genuinely trying to piece some things together.

"Early December."

She shut her eyes briefly. "Oh, Joshua." They fluttered open, two big blue pools of empathy and compassion.

He could see all the pieces fall into place for her as his aversion to Christmas suddenly became clear. It wasn't the whole truth, and he wasn't about to tell her about Bethany even if it was the perfect time, because empathy he could deal with, but pity only made things worse.

Pity amplified the tragedy.

Thankfully she didn't sling some kind of useless platitude his way or try and move closer, but her arms had visibly tightened around her middle like she was desperatcly trying to keep herself in check. "I am so sorry. I know it's never a good time to lose people you love, but I'm sorry in your case that it also ruined a traditional family time. And I'm sorry that I've subsumed all your grief and loss with my own family crap."

"No." He shook his head. "I liked it. I liked that you didn't know. Too many people around here know." That was another thing he hadn't realized until now. Suzanne St. Michelle's very presence might have annoyed the crap out of him, but she'd never treated him like he was damaged goods. Like he was fragile and needed to be handled with care.

She'd always told him exactly what she thought. She'd called him on his shit and not worried about his *feelings*.

"And that's a bad thing?"

"I don't like being pitied or talked about behind my back or have well-meaning people saying trite shit they don't mean. I put up with it for three years before joining the military, and I don't want to encourage any relapses from the good people of Credence."

"I'm sure they were just concerned."

"Maybe. It was just…too much. Too overwhelming."

"Yeah. I can see that." She stared at him for a beat or two. "Well...like I said, I'm sorry."

Once upon a time, Grady had a bunch of standard responses to well-meaning people, many of them strangers, expressing their sorrow. Something that was soothing to the person it was aimed at, that made him sound grateful and slid off his tongue easy as Teflon.

But there was nothing trite about Suzanne's emotions, so he went with the simplest response. "Thank you."

They stared at each other for a beat or two longer before she said, "Think I'm going to sit by the fire and watch the tree for a while."

Grady glanced at the frightening tree, then back to her. "I'm going to work in the office for a bit, then hit the sack." A barely there nod of her head was the only response. "Make sure you switch off the lights before you turn in for the night. I'm pretty sure we're breaking a hundred different electrical safety rules with that thing."

She gave a half laugh and said, "Sure," but sighed happily at the tree nonetheless.

Grady rolled his eyes. "Good night, Suzy." It was getting much easier to say.

"Night, Josh."

And hell if that wasn't getting much easier to hear.

CHAPTER TWELVE

By three o'clock the next afternoon, the only place Suzanne hadn't taken her parents was Jack's, and given that she needed a drink pretty damn bad, she couldn't get there soon enough. They'd met Winona at Annie's for lunch, which had been pleasant enough. The food was amazing—cherry pie and ice cream to die for—and Winona was great at conversation. Plus, her parents loved Winona's outrageous sense of humor and her lack of give-a-fuck about polite societal norms.

Winona had taken them on a Highlights of Credence tour. It hadn't taken very long. Then she'd driven them out to the lake. It was chilly by the water, a moderate breeze cutting through clothes and skin and bones, making Suzanne glad they'd stopped at Déjà Brew on the way for hot coffee to keep them warm. The murky-blue surface of the lake shivered beneath the ruffle of the wind, despite the mostly sunny day. Bare trees stood like frozen sentinels around the edges of the water, adding to the overall frigidity of the landscape.

Excited to be moving in to her house in the New Year, Winona took them to see the land and the progress so far. She chatted about her friends back in Chicago who were also contemplating buying land and moving and her vision for a thriving artist community. Her mother became quite animated about that. Apparently, she knew a few people who could be interested in something similar. Her father also suggested a couple of artists he knew who might be attracted to such a place, and by the time they left the lake, all four of them were talking about enough local art production to support a gallery in Credence.

It was a wonderful conversation—animated and stimulating and exciting. But therein lay the problem. Her parents were fine when there were distractions and third parties engaging them, but when it was just them, they barely said a word to each other. There wasn't hostility. There was just... disconnection. After they'd dropped Winona back at the boardinghouse, the conversation had completely dried up.

Which was what was driving Suzanne to drink.

No way could she face the silent trip back to the ranch without some kind of legal pick-me-up. She could have one and still drive and maybe it might loosen up her parents a little. They could do the ranch tour with Grady another day.

It was cozy and welcoming inside Jack's, like it had been last week when she and Winona had stopped in for a quick drink on their way home from Denver. And busy for a weekday afternoon. Several booths were full, and there was a line-dance class happening on the small area designated as the dance floor. Billy Ray Cyrus played on the jukebox.

"I'll have a shot of Wild Turkey, please, Tucker," Suzanne said, sitting herself down on a barstool. She'd sworn she'd never drink bourbon after her boozy night with Grady, but she'd developed a bit of a taste for it, and the man was safely out of reach.

Tucker quirked an eyebrow at her harried request but just said, "Coming right up." By the time her parents sat down, one on either side, he'd placed her bourbon on the bar. As tempting as it was to throw it back, Suzanne picked it up and took a sip before she introduced her parents.

"Pleased to meet you," Tucker said to her father before turning to her mom.

Simone St. Michelle smiled at Tucker in that way she did, super-sexy and über-confident, and he blinked. Her mom may be in her late fifties, but she liked to flirt. For as long as Suzanne could remember, men had been falling under her spell, and Tucker, a good-looking guy probably twenty-five years her junior, was no exception.

Her mother's work was highly sexual, highly eroticized, and she'd told Suzanne when she was fourteen that a good artist was always aware of sexual discourse between people because how art appealed to people *sexually* was what made it come to life. Suzanne wasn't sure she believed the sentiment, which probably explained why her paintings were lifeless and her mother was a lauded sculptress. Also why her mom got along so well with Winona and why charming men was as natural to her as breathing.

Even if that superpower seemed to have gone awry somehow with her husband.

"Hi, Tucker." She smiled. "What a great name—it really suits you. Can you point me to the restrooms, please?"

Tucker blinked again and pointed to his left. "That way." On the wall, a sign with an arrow indicated the direction.

"Thank you," she said and smiled again before heading off.

Tucker seemed a little bewildered as he asked Albie, "Can I get you something to drink?"

Her father ordered a beer, and Tucker delivered it promptly before pushing off to serve a couple of older guys and a young woman who had arrived at the bar. Suzanne seized the moment to talk to her dad one-on-one.

"What's going on with you and Mom?"

She dived straight in—there was no time for subtleties right now. She half expected her father to deny anything was wrong. He was the everything's-going-to-be-all-right parent. So it was quite shocking to hear him sigh heavily and say, "I don't know, Suzanne."

"She said you two might be...breaking up."

Even more shockingly, her father nodded. "Yes. Maybe..."

Suzanne threw back the rest of her bourbon, welcoming the burn. "But why? What happened?"

He shrugged. "She doesn't see me anymore but she's perfectly happy to flirt with other men." He lifted his chin in Tucker's direction.

"Dad..." This was ridiculous; her mother had always done that. "Mom has always been a flirt, you know that. Frankly, I thought you kinda liked it."

She'd watched her father watch her mother work a crowd, and even at a young age, she'd understood that *he* enjoyed her power over a room as much as *she* did.

"Of course," he said dismissively. "She is, and I do like it. But the problem is she used to also flirt with me like that, but now…we're both traveling so much and we're like ships passing in the night and everything feels like we're on autopilot. We used to talk about art and music and books and life, and we used to make love for hours when she was creating because it fed the passion inside her. We might be in separate bedrooms, but she'd crawl into my bed in the wee small hours and climb on top and the sex was wild and frantic and incredible like… animals, you know?"

Her father calmly sipped his beer while Suzanne wondered if it was too late to cut her ears off and if the feed shop sold brain bleach and what kind of dose it would take to permanently erase this conversation.

Good god almighty, what was *wrong* with him?

"And then she'd just…" He stared into his beer. "Climb off and go back to her work."

Oh good lord—*make him stop*. This was *too much information*.

"And now it's like we're just…roommates. And she's not been happy about me representing a more diverse range of art, either. That's creating quite a bit of friction."

Albie had expanded his artist base the last few years to include digital artists working in a variety of different mediums. He'd even taken on a controversial graffiti artist.

He sighed. "She has such a narrow definition of

art and thinks *real* artists will stop wanting me to represent them, which hasn't been the case."

Yes, her mother was a complete art snob and quite scathing of things she did not consider worthy of an artistic cannon. Suzanne cringed at the thought of her mom laying eyes on what she'd painted while she'd been here. "Does she know that's how you feel?" Suzanne asked.

"I have tried to have conversations with her, but she's so busy at the moment, working all the time, traveling to different exhibitions and guest lecturing, and she's working on several pieces for a major project."

Suzanne nodded. She'd learned a long time ago that her mom disappeared inside her work when she was sculpting with no room for the trivialities of life. And Suzanne got it. Having spent days in the grip of an obsessive creative fever, she finally got it. But that didn't mean it was without its casualties, that loved ones didn't live on scraps of time and affection and counted down the days until the fever passed.

"I still can't believe she's dropped everything to come here."

"She's worried about you guys, too, Dad. She's trying to get things back on track."

"I think it's too late. I think we've forgotten how to talk to each other."

If Suzanne hadn't been their daughter, if she'd been Winona, she'd have said, *Don't talk.*

Get naked. Do that wild animal stuff she could never now *un*know they did. But she was not going to counsel her sixty-year-old father to get boinking.

Not in so many words anyway.

"So use this time," Suzanne urged. Her mother reappeared near the arrow pointing to the restroom. "She's not working on a project; you're not pandering to clients. You both seem to want the same thing. Get to know each other again. Think of it as a second honeymoon."

He nodded just as her mother took her seat and Tucker said, "What can I get you to drink?"

Simone smiled at him and asked, "What do you recommend?"

Tucker looked dazzled again, and Suzanne glanced at her father. He was watching the exchange with zero malice or jealousy—in fact, she could see the same admiration in his eyes for her mother that had always been there. A lot of men might have been insecure seeing their wife so openly fascinated by other men, but her father understood Simone St. Michelle better than anyone. He knew she was an artist down to her marrow and everything was grist for the mill and that she studied and flirted with everyone she came across—men *and* women—and it was about art and artistic expression, not sex.

It was all kinds of madness that the two of them would even contemplate breaking up.

"Tucker has a great cocktail menu, Mom."

Tucker nodded. "I do a mean piña colada."

"Oh, hmm." Simone sat on her barstool. Her mother liked martinis and Chardonnay from the Loire Valley in France, and she didn't really believe in switching things up. For a creative, she was quite rigid in many ways. "I think I'll just stick with a martini."

"Simone."

The note of exasperation in her father's voice was surprising. He'd always said he loved how Simone stuck with certain absolutes because so much of her artistic temperament was unpredictable. But they'd clearly reached a point where all those things that had caused them to fall in love were now just bugging the crap out of each other.

"Why not try something different?" he suggested.

"Yeah, Mom," Suzanne broke in. "Winona tells me piña coladas are Tucker's specialty."

"They are; I can definitely vouch for that."

Suzanne glanced over at the young woman two stools down. She had some kind of insignia on her pocket and was sitting with two elderly men who were currently debating when it would snow.

"Tonight, I tell you, Ray," bar dude number one said. He was a spritely looking old white guy, with a twinkle in his eyes. "My hip never lies."

"That's horseshit, Bob," bar guy number two interjected. He was a tall African American man with snowy white hair. "Bureau says day after tomorrow."

There was an inelegant snort. "What do they know?"

"They have weather satellites, you old fool. I'll take that over your dang hip any day."

"Humph. Bureau should pay me to be their satellite."

The young woman glanced at Suzanne and crossed her eyes, and Suzanne laughed as Tucker said, "What do you want, Della?" in a surprisingly short kind of way.

Not a *hi* or a *hello* or *how are you*. Not a *what can I get you* or *how about those Broncos*. His body language was different, too. He'd been all loose and laid-back with them, but with Della, his expression was more masked. Definitely more brooding.

She called him on it, though. "I'm fine, Tuck, thank you for asking." She didn't pause for him to apologize, just put in her drink order. "I'll get a piña colada."

Tucker glanced at the two old guys still bickering like they'd been doing it for decades. "Aren't you supposed to be working?"

She looked like she wanted to deny it for a moment; then she sighed. "Yeah." She looked like it had been a long day, and Suzanne could totally relate. "Better make it a Coke."

"I'll have a Shirley Temple," Bob said like he was Dean Martin ordering a scotch on the rocks in Vegas. "And can you throw in an extra cherry? Doc says I gotta eat more fruit." Then he laughed, and Ray laughed with him, slapping the bar several times. "I'll have a Fuzzy Navel," Ray said after he'd recovered from his laughing, playing Sammy to Bob's Dean. "Extra fruit for me, too."

And they both cracked up some more.

Tucker glanced at Della. "You giving out some new kind of happy pill at the old folks' home?"

"Why?" she asked sweetly. "You want some?"

He scowled at her briefly before returning his attention to Simone. "What can I tempt you with?"

"Live a little, Simone," her father said, his words encouraging despite his tone implying she didn't know how to—not any longer anyway.

A hurt expression flitted across Simone's face for a second, and Suzanne shot her father a stop-being-a-dick look as she rubbed her hand on her mother's back. "Have the piña colada, Mom," she said, her tone gentler and a little more teasing. "You said you were willing to try anything, remember?"

Her mother looked at her father, then nodded firmly. "All right, then, Tucker. Looks like I'm being outvoted."

"Hey, if you're really willing to try anything," he said, "I can recommend the line-dancing classes."

Her mother's gaze skimmed to where the boot scootin' was going on. She looked like she'd rather eat a live bug. There was *trying new things* and then there was *line dancing*. Even her father, who'd been advocating for her to step outside the box, looked horrified at the prospect.

"I think I'll start with baby steps," Simone said with a laugh as she returned her attention to Tucker. "Get me one of those piña coladas." She dipped her head briefly to the side in the direction of the Rat Pack and said, "You can give them my fruit."

"Much obliged, ma'am," the one called Bob said with a chuckle.

"Hey," the one called Ray said, narrowing his eyes. "Aren't you Simone St. Michelle?"

To say everyone was surprised by the observation was a gross understatement. So much so that there were a few drawn-out beats of silence among them all.

Suzanne was used to her mother being recognized wherever they went, but she'd never expected anyone from *Credence* to know Simone St. Michelle. It wasn't that Suzanne thought people in rural areas were ignorant or didn't appreciate art. But sculpture was such a niche genre, and people rarely knew the names behind modern pieces in galleries.

Even though her mother was a veritable rock star of modern sculpture.

Her mother recovered first from the growing silence. "Why, yes I am," she said, obviously thrilled.

"I thought you looked familiar." Ray beamed at Simone as he slid off his stool. "May I shake your hand?"

Her mother nodded. "Of course." She turned in her seat, holding out her hand for Ray, who took it the second he got close enough.

"It's an honor to meet you." Ray encased Simone's hand and placed his other over the top like he never wanted to let her go. "Bob," he said, "we have a bona fide *artiste* in our presence."

A hot little stab of something that felt very much like jealousy thrust between Suzanne's ribs. Which was ridiculous. She'd never been jealous of her mother's art or the way people fawned over her. Nor was she now. No, it was the label of *bona fide artiste*.

She wanted that, she realized. She wanted it badly.

Bob rose from his seat and clapped his friend on the back. "Since when have you been a patron of the goddamn arts?" He also offered his hand as he smiled at Simone.

Ray reluctantly let go of Simone's hand. "My late wife was a huge fan of your work."

"Oh?" Simone said as she briefly shook Bob's hand. "Was she an artist? Did she sculpt?"

"A little. She dabbled. It was more a hobby, but we've been to a few of your exhibitions in New York and in Washington once, too."

General introductions were made then, including Della and Albie and finally Suzanne. "And have you met my daughter yet?" Simone asked Ray. "She's been in Credence for almost two weeks now."

"The pleasure's not been mine." He bowed a little as he held out his hand to Suzanne, which she took and smiled back politely.

"No, well, that rancher boyfriend of hers is keeping her very much to himself in that cabin of his," Simone said with an indulgent laugh. A sudden hot prickle shot up Suzanne's spine, warning her what was coming next, but her brain scrambled and her mouth felt gummy and she was too slow to interject. "Grady knows a good thing when he sees it."

Oh, crap. Crappity crappity crap. Grady was going to *kill* her.

She'd seen his barn—there were probably a dozen implements in there alone that he could murder her with and use to bury her body.

The entire little circle went quiet and motionless, blinking in unison. Like a parliament of owls. Della broke the stunned silence. "You're *Grady's* girlfriend?"

"Grady *has* a girlfriend?" Tucker added.

"And you're living with him," Ray said, studying her face. "At the cabin, you say?"

Bob just out-and-out stared in disbelief. "On the *ranch*?"

Everyone was staring at her like she'd announced she was the new linebacker for the Broncos, their doubt over her mother's claim evident. She sure as shit hoped it was because Grady having a girlfriend was preposterous and not that him having *her* as a girlfriend was preposterous.

Meanwhile, her mother suddenly realized her faux pas. "Oh dear." She looked around at the surprised faces and then at Suzanne with an apologetic look. "I didn't realize it was a secret."

"As I said on the phone, *Mom*," Suzanne said with a smile that felt like spackle drying on her face, "we're trying to keep it on the down low for a while."

"Well…yes, but…" The lines on her mother's forehead became more pronounced as her hands fiddled in her lap. "I thought you meant from *us*. Not from the town. Oh god, I'm so very sorry."

Suzanne had no idea whether Grady having a girlfriend would be a *big thing* in Credence or not, although the incredulousness on the faces surrounding her seemed to indicate that it would. But she did know it would be if she made a huge song and dance about it in Jack's. What she needed to do was put a lid on this and move the fuck on.

She had to act like people finding out was no biggie. That it was *just fine*. "Don't worry about it," Suzanne said with a laugh she didn't feel and a wave of her hand. "It's not a state secret," she dismissed. "We were just being a little selfish, wanting some *us* time."

And that hole just kept getting bigger. Christ... that's where he'd bury her, in the goddamn huge hole she was digging.

Suzanne could almost see the questions lurking within disbelieving gazes and flitting across crumpled foreheads, and the thought of digging herself in any deeper sat like a big old rotting fish in her intestines. *Move the fuck on, Suzanne—move on!*

"Ray," she said, jumping in, not sure what she was going to say, just knowing she needed to divert attention ASAP. "Which Washington exhibition did you attend? Mom's done several over the years, but there was that controversial one a decade ago that people still talk about."

Thankfully Ray took the bait, and all eyes were back on Simone. Well...Della was still eyeing her speculatively, but most of the heat had shifted. Which was just as well, because Suzanne already felt hot enough.

Shit...what a mess. The universe was really kicking her ass over this small white lie that was growing bigger by the day. And now she was going to have to tell Grady that their secret—based on a lie—was out. That was going to be *so much* fun. Not. He'd been pretty damn specific about their fake relationship staying on the ranch.

But...maybe she wouldn't have to tell him? Maybe she'd get lucky and find Credence wasn't the stereotypical small town full of gossipy busybodies? That was possible, right? And really, how would Grady even hear such gossip out at the ranch? It wasn't like he was the friendly type who encouraged visitors, who had a poker night with his buddies every Friday or invited the neighbors over for a cookout.

Hell, she hadn't even seen him with a cell phone, although she assumed he had one because who didn't own a cell phone, and surely it'd be necessary out in the middle of nowhere? For emergencies and the like.

And just like that, Suzanne was forgetting about the hundred and one ways Grady might kill her and thinking about the hundred and one ways he might kill himself out on that ranch without anybody knowing or maybe even caring for days. It was way out of town, and who did he really have looking out for him?

How often did Burl check in?

When would his ranch hands start to worry?

Up until a few days ago, Grady had been an infuriating enigma—a big, tough, taciturn rancher dude whom Suzanne would have said didn't need anybody. But she'd been slowly getting to know him since her parents had arrived, and after his big reveal last night, she thought she was actually starting to understand him. God knew she'd lain awake long enough thinking about the trauma he'd been through and how it explained a lot about why he hadn't wanted her here—particularly not this time of year.

It also explained a lot about why he was hiding away from everyone. Isolating himself from people because it was too hard to be constantly reminded of what he'd lost and that going through the motions of life, working hard every day, was much more preferable to having to deal with his losses.

Maybe he even told himself he liked it or that it was enough. That the life he had was *enough*.

But god…what a sad indictment. What was life without…joy? Without people to share it with? Would his parents have wanted him to shut everyone out? And surely there'd been a woman somewhere, sometime in the intervening years? There had to have been. He was too damn sexy for there to have been no one.

He'd been in the military, for god's sake. In a *uniform*. There *must* have been a woman. Probably even wom*en*.

Or was cutting himself off from those possibilities just another way he walled himself off from any more hurts? From the everyday human things that took little chinks out of your heart that never quite healed?

She didn't know why thinking about him all alone out here was like a hot fist in her gut, but it was, and she already knew that when she left here, when she went back to New York and left him behind, Joshua Grady was going to weigh on her mind.

If he didn't kill her first.

"That's a great idea; I'd love to. Sounds good, don't you think, Suzanne?"

Suzanne blinked and came back to the conversation as a bunch of eyeballs looked to her for approval. "Um…I'm sorry, I was miles away. What?"

She avoided Della's gaze that was saying, *Hell*

yeah you were, precisely twenty-six miles out on the ranch with Joshua Grady.

"Ray's going to talk to the mayor about holding an ice-sculpting competition. He's going to arrange for some big blocks of ice to be brought in to Credence, just outside on the main street along the sidewalk, and your father and I—" She slid her hand into his, and a spark of hope lit in Suzanne's chest at the gesture. "We're going to judge it."

"Oh, that's great."

"It'll take a few days to organize, but I reckon we could get it done before Christmas," Ray enthused.

"It's fine." Simone waved a dismissive hand. "We're here until after Christmas, aren't we, Suzanne?"

Suzanne nodded and smiled. *Not if she could help it…*

CHAPTER THIRTEEN

Grady was pissed as he strode toward the cabin at two o'clock the next afternoon. It was a bitterly cold day, but anger had his engines roaring hot. And Suzanne St. Michelle was about to feel the full force of it. She'd pretty much annoyed the crap out of him from day one, and despite their relationship taking an unexpected turn—one that involved way too much touching and goo-goo eyes and way, *way* too much fucking kissing—she still was a pain in his ass.

He may have made a deal with her for a fake relationship, but that didn't mean he didn't wake every morning and want to send her away in that ridiculous van.

This morning hadn't been any different.

And right now? Right now, thanks to his telephone conversation with Burl about his new *girlfriend*, he'd even leave his balls behind and drive her away in that hideous vehicle himself.

Slamming his hat on the outside hook and briefly stamping his feet on the mat, Grady yanked the door open. *"Suzy!"*

The house was warm, and the seductive aroma of baking cookies—sugar and vanilla and sweet spices—flooded his senses. But Grady was too ticked even for cookies as three happy faces greeted him from the kitchen.

"Oh, hey," Suzanne said as she looked up from a

mixing bowl with a warm smile of greeting. "You're home early."

Christ, that smile. She wasn't even acting with that smile, and his heart lurched, which rocketed his temper even further. Smiling at him like she hadn't told all of fucking Credence that she was his girlfriend. His pulse hammered at his temples; his lungs felt tight. He wanted to…kiss that smile right off her face. Kiss her hard and wet and deep until she wasn't smiling. Until she was breathless and moaning and clinging and she could feel how damn angry he was.

Jesus. *Fuck*. Grady gave himself a mental shake. *Get a grip, dude*.

He didn't bother to greet anyone. He just said, "I missed you so much, I couldn't wait to see you," forcing a lightness to both his voice and step he did not feel as he advanced.

He wanted to growl at her, wanted to fucking *stomp*.

Her parents smiled at him indulgently. Her mother was holding a bag of frosting, her father a tree-shaped cookie cutter, but neither of them held his attention as he closed in on her, their gazes meshing. God alone knew what was sparking in his eyes, but whatever it was, she read it well. Her big blue eyes widened slightly, her pupils dilated.

"We're making Christmas cookies," she said, and the low, raspy quality in her voice scraped along Grady's nerve endings.

"Suzanne says they're your favorites," Simone added.

Grady didn't bother responding to either of

them. He was rounding the bench now and she was right there, in reaching distance, turning to face him in a yellow shirt that hugged her curves like a fucking glove, her hip pressed into the bench. He didn't stop to think about what he did next, just stepped right into her space and slid his hands up her arms to her shoulders. Her breathing tumbled out all rough and choppy between them. So did his. She swallowed, and he could feel it all the way down to the *V* of muscle slung between his hips.

He'd come in here to confront her about the girlfriend thing, and she was smiling and looking good and smelling like fucking cookies, and the devil was riding him, whipping up his pulse and his libido, and he didn't know whether he wanted to yell at her or lay her on the bench and bury himself inside her.

Jesus, he'd never known this maddening push and pull with a woman. Bethany had been sweet and lovely, and every other woman he'd been with since had been more than happy to let him lead.

This woman… *God.* This woman was so damn infuriating. Why did he have to want her so fucking badly?

"Grady?" she whispered, her voice husky and uncertain.

"Mistletoe," he said, thanking all the sweet, sweet angels that Suzanne had gone mistletoe mad.

Then he lowered his head and crushed his mouth to hers. She gave a startled little "Oh!" but it got lost in the hard press of his lips and the sweep of his tongue as he swallowed her all up—the sugar, the vanilla, the spice. Her cookie dough lips. He kissed her like they were the only two people in the room, the rush of his blood through his head and the lash of heat in his veins a roaring, snapping imperative. He kissed her until she melted against him and made a sexy little noise in the back of her throat.

"He sure wasn't joking about missing you."

Grady was so inside the kiss, the rush of his breath, the hammer of his pulse so loud inside his head, he wasn't even sure which parent had spoken, but whoever it was, they ripped him right out like a kick to the balls.

Fuck. He took a step back, his hands falling from her arms. He stared at her, his chest rising and falling in unison with hers as she stared right back, her mouth wet and full. He could smell vanilla and taste cookies, and it didn't seem to matter how much he wanted to toss her out on her ass because he wanted to kiss her more.

"Sorry," he apologized, curling his fingers into loose fists to stop himself from doing just that as he switched his attention over her shoulder to her parents. "It's been a long, cold day."

Albie laughed. "Rather you than me."

Grady's gaze returned to Suzanne's face—she still looked dazed and thoroughly kissed and he had to locate his earlier anger to stop himself from yanking her back again. She had some explaining to do, and he wouldn't let his primitive masculine impulses derail him from the much-needed conversation.

Taking a steadying breath, Grady smiled at her parents. "Would you mind if I borrowed your daughter for a few minutes?"

Simone and Albie shot wry little grins at each

other. "Not at all," Simone said, shooing them with her hand. "I didn't realize how creative frosting cookies could be, and we've got plenty more to do."

"This is what I keep telling you, darling, *anything* can be a canvas." Albie switched his attention to Grady. "You'll have cookie masterpieces by the time you're..." He faltered, realizing the road he was traveling down. "In no time," he amended.

Grady didn't bother to correct them. Let them think he was taking Suzanne away to ravage her— it was the part he was supposed to be playing, after all. Grabbing her hand, he tugged, and she followed as he walked out of the living room, through the arch, and down the hallway to his office.

No way were they having a conversation any-where near a bed.

He gathered his anger as he went. He needed it as both sword and armor right now. Because this was not about picking up where they'd left off in the kitchen—he wanted an explanation, damn it!

But if he thought Suzanne was going to just stand there all dazed and pliant and let him rant, he was sorely mistaken. It was like the door clicking shut snapped her out of her altered state and instead of finding hazy blue eyes and a soft luscious mouth, she was staring at him through chips of ice, her lips tight.

"What's wrong with you?" she hissed, her arms folded tight around her middle as she backed away several paces, putting distance between them. "My parents probably think we're in here fucking."

Grady blinked at both the dirty word coming out of her pretty mouth and at her demeanor. She was angry with him? *She* was angry with *him?* Jesus, was she for real? "Isn't us *fucking* the whole point?"

It was not in Grady's nature to be crude around women. His mother had brought him up to be polite and respectful with the opposite sex—well, just generally really, but with women particularly—and the uniform had demanded the same standards. But Suzanne knew exactly how to push all his buttons.

"At two o'clock in the afternoon?" she hiss-whispered.

Grady laughed out loud. She was really something. Did she not know that if what was happening between them was real, they'd be fucking all hours of the day and night? Grady would have absolutely no compunction delegating as much as possible to his hands so he could stay in the cabin with her until one or both of them were injured or dead.

"Oh, sorry, when do all the cool, hip New York artists usually fuck?" he goaded.

Even now, with her eyes shooting daggers at him, with her looking at him like she did that first day when she'd accused him of being a cowpoke, he wanted to sweep everything off his desk and give her the kind of afternoon delight that inspired pop songs. That yellow shirt of hers hugging her breasts was distracting as fuck. He wanted to stride across to where she was standing, tear it open, yank down her bra cups. He wanted to shove his hands inside her pants and kiss her again like he had out in the kitchen.

But deeper and harder and dirtier.

He wanted to make her come fast and furious,

her eyes spitting chips at him even as she came apart and he whispered all the reasons why she should never piss him off again.

"Why did you drag me in here?" she demanded, wisely ignoring his deliberately crude inquiry.

Grady took a breath. He was too wired. Alert in a way that was reminiscent of night patrols in the Middle East. He needed to calm the fuck down or he was going to stroke out. He shoved his hands in his pockets, waiting several beats before he answered. "Burl seems to be under the impression that I have a girlfriend I'm keeping a big secret out here on the ranch. Could you enlighten me as to how he might think that?"

"Ah."

"Yes. Ah."

"I was going to mention it to you, but—"

"But?" he interrupted. Why was there even a but? Surely a heads-up would have been the only decent thing to do.

"I was hoping it wouldn't get out."

He snorted. "Guess what, Suzy? It did."

"Look, okay." She held her hands up in a placatory gesture. "I can explain."

"Oh, you better." He folded his arms. "Because I am sure we had a conversation about this relationship staying right here on the ranch. In fact, I'm pretty sure I insisted."

"It wasn't me. We were in Jack's yesterday, and Mom let it slip that you were my boyfriend. I'm sorry, I tried not to make a big deal out of it, and I changed the subject right away and honestly, there were only a few people in the conversation. It wasn't like we dropped a flyer in everyone's mailbox."

"This is Credence. Nothing stays a secret for long. Who was there?"

"A couple of guys from the old folks' home. Ray Carmody and Bob someone."

"Bob Downey? Well, Jesus." Grady shoved a hand through his hair. "She might as well have bought a billboard. He used to be the mayor here a long time ago and still takes a little bit too much interest in the goings-on."

"Crap, okay…I really am sorry. But surely it's not the end of the world? I mean, you live all the way out here—it's not like you're going to hear any gossip."

Grady's temper flared again. Of course someone who lived amid the anonymity of ten million people could be flippant about the repercussions. "It's not whether I hear it or not. It's that it's out there. My *aunt* is insisting she meet you."

Another deliciously distracting bob of her throat spiked his anger higher. She'd landed him in another mess, and he was angry—his aunt was involved now. This was *not* the time to let his libido take charge.

"Oh…shit."

"Yes." He nodded. "And she's a really nice woman who never had any kids of her own but didn't blink an eye when a pissed-at-the-world seventeen-year-old kid full of anger and attitude landed on her. She wrapped me up and loved me through all my rage even when I didn't want her to. And she's been breaking her heart over me for the last seventeen years, hoping and wishing despite my never giving her *any* reason to think otherwise, that one day I'd find the kind of love that she and my uncle have for each other. And now here you are, and she wants to meet you. My *girlfriend*. Because all she's ever wanted was for me to be happy and oh, maybe now she doesn't have to worry so much about me."

"God...Josh..." Her eyes melted from ice to two huge, warm puddles, and she took a step toward him, but Grady stopped her with an almost vicious shake of his head. "I'm so sorry..."

Grady couldn't bear the compassion in her eyes, the soft sympathetic hitch in her voice. It affected him on a level he'd spent a lot of years pretending didn't exist and that fed the anger already burning through his system. He'd rather she be angry. That way he could maintain his rage, too.

He didn't need it diluted by her sympathy.

"I may live outside Credence, but I'm part of this town whether I like it or not. And what I don't need is a line of well-meaning townsfolk appearing with their apple pies and their cobbler and their fucking platitudes the second you hightail it out of town. I had enough pity to last me a lifetime seventeen years ago."

She nodded. "I'm sorry." Her voice wobbled, and she cleared her throat. "How do we fix it?"

Grady blanched at her question. "*We* don't do anything. *I'll* fix it." Jesus, she'd done enough already. "I'll deal with it. I deal with things—that's what I do."

She looked like she was going to say something, opened her mouth, even, then shut it again and didn't say anything. "What?" he demanded.

"If you don't mind an observation? I don't think

you *deal* at all. Not talking about things isn't dealing with them. They don't go away just because you don't say their name, Joshua."

Grady hated that she'd known him for two weeks and had already nailed the way he coped with the crap that had come his way. Just one more thing pissing him off, itching like a fever in his blood. "Oh, you mean like how you didn't mention to me about your mom telling Bob Downey about *us* and just kept your fingers crossed that it wouldn't get out?"

"Yeah, sure," she said, compassion turning to sarcasm. "That's exactly the same thing."

"Well, you don't need to worry, because I'm not going to deal with it your way. I'm going to tell my aunt and uncle the truth."

"Wh-what?"

Suzanne's expressive face ran the gamut of emotions, from confusion to questioning to irritated, then finally alarm. He could watch her face all damn day.

"But—"

"Don't worry." He cut her off before she could object. "They'll keep your little secret."

"How do you know?"

"Because I'll ask them to," he said testily.

He knew Burl and Cora would play along with the deception if he asked, even though it would go against their principals of honesty and decency. Which made Grady feel extra shitty. *As if regular shitty wasn't bad enough.* This was exactly the kind of thing he knew was going to happen when Suzanne had brought this proposal to him.

"But I don't want them getting hurt in this process. They've been through enough, Suzy, and I will not give them any false hope."

He should have put his uncle straight on the phone when he'd first called. But Grady had been too stunned at the revelation and sideswiped by the genuine joy in Burl's voice to strategize on his feet, especially when he was missing a chunk of the background information.

"Okay," she said after a beat or two, her voice small. "Of course, you're right, I'm sorry. Whatever you want. I just wish…"

Grady waited for her to finish her sentence, resentment still ticking in his veins. He shouldn't care about what she wished, but he did. "What?"

"I don't know. I like Burl. I guess I don't want him or your aunt to think I'm some kind of flake who sets up an elaborate scheme with a fake boyfriend to lie to her parents." She took a step toward him, and this time Grady didn't try to stop her. "I'm really not this person, Josh. I know you haven't known me long enough to know it but god…I'm so by the book I don't even jaywalk, and *everybody* jaywalks in New York."

Her voice was thick with regret and, for what it was worth, Grady believed her. Maybe he hadn't known her long enough, either, but he knew enough to know that while she could be a spitfire, there was nothing of the rebel about her.

But the point was—she was this person *now*. "It's not too late to walk this back."

"Oh, Josh." She shook her head, her teeth pressing into her bottom lip, looking utterly miserable.

"This hole is so deep now, there's only one way out of it, and that's through the other side. And I need my parents concentrating on their relationship, not me and my fake one. I don't want to give them a distraction from getting their shit together or," she shuddered, "have my mother hounding me to see her therapist."

Grady, who had seen enough shrinks to last a lifetime, understood that shudder all too well. Understood also, thanks to his military experience, that sometimes pushing forward was the only option no matter how much retreat appealed.

"Well, you do what you gotta do," he said. The anger dissipated suddenly, leaving him weary. "And I'll do what I've gotta do."

"I really am sorry," she said. When he waved away her apology, she added, "I'll understand if you don't want to take us out to see the ranch now."

"No. It's fine. I said I'd do it, and I have time. I think we're in for a few days of snow, so it might be now or never."

A beat or two passed, and then she said, "Thank you," and smiled at him. A sweet smile full of relief and gratitude that curled up inside his heart, and just like that, he was angry again. Goddamn it, he didn't want things curling up inside his fucking heart.

What was wrong with him? Why were things so complicated with this woman? He didn't want her smiling at him like that, like they had some kind of normal relationship. Like they were friends. Like they could be…lovers.

He wanted her to look like she had when she'd first come into the office—royally pissed.

"I want a painting."

She blinked at him, her smile fading, and his heart thudded against his rib cage like it was trying to get out. He felt instantly better and worse. Accomplished and lower than a slug all at once.

"You said you didn't want a painting for the ranch tour."

He shrugged deliberately, callously. "I do now."

For a moment, a flash of something murderous glowed in her eyes and pulled her mouth into a taut line, and Grady thought she was going to say, *Screw you, buddy.* Hell, he almost wished she would, matching her anger to his.

She didn't. She just did that little chin-jut thing that he was starting to know really well and said, "Which one?"

He gave an indifferent shrug this time and injected a bored tone into his voice. "I don't care."

Another flare of murder in her gaze and something else, too—maybe distress?—but it was there and gone in the blink of her eyes. Not saying another word, she strode across the room, giving him a wide birth as she grabbed the knob and opened the door.

Grady breathed out, shoving a hand through his hair and letting his head drop down. The screaming tension in his neck and shoulders he hadn't even been aware of released suddenly in a rush of blood. His heart thudded like a bongo drum, so loud he was amazed she hadn't heard it from the other side of the room.

He didn't know why he was being such a dick about those paintings. Taking them from her one by one. But he knew they were precious to her—as precious as his peace and privacy were to him. And that was a fair trade as far as he was concerned.

He heard her footsteps returning, and his muscles pulled taut again as he shoved his hands into his pockets. She entered the office, not even acknowledging him as she crossed to the opposite side and propped the canvas against the wall, facing in.

Man, she was pissed.

Turning back, she didn't make eye contact as she headed to the door. "We'll be waiting outside for you when you're done being a prick," she said calmly, and Grady's barely leashed temper spiked again, his pulse pounding like the gallop of hooves through his ears.

She had one foot out the door when he said, "Wait."

His arm shot out, his fingers lightly circling her wrist, and he watched her in profile as she glanced down at where he had her shackled, then glanced at him, cool as a fucking cucumber. There was about three feet separating them as he gave a gentle tug. She went with it, but she was stiff, and she stumbled a little, her shoulder bumping into his sternum, but it didn't matter—he barely felt it as cookie dough and the rough jerk of her breathing filled up his senses.

Grady's hands found her face, his palms sliding onto her cheeks, then his fingers funneled into her hair, and even though her eyes still flashed blue murder at him, she was lifting toward him and he was lowering toward her and their lips met and he groaned as his mouth slanted over hers, opened, demanded hers open, too, groaning when she let him in, when her tongue touched his, when it licked along his lips, when her mouth moved hard and deep and frantic, spiraling heat and lust to his core—to his abs, to his thigh, to his ass.

And all the way deep inside his balls.

How he broke away from her, Grady would never know. But he did—a very deliberate move. "Now you look like we've been fucking," he said, the growl in his voice scratching like razor blades in his throat.

Panting hard, she stared at him for long beats, her gaze a curious mix of lust and calculation before she slid her hand to his neck and tugged, pulling him in for another brief, hard kiss. She nipped his bottom lip as she pulled away, and Grady reared back, cussing under his breath.

"Ow," he said at the hot little streak of pain, his tongue automatically touching the spot. Her gaze flared as it followed the movement, and she was still breathless as she said, "Now *we* look like we've been fucking, you asshole."

Then she turned on her heel and left him standing there, his pulse roaring, the aroma of cookie dough in his nostrils, and the taste of blood on his tongue. And fuck if he wasn't more turned on than he'd ever been in his life. Which was just what he needed about five seconds out from spending the afternoon with her parents.

CHAPTER FOURTEEN

If Suzanne was in her right mind, she'd have been amazed at the number of words Grady was speaking during their ranch tour. Poor guy was pretty much forced to as her parents peppered him with 101 questions. He did his best answering them in his preferred communication style of brevity while trying to be polite and respectful and fulfill the role of fake rancher boyfriend.

But throughout, his love and pride for this place—his uncle's place—was evident.

He drove the fence line and pointed out herds of cattle now grazing on the more sheltered winter pastures where there were gullies and treed areas for wind protection during blizzards. He drove past several large crude structures closed in at three sides that looked like big open barns, which could be used for animals to shelter in during the worst snowfalls in winter and for storage of hay or equipment at other times. They also passed two small, rough-hewn shacks right out of the Wild freaking West that were there for emergency shelter should anyone ever be stuck out on the ranch in inclement weather.

But Suzanne only really kept one ear on the conversation. Her stomach churned and her brain was spinning like a top as it gnawed on all that had happened in the last couple of hours. How Grady was going to tell his aunt and uncle about them, and how she hated that they were somehow going to think less of her even though she barely knew Burl and hadn't met Cora yet and might not at all, and, come the New Year, she'd never see them again.

How incensed he'd been about their secret getting out and how ragey she'd been that he'd dragged her into his office like a recalcitrant schoolgirl. And how he'd kissed her—twice—making her hot and needy and then angry. So angry she'd *bitten* him. God…she'd never bitten another human being in her life, let alone deliberately out of spite and malice and some wild sexual impulse she didn't even want to think about.

She'd never been aroused by that kind of edginess, by the need to *mark* someone, but the way he'd reared back, the way heat had flared in his gaze as his tongue had lapped at the injured flesh of his lip had been a heady kind of turn-on.

And then the final insult—him not caring about which painting she handed over. It was such a ridiculous thing to be hung up on, but there it was. He'd been so specific the last two times, like he'd committed them to memory, thought about them a lot. His shrug had probably hurt more than having to use the paintings as a bargaining chip in the first place.

Suzanne shouldn't care that he didn't care. But she did. She thought he was…invested in her paintings and for him to be indifferent…that had been gut-wrenching.

She hadn't looked when she'd chosen, just stormed into the walk-in closet where she was keeping them and grabbed the closest one. If he didn't care, then she wasn't going to, either. But she'd checked after and it had been Atlas.

The painting that had survived the great cottage flood safe on the high ground of the easel.

Her gut twisted thinking about the satisfaction that had unfurled through her veins as she'd admired him on that easel back when she'd been in the throes of her creative flush and anything had seemed possible. Each and every one of those five paintings had a memory attached to it; they *meant* something to her, and now there were just two. Suzanne couldn't help but wonder how long it was going to take him to get them, too.

Not long the way they were going.

It made her not like him very much right now. Even though she knew she was lying in a bed of her own making.

"Don't you think, darling?"

Suzanne suddenly realized her mother had been talking to her and she had no earthly idea what she'd said. "I'm sorry, I was miles away."

"I said, it's so wild and barren and still out here. I hope you get a chance to get some of this on canvas. I know you're not an original artist, but a month is a long time to go without painting, darling. Don't forget, it's just like a muscle—it needs to be exercised, and you can't get more inspirational than this. I'd hate you to regret wasting an opportunity."

Oh, there were going to be plenty of things Suzanne regretted about her time here—but *not* painting the landscape was *not* one of them.

"Yeah," she said, glancing out her window, as uninspired by the landscape today as she had been two weeks ago when she'd tried to capture it on canvas. "I might wait until the first snowfall."

Grady's intensely curious gaze was hot on her profile, but she ignored it, hoping valiantly that a blanket of white would be the shot in the arm her muse needed to paint what she'd come to Credence to paint. Snow *was* pretty damn inspiring.

Maybe not as much as Grady stripped to the waist in the mudroom, but she could at least set up a canvas again and see what happened, right?

"According to Bob's hip, it should have snowed last night," Albie said.

Simone laughed. "Ray said not, though. He said tomorrow. What do you think, Grady? Do ranchers have hunches about these kind of things?"

"Plenty do," he said. "I prefer science. Bureau says light snow tonight, and I'll back it over Bob Downey's hip any day."

More laughter from Simone. "Well, it's cold enough to snow, that's for sure. I'm pleased to be in the vehicle and not out there." It was toasty warm inside the cab. Way warmer than it would have been in Ethel. "I don't know how you can bear being out in this all day."

"It can get a bit cold from time to time," he agreed with his typical flair for understatement.

Saying it was a *bit cold* out here was like saying it was a *bit warm* in the middle of the Mojave Desert. Of course, she expected no less. Grady wasn't someone who moaned and bitched about his lot. He worked a ranch, he'd been in the military, and both those things weren't conducive to luxury indoor working conditions.

He was tough. As nails. And why in the hell she'd thought he'd just roll over and play nice after she'd essentially bribed him into being her fake rancher boyfriend, she'd never know. He might have agreed, but there was only so far she could push him, and he didn't have any compunction pushing back, as he'd proved earlier in his office.

Something she'd be wise to remember as he switched on his vehicle headlights. The light was fading quickly now as the night drew in. "Time to head home," he announced.

"How do you even know the way back?" her father asked as Grady turned the vehicle around. "We've been driving all over, and there's no real road."

"Well…" Grady's voice was dry as the cold, cracked ground under their tires. He turned the wheel and pointed straight ahead. "It's kinda easy at the moment."

And there in the distance was the cabin lit up like a Vegas slot machine. Grady's mouth had flattened into a thin line, and she heard a swift intake of breath from the back seat, which could have been either or both of her parents. The house blinked and flashed, but Suzanne didn't care how tacky it might appear, she got a little teary just looking at it.

It was Christmas, damn it.

She knew Grady had legitimate reasons to be all bah humbug, but she was annoyed enough about everything that had gone down these past couple of hours—she didn't need his or her parents' festive derision. They were just lights for crying out loud.

"I'm so pleased you decided on the blinking lights, Josh," she said, forcing a breathy kind of excitement into her voice.

His knuckles whitened around the steering wheel, and there was a spark of irritation in his gaze as he shot her a phony, overly bright smile. Her gaze automatically zeroed in on the slightly reddened area of his bottom lip where she'd nipped him. It stood out like a beacon to her, but if her parents had noticed it, they hadn't said.

"Well, as Uncle Burl says, Suzy, it's not Christmas until we're giving the horses seizures." He laughed, but his eyes did not. "You don't think it's too much, do you?"

"Oh no, absolutely not," she enthused, shooting laser beams at him from her fake *goo-goo* eyes. "It's perfect."

He reached across and gave her hand a very firm squeeze. "I'm so thrilled you love it. There'll never be another Christmas like this."

The double message behind his words was clear as he withdrew his hand. And, despite the undercurrent of hostility that had flared between them again, Suzanne couldn't help but think how sad that was—for both of them.

• • •

Her parents came to the cabin for dinner and left just after seven as the first light drift of snow was falling. Grady promptly disappeared through the archway, too. Suzanne assumed he was doing work in his office, but two hours and four batches of cookies later, she figured he'd gone to bed. A fact that seemed to be confirmed when there'd been no strip of light under the office door as she'd passed by twenty minutes earlier to have a quick shower while the cookies cooled.

She didn't usually frost cookies at nine at night. Hell, she couldn't even remember the last time she *had* frosted cookies prior to today. But the two movies she and Grady had watched seemed to make a big deal out of Christmas cookies, and the batches she'd made earlier with her parents had been a bit of a hit. Despite her mom's initial resistance, citing the perils of butter and refined sugar, she'd really gotten into the frosting side of things.

Her father had not been wrong when he'd said they'd have cookie masterpieces. Simone's renowned artistic flair was evident even with cheap tubes of frosting.

And now it was Suzanne's turn, because it was this or go to bed, and it was way too early for that. She would only lie awake for hours, and that was not a good idea when her head was full of Grady. For the first time in her life, despite the coziness of the fire and the low murmur of traditional Christmas carols from her playlist and the absolute delight of the twinkling tree, she wished she didn't prefer the night hours. It was hardly conducive to ranch life when everything was about early to bed, early to rise.

She'd *never* make it as a rancher's wife.

Suzanne's hand paused abruptly above the cookie she was frosting. Where in the hell had that come from?

Sure, over the course of her life, she'd thought about being a wife. Somebody's wife. She hadn't thought too much about her mysterious husband, but deep down she'd always assumed he'd be an artist like her or in one of the associated industries. Maybe an agent like her father. Or a gallery owner. Or…someone who worked at Sotheby's. But never in her life had she ever thought she'd be a *rancher's* wife.

It was…utterly ridiculous.

She was here for a month. And this relationship was fake. *A big, fat fake*. She didn't know the first thing about life out here, and two weeks on a ranch did not make her rancher wife material. Not to mention the fact that Grady didn't want her here. Hell, he probably had some calendar somewhere he was crossing off the days on with a big red marker.

Besides, she was a New Yorker. Her life was in New York. Her work was in New York. Her friends and family were in New York.

But even as she thought that, she knew it wasn't true. Not really. Sure, she had friends in the city, and her parents and the house she'd grown up in were there also. But her work often took her away from New York and, frankly, she could paint anywhere—she'd just proven that.

Especially if she wasn't traveling for commissions and decided it was time to concentrate on her own art for a while.

Her heart fluttered like wings inside her chest as her muse stirred. Her own art. Grady might want her gone at the end of her rental period, but that didn't mean she had to leave Credence. What if she got her own place by the lake, like Winona? Set up a studio out there? Finally left home and found out who she was without the constraints of the familiar?

The thought was both preposterous and exciting at once.

"I thought I could smell cookies."

Suzanne startled and almost dropped the frosting tube, glancing to the side to find Grady paused under the archway. He was in track pants and that soft faded T-shirt, looking like the best kind of Christmas present. His hair was a little messy, as if he'd been shoving his fingers through it, his jaw dark with stubble and his feet bare.

And the way that T-shirt stretched just right over his shoulders was the most indecent thing she'd ever seen.

She straightened. "I…thought you were in bed."

He shook his head slowly, the working of his jaw visible across the distance. "Nope." Then his eyes took an inventory of what she was wearing—baggy plaid fleece pajama pants and a thin navy T-shirt with a V-neck and tiny navy buttons that ran all the way down the front to the hem. The buttons pulled a little at her cleavage, and Suzanne thanked God she'd decided to wear a bra beneath her pajama shirt—just in case.

For a beat or two, she thought he was going to

turn around and go back to wherever the hell he'd been hiding. But the moment passed, and he moved toward the kitchen instead, saying, "We need more cookies?"

No, they had enough cookies to feed all of eastern Colorado, but she *had* to do something. "I'm making some for Winona. We give each other a fun, gimmicky gift every year so I thought, in the spirit of hokiest Christmas ever, why not?"

She didn't mention the cookies were more risqué than hokey. Not the type you could put out for Christmas day, although no doubt Winona would.

Conscious of Grady's every move as he stepped into the kitchen area, she took a quick swallow of her wine and went back to the frosting, hoping he'd grab whatever he'd come for and leave again, although he didn't seem to be in any crashing hurry to do so. He crossed to the cupboard where the glasses lived, then headed for the sink. She heard the faucet turn on and the sound of running water into the glass seemed extraordinarily loud. A beat or two later, the hair on Suzanne's nape stood to attention as she sensed a heated gaze fixed firmly on her ass.

Crap, she squeezed her butt cheeks together. Plaid was not a flattering pattern if you had an ass like hers, especially with them being so baggy. Stripes—why didn't she bring her stripy pajamas?

"It smells good in here." His voice was all low and rumbly. "May I have one?"

Suzanne shut her eyes at his low request, knowing it would be a particular kind of torture watching him eat cookies lounging in his pajamas. With bare feet. Maybe crumbs on his lips.

He didn't wait for permission, and the hairs on her neck actually prickled as he sidled up. His arm, his shoulder, his hip were about an inch from hers, and the warmth radiating from his body was like a furnace. She was excruciatingly conscious of him—of his heat and his hardness and the heady aroma of his soap. Hell, she was conscious of his *breathing*.

His big hand slid out to snaffle a cookie but paused halfway to the tray. "What the hell?"

Suzanne was confused for a second, so caught up in her awareness of him that she'd temporarily forgotten what she'd been frosting.

He stared at the bench top. "Are they…?"

Her gaze refocused on the dozen cookies in front of her. "Penis cookies?" She cleared her throat of its sudden highness and tried to affect an air of nonchalance, like she shaped dough into phalluses every day. "Yes."

He glanced at her. "You're making cock and ball cookies?"

Suzanne didn't return his gaze as her cheeks flushed hot. "Yes. For Winona. Like I said, something gimmicky. You know…because she's an erotic romance author."

"Yeah." He returned his attention to the cookies. "I get it. I just didn't realize they made…penis cookie cutters."

With her gaze firmly fixed on the cookies, she said, "Well, I'm sure you can get penis paraphernalia online, but that obviously wasn't much help to me now. And I guess you can probably get all kind of penis-related cooking items in sex shops and the like, but I didn't think Credence had one of those."

Suzanne cringed internally as she ran off at the mouth again, the words spewing unchecked from her lips. "So I just kind of improvised. I wouldn't be much of an artist if I couldn't do a bit of freehand, would I? And I figured how hard can a penis be, right?"

Oh dear god. *Shut up, Suzanne.* For the love of god, *shut up*!

"Anyway," she rushed on (for reasons known only to the universe), "they're just for fun, and I'm going to put them in some little clear bags and tie a red bow around them—the bags that is, not the penises—or is that peni for plural? I never know!" Suzanne shut her eyes. *Oh Jesus, please make it stop.* "And I'm going to do a fancy label because nothing says Christmas like a bag of dicks, right?"

Suzanne didn't know how many times she'd said the word "penis" just now, but she did know saying it less in front of Grady while they stared at a dozen of them would have been a better strategy.

Mercifully, he took her question as rhetorical and left it alone. "They're quite…big."

"Well, yeah…small dicks aren't as funny."

He opened his mouth as if he was going to say something, then shut it, and there was a beat or two of silence before he tried again. "They're also quite…" He pointed at the one nearest him. "Embellished."

"Oh yes…well." The cookie in question was sporting a cock ring. "I mean, they're supposed to be fun, so…"

Apart from the cock ring, she'd also frosted two cookies with bow ties, one dressed as Santa, one wearing a leather-studded jockstrap and two more where the testicles had been decorated as Christmas baubles. She'd just finished piping words onto one when Grady had appeared, and that was the one he pointed to next.

"Lick me?"

The timber of his voice changed. It was deeper, rougher, and sparks of heat turned on like switches all along her pelvic floor. "A character in"—she stopped and cleared her throat—"one of Winona's books has a lick-me tattoo on his…"

Jesus, *do not say penis one more time*. Suzanne let the sentence drift off.

"I see."

He didn't sound like he *see*'d at all. He sounded bemused and disbelieving and maybe even slightly intrigued. "And what's your next decorative move?"

"I was just going to do a couple with blue balls."

"Blue balls aren't very funny, either."

Suzanne could hear the wince in his voice loud and clear. She didn't know if he was talking from experience or implying the current state of his testicles. Both thoughts led down unhelpful paths—like ways in which she could help him out of that predicament.

"You can take one if you like. I have more than enough, and they taste delicious if I do say so myself."

"Thanks, but—" He held up his hands. "No thanks."

She noticed his slight recoil and rolled her eyes

at his macho bullshit. "It's a *cookie*."

He chuckled. "I know."

Suzanne's breath caught as his smile warmed his face and the vibrations from his low laughter enveloped her. "What?" She raised an eyebrow. "You think eating a cookie dick is going to make you gay?"

He laughed again. "Nope."

None of the men—straight or gay—she knew in New York would think twice about eating a cookie shaped like a penis. They'd probably make crude, witty jokes that made her laugh as they munched.

"I'm just more of a female genitalia cookie kinda guy. You make any of them?"

"No. But pussy cookies would have been a good idea." One she might have thought of had Grady not been on her mind so much. "Winona's all about equal genitalia opportunity."

He grinned and gave a little fist pump. "Viva la vulva."

Suzanne blinked. Then she laughed. *Viva la vulva?* The man was full of surprises. It should have sounded ridiculous, something so feminist coming from a guy who pretty much represented one of the country's last bastions of masculinity, but it didn't. Her pulse tripped and she felt a little light-headed. How could she be so damn angry with this guy 50 percent of the time yet still want to climb all over him?

It had to be the surroundings. It had to be the fire crackling in the hearth and the Christmas tree lights blinking haphazardly and the carols. Add in the aromas of sugar and cinnamon and the wine that must be going to her head, and it was no wonder a shot of recklessness jettisoned into her system.

Picking up one of the unfrosted cookies, she bit into the head. It crumbled in her mouth, and the sugar and butter melted on her tongue, and she moaned a little because it tasted amazing and because it made Grady's eyes darken and his nostrils flare.

"Good?" His gaze dropped to her mouth and lingered.

"Uh-huh." Swallowing her mouthful, she licked the crumbs from her lips and enjoyed the way his eyes tracked the movement. "Best dick I've had in a long time," she murmured with a smile.

He laughed, and Suzanne's gaze was drawn to his bottom lip, to the reddened area where she'd marked him earlier today. A prolonged inspection revealed a slight bluish discoloration to the mark. "I'm sorry…about biting you."

He shrugged. "I was being an asshole."

Suzanne blinked, surprised by his easy admission of guilt. "Yeah, you were." He laughed again. "But that doesn't make it right. Is it sore?"

He shook his head. "Only when I laugh, talk, eat, drink, or breathe."

It was Suzanne's turn to laugh. "I *am* sorry," she said, and without giving it much thought, she lifted her fingers to his mouth and lightly touched the spot.

He didn't pull away or wince, he just went very still, his eyes fluttering shut for a brief moment before opening again. "It's fine," he dismissed, his voice like gravel as he stared at her mouth, and heat bloomed between them.

"Maybe," Suzanne whispered, blood throbbing through her veins, the air in her lungs heavy, "or maybe it needs kissing better?"

He swallowed, and the bob of his Adam's apple seemed thick and painful, and she knew all sense of rationality had left the building when she seriously contemplated kissing it better.

Kissing all his boo-boos better. The ones she could see and the ones she could not.

"Maybe it does," he agreed, his voice rumbling into the air, his eyes glued to her lips, making her breath hitch and her pulse whoosh through her head as every reason she shouldn't be doing this fled.

It was just a kiss, right?

CHAPTER FIFTEEN

Slowly, rising on her tiptoes, excruciatingly careful to maintain the paltry distance between their bodies, she leaned in, her mouth—just her mouth—closing the distance. Kissing Grady's lip better didn't require their bodies to touch. Just their mouths.

Only their mouths.

Carefully, gently, Suzanne touched her mouth to the mark on his bottom lip. He kept still as her mouth lingered for one second, two. But she could hear the rough draw of his breathing. And hers. Pulling back slightly, she asked, "Better?"

"A little." His voice was somewhere between a pant and a whisper.

Her pulse so loud between her ears now that she couldn't think straight, Suzanne put her mouth to his bottom lip again, lingered again, touched her tongue to the swollen area.

He made a rumbly kind of noise in the back of his throat, and she did it again and again until her tongue was swiping along his entire bottom lip, until he groaned and a hand slid into her hair and his mouth parted.

They were truly kissing now, tentatively at first and then not at all tentatively as he deepened the kiss, his hand sliding onto her hip, hitching her close, their bodies bumping deliciously together, his hand sliding to the small of her back, locking them in place.

A momentary slither of clarity had her mouth breaking away slightly, the pant of her breath mingling with the pant of his. "Does it hurt?"

His rough "Hell no" was all the encouragement she needed to go back for more, one arm sliding around his neck, the other hand fisting in his shirt.

Things went wild and hazy then, his mouth devouring hers, hard and demanding, his tongue licking along her lips and into her mouth, thrusting and seeking and devouring. "God, you taste good," he said on a groan, his lips the merest of a fraction away from hers. "I want to taste all of you."

Then he was kissing her again, so deep and so good and pressed against her so close and so tight that Suzanne was barely conscious of him turning her and lifting her onto the bench. Her knees spread automatically to admit him closer, and his hands found her ass and hitched her forward. The bench was just the right height, bringing the heat and tingling between her legs flush against the heat and hardness between his. It felt electric, arcing and sizzling, tearing a gasp from her throat and a groan from his.

"Fuck," he whispered as their lips broke apart and they held, panting together, suspended in the moment for a beat or two before Suzanne ground against him.

"Yes please," she said, her voice low and urgent.

Grady groaned again, his lips sliding kisses to her jaw and down her neck and along her collarbone and to the swell of her cleavage as she rode the hard ridge of his erection, the sensation both soothing and stoking the roaring ache between her legs.

The tip of his tongue licked along the edge of the V neckline before his lips traveled to the hard point of her nipple pressing against the T-shirt and sucked into his mouth. Even with the barrier of fabric, it was a jolt through her system, and Suzanne cried out, her hand finding the back of his head and holding tight.

He broke free, lifting his head, and said, "Off." His eyes hot green pools as he glared in frustration at her shirt. "I need to see you."

He didn't wait for her to comply, just lifted his hands to the front of her shirt, grasped either side of the buttons, and yanked them apart. Suzanne gasped as buttons flew everywhere and she sat exposed before him, her shirt ruined, her chest rising and falling unevenly, her breathing a rough pant as his eyes roved over her satiny red bra with black stitching and a black lace trim.

"Christ." His eyes roved over her breasts like he'd just discovered gold. "These are so much nicer than my fantasies," he said in a hushed, husky kind of reverence that Suzanne felt all the way down to her clitoris.

"You fantasized about me?" Her stomach clenched and her heart fibrillated, and she was hot and trembling all over. It was good to know she hadn't been the only one unable to master her subconscious.

But had he fantasized about her with the level of detail she had him?

He nodded. "All the time." Dragging his gaze off her breasts, he met her eyes. "While I'm fixing fences, feeding cattle, talking to my men, freezing my ass off on a horse. And every fucking night since you moved into the cottage."

His voice was rough with desire and indignation, like he hated himself a little for his lack of control, and that only made Suzanne hotter. Because she knew exactly how he felt. Streaks of need darted from her inner thighs to her belly button and undulated along her pelvic floor.

"And these." Grady dropped his gaze to her breasts, his hands sliding up her thighs, over her stomach and ribs to slide onto the satin-covered mounds. He squeezed them, Suzanne's breath caught, and when he swiped his thumbs over the visibly erect nipples, she made a little noise in her throat and arched her back. "I've thought about these more than I've thought about boobs in my whole life combined."

He traced his index fingers along the lacy edge where fabric met flesh and then, hooking his fingers under the edge, he pulled both the cups aside. Suzanne panted heavily as her breasts spilled out, and Grady groaned, his hands moving to capture the fullness of them, squeezing them, playing with the weight of them in his hands before lowering his head.

Suzanne cried out as he sucked a nipple into the wet heat of his mouth, rolling it around, flicking it with his tongue, grazing it with his teeth. He switched quickly to the other, and everything dissolved around her as her body succumbed to the hot, wet tug of his mouth, her fingers winding in his hair.

But even as she gasped and writhed beneath his

tongue, the growing need to touch him, to slide her hands over him, to feel him, grew until she was clawing at his soft shirt. She yanked it up over his head, forcing him to release her nipple, but that was okay because *oh dear god* it was the mudroom all over again. Except his skin was flushed and warm and his eyes were hot as they bored into her and his mouth was wet and he was looking at her with the kind of feral need she knew echoed in every beat of her heart.

Grabbing his shoulders, Suzanne pulled him close, her mouth landing on his, her breasts flattened to his chest as she ground against his erection. His hands slid to her ass to keep them locked in place, and she blasted him with a kiss that gave and took in equal measure as her hands explored his back, stroking up and down the length, feeling the play of muscle, the hardness of bone, the furrow and notches of his spine. Exploring the dip that was the small of his back, the rounded well of two dimples and the slope leading to the waistband of his track pants.

Suzanne didn't think twice about slipping her hands into the waistband. Her palms were greedy for the feel of his flesh, and they moved on autopilot, enjoying the contraction of muscles as she palmed the smooth naked globes of his ass and gave them a squeeze.

God…Grady was built. This was an ass that out-assed anything she could have ever painted. Suzanne stroked her tongue in and out, mimicking the rhythm of her hands as they kneaded his glutes. The deep well of his groan was like a sexual sugar rush to a system already buzzing with high-octane arousal.

But, as good as it was, his ass was never going to be enough. She needed more than his ass in her hands; she needed the hardness between his legs in her hands—in *other* parts of her. Greedily, her fingers moved to his front, dipping into his boxer briefs, seeking out his erection, trembling with a need that bordered on feral, finding it all hard and heavy and solid, moaning in satisfaction as she curled her fingers around its girth.

A noise that didn't sound quite human spilled from Grady's lips as he tore his mouth away, pressing his forehead to hers, their heads bowing as she wrapped her fingers around his dick, a bead of liquid pearling at the slit in his flushed crown.

"Jesus…" He gasped, his breathing short, sharp pants. "We should not be doing this."

Suzanne's chest rose and fell in unison. "I know." And she did know. He was absolutely right. They really needed to stop. This wasn't real, and making it real wasn't an option.

But he felt so good in her hand—so thick, so right—the taut skin deceptively velvet, the core like forged steel. And it felt like that all the way from the root to the tip because she tested it to make sure. She couldn't *not*. Not with her heartbeat like a tempest in her blood.

Groaning again, he buried his head in the crook of her shoulder, and she knew that his gaze was locked on her hand as she worked up and down his length. Once, twice, three times. A series of rough pants spilling from his mouth.

"Suzy..." he muttered, his hand on her ass tightening.

The use of *Suzy* was like a lit flare to a vat of oil. *Suzanne* might just have been able to pull her back from the brink. After all, Suzanne always did the right thing. She was the good daughter, the good friend. She didn't push or make waves. Her path had been cut out for her in life, and she'd been happy to tread it. She was Simone St. Michelle's daughter; she forged other people's art and was happy doing so.

Suzy, on the other hand, was none of those things. Suzy yelled at tough rancher dudes and bribed them and bit their lips. She lied to her parents. Suzy painted her own stuff. *And* made out on kitchen benches.

Suzy was freaking awesome.

"I need..." His voice trailed away as his gaze searched her face like he was trying to fathom if she also felt this wild kind of recklessness. "I need..."

She nodded. She knew exactly what he needed because she needed it to. She needed him inside her, moving inside her, to be as connected to him as was humanly possible.

To be one with Joshua Grady.

"Me too," she whispered, releasing his dick to circle her arms around his neck, her nipples brushing the smoothness of his chest. "Me too."

She kissed him again, their lips meeting in a desperate kind of mashing that had her gripping his hair and locking her legs around him, clinging and grinding herself against him until they were both groaning and panting.

Suzanne wouldn't have thought it was possible to come from dry humping, but she was damn near there, and she wanted him inside her when she came.

"Condoms," she rasped, pulling out of the kiss, the air in her lungs thick with desire.

He stared at her, his hair all messed up, the spot where she'd bitten him even more pronounced, his chest rising and falling as he dragged air into his lungs. "Wh-what?" His green gaze was clouded with confusion for a second before it cleared. "Oh shit." His eyes went distant as if he was doing a mental inventory of his bathroom vanity. "I...don't think I have a single condom in this entire house."

Suzanne, her breath chugging, too, sat back a little. She hadn't expected him to have them in the back pocket of his track pants, but what single man didn't have quick, easy access to a stash in his own home? Just in case he was called on to be someone's fake rancher boyfriend and things got out of hand. "You don't use condoms?"

He shot her a frustrated scowl. "I *always* use condoms. I just...don't do *this* all that regularly... and never here. I usually get them on the way..."

Suzanne supposed it made her a bad person to like that Grady wasn't putting it out for every woman he came across. It probably made her a truly heinous person to admit the thought even turned her on a little. Grady was a seriously hot guy. She imagined—if he actually smiled—he could crook his finger and have just about anyone.

And he'd chosen her.

It was ridiculous to be aroused by what essentially amounted to a lack of practice. It probably made him lousy in bed. But some things were innate, and Grady sure as hell hadn't taken a wrong step yet.

"I have condoms," she said, sliding her arms around his neck, tightening her thighs around his waist. She always carried them in her handbag. "In my room."

Grady did not need any further direction. He just grabbed her ass and pulled her off the bench top, kissing her with deep, drugging kisses as he carried her, navigating from the kitchen past Zoom's tank through the archway to her bedroom at the end of the hall without dropping her or running them into a single wall. Not that Suzanne was conscious of anything outside of Grady. All that existed was his mouth and the play of his tongue and the heat of his chest and the hardness between his legs. It was as if she were floating.

Floating in a sea of fake rancher boyfriend.

It wasn't until he urged her legs to unlock and her feet were sliding to the ground, the backs of her calves brushing the mattress, that she came back to herself. They broke apart and just stared at each other for long moments, the only sound between them the husky fall of their breaths.

God…he was sexy. His naked chest, his hair all messed up, the stubble on his jaw. The heat radiating from his body mixed with the soapy scent of his skin to form some kind of intoxicating hit of pheromones. The glitter in his eyes was full of desire and longing and absolute purpose.

Her legs suddenly weak as cotton candy, Suzanne sat on the mattress and eyed the tie of his track pants. It was dark in the room, but her night vision was in full working order, allowing her to see the prominent bulge at just the right level.

Yay for night vision!

Her mouth watered at the thought of tasting him. "Take them off."

It was satisfying to hear the rough intake of his breath and see the slight tremble of his hand as he tugged on the tie, then pushed them down his legs.

"Those too," she said, pointing at his boxer briefs even before his track pants had hit the floor. He looked hot as fuck in the crimson fabric, his erection filling them out the way God and Calvin Klein had no doubt intended, but right now all they were doing was stopping her from getting to his goods.

They were soon gone, too, and his erection sprang free, standing out—thick and proud. And hard. And *big*. The kind of big that made *tumescent manroot* an entirely acceptable way of describing a penis.

He was certainly no *David*—that was for sure.

"Come closer," she whispered, her exposed nipples aching, her mouth dry with the need to taste him.

He stepped in close, and their gazes locked. The groan he let out when she slid her fingers down his length went straight to her ovaries. The swift, harsh suck of his breath when her mouth followed went straight to her clitoris.

"Jesusssss," he hissed. *"Fuck."*

His eyes closed as he slid his hand onto her shoulder, and Suzanne's eyes closed, too, reveling in the silky hard contradiction of him against her tongue, in the scent of him filling her nostrils and his clean salty flavor playing on her taste buds. She swallowed him up, her hand sliding onto one of his ass cheeks as she took him as far as she could before backing off, to swirl her tongue around and around and around the taut crown, lapping at the salty residue there.

"Christ," he muttered, opening his eyes. "You drive me crazy."

Suzanne didn't know if he meant right now or the past two weeks or both, but he sounded so undone, and hell if that didn't do loopy things to her insides. Her eyes fluttered open to find him staring down at her, and the craving in his gaze was arousing in ways she never knew existed.

He wasn't the tough guy rancher or the badass military dude anymore. He was just a man—totally stripped back. It was humbling and powerful all at once that he was laying himself bare to *her*. A guy as hard and stoic as the elements he battled every day, who didn't seem to open up to *anybody*. To *need* anybody. But he was looking at her—the woman who talked too much and sassed him too much and was just *there* too much—with such naked hunger, her bones dissolved.

It was hot as fuck, and she had the giant lady boner to prove it.

"The feeling's entirely mutual," she whispered, her lips brushing the head of his penis as she spoke before she opened them over him again, shut her eyes, and took him in as far as she could.

He groaned, and it was like an electric charge spurring Suzanne to take him deeper, suck him harder. A hand slid into her hair and tightened, and for long moments there was just the bob of her head, the taste of him on her tongue, the ragged pant of his breathing, the tingle in her scalp and the rhythmic contraction and relaxation of his ass cheek under her hand.

And just when that ass cheek started to clench and get harder, he groaned something unintelligible and wrenched himself from her mouth, reaching down for her, hauling her up, pulling her roughly against him, breathing hard as his eyes glittered for long, charged seconds.

"I wasn't done yet," she said, her voice breathy, her pulse fluttering at her temples.

"I'm not going to last very long if you keep doing that, and I want to be so deep inside you when I come, you're never going to forget my face."

He kissed her then, the pressure almost punishing, but it was exactly what Suzanne needed as she rose to meet the kiss with equal vigor, trying to assuage the desperate passion his words had ignited. She didn't understand the passion. His words were so *possessive*, so…bullshit patriarchal, so *caveman*. Like his cock was the one cock that ruled them all.

Like it was going to ruin her for all other men.

He didn't even *like* her. Hell, right now she wasn't sure she liked him. But *he* wanted to be the face she always saw? It was breathtakingly arrogant.

Also *seriously freaking hot.*

With his cock jammed between them, his mouth devoured hers, his tongue lashing hers, his hands stripping off her shirt and her bra and pushing at the waistband of her plaid pajama bottoms, then at the waistband of her lacy red underwear. They weren't even fully down her legs before he was easing her backward, bouncing her softly against the mattress and following her down, stripping her pants off her legs before rolling on top, his weight solid and perfect, their hips aligning, his erection pressed like hot lead into her belly.

And then his mouth was on hers again, devouring her, possessing her in a frenzy that stole Suzanne's breath. It was like he couldn't get close enough. Kiss her hard enough or deep enough, and she met him with equal ferocity. Kiss for kiss, tongue stroke for tongue stroke, licking into him, her pulse washing through her ears, her breathing struggling to keep up and then spilling out on a moan as his hand slipped between them to guide his dick through the slippery folds of her sex.

Her fingers dug into his shoulders as he notched at her entrance. He felt so good. Thick and blunt and all she could think about was that heat and hardness inside her.

Grady inside her.

Not about tomorrow or about their pretense or her parents or Christmas. There was nothing but Grady.

And he didn't pause, didn't slow down, didn't stop kissing her to take a breath, he just entered her in one stroke, sliding in high and hard, tearing a gasp from Suzanne's throat and a groan from his,

his mouth breaking away as he buried his face in her neck, pressing his lips to just below her ear.

He didn't move for long moments, and neither did Suzanne. They just lay still, breathing heavy in the aftermath of that first thrust. It was better than anything she'd ever imagined—and she'd imagined *this* far more than was good for her. Fireworks popped behind her closed eyes as she reveled in the weight and the heat and the hardness of him on top.

If this was how good he was at *entry*, Suzanne was going to be a dead woman when it came to actual thrusting.

He moved then, levering up on one arm as he withdrew and looming up over her as he thrust again. Suzanne gasped, twining her legs around his waist to take him deeper, and he kissed her, cutting off her gasp as he nudged higher, thrusting his tongue in time with the piston of his hips, turning her gasps to moans and then whimpers.

He fucked her *hard*. The tension in his muscles ratcheted tight, his back a taut, tight bow, a fine tremor fibrillating through his frame as he hunched into every thrust. It was almost like he was punishing her, or punishing himself anyway. Like he was trying to exorcise her from his head if not his life. Suzanne knew exactly how he felt—she didn't want to want him, either—but if this kind of pleasure was punishment, she'd take it any day.

This frenzy was *exactly* what Suzanne craved, and she met his every thrust, feeling it ripple over her skin and rattle through her bones and streak straight to her clitoris as her heart galloped inside her chest. And whether it was from Grady's barely contained arousal or the way his grinding provided such a direct stimulus to just the right place, Suzanne knew she was close to climax.

She cried out at the first deep pull spreading through her pelvis. "Josh," she whimpered, her lungs on fire as they desperately grabbed for air.

"Fuck," he muttered, panting hard as he rose up on his forearms, the tendons in his neck like ropes. He stared down at her with a mix of lust and helplessness more potent than his bourbon.

The pull became a hot ripple of pleasure. *Frickin' hell*, she was going to come. "Oh god…I…I'm…"

"Yes," he said, his voice so rough it scraped like gravel along her skin; then he slid his hand between them, found her clitoris, and rubbed. "Yes."

At his touch, Suzanne's orgasm flared like a firework, and her thighs gripped his convulsively as it exploded to life. She cried out as it hit, and so did he, the muscles in his back turning to rock, a guttural kind of curse escaping his lips as the fierce piston of his hips became discordant—but no less effectual—under the influence of his climax. Each thrust sent her higher and higher as he pulled her close, buried his face in her neck, and they panted and shuddered through their orgasms together.

Suzanne didn't know what to expect as the glow settled and Grady, who had collapsed against her, stirred. She didn't want him to go. She liked the weight of him, the smell of him, the fact his frame dwarfed her. But she didn't protest as he eased off, just shivered deliciously as he withdrew from her and rolled onto his back. Then, surprisingly, he slipped an arm under her neck and a hand around her shoulder, scooping her closer until she was on her side snuggled into him, her knee sliding over the top of his, her hand anchored on his chest.

Her heart thudded at the intimacy as Suzanne held very still in the quiet surrounding them. She had no idea what to do now. With a normal guy, she'd just let the warm rush of endorphins flooding her system and tugging at her eyelids have its way, but Grady wasn't a normal guy. She didn't have a rule book for him. The fact they were snuggling being a good case in point. She'd have laid money on Grady not being a *snuggle* kind of guy, yet here they were.

The silence between them deepened, and she wondered what he was thinking. Was he holding her because it was the expected thing? Was he regretting their loss of control? Was he searching for small talk? Was he thinking about the condom they'd come to her bedroom specifically to use and then completely disregarded?

Or was he wondering how long he had to lie here before he could leave?

That particular thought felt the most barbed. She had a contraceptive implant, and Grady had told her he always used protection so the lack of condom, while irresponsible, didn't alarm her so much. But the thought he was plotting his escape while they lay in this bliss bubble, her cells still half scrambled, was the most disturbing.

A soft, snuffly noise broke through her increasing anxiety and for a moment, Suzanne was confused as to its origin—it sounded like a dog or a cat—until she identified it as coming from Grady. Rising slowly up on her elbow, she looked down at his face.

Sleeping. He was sleeping. Deeply if that soft, snuffle snore was any indication.

He looked peaceful. And younger. That almost constant scowl he wore was ironed out in slumber. The dark shadow of his whiskers was tempting, inviting her to touch, the slack fullness of his mouth even more so. She'd kissed that mouth far more than was good for her peace of mind.

And, god help her, she didn't want to stop.

CHAPTER SIXTEEN

Joshua woke at five thirty the next morning with a numb arm, a warm woman plastered to his side, and a raging hard-on. He'd slept like the dead, and he was momentarily disorientated by the unfamiliar room and not being alone. What the hell? He didn't *sleep* with women. On the rare occasions he indulged in some female company, it was always a limited transaction—date, sexy times, then leave.

So it took a few seconds for the pieces to fall into place, for the memories from last night to return. For the self-flagellation to kick in as he'd known it would when he'd drifted to sleep but had been too damn sated to care.

He cared this morning. He cared a lot. Not least of all because his men would be here soon, and he was still bare-assed naked in his fake girlfriend's bed—the woman he *should not* have done the wild thing with and definitely *should not* have stayed in bed with all night.

Turning to gently ease his dead arm out from under Suzanne, Grady was stopped momentarily in his tracks by a strange twist in his chest. A slice of her hair had curled around her cheek, the tips brushing the corner of her mouth, which was temptingly full, and Grady wanted to put his lips on hers so badly, it rang warning bells that could probably be heard in Kansas.

He'd never craved this scenario—waking up to someone every morning—but that twist sure as hell felt a lot like regret.

Or maybe yearning.

Whatever it was, it didn't make getting his ass out of this warm bed a very appealing prospect.

Christ. A trickle of panic dripped into his veins. He didn't need this—it was just his hard-on talking. He didn't need a woman to wake up to every morning, tempting him to shirk his duties around the ranch. Sure, his ranch hands could pick up his slack and do what needed to be done without him, but that wasn't the way he ran things around here.

And nor was it about to be.

Ignoring the little voice urging him to stay, he extracted his arm, praying she didn't wake. They were going to have to have a conversation about last night at some point, but he sure as hell didn't want it to be now. She stirred a little, muttering something nonsensical before turning away from him, rolling in the opposite direction, exposing her back and her naked ass to his view.

Grady's dick twitched, and he shook his head. *Get your butt out of bed, man.*

Now!

All but leaping off the mattress, Grady was out of Suzanne's room and in and out of his, dressed and ready for work, in ten minutes flat. It was still dark outside, but the house was fully lit as he paused in the archway to the living room, grimacing anew at the assault to his senses from the Christmas overdose. The room *blazed* with light, from the wagon-wheel chandelier to the epileptic blinking of both the lights on the Christmas tree and the ones wrapped around the outside of the cabin, flashing like some giant fucking bat signal.

But the lights weren't the only thing that had been neglected in their rush to bed last night. Trays of unfrosted dick cookies sat on the kitchen bench, and the pile of ash in the fireplace reminded him he hadn't even banked the fire.

"Christ," he muttered, shaking his head at his careless behavior.

The whole goddamn cabin could have caught alight and burned to the ground in minutes, what with all the goddamn tinsel acting as an accelerant.

A noise to his right distracted him, and Grady glanced over to find Zoom taking a swim. "Hey, Zoom." He took the two paces to the tank, reaching for the pellets as he made eye contact with the turtle. Zoom bobbed around, his head above water, his beady little eyes fixed firmly on Grady. Eyes that seemed to say, *I know what you did last night*.

That would teach them to make out on the kitchen bench in full view of an impressionable turtle.

"Give me a break, dude," he said as he dropped in a handful of food. "I didn't plan it."

Zoom made no attempt to go after the food, just kept staring at Grady with what he swore was a little turtle lip curl. "Hey, man, don't judge me. She was making *dick* cookies."

Grady's stomach grumbled at the thought. Ordinarily he'd have had two cups of coffee by now and made himself some eggs and beans on toast with a side of hash browns. But, ordinarily, he'd have woken an hour ago. *Alone.*

This was no ordinary morning. Hell, nothing about these past two weeks had been ordinary.

Zoom, however, didn't stop with the judgment, and they stared each other down for long moments. "What? Just because she's fed you occasionally, she gets a pass?"

The distant sound of a car engine coming down the drive broke the impasse between man and turtle, galvanizing Grady into action. He turned off all the lights, crammed two cookies into his mouth and his feet into his boots. Grabbing his hat and his coat, he stepped outside into the pitch-black of a freezing Colorado morning, making his way to the barn as he pushed all thoughts of the warm bed and the even warmer woman he'd left behind from his mind.

• • •

To say Suzanne was distracted later that morning was an understatement. She'd been able to think of little else but her nighttime tryst since she'd woken at seven. All alone. She had no idea when he'd slipped out of bed—she certainly hadn't felt him leave. Although she'd slept so deeply, she doubted she'd have felt a twister touch down. But his side of the bed had been cold, which meant he'd been gone for a while.

So…how long *had* he stayed? Had he just been pretending to sleep, waiting for her to nod off so he could leave as soon as possible? Had it been half an hour? An hour? Or had he stayed longer?

Had he stayed all night?

And if so, what had he thought when he'd woken? The same as her? *Holy shit?* And *what have we done?* And *why do things so damn bad always feel so good?*

Because it had been *so very good.*

Suzanne had had her fair share of good, so she felt she was a reasonable judge. But Joshua Grady, who walked around like he didn't need any kind of human connection and admitted that he didn't *do this all that regularly*, may just have been the best she'd ever had.

"Don't you think, darling?"

Her mother's inquiry dragged Suzanne out of her head. "Hmm?" She frowned. "Sorry, I...checked out there for a moment."

In truth, Suzanne hadn't heard a word of the conversation going on between her parents and Winona since they'd entered Déjà Brew for one of Jenny Carter's sinfully good pumpkin spice lattes. It was seriously as good, if not better, than anything you could find in New York.

Jenny had apparently come to town with the other women in summer and had fallen in love with Wyatt Carter, who just happened to be the brother of Wade Carter—famed ex-quarterback for the Denver Broncos. She'd brought her five-year-old son, Henry, with her and set up Credence's first-ever coffee shop.

"That Renoir you painted for that private client in upstate New York is your best work to date."

"Oh." Suzanne had to shake away the sticky web of unhelpful images in her head that had nothing to do with Renoir before she could even recall that particular commission. "Yes, I think you're right."

Except she wasn't. Suzanne's best work to date was her interpretation—no doubt her mother would say bastardization—of *David*.

Which led her thoughts straight back to Grady.

"Here you go," Jenny said as she handed Suzanne her order in a to-go cup. "You look like you need some fortification."

Suzanne blinked. "Oh?"

"You look tired. That new guy of yours keeping you up all night?" she said with a smile.

Several sets of eyes swung in her direction. At least half a dozen of them did not belong to her family or Winona, who were all grinning at her indulgently as heat flooded Suzanne's face.

Winona was barely controlling a laugh.

Obviously everyone knew about her and Grady, but…could Jenny Carter tell she had sex last night? Could *every*one?

"You should watch out," she quipped, rubbing her hand over the roundness of her flowering belly, "or you'll be next."

Suzanne blanched. It was bad enough news that her and Grady's *relationship* was apparently all over town—as he'd predicted—they didn't need a pregnancy rumor as well. She could only imagine how furious Grady would be about that.

What was it with pregnant women thinking the whole damn world should be knocked up? She placed a hand over her stomach to ward off any weird pregnancy juju floating around inside Déjà Brew.

"You're pregnant?"

The startled voice behind Suzanne had her swinging around to find Burl standing just inside the door, his arm around a woman about his age with a cute salt-and-pepper pixie cut and kind eyes. Cora, she presumed.

Crap.

Cora's gaze fell to Suzanne's hand still resting against her abdomen, and she beamed. "Oh, Burl." She looked at him like they'd just won the lotto. "We're going to be grandparents."

Suzanne dropped her hand like it had been scalded. "Oh no." She shook her head vehemently, waving her hands in front of her in a universal sign of denial. "Absolutely not."

Shit! Grady was going to be pissed.

"Now, now, Cora." Burl laughed, obviously taking in the alarmed denial in Suzanne's gaze. "Don't get ahead of yourself. Come and meet her first."

Cora rushed forward and pulled Suzanne in for a hug. "My dear, dear girl. I'm Cora. And you must be Suzanne. It is so very nice to meet you. Now let me get a look at you."

She stepped back and held Suzanne at arm's length. There were tears in her eyes, which made Suzanne feel totally shitty. Deceiving her parents was one thing. Her parents, she knew, would move on quickly from Grady when Suzanne announced it had all fallen through. Deceiving this woman who plainly loved and worried about Grady and who clearly wore her heart on her sleeve was terrible.

And, if they'd been alone, she'd have fessed up right then and there even before Grady had the chance. Because it was obvious Cora had bought in to the gossip about her and Grady and that she was *thrilled*. But her parents were hovering, and there wasn't one single person in Déjà Brew who wasn't watching the exchange with interest.

"Oh yes," Cora said with a sniff as she blinked back the moisture in her eyes. "You'll do nicely." She beamed at Suzanne, then shook her head wistfully. "I'd always hoped he'd find someone after Bethany but—" Cora stopped abruptly, as if she'd said too much, then pulled Suzanne in for another hug. "Never mind," she said, her voice muffled, "you're perfect, I can see why he's sweet on you."

Bethany?

Suzanne frowned into the other woman's neck. Who the hell was *Bethany*? An ex? Wife? Or maybe long-term girlfriend? It made sense that there would be someone—frankly, Suzanne had found it difficult to believe there wasn't. And a bad relationship breakup would certainly explain his determination to not get involved with a woman. But how long ago? There were no pictures around the cabin of her—or his parents, for that matter—and no evidence that a woman had ever lived there at all. Those little touches like pretty hand towels and candles, nice china, or a cupboard with vases.

Grady's cabin was so masculine, she could practically smell the testosterone.

But…there'd been a Bethany?

Burl laughed. "Cora, let the poor girl breathe." He gently pried his wife away from Suzanne, who felt weirdly bereft despite the clash of her inner thoughts. It had been nice to be welcomed with such unfettered delight by someone who was, in essence, a complete stranger.

Burl introduced Cora to her parents. She gave them a hug, too, much to her mother's surprise, but Cora went right on and did it anyway. "Sorry," she said with a rueful smile. "I'm a hugger from way back, aren't I, Burl?"

Suzanne felt a swell of emotion in her chest just thinking about how much Cora must have hugged Grady when he'd arrived at their house, a grieving teenager. Had he let her? Was that why they were so close today?

Burl gave another indulgent laugh. "You sure are." And he slid his arm around her waist, giving her a squeeze as they smiled at each other like they were newlyweds.

It was a stark contrast to her parents, whose definition of public displays of affection was air kissing at gallery openings. Sure, Burl and Cora may not have been as stylish as her parents, who were dressed head to toe in the latest high-end winter labels from Saks, but their closeness was unmistakable. They might be more homespun in their faded denim and plaid, but the way Burl's hand rested gently on Cora's hip made them richer by far in Suzanne's eyes.

Her parents' body language was terrible. They were separated by a couple of feet and had barely said two words to each other this morning. Suzanne began to wonder if this whole plan had been doomed to failure from the start. That forcing them to spend time in each other's company to get away from all the unsightly Christmas spectacle at the cabin had been for nothing.

Damn it all, what were they doing in that cottage?

"Burl tells me your parents are here for Christmas," Cora said, reaching for Suzanne's hand and giving it a squeeze. "I insist you all come for Christmas lunch."

"Ahh—" Suzanne glanced at Winona, then back at Grady's aunt. *Shit.* What did she do now?

"Oh." Cora's face fell a little, but she kept a smile on her face. "You already have plans? That's fine." She dismissed her invitation with a quick flap of her hands. "We'll catch up with you and Joshua over the holidays at some point."

Cora's smile was still bright and bubbly, but it didn't take an expert to see she'd been looking forward to spending Christmas with them. Winona obviously saw it.

"Oh no, please." Winona stepped forward. "Why don't you both join us at the boardinghouse? All the newbies are gathering there for our first Christmas in Credence celebration, along with Grady and Suzanne and her parents, and we'd love your company, too. The more the merrier, really."

Cora's full-wattage smile returned. "Oh yes. There's nothing nicer than sharing the Christmas spirit and welcoming new neighbors." She glanced at Burl. "That sounds lovely, doesn't it, honey?"

Burl chuckled indulgently. It was clear he didn't care where they spent Christmas as long as he and Cora were together. "Reckon it does," he said with a nod.

A general discussion followed about the logistics of the day and what Cora could bring, but Suzanne barely heard any of the conversation. She was too busy thinking about the warning text she was going to send to Grady as soon as she could about the possibility of a pregnancy rumor circulating around town.

And, oh yes, there was also Bethany...

• • •

Grady was totally, 100 percent avoiding going back to the cabin as he strode into Jack's at four that afternoon after stopping off at the supply shop to pay his account. The god-awful rendition of "Jingle Bells" playing on the jukebox reminded him he'd made a mental note not to come here until after Christmas, but desperate times required desperate measures.

He'd have a couple of light beers before heading home. Finally look at his phone with the text from Suzanne that had been burning a hole in his pocket ever since it had come in around lunchtime—he should never have given her his number. He'd seen her name pop onto his screen and promptly ignored it, not ready to face what she had to say about last night, especially when it was something he was still processing. He sure as hell hadn't wanted to run an analysis on it via text.

But he was going to need to look at it before facing Suzanne again, and for that he needed beer.

Jack's was—thankfully—quiet as he strode across the room. "Tucker," he greeted as he came to a halt at the bar.

"Grady."

"Bud Light, please."

Tucker reached for the drink, cracked the lid off, and passed it over. Grady picked it up and swallowed half of it down in one go.

"Been that kind of day, huh?" Tucker asked when Grady finally came up for air.

Grady wiped his mouth. "Been that kind of month." He threw some money on the bar. "Give me ten minutes and bring another one over," he requested. Grady had absolutely no intention of sitting at the bar, inviting the kind of attention he'd garnered last time he'd been in Jack's. He didn't want or need anybody's unsolicited opinions.

Tucker nodded, and Grady made his way to his usual booth that faced the door. Placing his beer and his phone on the table, he stared at both. He pressed the home button, and the notification that Suzanne's text was waiting flashed on the screen. There was also one from Cora.

Which reminded him he needed to go and tell his aunt and uncle about the predicament Suzanne had landed him in before it got any more out of hand. He'd head there after he left Jack's.

The phone taunted him for the next ten minutes as he sipped more slowly at his beer. By the time Tucker came over with his second drink, he'd picked it up and put it down twice.

"You get a call from the IRS?" Tucker asked as he slid into the chair—*uninvited*—on the other side of the booth.

Grady shook his head. "The IRS would be

easier." Reaching for the new beer, he took a swig.

"You want to talk about it?"

Grady cocked an eyebrow. *Jesus.* It was like his last visit all over again minus the peanut gallery. "You that hard up for conversation?"

Unperturbed by Grady's clear back-off signals, Tucker pressed. "Looks like something's bothering you. Sometimes it helps to talk."

Grady snorted. He'd heard that practically his entire life, and he wasn't doubting it. He'd even seen a military shrink a few times, but talking wasn't his preferred state of being. "I'd rather be bare-ass naked and staked to an ant hill."

Tucker laughed. "Aww, man. You sure know how to hurt a guy's feelings."

"Don't you have a business to run?"

"I can sit a while." Tucker looked around at the five other people in the bar taking up another two booths. "Slow day."

Grady grimaced. "Lucky me."

"I'm thinking about Christmas carol karaoke. Thoughts?"

If Grady had been asked to guess what would come out of Tucker's mouth next, it would not have been Christmas karaoke. "I have no thoughts other than *ugh*."

"Not something you'd come to the bar for?"

"Do I look like the kind of guy who enjoys karaoke? Of any type?"

Tucker regarded him for long moments. "Nope." He shook his head slowly. "Can't see you belting out 'I Saw Mommy Kissing Santa Claus.'"

"Right." Grady nodded.

"You're kind of antisocial—anyone ever tell you that?"

"It's been said."

Just then, the bar doors flung open, and for a split second, Grady could have kissed whoever the hell had chosen that moment to enter. Then he realized it was Arlo and Drew Carmichael and, spying Tucker, they both made a direct beeline for his booth.

Fucking *awesome*. The peanut gallery.

"This where the action's at?" Arlo said.

Grady threw him a tight smile. "Apparently."

"You want beers?" Tucker asked, finally shifting his ass out of the booth, and Grady dared to hope he'd be left in peace.

"We'll have what he's having," Arlo said, speaking for both of them. And then he slid *his* ass into the booth, followed closely by Drew as Tucker left to get their beers.

"I hear congratulations are in order," Drew said as he settled into the chair.

Drew had taken over his father's funeral home business a few years back. He seemed like a nice-enough guy from the limited time Grady had spent in his company. He looked more like an old-fashioned Hollywood screen idol than a dude who drove a hearse around bumfuck nowhere. But apparently even he had heard the rumors about Grady and Suzanne.

And wasn't that just dandy?

Grady raised his beer bottle and mumbled a "Thanks" before taking another swallow.

"Fast work there, bud. I didn't realize she'd been

in town long enough to put a bun in her oven. You should enter those swimmers of yours into the next Olympics. You've got some golden medal spunk going on there."

Grady blinked, placing his bottle down on the table with a loud *thunk*. An itch started at the base of his spine, his bloody pressure spiking. *What. The. Fuck?*

"Who's got a bun in the oven?" Tucker asked as he reappeared with three bottles of beer and handed two over.

"According to Dolly Watson at the Gerald funeral this afternoon," Drew supplied, "Suzanne St. Michelle."

Arlo nodded. "I heard it from Shirley at the bakery."

Grady stared at Drew and Arlo as his brain tried to process the most preposterous gossip he'd ever heard. And that was saying something for Credence. There was no way—despite the lack of condom, which had been monumentally stupid given they'd moved *to* her bedroom to get one, for fuck's sake—Suzanne could be pregnant now.

Correction. Grady's blood pressure spiked again. No way she could *know* she was pregnant now, because ultimately, he supposed, she *could* be pregnant. If she wasn't using some other kind of contraception.

Grady's heart pounded. *Oh. Holy. Jesus.*

He came back to the conversation, which somehow had moved to prenatal vitamins. "Folic acid," Drew was saying. "It's important she get started on that ASAP."

Arlo snorted. "Dude, you sell fancy coffins for a living. What you'd know about pregnancy vitamins could be written on the back of a postage stamp."

"I can read, dickwad." Drew shot Arlo a withering look. "And please, we in the terminal-care industry prefer the term *eternity suites*."

Which cracked up Arlo and Tucker.

Grady barcly registered the laughter and banter going on among the three guys who had not only crashed his peace and quiet but blown it to smithereens. His gaze fell on his phone, and suddenly the presence of those text messages took on an urgency thcy hadn't before. He picked it up, his hands shaking, his pulse tripping.

Tapping on Suzanne's message, he mentally braced himself as it opened.

God I'm so terribly, terribly sorry, Grady. Wish I didn't have to give you a heads-up but here goes… There may or may not be a rumor going around Credence about me being preggers, so I wanted to forewarn you. I DID NOT start it and there's ZERO chance of it being true because I have a contraceptive implant, but I think it's out there and I think your aunt (who is so so so lovely btw) thinks it's true even though I DENIED it most vehemently. I promise I did.

Grady stared at the lengthy message. God… even her texts suffered from verbal diarrhea. He read the message several times over, that awful, all-too-familiar sinking feeling in the pit of his stomach making itself known. Fucking hell. What was happening to his life? Not only were he and Suzanne supposedly in a *relationship*, but now he'd knocked her up as well?

Christ. *Cora…*

Quickly, he scrolled to his aunt's text, hoping against hope it was about something as innocuous as her semi regular reminder he hadn't attended church in forever.

Nope.

Met your Suzanne today. She's perfect, Joshua. I'm so happy for you. And is there something else you haven't told us yet, young man?

Well, crap. When his aunt called him *young man*, she was already convinced.

"There's fascinating new research on neural tube defects, in fact—"

Whatever tidbit of information Drew had been about to impart was cut off abruptly by Grady practically leaping out of the booth.

All three guys looked at him quizzically. "Where's the fire?" Tucker asked.

"Gotta go and see Burl and Cora," Grady replied, not stopping to finish his beer or even to say goodbye as he strode out of the bar, his mind grappling with the conversation he was about to have and the strange cramp in his chest at the thought of being a daddy.

Even a fake one.

CHAPTER SEVENTEEN

It was almost eight by the time Grady stepped into the cabin. The immediate warmth was a welcome relief from the already freezing temperatures outside. Most of the snow that had fallen last night had melted, but it was going to be another cold one, and the weather bureau was predicting blizzards to sweep across the country in two days' time. Which meant he was going to be busy around the ranch getting everything ready for the cattle to survive what could be a potentially catastrophic weather event.

He didn't generally welcome blizzards, but they could always count on at least one during winter, so it might as well work to his advantage. The less time he had to spend in Suzanne's company, the better. A fact reinforced by the lurch of his body as he spied her all the way across the kitchen. She shot him a nervous smile and took a gulp of wine from the glass she was holding. Her parents were nowhere in sight, and the lights were on in the cottage, so he presumed they'd retired for the night.

"Hi." She cleared her throat as she placed the wineglass down on the bench. "I was starting to worry about you."

Grady's hackles were immediately—irrationally—raised. He didn't need anybody worrying about him. He'd done just fine by himself these past seventeen years, and he'd do just fine after she left for

New York. Add to that the eyeball assaulting interi-
or, her ridiculous candy-cane earrings, and another
hideous sweater sporting pom-poms that were begging to be touched, and Grady's mood was swinging
around more wildly than a wind chime in a blizzard.

How could he be so simultaneously annoyed
and aroused?

It made no sense. Particularly given he'd just
had to tell his aunt that he and Suzanne weren't a
couple and definitely *were not* having a baby.
Which had been awful. Sure, she'd taken it in stride
and had understood how Suzanne's little white lie
had escalated, but Grady had still felt like pond
scum that she'd had a period of false hope, no
matter how brief. So how could he want this
woman, who had brought this unholy mess down
on his head, so much?

How?

He'd thought—hoped—he'd fucked her out of
his system last night, but apparently not, if the pull
in his groin was any indication. Which only made
him madder.

"I was at my uncle's place."

"Oh."

"Yeah." Grady nodded. "Oh."

She picked up her wine and took another slug
before putting it down again. "I really am sorry,
Grady. I don't know what happened. Jenny said I
looked tired; then she said I looked like she looked
at the beginning of her pregnancy and I better
watch out or I'll be next, which everyone in the
shop overheard and presumed, including your aunt
and uncle, and it didn't seem to matter how much I

denied it. They all just nodded and smiled at me like I was trying to be coy."

"Maybe you just shouldn't…go into town again?" Grady suggested. Lest they suddenly start expecting triplets.

She gave a half laugh. "Maybe you're right." Folding her arms, she asked, "How did your aunt take the news?"

"Fine," Grady said dismissively. Because she had. She'd taken it like a trouper. Grady suspected that was because, deep down, Cora was a romantic, and despite him stressing it was all an act, she had that speculative little gleam in her eyes his uncle called her *knowing* look.

"I hope you apologized for my behavior. God…" Suzanne wrung her hands in front of her. "Does she hate me?"

A small part of Grady wanted to pretend his aunt had been hysterically upset by the news just so Suzanne could feel a little bit of the discomfort and angst this predicament has caused him, but her expression told him she was pretty much feeling every one of the consequences as acutely as he was.

"No. She doesn't. She likes you. She likes you a lot." Which meant that Cora was already picking out china patterns. "She understands that you're trying to help your parents' marriage, and she won't rat you out, but she thinks you've overcomplicated things."

Which was the fucking understatement of the year as far as Grady was concerned.

Brittle laughter punctuated the air. "Cora is a wise woman."

They stood staring at each other for long moments. Suzanne looked miserable, and no matter how much of it was of her own making and how she'd caught him up in this web of lies, Grady felt strangely protective of her. She was a screwup, but right now, whether he wanted it or not, she was his screwup, and the urge to cross the room and pull her into his arms and tell her it'd be okay was almost overwhelming.

Which made him want to run in the other direction. "I'm going to work in the office for a while." He knew they should probably talk about last night, but dealing with being a fake baby daddy along with a fake boyfriend had been more than enough for one day.

"Oh—" She took a step toward him. "Don't you want something to eat? I made meatloaf."

Grady shook his head. "Cora fed me."

He didn't wait for her acknowledgment, just headed in the direction of the arch. He only had two days to make plans before the weather came in. Suzanne was a big girl who could entertain herself.

He hadn't quite reached the arch when her voice—quiet, almost plaintive—asked, "Who's Bethany?"

The question stopped him in his tracks. A niggle started in his chest as he slowly turned to find her watching him, her teeth digging into her bottom lip. "Who told you about Bethany?"

"Cora mentioned her in passing. I got the impression you and she used to be an item."

His aunt—of course. He supposed it was better

from her than a gossipy member of the Credence community, but he'd rather not go there at all. "Yes."

She stared at him as if she thought he was going to elaborate, but she was wrong. He didn't talk about Bethany to anyone, and frankly, he didn't understand why he hadn't just kept on walking.

"Were you married to her?"

"No. I've never been married."

"So she was what…a girlfriend?"

"Yes."

"She must have been significant for Cora to have mentioned her?"

"She was." She'd been his *only* girlfriend.

"What happened? Did you break up? It must have been bad, because there's nothing of her here at all. Not a photo or anything even remotely girlie."

"There's Zoom."

Suzanne glanced at the tank to Grady's right. "Zoom was Bethany's?"

"No. She gave him to me as a birthday present."

"For which birthday?"

Grady contemplated not answering. Or lying. But he didn't lie—not to other people anyway. "My seventeenth."

She frowned, obviously trying to piece together his sparse information, and he watched as realization dawned. "That's a…long time ago."

He sighed. He could stand here slowly bleeding to death while she eked the information out of him one question at a time, or he could just rip off the Band-Aid.

"Bethany was my high school girlfriend. We started going out when we were fifteen. She died in the same accident that killed my parents."

"Oh god, Joshua…" She pressed a hand to her chest, her blue eyes stricken as she searched his face for Grady didn't know what. "I'm so sorry. I didn't… Why didn't you say something back when you told me about your parents?"

Even from across the room, he could see the shimmer of moisture in her eyes, and it was like a hot fist to his gut. As was the way she said *Joshua*, all soft and brimming with emotion. He hadn't said anything because of *this*. Because he didn't want to be the object of anyone's pity, especially not almost two decades later. The deaths of Bethany and his parents had been a terrible tragedy, but they were in the past.

He shrugged. "Like you said, it was a long time ago."

And it was none of her damn business. Sure, maybe it was something a guy confessed to a girlfriend, but Suzanne *wasn't* a real girlfriend, and he couldn't bear the thought that she'd look at him differently now.

"Maybe," she conceded, her voice soft. "Doesn't make it any less shitty."

Grady gave a soft snort. Wasn't that the truth? But he didn't have time to discuss ancient history. "I really have to get to my office. Bureau says there's going to be a blizzard night after next, and there are things I need to do."

"Okay. Sure." She nodded. "I…left a painting in there for you. It's Adam."

He cocked an eyebrow. "Oh?"

She shrugged, but a melting pot of emotions brimmed in her expressive blue eyes. It obviously hadn't been easy. "My penance. For the pregnancy thing."

Grady blinked. He hadn't thought to ask for one. He must be getting soft. But the pregnant thing was just another example of the collateral damage caused by her lie, and he sure as hell wasn't going to knock it back. The painting reminded him what they were doing here was fake, because coming home to her every night was starting to feel a little too real.

The fact it was clearly hard for her to part with would hopefully remind her, too. Even if it did make him feel like a fucking ogre. It was better all around that she think he still wanted to use her paintings as a bargaining chip, that he was still pissed off about her painting him without his permission, even though he wasn't entirely sure he was anymore.

Better for both of them.

He cleared his throat. "Thank you."

"Sure." He thought he detected the slightest wobble in her voice, and he felt absurdly like going to her, but he shut that thought down and locked his knees. Christ—this was not his fault. The woman had bribed him into being her fake boyfriend. This was a bed of her making.

"I won't be around much the next couple of days," he said, his voice gruff. "Don't wait up for me, and don't count on me being here for dinner."

"Oh…sure. Okay."

If anything, her voice sounded smaller the more businesslike he became, and Grady hated himself for his abruptness. But this was his life—there was work to be done. She wanted to pretend to be his girlfriend? Well, this was the reality of being with a rancher. He turned away again, heading for his office.

"Joshua," she called after him, "be careful out there."

He faltered momentarily before continuing through the archway.

. . .

At midday the next day, under a dark-gray sky, Suzanne was standing on the wide sidewalk leading to the four steps in front of the municipal offices waiting for the ice-sculpting competition to get underway. So apparently was half the town, all huddled in their scarves and jackets and boots on this below-freezing day, which was good, at least, for the ice.

There were eight large blocks of it all measuring two foot by two foot by two foot, mounted on tables, and a variety of ice-sculpting tools supplied from chisels to power tools such as angle grinders and small hedge trimmers.

"Not sure this is going to do the job, Ray," Bob said as he started the trimmer and revved the engine, brandishing it like some kind of weapon. "Chain saw'd be better."

"Put the damn fool thing down, Bob," Ray grouched, reaching over to switch off the implement. "You've never used a chain saw in your life. You'll have my ear off waving it around like that."

"Van Gogh painted *Starry Night* with only one ear."

Suzanne suppressed a smile as the two men bickered good-naturedly like they'd been doing it for decades. They were entering as a team, as were three other local couples Suzanne wasn't familiar with. At the station next to Ray and Bob, where Suzanne stood, was Winona. She was entering by herself.

On the other side of the octogenarians were Molly and Marley, twin sisters from New York who had come to Credence with the influx of women during the summer. There were also Jenny and Wyatt and a very excited Henry, who was chattering on about the hog they were going to carve from the ice. With them was Wyatt's mom, Veronica Carter, one of the town councilors.

The last block of ice had been reserved for Simone. Yes, her mother was judging the comp, but everyone agreed they wanted to see what she could do with a frozen medium, and Simone, always happy to play to an audience, graciously agreed. She and Suzanne's father were currently discussing the block of ice, their conversation animated, their bodies close. Maybe the closest Suzanne had seen them in a long time.

Maybe things *were* changing for the positive between them?

"I presume you'll be creating something phallic?"

Suzanne started at the authoritative voice behind

her, turning to find Arlo looking all tall and hot-cop imposing as he peered at Winona.

"But of course," Winona said, plastering a sweet smile on her face. "I'm thinking giant dong. Every ice-sculpture competition needs at least one. What do you think, Suzanne?"

"Oh yes." Suzanne nodded, trying to keep her laughter in check. "The bigger the better."

He scowled at Suzanne. "Do not encourage her." Then, turning to Winona, he said, "Try and keep it PG, huh? Let's not traumatize the kiddies."

Winona rolled her eyes. "Fine," she said, sighing dramatically. "What are you doing here, Officer Spoilsport? Didn't picture you as a patron of the arts."

"Crowd control."

An inelegant snort slipped from Winona's mouth. "You expecting the great Credence ice-sculpture riot or something?"

Suzanne tipped her head in the direction of Bob and Ray still fighting over the hedge trimmer. "I'd have thought we'd need paramedics more than the police," she said.

Someone *was* going to lose an ear if they kept it up.

Arlo glanced across and shook his head. "Oh for the love of—" He cut off abruptly, shooting a quick "PG" in Winona's direction before he nodded at them both and said, "You have a nice day now, ladies," and striding off to intervene in the impeding bloodbath.

"Jackass," Winona muttered under her breath.

Suzanne laughed, but it was cut off by Don

Randall, the mayor, in his full mayoral robes and chain, calling everyone to order and running through the rules of the competition. "Okay then," he announced finally. "You have two hours to complete your work of art, which will then be judged by our guest judge, world-renowned sculptor Simone St. Michelle."

The crowd clapped and cheered as her mom took an impressively artistic bow.

"Are we ready?" Don asked, bringing the applause to an end.

"We've been ready for ages, you fool," Bob called. "Get on with it."

There was general laughter that Don chose to ignore along with Bob's bellyaching. "On your marks…get set…"

"Good luck," Suzanne said to Winona as she stepped back from the table to give her friend space to create.

"Go!"

"Yee-haw!" Bob started the hedge trimmer with a mighty roar that caused several looks of alarm among the crowd before he handed it over to long-suffering Ray.

Suzanne spied Cora and Burl through the crowd as chisels went to work and ice shavings flew through the air. Cora gave an enthusiastic wave, which Suzanne returned, but she felt so bad about her deception, she made no move to join them. Grady had told her last night that his aunt had been fine with the situation, but what did Cora really think of her?

Grady wasn't exactly in touch with such esoteric

things as emotions, so maybe he couldn't read those kind of cues?

Just like she hadn't been able to read his cues last night about Bethany. Suzanne had lain awake into the wee hours thinking about Grady's high school sweetheart who had died so tragically. Died too young. Wondering if, had she lived, would she and Grady have still been together today? Wondering if he was still in love with her and that's why he'd shut himself off to the possibility of another relationship. Why he was happy to settle for nothing and nobody out here in the wilds of far eastern Colorado if he couldn't have the woman he loved.

Just because there wasn't a single picture of her, no shrine to her memory, didn't mean she'd faded from his mind. All he had to do was look at Zoom and be reminded of her, right?

Did he? Did he think of Bethany every time he laid eyes on the turtle?

God…had he been thinking about Bethany that night in her bed?

"You okay, dear?"

Suzanne startled at the intrusion, blinking twice before she realized Cora and Burl had joined her at Winona's table. "Yes. Thank you." She smiled at Cora, who returned it as she looped her arm through Suzanne's.

"We thought you'd be competing as well," Cora said.

"Figured you'd be a chip off the old block," Burl added, then laughed at his own pun.

Suzanne laughed, too, but she wasn't really

feeling it. She'd been looking forward to joining in the comp, but giving up her fourth painting yesterday had killed whatever paltry creative urge she still owned that hadn't been decimated by the arrival of her parents.

It'd been ridiculously hard to hand over Adam, and Suzanne had been acutely aware, as she'd put the painting in his office, that there was only one left. The fact that Grady hadn't seemed to know or care had only compounded her feelings of loss. Even now, talking to his aunt and uncle, she could feel the tight knot of emotions in her chest.

"It didn't seem right to compete with my mom judging," Suzanne said, keeping her voice light.

They nodded like they thoroughly approved of her decision. "Your mom makes it seem effortless," Burl said. "She's amazing."

Glancing over at her mom's table, Suzanne could already see wings emerging from the block of ice. "She is," Suzanne agreed.

Her mother was a true artistic genius, and Suzanne was proud of her, but she couldn't deny the spike of professional jealousy. One day she hoped to be as proficient, as effortless, and as sure of herself as her mother. If her muse ever decided to come out and play again.

They watched in silence for a few more moments, but Suzanne was too acutely aware of Grady's aunt and uncle to take in much of her mom's evolving piece.

"I'm sorry," she said eventually, barely hearing the softness of her voice over the thump of her heart as she turned her face toward Cora. "About deceiving you. It's—"

"Now, now," Cora cut in, placing her arm around Suzanne's shoulders and giving her a tight squeeze. "You got yourself into a fix; we understand that. Burl and I don't condone dishonesty, but your intentions were pure and...well...whether Joshua knows it or not, you're good for him. And I do think there's a little zing between the two of you—"

"Oh no," Suzanne interrupted, panic descending. She could just imagine how annoyed Grady would be if she didn't at least attempt to put his aunt straight. "There's no zing," she lied. "It's just an act."

"Hmm. Is it?"

Those old, searching eyes seemed to bore right into Suzanne's soul, and she swallowed at the shrewdness she found there. "Yes."

Another "Hmm" as Cora patted Suzanne's arm in a way that felt very much like she was being humored. "We'll see. But the point is, there's no need to worry. We'll play along with the fake relationship thing."

"Thank you." Suzanne smiled.

"Of course," Cora said, waving her hand dismissively, but her eyes gleaming with speculation.

By the time two hours was up, there was a surprisingly good array of ice sculpture art for her mom to judge and, despite Bob's reckless use of a power tool, a zero injury tally. Jenny and Wyatt's hog—or hog's head anyway—wouldn't win a blue ribbon at the state fair, but it was cute with a quirky bend to one of its ears, and Henry was thrilled to bits at how it had turned out. Ray and

Bob had sculpted a Christmas tree, and Winona, much to the chagrin of Arlo, had fashioned a gorgeous hothouse flower that bore a striking likeness to female genitalia if one was old enough to understand anatomy.

It definitely had sexual overtones.

The other three sculptures were a fish, a mermaid, and a star.

The quality varied across the pieces but, considering everyone but her mother was an amateur, they were all quite good. Simone exclaimed as much as she went around critiquing the pieces, giving constructive feedback. She praised Ray's use of the chisel to give the leaves a tactile quality, Henry's suggestion for the floppy ear, and Winona's wild imaginative streak. But in the end, she gave the award to the mermaid.

Technically it wasn't the best piece, that was quite clear to Suzanne's trained eye, but there was a liveliness to the sculpture that drew the gaze, and Suzanne knew that was a hard quality for a professional to pull off, let alone a corn farmer from Credence whose last *work of art* had apparently been a scarecrow.

Simone shook Chuck's and Denise's hands as she congratulated them. "We're utterly impressed, aren't we, darling?" she said, smiling at Albie, who nodded enthusiastically, his arm around his wife's shoulders. "I'd like to send you a little something as a prize, so I'll grab your address before we leave Credence and get it sent to you in the New Year."

"Oh…thank you," Denise said.

The poor woman seemed totally starstruck, and

Suzanne swore she was about to curtsy. It was a generous offer from her mom, who would no doubt send one of her smaller pieces she regarded as *seconds*. In the eyes of Simone St. Michelle, they weren't good enough—but in the eyes of the art world, they were still exquisite quality and worth a lot of money.

Then everyone's eyes turned to Simone's creation, gathering around it to admire and compliment. As far as Suzanne knew, her mother had never carved ice before—in fact she'd put money on her mom not even having considered ice sculpting *art*—but there was certainly no evidence of that in the delicate loveliness of the angel glistening in a stray sunbeam that had managed to poke through the blanket of gray. She supposed her mother had worked in much more difficult mediums but to make a figure carved from ice so vibrantly warm and alive was a true skill, and her mother had outdone herself.

The icy wings were gossamer-thin and practically translucent as water droplets dripped off the bottom, but more than that was the tangible *supplication* in every curve of the angel's body and the beatific devotion on her face angled toward the heavens. The bodice of the gown was made up of fine icy strands, like silken webs, and the skirt flowed effortlessly as if being stirred by a breeze.

"I wish my wife was here to see this!" Ray exclaimed, stepping forward to examine the statue as the crowd started to disperse. He slid his glasses on his face as he bent to get a closer look at the bodice. "She'd think it was the most divine creature she'd ever seen."

"Why thank you, Ray. I wish your wife were here, too. If this statue wasn't doomed to melt, I'd have given it to her."

Ray stood momentarily surprised by the suggestion before sending a warm smile in Simone's direction and reaching out his hand, which she took. They stayed clasped like that for brief seconds before their hands slid away and the moment passed.

"What inspired you to sculpt an angel?" someone asked from the crowd.

Simone didn't answer for a beat or two, clearly giving her response some thought. "Well," she said slowly as if she wasn't absolutely sure from where the artistic creation had sprung, "it's Christmas, isn't it?"

Suzanne blinked. She doubted her mother had ever been inspired by the festive season. In fact, she always said that December was her least creative time because there was so much *artifice*. But the crowd ate it up. So did her father, who bent his head to kiss his wife on the mouth.

It was brief, but Suzanne's heart sang a little at the intimacy both in it and in the smile they were sharing. It was just like old times, and Suzanne hoped like anything that this icy Christmas angel was the start of something wonderful.

CHAPTER EIGHTEEN

Suzanne woke the next morning to an empty cabin—again. She had seen Grady last night, but only briefly when he'd come in at eight thirty and headed straight for his office. There was a note waiting for her, though, as she entered the kitchen. A note with instructions in his big, bold handwriting to go into Credence and pick up supplies for her parents' cottage so they were prepared for the blizzard that was supposed to touch down later tonight.

She assumed Grady was always prepared, so nothing was needed for the cabin.

Candles and matches were on the list as well as spare batteries for the two large flashlights he'd left on the bench top. Also on the list—a supply of bottled water and some cans of food.

Beans are good.

That's what he'd written. Suzanne struggled to think of a time she'd ever seen her parents eat baked beans, or any kind of ready-to-eat meal out of a can, and failed. But if the power went out, which it probably would at some point, they'd only have their gas cooktop so cans it was. Thankfully, the gas fireplace in the cottage meant there was no need for Suzanne to worry about her parents running out of firewood and risking a trip outdoors for more in the middle of a blizzard.

Unlike Grady's cabin with its wood-burning fireplace.

But Suzanne had noticed yesterday that Grady—or somebody anyway—had stacked up a supply of wood and two huge baskets brimming with pine cones around the fireplace and against the cabin on the back porch under the overhang of the roof. The wood was neatly piled and tightly packed, looking like enough wood for a week and, as far as she knew, the weather station said the worst of it should be over in two days.

Fingers crossed.

Suzanne shivered. The wind was already picking up outside, and she was grateful to be inside, unlike poor Grady and his men, who must be freezing their balls off out there. Sure, it seemed right up his ex-military, tough-guy alley to be out battling these kinds of elements, but yikes...

Rather him than her.

• • •

At eight that night, Grady still wasn't home as Suzanne waved her parents off at the door. "Are you sure you don't want to wait the blizzard out here with us?" she asked them. "There's a spare room."

Her mother looked around at all the tinsel and other Christmas tack and shook her head. "No thanks, darling, we'll be fine."

At another time, her mother's obvious distaste might have annoyed Suzanne, but frankly, she was relieved her mother had declined. For starters, it meant she and her father would spend more alone time together, and then there were the sleeping arrangements...

Yes, there was a spare bedroom. Right next to Suzanne's. Except Suzanne was supposed to be sharing Grady's room—Grady's bed—so it could be hard to explain if that little fact were uncovered.

God…she couldn't wait for her parents to return to New York so this pretense could end.

"When did Grady say he'd be home?" her father asked.

Suzanne shook her head. "He didn't." She was trying not to think about him out there in the increasing wind. She hoped he wouldn't be too much longer. The bureau had predicted the blizzard currently making its way across Kansas and Nebraska to arrive just before midnight.

"Before the blizzard hits, I hope," he said.

"Me too."

"Oh, hey." Her father pulled her in for a hug. "You're worried about him."

Yes. She was. Surprisingly. She knew Grady knew what he was doing and that he wasn't out there alone, but she was still antsy. She supposed seasoned rancher wives/girlfriends were used to this kind of thing. They were probably cool and calm in the face of an approaching biblical-ass storm. Hell, they'd probably be out there among it with their men.

But Suzanne couldn't help but think of a hundred things that could go wrong. "At least with all these lights, he'll be able to easily find his way home," Albie said, attempting to make a joke but hugging her a bit harder.

Suzanne laughed. "Grady does love his Christmas."

The lie didn't sit well. She had zero doubt the

lights would be gone as soon as her parents high-tailed it out of Credence. But her father was right, the lights flashing outside the cabin were visible for miles and, on a night like this, she was relieved to have them blinking away.

She hoped Grady was, too.

"Do you want us to stay?"

Suzanne shook her head and pulled back. "No." She wanted her parents to spend as much alone time together as possible. They'd been smiling at each other a lot today, and who knew what being snowed in could lead to? "Josh will be home soon. You two go and batten down the hatches while you've got the chance. It's already starting to really blow out there. Just remember you'll probably lose power and phones, so if anything happens and you need us, either come across or tie the red washcloth around the outside doorknob."

"We'll be fine, darling," her father assured, and, with one last round of hugs, Suzanne opened the door.

The wind whistled, pushing Arctic fingers into the warm cabin. Her parents braced themselves for the short walk to the cottage, and Suzanne watched them from the doorway as her parents trudged away, hunched into their coats, their flashlights lighting the way on the cold, dark night, gusts of wind making the short walk challenging. When they reached their door, they turned and waved, and Suzanne waved back before shutting the cabin door and the inclement weather outside where it belonged.

Outside with Grady.

• • •

Nine o'clock came and went. Ten o'clock did, too. Grady had told Suzanne to not wait up, but she couldn't go to bed with the wind howling outside and him still out there in it. True, it hadn't started snowing yet, but it wouldn't be long.

Where was he? She'd texted him half a dozen times, and her head was full of worst-case scenarios.

In an effort to keep her mind off Grady's absence and her infuriatingly silent phone, she'd kept herself busy. She'd showered and regularly stoked the fire so the cabin would be toasty warm when Grady finally did arrive home. She'd baked a batch of brownies that were cooling on the kitchen bench top, and she had a saucepan full of warmed milk ready to go because surely a hot chocolate would be appreciated after coming in from the storm?

She'd turned on some Christmas carols for company, painted her toes, and cleaned out her handbag sitting on the rug in front of the fire. And now she was on the couch, her legs pulled up under her, a fleecy blanket over her lap and a glass of red by her side, trying to concentrate on her e-reader. She'd turned off the carols in an effort to improve her concentration, but it hadn't worked, as she stared once again at the Christmas tree, her thoughts whirring.

Not even the tree gave her any pleasure tonight, despite the small pile of presents beneath it now. One each for her parents, even though they didn't believe in gift giving. And Winona's wrapped cookies. There was also a little something for Burl and Cora. And there was a present for Grady, because it would be weird if she hadn't gotten him anything. And one from him to her that she'd wrapped and placed with the others because, *ditto*. They were just matching sweaters to wear to Christmas lunch, but there was still a pretense to be upheld.

Glancing out the windows into the dark, Suzanne was grateful the power hadn't gone out yet. The lights inside were comforting while she was here alone, and knowing the ones outside were shining like a beacon for her rancher was also welcome.

She blinked. *Her* rancher? He wasn't *her* rancher, she knew that, but right now with Grady somewhere out there in the wild weather and her safe on the inside, he very much felt like her rancher. He sure as hell was all she could think about.

And she was getting madder by the second.

Okay, sure, he couldn't stop and answer every text she'd sent when he was working his guts out to get the ranch prepared for the havoc that was about to be brought down upon it, but surely he could answer just one? A quick *I'm fine. Home in xyz amount of time*. Was that so freaking hard?

If he'd answered just one of her inquires, she wouldn't have had to send a half dozen others. God…what if he'd slipped and fallen into a gully and was unconscious and his men couldn't find him? What if he'd had an accident in his vehicle and they couldn't find him? What if he was trying to pull another calf out of another bog and had been pulled headfirst into the muddy quagmire and they couldn't find him?

Not even the full-bodied red and the romantic flicker of firelight could soothe the slick of adrenaline stalking her system. She'd give him one more hour. And if he wasn't back by then she'd… Hell, she didn't know what she'd do, but she sure as hell was going to do *something*.

Call someone. Burl maybe? He'd called earlier to check on her and assure her Grady would be home when the work was done, so he'd know if Grady's prolonged absence was normal.

That's what she'd do. In one more hour. With that decided, she tamped down her fears and returned to her book, to the same page she'd read at least a dozen times now.

The door opened abruptly fifteen minutes later, the wind nipping and snarling before it was shut out again. Suzanne's nerves jumped and her heart leaped as she scrambled off the couch toward Grady, who was shaking snow out of his hair and stepping out of his boots saying, "Oh yes, thank you… It's like the Bahamas in here."

"*Grady!*" She all but ran to him, launching herself into his arms, hugging around his shoulders.

"Whoa there, slugger," he said on a half laugh as his body absorbed the impact of hers.

His jacket was freezing, as was his neck where she'd pressed her face, but she didn't care. She hugged him fiercely, her pulse hammering madly at all her pulse points. Grady was here. Grady was safe. Grady was whole.

"God," she said, her voice husky, tears stinging her eyes, "I was so worried about you."

"As you can see, I'm fine."

The amusement in his voice grated. Grady was here and he was safe and the adrenaline that had held her hostage drained away like dirty dishwater down the drain, leaving her wrung out and nauseated. She pushed away from him and whacked his arm.

It had all the impact of a feather through the thick layers of his jacket.

"Where have you been?" she demanded and whacked his other arm. "I've been worried *sick* about you."

He chuckled. "I told you not to wait up."

She blinked hard to dispel the threatening tears. She would not cry when he was smiling at her like he was indulging a two-year-old's temper tantrum. "I've been picturing you dead in a ditch," she yelled, giving his chest a shove this time. It barely moved him, which made her madder. "Why didn't you reply to one of my texts to let me know you were okay?"

She shoved again, but he caught her hand this time, his smile dying. "Suzy…" His brow crinkled. "It's okay. I'm fine. See?"

He held out his arms to show her he was whole and intact, and had he used any other name, she might have stayed stoic, but the way he said *Suzy*— the only man who had ever called her that—was her undoing. She felt absurdly like bursting into tears, but she didn't. She threw herself at him again instead and just hugged him, his big, broad shoulders feeling like boulders in her embrace.

He was fine. *Grady was fine.*

"God, you're so cold," she said after a beat or two, the icy feel of his jacket permeating her pajama top.

"It's just the outside of my clothes," he dismissed. "I'm warm underneath."

"Come over to the fire." She let him go but tugged on his freezing hand, not prepared to take no for an answer. Thankfully, after a moment of resistance, he followed, that bemused look back on his face. He was humoring her again, but she was okay with that.

"Stand here in front of this, and warm your hands. I'll make you a hot chocolate."

Again she didn't wait for his consent, just scurried to the kitchen on a cloud of relief.

"I'd rather bourbon."

Right. Of course. He was a grown-ass man who'd been out doing hard physical labor for the last seventeen hours. The man deserved alcohol.

"Good plan."

Suzanne headed for the drinks cabinet. She had to pass Zoom's tank, which made her think of Bethany, but she quashed it as she opened the cabinet doors and grabbed the Wild Turkey bottle. Her hand shook as she reached for a heavy lead crystal tumbler and poured a hefty slug. Picking up the glass and the bottle—he'd probably want more than one—she headed back toward Grady.

He'd taken his jacket off and was facing the fire, and even in this huge living room with its soaring ceiling and massive wooden beams, Grady dominated. Tall and broad, his back straight, his stance wide and confident. He was king of his domain, and damn if that didn't send a delicious little trill right through her abdomen.

Stopping to place the bottle down on the side table next to her wine and handbag, she picked up her glass and ferried both it and Grady's bourbon over to where he stood. He had his hands thrust toward the fire, warming them as she'd directed.

"Here." She nudged his elbow with the tumbler.

"Thanks." He relieved her of it and immediately raised it to his mouth, taking a big swallow.

Suzanne, still feeling edgy from the remnants of adrenaline, almost did the same with her wine but forced herself to sip it instead. Neither of them said anything for long moments as they stared into the fire. She snuck a look at Grady's profile as he took another mouthful of his drink. His eyes were shut as if savoring it, and then he tipped his head from side to side, stretching out the muscles of his neck.

"You must be exhausted," Suzanne said, noticing the fine lines around his eyes.

His lids fluttered open, and he stared into the fire again. "I'm okay."

Of course he was okay. Couldn't have surly rancher dude admit to anything as human as tiredness after two full days of manual labor.

A sudden howl of wind shook the cabin, and Suzanne glanced out the window at the horizontal snow whipping past. "Did you get everything done?"

"Yeah." He nodded. "Just gotta hope for the best now."

"I'll drink to that." Suzanne raised her glass toward him, and their gazes met as he tapped his tumbler to hers. The glasses *tink*ed, and Grady took another swallow as he returned his attention to the fire.

"You must be hungry. I kept some food for you. There's also a batch of brownies that's probably still warm."

"Thanks." He nodded. "I'll get something soon."

"I can do it; you've done enough today."

She turned to go, but he put a stilling hand on her arm. "Suzy…"

Suzy. God… Her belly looped the loop. Talk about heat. How did the man manage to make that name sound so damn sexy?

"It's okay. I just want to enjoy the warmth of the fire and the heat in this drink for a little while longer."

"Of course," she said, standing beside him again, her gaze returning to the fire.

The silence grew between them as they sipped on their drinks, which only made Suzanne more and more aware of him, of his brooding presence. What was he thinking about? Was he worrying about the storm? The ranch? That he hadn't done enough? Or was he thinking about the long hours ahead with just him and her—alone. In this cabin.

Like she was.

"So what happens now?" she asked eventually when the quiet became too much.

He shrugged. "There's nothing left to do. The blizzard's upon us, and we can't go out again until it's blown over, so…" He turned slightly toward her and smiled. "We just wait it out."

Suzanne swallowed. Exactly. Just her and him. Waiting it out. How *were* they going to keep themselves occupied?

"How long do you think it'll last?"

"Figure it'll go all night and all day tomorrow and into tomorrow night. We can follow the progress of the storm on the computer."

Just then, another powerful blast of wind shook the cabin, and the lights flickered out. Had it not been for the fire, they'd have been plunged into darkness. Suzanne shivered and took an involuntary step closer to Grady.

"Or…maybe not." He pulled his phone from his back pocket and swiped at the screen several times. "No cell or internet, either. Looks like we'll have to go old-school."

Draining the last of his bourbon, he placed the glass on the mantelpiece next to Christmas Elvis riding a reindeer and headed for the kitchen. Suzanne didn't bother to follow him, preferring to stay near the source of light. She wasn't afraid of the dark, but the howling was really ramping up outside. It sounded like wolves. Rabid wolves.

Suzanne didn't mind admitting she was feeling quite vulnerable out here in the middle of nowhere with all that frothing, wailing nature just outside the door. She had absolutely no doubt that Grady would be able to handle any calamity that arose and that he wouldn't let any harm come to her but, despite the solid shelter of four walls and a roof, she suddenly felt every inch the city girl.

And very, very small.

There was some clattering from the kitchen, then the scratchy crackle of static before a tinny voice grew louder and louder but fading in and out as it talked about wind speeds and temperatures. There was nothing but the voice for a minute, and Suzanne assumed Grady was listening attentively, but then there was an "Oh my god" followed by a groan.

Already on edge, Suzanne tensed. What? What was wrong? She couldn't hear the weather guy well from here. Had he announced that an asteroid had been sighted on the satellite hurtling toward Earth? It sure as hell felt like the end of the world was nigh. She heard footsteps and turned, panic rising in her chest to see Grady advancing toward her with the baking dish in hand.

"This," he said, around a mouthful of brownie, pointing to the gooey dark chocolate cakey goodness still in the pan, a corner missing, "is amazing."

She blinked, uncomprehending for a beat or two, then smiled at the genuine, clearly heartfelt compliment as panic subsided to pride. And pleasure. There was something ridiculously primal about being appreciated for her ability to feed her man.

God…*her man*. Her *rancher*. What was wrong with her? Where were her feminist sensibilities? Had the storm reduced her to some kind of cavewoman? "I figured you might want something sweet when you got in."

Suzanne hadn't thought too much about that sentence before it came out, but his chewing faltered, and suddenly his gaze heated as it drifted to her mouth and the V neckline of her pajama shirt, and the static seemed to jump from the radio to fill the space between them.

"I didn't," he said, dragging his gaze off her mouth. "But I do now."

Suzanne knew exactly how he felt. She was hungry just looking at him. The static arced between them, coursing and sizzling.

"If you want some of this, you'd better speak up, because I'm probably going to eat the whole thing."

If you want some of this?

God…she wanted, all right, and it had nothing to do with the pan of brownie and everything to do with the man holding the damn thing. She'd been so worried about Grady, and now he was here all hale and hearty, and it was like every instinct she'd had to deny their attraction—and there'd been many—had been swept away by the blizzard.

Who'd have thought a rancher in plaid and denim appreciating her cooking would be such a freaking turn-on? Suzanne tried really hard not to think about drizzling bourbon on his body and smearing it in chocolate brownie.

"You're going to eat it all now?"

His gaze dipped briefly again, and her nipples hardened before his eyes returned to her face. "If that's okay. I didn't realize how hungry I was."

Yeah…neither had she.

Swallowing hard, Suzanne forced herself to take a mental step backward. What in the hell was wrong with her tonight? Just because there was an apocalyptic blizzard raging outside didn't mean she could just throw out all her inhibitions. "Of course it's okay," she said, her voice way shakier than she'd have liked. Then an idea struck. "Wait. Hold that thought."

Shoving her wineglass on the mantelpiece next to his tumbler, she headed toward the kitchen, thankful for the strong glow from the fire. Opening the cutlery drawer, she grabbed two spoons, then the roll of kitchen paper and briefly considered ice cream or the whipped cream before dismissing both as a very bad idea.

For one, the power was out, and opening the fridge and freezer should be limited to emergencies and two, she didn't think either of them needed such a blatant sexual cue between them. In her current state of arousal, a can of whipped cream was the equivalent of bringing a vibrator into the room.

With that inappropriate thought nipping at her heels, she hurried back to find Grady had moved close to the fire again, the brownie pan still in hand.

"Rug picnic," she announced as she brandished the spoons in the air.

He turned as Suzanne made her way around the couch, grabbing up the blanket she'd had over her knees earlier.

"That's not a thing,"

"Of course it is."

"Not when you're an adult."

Suzanne spread the blanket out on the rug. "Who says?"

"Rules of being a grown-up 101."

"Pfft." Suzanne's bangs fluffed out as she made the sound. "Rules of being a grown-up don't apply when we're stuck in a blizzard in the middle of nowhere." Suzanne had been through blizzards before but in a city, there was safety in numbers.

He gave a surprised half laugh. "You're in a house that's been surviving blizzards for forty years. In front of a fire. Drinking wine and eating brownies. Not a tent."

"Whatever… It's too *Little House on the Prairie* for my liking."

He cocked an eyebrow. "You're serious?"

"Absolutely." She sunk to the floor, sitting lotus-style, as close to the fire as possible while still being on the rug and glanced up at him. His legs looked six feet long from down here. Man…was there an angle from which Grady didn't look great?

"What?" she demanded as he continued to stare. "Too manly for a picnic? Will it ruin your reputation in the Surly Rancher Dude Club?"

"Surly rancher dude?"

"What, no club?" Suzanne feigned disappointment. "I was sure you'd be president."

He clutched his chest. "Who me, ma'am? A simple cowpoke?"

She rolled her eyes. "Just sit already. I promise your secret is safe with me. What happens in the blizzard stays in the blizzard, right?"

Firelight caught the clench of his jaw as a whole world of possibilities opened up in Suzanne's head. And if she was reading the sudden mushroom cloud of heat in his gaze right, Grady was on the same page. "To coin a phrase," she added lamely, and then, quickly changing the subject, she held up the spoons, one in each hand. "So are you going to share the brownies or keep them all to yourself?"

For a beat or two, Grady didn't say anything. Nor did he move. He just stood there looking down at her, his gaze like a heat wave as it raked over her body. Then he passed her the pan. "My aunt would whoop my ass if I didn't share."

Suzanne let out a shaky breath as she took the pan and placed it on the blanket. "You want to grab our drinks?"

God knew she was going to need some kind of fortification if she was going to share a pan of brownies with a guy who looked, even now, like he'd walked out of the Wild West and whom her body had decided was just her kind of Christmas crack.

He grabbed both his tumbler and the bourbon in one hand and her glass and the wine bottle in the other. Crouching at the edge of the rug, he placed them on the floorboards, pouring another slug of bourbon for himself and topping up her almost empty glass. He handed her wine over, then picked up his tumbler before settling opposite her, also lotus-style, nothing but a pan of brownies and one very long night between them.

There was about a hand's width between their knees, and damn if she wasn't aware of every charged inch of that space. And how easily she could just slide her palm onto his thigh. She thrust the spoon at Grady instead, which he took with one hand, then raised his tumbler between them with the other. "To rug picnics," he toasted with a touch of derision in his voice.

Suzanne tapped her glass to his tumbler. "I'll

drink to that." She took a sip of her wine, placed it down on the floor next to the rug, and said, "Dig in."

He dug in, so did she, and for the next five minutes, there was nothing but the sound of spoons scraping the bottom of the pan, the crackle of the fire, and the wind yowling outside. Suzanne stopped after eating a quarter of the pan. She was getting full, and the brownies were too rich for someone who didn't have a huge sweet tooth.

"I'm done." She splayed her hand over her belly as she took a sip of her wine.

Grady, who obviously did have a sweet tooth, smiled at her like she was some kind of lightweight. "That is a tragedy," he said, faking a crestfallen expression for a beat or two before shoveling up more brownie and spooning it into his mouth.

Suzanne didn't bother *not* to look as he continued to eat. He was mesmerizing to watch devouring the food *she'd* cooked. It was causing a happy little glow in her chest and a raging inferno inside her pajama pants. Stopping to draw breath, he took a swallow of his bourbon and moaned, which didn't help the emergency fire situation going on inside her panties.

"Mmm," he murmured appreciatively. "Bourbon and brownies are good together."

"Yeah?"

He dug some more brownie out with his spoon, dribbled some of the bourbon from his tumbler onto the dark chocolate mass, which soaked it in. He held the spoon between them and said, "Open up."

Suzanne should probably have declined. But she was no more capable of that than stopping the blizzard raging outside. She parted her lips, and he slipped it in, her mouth closing around the spoon. Shutting her eyes, she savored the taste as he withdrew the implement. The bourbon supercharged the sweetness but gave it a little kick of something else.

"Mmm," she murmured as the flavor infused her taste buds. She swallowed, her eyes fluttering open to find him staring at her lips.

Her stomach clenched at the heat, at the intensity of his gaze. Her breathing faltered.

A beat passed. Then another. Then, before she could catch her breath, his head swooped and he kissed the corner of her mouth, his tongue flicking out and lingering for long, pulse-skittering moments before he withdrew.

Suzanne sucked in a hasty breath, filling her lungs and her senses with the aromas of pine cones, bourbon, and Grady.

"Sorry…you had"—he pointed to the corner of her mouth—"some crumbs…"

Her breathing husky, Suzanne swallowed. She wasn't sorry at all.

CHAPTER NINETEEN

Grady's heart thumped in his chest as he stared at Suzanne. He shouldn't have done that. He *should not* have done that. A buzzing noise in his head grew louder and louder, obliterating the noise of the blizzard and every modicum of common sense. All he could see was Suzanne's mouth, and all he could think about was kissing it—again.

Longer. Deeper. Wetter.

Everything since he'd stepped inside the warm, welcoming cabin tonight had felt like it was leading to this moment. The fire and the bourbon and the brownies. And the woman waiting up for him. Worrying about him. It had irritated him a couple of days ago, but tonight...

This wasn't Grady. He wasn't the kind of guy who craved all that home and hearth bullshit. He'd resigned himself to going without those trimmings years ago, and he'd never allowed himself to think about what he might be missing. Not even with all the guys tonight talking about getting home to a warm house, a warm meal, and a warm woman.

Grady had been looking forward to a drink in front of the fire and spending a couple of hours in his office following the progress of the storm. But then he'd opened that door and Suzanne had been there, worried and cranky, alternating between yelling at him and hugging him, and the desire to come home to this every night—to *her* every night—had slugged him right in the center of his chest, making it impossible to breathe.

To think.

It was utterly ridiculous even entertaining such a thought. Grady had never met a woman more *city* than Suzanne—except possibly her mother. And as much as she seemed to have taken to the whole fake rancher girlfriend role, Grady would bet his last cent she bled concrete. So even if he did suddenly want to ditch seventeen years of tightly leashed control, there was nothing that could possibly ever come from this.

But there was a little voice whispering, *What happens in the blizzard stays in the blizzard*, and it was lethal. Ever since they'd slept together, he'd been trying to convince himself it had been a one-off thing, but the truth was, he wanted Suzanne St. Michelle so fucking badly, he could barely see straight.

"Did you…" Her voice was a ragged whisper, breaking into the silence stretching taut as a bow between them. Her throat bobbed. "Did you get it all?"

For a second, Grady was confused as to her meaning, but then her tongue flicked out to wet her lips, and he was back at ground zero. He shook his head and whispered, "Nope."

He wasn't sure who made the first move; if he'd been forced to guess, he'd swear they'd both moved together, reaching for each other simultaneously, their mouths meeting in the middle, their tongues melding in an instant. Then he was pushing aside the cake pan and his hands were palming her ass, and he didn't know if he yanked or she scrambled, but she was in his lap, straddling him, her hands pushing into his hair, rocking against him and moaning as the seam of her jeans rode the bulge behind the seam of his, and it felt so fucking great. He thought he might just come from that alone.

"Suzy," he murmured, breaking off their kiss, his lips on her neck as he held her tight and they rutted against each other, enjoying the heat and the friction and her wanton abandon.

But it wasn't enough. He wanted more. He wanted it all.

With Suzanne still clinging to him, he rose to his knees and tipped her backward, guiding her gently down to the rug, her head and shoulders and back flat on the floor, her ass still anchored firmly on top of his thighs as he sat back on his heels.

"I want to look at you," he said as he pushed the flats of his palms under the hem of her shirt, over her stomach, and up her ribs to her breasts, taking the shirt with him. His hands found the soft satin of her bra but didn't linger—not yet anyway—just moved inexorably north, leaning forward slightly as he removed her shirt inch by inch until it was close enough for her to duck her head through the opening and he could pull it off her arms and toss it away.

"Yes," he hissed.

Firelight played on the pale hue of her skin and emphasized the two firm mounds clad in ice-blue satin. His fingers traced the edge of her bra cup all the way down to the front-opening claspnestled in her cleavage.

Christ…he *loved* a front-opening clasp.

Grady's gaze locked with hers, his breathing ragged as he twisted and the bra sprang open. She gasped, arching her back a little, and Grady's gaze dropped to the spill of her magnificent breasts, her nipples tipped rose gold in the firelight. He sucked in a breath, his hands automatically reaching for all their ripe fullness.

She shuddered as his hands closed over her, and Grady could no more have stopped himself from leaning in to suck her nipples than he could stop the world turning. Her moan and the desperate clutch of her hand at his shoulder as his mouth closed over a taut peak stoked the fire blazing out of control in his loins.

"Grady," she said on a pant, her back arching more as his tongue flicked back and forth over the hard tip. But he wanted to hear her yell it. Hell, he wanted to hear her scream it as she scratched up his back.

It wasn't like anybody was going to hear her over the racket of the blizzard.

He switched to the other nipple, and she moaned again, louder this time, her back bowing at the pleasure. He sucked it hard, reveling in the rasp of it against his tongue.

"Grady," she said again, her hands grabbing at his shirt, dragging it up his back and pulling it over his head, breaking his lip-lock on her breast. He straightened to rid himself of the shirt, looking down at her, looking at the flames dancing patterns on her belly and the hard, wet peaks of her nipples, the red marks just below her breasts where his whiskers had rubbed and the soft flare of her hips. Her hair was loose around her head and her mouth was full and red.

She looked wrecked, and he hadn't even started yet.

Easing her ass to the ground, he stripped off her pajama pants and her ice-blue panties until she was lying in nothing but her birthday suit and the firelight. And *holy fuck*, his balls ached and his loins ached and his eyeballs ached at the sight of her before him like some pagan sacrifice to the gods.

Hell, his heart was hammering so hard, his chest *ached*.

"Your turn," she said, tipping her chin at his jeans.

Grady heaved in an unsteady breath to match the unsteadiness of his hands as he undid his belt, then the button of his fly, then made short work of his zipper. Rising on his knees a little, he eased his jeans and his underwear down in one move. His cock sprang free, and the way her gaze latched on to the rampant jut of his dick was like a squeeze to his balls. With nowhere near as much finesse as he hoped, Grady wriggled out of the denim without falling on top of her or face-planting into the floor until he, too, was naked, kneeling between her spread thighs.

Nerve endings in his buttocks tingled as her gaze, as hot and urgent as her mouth had been that first time, devoured every inch of his dick. It was hard to believe that anything much could be heard above the howl of nature outside the cabin, but he could hear the unsteady timber of his breathing. And the husky rasp of hers.

"Condoms in my bag on the table beside the couch," she said.

Grady raised an eyebrow. "Suzanne St. Michelle—did you plan this?"

She shot him a lazy smile that curled deliciously in his belly. "No. I was cleaning out my bag earlier, trying to keep occupied and not worry whether you were dead in a ditch somewhere."

She was still smiling, but the fact that she had obviously been very worried about him curled around his heart. "As you can see…" He glanced down at his cock. "I am very much alive."

She reached for him, closing her hand over the taut girth of his dick. Grady sucked in a breath as the muscles deep in his pelvis shuddered and tightened. "Prove it," she whispered.

That was all the encouragement Grady needed as he slid out of her grasp and pushed to his feet, grabbing her bag.

"Side pocket," she said.

Grady shoved his hands in the side pocket as he walked back toward her, his fingers immediately finding a foil strip and pulling it out. Dropping her bag to the floor, he tore off one of the condoms and tossed the rest on top of the bag as he opened the foil and hastily donned the protection. "Mmm," she murmured. "I like watching you touch yourself."

His breath hitched at the desire in her eyes. "I like touching you better."

And then he was down on his knees again, between her legs and feeling so damn at home there, it stole his breath. She reached for him, her palms sliding onto his shoulders, and every nerve ending from there right down to his buttocks contracted and sparked to life as he settled over her, his dick gliding through the slickness between her legs, finding her center and, as he claimed her lips in a kiss that was deep and wet and long, he pushed inside her, sliding all the way home.

She moaned against his mouth, breaking their kiss to pant, "God, yes…Grady," and then she kissed him again and he was lost.

Lost to the touch and the feel and the taste of her, to the tight, wet clench of her and the soft breathy sounds of her as he entered and withdrew in slow, easy strokes, caught in a rhythm that was purely theirs. His blood flowed thick and hot through his veins and pulsed with the tempo of their joining through his belly and his temples and his groin.

The pleasure built slowly—so slowly—like musical notes layering one on top of the other to a crescendo, and Grady wrung every moment out of the build. Enjoying the feel of her under him, around him, reveling in every hitch of her breath, every moan, every desperate clutch of his ass pushing him closer and closer. When she started to tighten around him and gasp, "Yes, yes," against his mouth, his own orgasm rumbled through his system, and when her back bowed and eyes flew open and she clamped tight around his length, he broke, too, their gazes locking as they came together, crying out into the night, two hearts and two souls intimately entwined.

• • •

Suzanne stirred a while later. She didn't know how long she'd been asleep or what had even woken her. For a moment, she thought it was the vicious howl of the wind that seemed to have ratcheted up to banshee status—not an official meteorological term—but then she became aware of a pair of hot lips kissing her neck and an even hotter part of Grady's anatomy pressing into the cleft of her buttocks.

She vaguely recalled that he'd moved not long after they'd collapsed in a heap and that she'd made some kind of protest, but he had hushed her and said he'd be back and he'd returned shortly after, his arm sliding possessively around her waist as he'd spooned her, and she didn't remember anything after that until now.

Opening her eyes, the low flame and bright-red coals of the fire were the first thing she saw, the warmth on her face and body deliciously toasty. Sighing, she snuggled into Grady, squirming against him appreciatively. A deep groan caused her nipples to harden, and she shivered as his tongue stroked up the side of her neck to just under her ear.

"You're awake," he muttered, his breath hot, goose bumps prickling over her scalp.

"What's the time?"

"Just after one."

Suzanne rolled onto her back, and he shifted, propping himself on an elbow to look down at her, his other hand drawing circles on her stomach, striking sparks beneath her skin. "Sorry, I passed out." She lifted her hand to smooth her palm along his soft, scratchy whiskers, which caused a few more sparks.

"So did I," he said, shutting his eyes briefly as she traced the pads of her fingers over each of his lids.

"Yeah, but you've been working like a dog for the last two days."

He shrugged. "I'm used to it."

Something Grady had said earlier came back to her, and Suzanne dropped her hand. "I didn't plan this, Grady. I hope you know that."

"I know." His fingers stroked up her middle, from her belly button all the way to her mouth, brushing along her bottom lip. His touch was light, but she felt it *everywhere*. "It just happened."

"Yeah," she acknowledged. "I guess we should probably talk about that."

Like they should have the first time they'd hit the sheets together.

"Probably." His fingers slid down her throat to play in the hollow at the base. "But honestly…right now I'd rather just spend the next however many hours we have making you come as many times as possible. The blizzard will be over soon enough and reality will intrude, including all the reasons why you and I doing this is a bad idea. So I'd rather not have to think about them now. I'd rather show you that it's not just my hands I'm good with."

Suzanne swallowed at the blatant imagery he'd invoked. The man sure knew how to negotiate. But this was classic avoidance and 100 percent the Grady she'd come to know. The guy who didn't talk or dwell or analyze anything that couldn't be changed. Who didn't look back. Who moved forward. Who got on with things.

Just like he would when she left.

"You should use words more often," she teased, a smile nudging her mouth because whether he was indulging in his usual avoidance or not, if all she went back to New York with was this one night, then it was better than some people got in a whole lifetime. "You're good at them."

He chuckled. "I prefer actions."

His hand slid to her breast, and her nipple hardened beneath the stroke of his fingers. He followed it up with the hot, wet suck of his mouth, and Suzanne arched her back and surrendered to him as he kissed and nibbled and sucked all the way down her body, teasing her map-of-Texas birthmark with his tongue before settling between her legs and licking right along her center, causing Suzanne to moan so deep and sonorous, she wouldn't have been surprised had a pod of whales come crashing through the front door.

And when she climaxed, which she did so damn quickly, the wild nonsensical mutterings falling from her mouth were so foreign, they might as well have been Portuguese. But she was barely conscious of them as she buried her fingers in his hair and rode his tongue all the way until the end, until she was gasping and panting in the aftermath.

He took his time kissing his way back up her body so by the time his lips were brushing along the ridge of her throat, she'd finally come back to herself.

"See," he said, lifting his head, his smile big and smug, the firelight softening the hardness of his features. "It's much better when I don't talk."

He looked cocky and sexy and his dick was still hard and pressing into her side and damn if she didn't want to show him how the two—sex and talking—weren't necessarily exclusive. Pushing on the center of his chest, she followed as he fell to his back; then she straddled his hips, settling herself over his hardness, her hair falling lightly against her shoulders.

"If you were a woman," she said, reaching over to snag a condom off her bag about a foot from his head, "you could do both."

He quirked an eyebrow. "That a fact?"

"It is," she said and proved how skilled she was by giving a running commentary as she opened the foil with her teeth and pulled out the condom and applied it to his cock with expert precision.

He sucked in a breath as she positioned him at her center. "Impressive."

"You ain't seen nothing yet." And slowly but surely, she sank down over him, taking all his rampant hardness into the tight sheath of her sex, reveling in the stretch and the fullness as she took him all the way to the hilt.

"God." He groaned as his hands glided up her ribs to her breasts, cupping them. "You're beautiful."

His fingers brushing her nipples was exquisite, and she wanted nothing more than to let her head loll back and enjoy, but she was trying to make a point. "I have a plain face, and I'm too curvy," she dismissed.

"No," he whispered. "You're perfect."

Suzanne's breath caught in her throat. He said it so reverently, she actually believed him.

Looking down at herself, at the way his work-calloused hands covered her smooth, pale breasts so possessively, was arousing on a whole new level.

She'd never wanted to be possessed by a man before, but hell if she didn't want to be branded all over by this man. She moved then, circling her hips, needing to steer them away from useless thoughts she didn't know what to do with. Sliding her finger to the puckered wound near his collarbone, she said, "Tell me what happened."

He squeezed her breasts, pinched the nipples. "Seriously?"

"Seriously."

"I'm a little busy here."

Suzanne smiled as she leaned into his hands, angling her body for freer movement. "Multitask," she murmured as she eased herself off him a little, then back down again, her pulse tripping, her body shuddering at how damn good he felt sliding in and out.

He shuddered, too. "Wrong place, wrong time," he said on a harshly expired breath.

She rocked forward again, moaning, her voice a rough pant. "IED?"

"Car bomb."

God…a *car bomb*. Suzanne couldn't even stand the thought of it as she took him inside her again. "Did it hit anything vital?"

"No."

"How long were you in the hospital?"

He didn't answer for a beat or two, and they just stared at each other as Suzanne took full advantage of her position to ride him. His hands were firm on her breasts, his arms extended, his elbows locked, which allowed her to lean in hard, to get just the right amount of leverage to slide up and down the length of him.

She pulled off him almost all the way, and he groaned and said, "A few days."

"A few *days*?"

Suzanne was so shocked, she rocked back onto him with a quick snap of her hips.

He grunted as she stared down at him. "It's not much more than a scratch."

A scratch? Yeah right. But she didn't stop rocking, greedy for every magnificent inch of him. He was solid and very real between her thighs. He was okay. "You went back after that?"

"Cleared for duty…" He shut his eyes and pulled in a couple of short breaths. "A week later."

Jesus. That sounded ridiculous. "But you left eventually, right? Why?"

"After three tours, my time was up." He opened his eyes. "And I was sick of being shot at."

Suzanne gave a half laugh, circling her hips now, causing her to shiver as Grady's dick hit a completely different spot. "Was there anybody else injured? With the car bomb?"

His eyes locked on hers, intent. Serious. "Two."

Suzanne ground down hard against him, her pulse hammering. "Bad?"

"Yes."

He didn't have to tell her they hadn't made it. It was in the finality of his tone. She leaned into him more, easing off him a little but not intentionally, just to get closer. "I'm sorry," she whispered.

"So am I," he said, then thrust, hard and high, wrenching a gasp from her throat and a groan from his as he vaulted up, his chest pressing to hers, his arm snaking around her waist, his lips so close to hers, they were almost brushing. "I don't want to talk anymore."

And then he kissed her—hard—his tongue tangling with hers as he fell backward, bringing her down with him, his hands splayed on her ass, his thrusts deep and sure, fucking her like Armageddon was knocking at their door, fucking her till the pleasure rained down and they were spent.

· · ·

It was light when Suzanne woke hours later. She half expected to find Grady up and about, but he was lying on his back beside her, sleeping peacefully, the discarded foil from the third condom they'd used about two hours ago an inch away from his elbow. She smiled, remembering Grady's voraciousness. Remembering hers.

She was struck again by how much younger he looked in sleep. His mouth wickedly tilted, his frown smoothed out, his jaw, covered in delicious whiskers, relaxed. She wanted to touch those whiskers, to trace her finger along his mouth and his cheekbones, to run it down the hard ridge of his throat and lower, to the ridges of his abs and lower again to the flaccid fullness of his cock, still impressive.

A tingle of desire squirmed through her belly. She knew she'd only have to touch him and it'd spring to life. But…the man needed sleep. He hadn't exactly had a lot of that last night, not to mention the previous two nights, and she'd bet her mom's most expensive piece of art that Grady had rarely, if ever, slept the day away.

So she'd leave him be for now.

Judging by the unrelenting noise of the wind, they had all day to, how had he put it? *Making you come as many times as possible.* She shivered at the carnal eloquence and deliberately rolled away from the temptation of Grady, getting to her feet and heading for the bathroom.

Returning fireside a few minutes later, she stepped into her underwear and put on her pajama shirt, planning to check on her parents but getting distracted, once again, by a naked Grady, whom she blatantly ogled. Her muse, which had been MIA since her parents had arrived, suddenly perked up. Now *that* she could paint. Grady reclined and, in the buff, his work-honed body looked all long and loose and relaxed, that slight uptilt to his mouth suggesting the kind of satisfaction that came only from the type of carnal activities in which they'd indulged.

The title? *Waiting out the weather.*

Her muse whispered heady sweet nothings in her ear, which Suzanne steadfastly ignored—painting Grady had gotten her into this mess in the first place. Turning her back on him, she crossed to the window near the Christmas tree. It was blindingly white outside, from the foot of powdery snow that had fallen overnight to the stuff that was currently being whipped around by the relentless wind, but Suzanne could still make out the cottage door and was relieved to see no red cloth tied to the knob.

Leaving the window, she made her way across the cabin to the one opposite that overlooked the porch and the front field. It was, as expected, a total whiteout. The dark line of fencing and the bare trunks and branches of trees were the only flashes of muted color visible through the windswept flurry of horizontal snow.

Suzanne shivered. There was a wildness and a beauty to nature that was compelling, something so elemental that a person couldn't help but be drawn to it. Suzanne could see why so many of the great painters through the ages had put it on canvas, capturing it in all its beauty and its terror.

She could even see how an artist could paint the same scene over and over again, as so many of them had. Nature was so changeable. Depending on the time of year, or even the time of *day*, it never stayed exactly the same. She just wished she felt similarly compelled. Wished that it excited her muse the same way. Looking out at the harsh reality of this winter landscape, she felt a lot of things—small and awed and…human.

But she didn't want to paint it.

Grady, on the other hand… She glanced over her shoulder at him, and her muse purred. She actually *purred*!

Sighing, Suzanne headed to the fire, removing the screen to build it up, throwing bigger logs on it and topping it with a handful of pine cones because they burned so prettily and smelled like Christmas.

"Good morning."

The low, lazy greeting shot a shiver up her spine and wrapped around her heart. That voice wouldn't be a terrible thing to wake up to every morning.

She turned, and her breath caught at the rugged beauty of him. It didn't matter that she'd already ogled the bejesus out of him; she just couldn't get enough of him stretched out naked like this—for her eyes only.

Paint him, her muse whispered. *Paaaaaint him.*

Taking a deep breath, she smiled at him and let her muse have her way. "Can I paint you?"

CHAPTER TWENTY

Grady, trying to clear the heavy malaise of sleep from his head, blinked at the suggestion. Was she serious? But he could see that she was, as the hot flick of her gaze raked his body in what he assumed was her critical eye—professional and businesslike.

Not that his dick knew the difference.

If she stared at his junk any harder, there'd be no way she could paint another of those little wieners on him. Which was something, at least.

"Haven't you already painted me enough?"

She shook her head, her teeth biting into her bottom lip as she continued to peruse his body like maybe she wanted to put the paint *on* him rather than a canvas. "No, not like that. Not like the other times." Her gaze met his. "You, as you are now. Lying on this rug, sleepy and lazy and…"

"Sated?" Grady didn't know how he looked, but he knew how he felt.

A slight smile tugged at the corners of her mouth. "Exactly."

Exactly. Grady couldn't ever remember a time when he was so damn *replete.* There was a blizzard outside for God's sake, and while there wasn't anything he could do until it blew over, he could still be pacing the floor and looking out the window every ten minutes for some kind of break in the weather. He could be tuning in to the radio and strategizing the cleanup.

Instead of lying here letting her ogle him like one of his prize bulls. But man…he *liked* being ogled. He liked how *she* ogled.

He glanced down at his burgeoning cock. "Will it be anatomically correct this time?"

Her eyes drifted to his crotch, which did not help with his swelling problem. "Oh yes."

Grady regarded her, seriously tempted and completely unable to fathom why. Vanity didn't seem to be a very good reason to consent to something that had gotten them into this predicament in the first place. She must have taken his silence as a precursor to a no and quickly jumped in with a "Or I could make it bigger if you like?"

A chuckle rose in his throat. "Why?" he asked, rolling up onto his elbow. "Why do you want to paint me when you have all that"—he gestured with his free hand to the winter wonderland outside the window—"out there to inspire you?"

She sighed. "Because for some reason, my muse has a thing for surly rancher dudes. And the muse wants what the muse wants."

He laughed at the note of frustration in her voice. "That's inconvenient."

"You have *no* idea."

Oh, he did. He really did. Having Suzanne here had been extremely inconvenient to the strict confines of his life. And yet here he was, contemplating letting her paint him in his birthday suit. "And the muse always *gets* what the muse wants?"

She nodded. "It's kinda the way it works."

"Inconvenient," he repeated.

"Yeah, but…" Suzanne's eyes met his, sincere and earnest. "She's been missing for so long now. To have her back…" She pressed her hand to her chest. "It makes me feel whole again."

The soft catch in Suzanne's voice slugged Grady hard. She *really* meant it. "Who will it be for?"

"For me. Only me." She patted her chest for emphasis. "My first true piece of art that's all my own. Not a replica. Not a caricature. *My own work.* If you'll allow me to take it home with me?"

Home. Grady knew from bitter experience that one word could have a massive impact on a life. Accident. Dead. Orphan. Credence. Bomb. Shrapnel. He'd just never considered *home* would be one of them. But…*I'm a New Yorker.* That's what she'd said that very first day. And he was a cowpoke, and she was leaving, and that was fine because he didn't need anybody no matter what the sudden niggle in his chest said.

This thing that was happening now was an aberration—like the weather—and it'd be over just as quickly. He'd been alone before; he could be alone again.

"What do you think?" she prompted.

Grady pulled his clashing thoughts into some order. They were for the future. "I…think it's nice to be asked this time."

"Yeah." She shot him a sheepish smile, her cheeks tingeing pink. "Sorry 'bout that."

The niggle in Grady's chest became an ache, and a warning signal went off in his head. It would be easy to forget in this cozy little sexed-up bubble that they were only here because of the predicament

Suzy had landed them in. And soon the blizzard would be over.

He needed to remember—for them both to remember—that *nothing* here was real. "I want the last painting."

If he thought he'd felt bad being all hardass over the fourth painting, it was nothing on the way he felt now with those big blue eyes staring him down and the bob of her throat as she visibly swallowed. He instantly regretted the request. Sure, he knew the whole fake rancher boyfriend thing wasn't over just because he'd have all the paintings in his possession. They were only ever supposed to be a reward for his help once her parents had gone back to New York. But, symbolically, it felt like an ending.

Which was what he wanted, *damn it*. So why was part of him tempted to call back the request and hope she told him to go to hell?

She didn't. After what seemed like forever, she took a deep breath and said a quiet "Okay."

Grady blinked, not expecting such easy capitulation. "I thought you'd put up more of a fight."

"If you think letting go of the last painting doesn't hurt, you're wrong. Those paintings might be frivolous to you, but they mean something to me. Right now, though, I *need* to do this painting. Of you. I need it in here." She tapped her chest. "I need it like I need oxygen. *Nothing* else matters as much as that."

It was Grady's turn to swallow, the conviction in her voice so compelling that it was almost as if he could *see* her need. It didn't make him feel any better about the price he'd demanded, but the fact she was willing, no matter how reluctantly, to sacrifice the painting to a greater cause helped.

And he could no more deny her her oxygen than he could deny his own.

"Then let's do it."

• • •

Half an hour later, after having the last of the brownies soaked in bourbon for breakfast—end of the world adulting 101—Suzanne had a five-foot canvas set up landscape style on her easel. The light from the window behind her was good, and Grady had given her one of his old plaid shirts on the proviso she didn't wear anything underneath, so she wasn't.

The sand in the hourglass was running out in this bubble of theirs, and she wanted to wring every sexy, lighthearted moment she could from it. If that included him getting off on catching an occasional glimpse of her bare ass, then fair enough, considering he was lying buck naked on the rug amid a nest of duvets, pillows, and blankets.

He looked warm and comfortable and exceedingly sexy in the firelight and very at home in this cabin as rough-hewn as himself. Very...*frontier man*, lying so casually, unconcerned while the storm raged outside.

Even naked and horizontal, the man was king of his domain.

A thrill, the same thrill she felt when she'd first started painting him, gripped her as Suzanne made the first slash on the canvas. Magic tingled in her fingertips and tapped in her toes, and she knew that all the painting she'd done of Grady up till now had been leading to this moment.

Suddenly the heaviness in her heart over losing those paintings lifted. They had meant a huge amount, but they'd merely been signposts in her journey to *this* painting. Signposts to the starting point of her career. It didn't matter that they weren't in her possession, because she would always carry them in her heart.

"What do you want me to do?"

Suzanne glanced up from her palette. "Do?"

"Yeah. Am I supposed to lay a certain way? Do you want me to…pose?" He turned on his side, with his top leg splayed wide, showing off his wares like a bad seventies porn star.

She laughed. "This ain't that kind of portrait." He laughed, too, but she could see he was finding the whole experience a little discomfiting. "Just be yourself."

He snorted as he rolled onto his back again. "This is so far from myself, I don't even know where to start."

"Just lie like that for a while and talk to me."

"What if I need to scratch my nose? Or use the bathroom?"

Suzanne rolled her eyes as she made the broad brushstrokes of his outline. "Then use the bathroom. If you need to scratch your nose or take a break, that's fine; you don't have to lie there not moving for hours."

"Good. I'm not someone who can just lie around

for hours. In fact, I doubt I've been this inactive since…since before I came to Credence."

Since before his parents and girlfriend died and his life was shot to hell.

He hadn't said it or even implied it in his tone, but Suzanne couldn't help wondering if he was back there right now, in that moment. "Oh, I don't know," she said with a smile, desperate to have him here with her, in *this* moment. "I wouldn't say you've been *inactive.*"

He laughed, and his heated gaze fanned across the tops of her thighs barely covered by his shirt. "That's true." He shoved his hands under his head. "So what shall we talk about?"

Suzanne could think of a million things—his parents, Bethany, coming to Credence, his time in the military. Loss, grief, recovery. But she wanted him to relax and talk to her, not clam up. "Tell me about Bob Downey. He seems to have a lot of influence for an octogenarian who lives at the old folks' home."

"God…" Grady gave a short, sharp half laugh. "This blizzard would need to rage for a year to tell it all. Let's talk about you instead."

Suzanne glanced up sharply. "What about me?"

"Tell me why your muse was missing all those years."

Jaysus. So he wanted to start with the easy stuff, then? She painted on for a minute, not answering, contemplating not answering at all but wanting, strangely, to tell him if only so she could figure it out herself.

"That hard, huh?" he said as the silence stretched.

She stopped painting, trying to find a way through the mental minefield. "I'm good at forging… At replicating. Like, *really* good. But it doesn't require any…creative spark. I just literally copy what I see."

"You make it sound easy."

"Well, no, the process is often long and laborious, but the act of copying has always come easily for me. Except it put my muse into hibernation, you know? Which isn't good when you're trying to paint originals."

"It's like your mom said: The muse has to be exercised, right?"

"Right. And also…"

"Also?" he pushed after she'd been silent for a while.

Suzanne shrugged. "I've been…scared, I guess."

"Of what?"

"I…don't know." Suzanne put brush to canvas again. "Scared that I didn't have it in me. That I wasn't capable of something original."

"I think sticking my head on a cherub is pretty damn original."

She laughed. "I don't mean that kind of original. That's not art."

"It's not?" He frowned. "Who says?"

"Serious art people. Capital *A* Art People."

"Like your mom?"

Suzanne was fast coming to recognize that Grady was no stereotypical, slow-off-the-mark cowpoke. He was sharp and missed nothing. "Yes."

"Is that why you haven't told her what you've painted when she's asked?"

"Yeah. She wouldn't understand."

"I guess it must be hard being Simone St. Michelle's daughter."

"It can be." Suzanne didn't want to dwell on that, though. She'd grown up with enormous privilege thanks to her mother's success—it was such a first-world problem.

"You're intimidated?"

"No." She shook her head. "It's just been easier to replicate other people's art than create my own because I'm good at it and I love doing it. If I tried something different, there would be a lot of... expectation. There would be comparisons. And if I wanted to stand on my own, as an artist in my own right, *which I do*, I'd have to be..."

"Better?"

"No." She gave another quick shake of her head. "We work in different mediums; it wouldn't be about better. It's about being...*more.*"

"Sounds like a lot of pressure."

"Yeah. Hence the muse problem. I mean, what if it's all crap and lifeless, like I'm still copying instead of creating? What if I'll never be any good in my own right? What if I'll always just have to stick with painting other people's paintings? It's why I jumped at Winona's suggestion to come here." She glanced up to find his warm gaze trained firmly on her face. "To get away from the *art world* and see what I could create without a bunch of people in my head. I thought I'd paint the landscape, but then my muse perked up when she saw you, and—"

"The muse wants what the muse wants."

"Yeah." And the muse had wanted Grady. Even

if Suzanne had fought her tooth and nail.

"Well, then, maybe I should turn this way." He rolled onto his hip, baring his ass to her view. "I'm told it's my good side."

Suzanne laughed. It was a *mighty fine* side, complete with a shoulder blade tattoo, but the man didn't have a bad one.

He rolled back again, his face suddenly serious. "You've already painted the hardest part of me five times, and each time you managed to perfectly capture the exact thing I see in myself every time I look in the mirror. Now, I know jack about art, but I figure that's something pretty damn special, Suzanne St. Michelle. Just like what you're painting now will be."

Suzanne blinked, surprised and humbled by the utter sincerity of his compliment. She had no idea he'd done more than give her paintings a cursory glance. But to see what he'd seen, he had to have looked closer.

"Thank you," she said, her voice husky.

But she didn't need him to tell her what she was painting was special. She'd known that from the very first brushstroke. It was going to be a keeper.

Even if the real Joshua Grady wasn't.

• • •

For the next few hours, she painted and they talked. Not about anything deep or meaningful, just daily life kinda stuff. He told her about a typical day for him, and she told him about a typical day for her. Grady made coffee and fixed them baked beans on toast by cooking the bread over the gas flame—all while naked. He kept the fire stoked and occasionally tried to convince her to let him take a peek at her progress, which she resisted.

Like her mother, she never showed anybody her art before it was finished. The need to protect her process was paramount, and if she opened it up to opinion before it was done? Well, that could wreck her. It could certainly mess with her flow.

At one point, he asked if she would mind if he did some work on his laptop, and when she shook her head, he'd sat in the buff, the computer on top of the blanket and balanced on his outstretched thighs and did just that. "What are you working on?" she asked, her gaze firmly trained on the canvas as she added definition to his abdomen.

"Stock feed spreadsheets," he murmured.

Suzanne glanced up to find his concentration wholly focused on the screen. She almost laughed. Could they be any different? She was painting a nude portrait of him, and Grady was looking at numbers. But there was a homeyness to the scenario that was appealing on a level Suzanne didn't dare let herself explore. Normally she needed music, *loud* music, to be productive, but not today. Today the crackle of the fire, the dull rub of brush against canvas, and the tippy-tap of keys were totally doing it for her.

And the art was flowing.

After twenty minutes, he put the laptop aside and reached for the radio, squirming down onto his back again, bending his elbow and shoving his right hand behind his head to prop it a little as he turned it on. The static almost drowned out the voice broadcasting the progress of the storm.

"They're still saying it'll be midnight before it starts to ease," he said.

Suzanne nodded absently at the update, knowing it was a rhetorical statement not requiring her response but informative given she hadn't really been listening to the report. She'd tuned in to the static instead, the scratchy white noise just the right pitch to sharpen her focus on the image of Grady coming to life on the canvas.

She glanced up ten minutes later to find he'd fallen asleep, radio still on, and Suzanne's heart gave a little squeeze at the sight. His head had lolled to the side, his lips had slackened, and his left hand was resting low on his abdomen, perilously close to his junk. This was the essence of the man, and her muse lapped it up, the brush flying over the canvas as she rushed to capture his lazy masculine potency.

An hour later, with only the static for company, Suzanne put her brush down and stretched out the muscles on either side of her neck. *It was done*. Oh, she had no doubt she'd tweak it a little over the days and weeks to come, but essentially she was finished. And it was good.

So damn good, she almost cried.

All that worry about not being able to create something original, about her art being stiff and two-dimensional, fell away as she stared at a painting so fluid, so full of life and vitality, it sucked her breath away.

She *was* an artist, damn it. She was a *portrait* artist. That was her niche. *That*'s who she was.

She realized something else, too, maybe even more startling. Something she hadn't seen until now, until taking in the whole. It was full of love. Infused with it. They said a picture was worth a thousand words, but this one was worth only one. If she'd seen this painting hanging in a museum or a gallery, there'd be no doubt about what she was viewing—a portrait of a man painted by the person who loved him, every brushstroke a love letter.

Tears blurred Suzanne's eyes, and her ribs felt tight around her lungs. It couldn't be—she *couldn't* be in love with him—she'd known him three freaking weeks. Not that she *knew* him at all, really, which made this even more preposterous. How could she be in love with someone who kept himself so closed off? But it was no use trying to deny it when the truth of it was staring back at her from the canvas. The heart wants what the heart wants, and her damn fool heart had decided on Joshua Grady.

What an *idiot*. To fall for a guy so emotionally unavailable that she might as well have fallen in love with a rock. *Brilliant, Suzanne. Good job.*

Shit…what a mess.

Suzanne started as she heard movement from behind the canvas, blinking rapidly to dispel the blur of tears, wishing she could blink her pulse back to normal. It skipped madly at her wrist as she tipped her head to the side and peered around the canvas to find Grady stretching languorously by the fire.

Her breath hitched at the dominantly male display, the action rippling through every muscle group from his toes to his head, emphasizing every nuance of his nudity.

"I fell asleep."

It was a statement rather than a question, and he sounded so nonplussed, it surprised a laugh out of her. "You did. It looks good on you. Maybe you should do it more often."

"Sure." He chuckled. "I'll book it in for after my regular spa day."

Suzanne rolled her eyes at his easy dismissal of being pampered. But she couldn't help but think he needed someone in his life to make him sleep in once in a while.

If only he hadn't decided he didn't need anyone.

"You done yet?" he asked.

Dragging her mind back to the painting, Suzanne glanced at it one last time. "Yeah," she said with a slow nod. "I am."

The change in Grady's expression was priceless as he vaulted upright. "Really?" He glanced at the clock hanging above the mantelpiece. "In four hours?"

Suzanne nodded. Her other paintings had taken longer because she'd spent so long getting his face right—the angle of his head and the hardness of his jaw and the exact expression she was trying to capture—but having painted it so often now, it was second nature. No doubt her love had also guided her hand.

Pushing to his feet, Grady strode toward her, and Suzanne thrilled at how comfortable he was being naked in front of her, at the easy intimacy between them. It would disappear in a puff as soon as Grady left this cabin to get back to work—she knew that. But for now, she was going to cling to it and always remember these hours they spent together while a storm worthy of Noah raged over their heads.

He rounded to her side of the canvas, and a knot of nerves pulled tight in her chest as he stood behind her, sliding his arms around her waist and propping his chin on top of her head. He didn't say anything for the longest time, and there was nothing but the sound of the gale and the roar of her pulse in her ears as she waited for his verdict. She felt for sure he must be able to feel the wild slam of her heart thumping just under where his hands were clasped.

Could he see it, what was so obvious to her? Did she want him to?

"It's…" His chin slid back and forth across her hair as if he was shaking his head. "It's incredible. I look so chilled and relaxed, like…"

"Like?" Suzanne held her breath. What did he see in this labor of love?

"Like I've just gotten laid."

Suzanne laughed to cover up the surge of disappointment. He didn't see it. At least not *all* of it anyway, because there was no doubt Grady looked like he'd been thoroughly debauched. But he'd totally missed the underlying emotion, the deeper resonance.

Maybe that was something only a person with a trained artistic eye could see? Or a person who was in love.

"I know I'm not an expert, but…it's stunning, Suzy. Really stunning," he said as he continued to peruse the painting. There was awe and respect in his tone, and Suzanne totally let it go to her head. "How do you even do that in such a short space of time?"

Suzanne gave a half laugh. "Practice."

He chuckled against her hair and pressed a kiss to the top of her head and Suzanne shut her eyes, enjoying the simple yet intimate caress. "Do *you* like it?" he asked. "Are you happy with it?"

Suzanne nodded. "Yes. Very." She didn't need anyone else's opinion; she knew it was good. The best paintings were the ones where emotion leaped off the canvas, and this portrait had that in spades.

"You haven't signed it."

She blinked at his statement. It hadn't occurred to her to sign it. Due to the nature of her work, she didn't usually sign any of her art. Her name was usually printed on the back and in catalogs as the reproduction artist, but that was it.

"It doesn't matter. It's not like anyone but me is going to be seeing it."

"Of course it matters." His arms tightened around her waist. "You painted it. And this is your first original piece of work, and it's wonderful. You told me you wanted to be an artist in your own right. Don't artists put their name on their work?"

A giddy rush of artistic pride filled her chest at his words. Grady was right. Artists signed their work. Her hand shook as she reached forward for her smallest brush, and Grady dropped his arms.

She took a step, dipping the brush in an ochre-colored oil and swiftly, without thinking, painted her name in the bottom right corner where the edges of the rug became ill-defined.

Suzy.

Replacing the brush, she took a step back, welcoming the bands of his arms as they enveloped her again, resting the back of her head against his chest. "Suzy, huh?"

She nodded. "Yes."

"Not Suzanne St. Michelle? Because you…don't want to trade on your mom's name?"

"Because *Suzanne* paints forgeries. Suzy is the *artist*."

"Mmm," he murmured, his lips playing at her neck. "I like it. In fact…I'm a little turned on by it." His hands slid under the hem of her shirt, his palms sliding up her body, taking the shirt along for the ride. "That's wrong, right?"

His palms found her breasts, the nipples already taut and aching for his touch. A hot wave of arousal washed through Suzanne's belly, and she shut her eyes and arched her back. "Only if it's wrong for me to be turned on, too."

"Absolutely not," he said, his thumbs stroking her nipples. "You're the *artiste*."

Suzanne moaned as the aching spread to her thighs and her butt and right between her legs. She turned in his arms, needing to be closer, whimpering when she found his mouth right there ready for her, losing herself in the heady heat of his kiss. But still, she needed to be closer, snaking her arms around his neck and rising on her toes.

As if sensing her need, Grady slid his hands under her ass and hauled her up, separating her legs, fitting them on either side of his hips and holding her tight as he strode her over to the rug, lay her down, and showed her art came in many, many forms.

CHAPTER TWENTY-ONE

Suzanne didn't know what time it was when she woke to Grady stirring beside her and the lights blazing in the house.

"Electricity's back," he said, rising to his feet.

Suzanne squinted at the clock, battling the sudden assault to her pupils and the sticky cling of deep sleep fogging her brain. Just after eleven p.m. A little over twenty-four hours since Grady had come back to the cabin to wait out the storm. "Something's different," she murmured.

"The wind. It's stopped."

Suzanne blinked, tuning in to the sounds instead of the sights of tinsel and a butt-naked Grady. It was eerily quiet after the banshee howling that had been creeping her out. "You're right."

The overhead lights suddenly flicked out, and Suzanne's eyeballs relaxed. The lights around the windows went next, then the flash of the lights outside the cabin. All that remained was the red glow of coals from the fire and the tree lights blinking merrily, as if to celebrate the passing of the blizzard.

It was so pretty, Suzanne's heart ached with it. She'd always wanted this—the tree, the presents, the lights. It was like a Christmas trifecta. Add in the fire, the cabin, the snow, and the bittersweet ache of new love, and she'd hit the Yuletide jackpot.

Grady went to the window near the tree and

peered out. "It's stopped snowing as well."

A sudden spike of alarm smashed through her romantic Christmas fantasy. "You're not going out there in it now, are you?" Surely that was not advisable?

He gave a half laugh. "No." He strode back to her then, rejoining her on the rug, rolling on his side and propping one hand under his head, the other on her belly. "The guys are coming at six."

The spike crashed, and so did the surge of adrenaline, settling like an oily slick in her stomach. "I guess there's going to be a lot to do."

"Yes. But fingers crossed we prepared everything well enough and there'll just be snow clearing and feeding."

She raised two sets of crossed fingers, and he smiled and kissed the fingertips of the closest. Suzanne's breath hitched. Their time was almost over. The wind had been dreadful—a rabid beast yowling and moaning—but she'd have given anything right now to have it back. She ran her kissed fingertips through his stubble, over his lips, along his jaw to his ear and pushed them into his hair. He shut his eyes and angled his head and she massaged his scalp for a beat or two until his eyes opened and their gazes locked.

"There's one condom left," he said, his voice low and husky.

Winona had teased Suzanne once about the number of condoms she carried around, especially considering Suzanne had never used more than two when she'd been with a guy. But hell if she wasn't coming out on top now.

One condom. One last time. Because that's what it would be. She could see it in his eyes, hear it in his voice. When he got up out of their makeshift bed in the morning, whatever had happened here would be over.

Suzanne swallowed back the painful lump building in her throat. She would not dwell on tomorrow. She had tonight to be with the man she loved—to make love with the man she loved—and she'd take whatever she could get. "It would be a shame to see it go unused," she replied.

He grinned. "My thoughts exactly." And lowered his mouth to hers.

• • •

A kiss on her shoulder woke Suzanne some time later. It was still dark outside, but it took about three seconds for her to remember that Grady was going back to work and the slick of nausea from last night made itself felt again. "I have to go," he whispered.

Suzanne nodded, pretending to be only half-awake even though her heart thudded painfully and every sense was on high alert. At least he wasn't leaving without saying goodbye this time—that was something, right?

Even if it felt horribly, horribly final. She'd known this interlude had only been temporary, known deep in her bones that as soon as he went back to work that he'd revert to the old Grady. But that didn't make it any easier to face.

"'Kay," she murmured, feigning a sleepy smile.

"Be careful out there."

"Of course." Another brief kiss landed on her shoulder, and then he was gone.

She waited for the sound of his footsteps to retreat before the first tear fell and a sob rose in her throat. She choked it back because Grady hadn't left the cabin yet. He had to get dressed and grab something to eat, and she was going to have to lay here and pretend she was still asleep until he was gone. Hold it together like her heart wasn't breaking in two and only when he left could she fall apart.

Because she wouldn't do it in front of a guy who could spend twenty-four hours in bed with her and walk away without any indication that it had meant anything at all.

It was a long twenty minutes, but Suzanne did it. She listened to his footsteps retreat. To the sound of water running through pipes while he took a quick shower. To the sound of the fridge door opening and the smell of coffee brewing and bread toasting. She listened to the radio static as he turned it on low and then the trek of his feet over to where the painting still stood on its easel, counting the seconds until he trekked back to the kitchen again.

Then the keys jingled as he pulled them off the hook on the wall, and several seconds later the door opened. Suzanne lay very still, hardly breathing as she waited for it to close. Waited and waited, the pressure building behind her eyes and in her sinuses.

And for long moments she swore she could feel

the weight of his gaze on her back and she stopped breathing altogether, her heart beating like a train. Until finally—finally—the door clicked shut and the dam burst.

Suzanne allowed herself half an hour. One half hour before she picked herself up off the floor, literally and figuratively, and got on with the day. She needed to check on her parents. And clean up in here. Put the painting away. It was three days until Christmas, and she couldn't spend them curled up in a fetal ball because she'd gone and done something monumentally stupid.

There was cooking to be done and last-minute things to buy. She'd told Winona she'd go to the boardinghouse and help her with some table favors she wanted to make. Her mom had promised she'd give a talk at the old folks' home. She had too much to do to feel sorry for herself.

In the end, she only got twenty minutes into her pity party before being interrupted by the roar of an engine that sounded like it was bearing down on the cabin. Adrenaline surging, she sprang to her feet, dashing away tears as she dragged the duvet around her. Rushing to the window, she saw a huge yellow machine with a massive bucket clearing the snow between the cabin and the cottage. It was light enough to see that Grady was not the driver. Light enough for the driver to see her and give her a cheery wave.

Stepping back from the window, she crossed to the kitchen and grabbed her phone where it had been charging on the bench, grateful to see the usual three bars indicating the network was up again. She dialed her mom, who picked up on the second ring.

"Hey, Mom. Everything okay over there? How'd you guys do?"

"Yes, darling, all good here. It was quite terrifying, though, wasn't it? The howling was really very spooky."

"Yes." It had been.

"But it was good to have all that downtime. I've been so inspired since the ice-sculpting contest, I've been sketching up a storm. *Angels*, Suzanne. I have this most magnificent idea for an angel. I'm seeing angels in my sleep."

Oh *no*. Suzanne didn't like the sound of that. She knew how her mom got when inspiration struck. How everything else became secondary. Including the man to whom she was married and supposedly trying to rekindle the flame.

So much for taking advantage of the one bed and the romanticism of being snowed in. Her mother probably hadn't looked up from her sketch pad.

"That sounds a little too…Christmas for you."

"I know. Weird, isn't it? Remind me to thank Grady—I think all the lights and tinsel must have rubbed off."

Suzanne blinked. Well…she certainly hadn't seen that coming.

"You guys want to come over for breakfast in a couple of hours? Actually, no… Let's go to Annie's."

Whether the diner or anything would be open in Credence this morning, Suzanne had no idea.

Hell, maybe the roads were still closed. But she suddenly had cabin fever in this place where the rug she was staring at was a constant reminder of what had happened between her and Grady. And she would bet her father was feeling a little cottage fever, too.

"Oh no, I'm just going to keep on sketching. But you and Albie should go."

A rumble of anger swept through Suzanne's gut. Maybe if she hadn't just spent the last twenty minutes crying, she'd have taken her mother's dismissal in stride. But her mom had a man who loved her and wanted to be with her—how *dare* she let anything come between that.

Not to mention Grady and her were in this ridiculous situation so her Mom and Dad could *work on their relationship*.

"*Mom*. No. Just *no*. We are going and you are coming with us—*without* your sketch pad."

"Suzanne." Simone's voice had that stubborn edge Suzanne knew all too well.

"*Mom*," she repeated. "You came to Credence to rekindle your relationship with Dad. You know, to avoid a *divorce*. Remember?"

"Oh…" Simone's voice sounded suddenly small, and Suzanne actually heard her swallow. "Yes. God, you're right. I'm so sorry. I'm doing it again, aren't I?"

Yes, Suzanne almost snapped. But she hadn't expected to cut through to her mother so easily, and the fact that Simone appeared to finally have some insight into her behavior tempered Suzanne's response. "Yes," she said gently.

"Right, of course. Yes, let's go to Annie's. Your father will love it. And so will I."

"Good." Suzanne nodded.

She may not be able to get a positive relationship outcome for herself in all this mess, but she sure as hell was gunning for her parents.

• • •

The next three days passed in a blur of activity. The sun was out, and the skies were blue, and even though it was still cold, the mercury managed to rise above freezing and helped melt the two feet of snow the blizzard had dumped all over Credence. Suzanne kept her parents busy and together, with her mother's full cooperation. They even agreed to Christmas karaoke.

No one could get them up onstage, but the fact that they bore it in good spirits was welcome.

Grady was absent, busy with the cleanup until well after dark. She waited up for him each night, but it was like their interlude had never happened and he'd reverted to the grunting man of few words she'd first known.

She'd expected awkwardness and avoidance—that was what Grady did—but she hadn't expected to be shut out. It hurt, Suzanne couldn't deny that, and she wanted nothing more than to call him on his bullshit. But…he was beat. She could see that. And there'd been some stock loss, which he'd obviously taken hard. The last thing he needed was a nagging fake girlfriend whining about not getting any crumbs of his time.

So she held her tongue.

But it didn't stop her stupid romantic heart from hoping he might come to her bed each night or her ears straining for his footfalls outside her door. Which was...*pathetic.* How could she even think about opening her legs for a guy who could barely spare her a word?

Where was her pride, damn it?

Christmas Eve was probably the worst night of all. Suzanne had cooked roast beef with sweet potatoes and green bean casserole and insisted they all watch *It's a Wonderful Life* together because it was Grady's favorite. She sincerely doubted it actually was—he seemed more of a John Wayne guy, maybe Rambo—but fake Christmas-loving Grady totally dug the film. Unfortunately, he didn't get in until after it was over and her parents had left for the cottage.

He grunted his usual cursory greeting before heading directly to Zoom's tank, his long legs easily eating up the distance. "I fed him already," she said.

He faltered. "Oh, thank you."

He detoured to the drinks cabinet instead, grabbing a tumbler and the bottle of bourbon, which reminded her of the blizzard and made her cranky. And horny. Which made her crankier.

"You want one?"

Suzanne shook her head. The way she was feeling right now, she'd probably dump it over his stupid fat head. "Please tell me you get a day off tomorrow?"

He downed the first slug of bourbon. "There's

no such thing as a day off for a rancher," he said, talking to the bottle as he poured himself another.

Suzanne blinked at the belligerence in his tone. Was he trying to prove some kind of point? Apart from how much of an asshole he could be? "Your men also work Christmas Day? Don't they have families?"

"They get Christmas off."

"We're expected at Winona's at eleven." God, she sounded like a...*wife*. "The snowman competition kicks off just after that."

"Of *course* it does," he muttered as he lifted the tumbler. "Don't worry. There's only a couple of hours' work in the morning." He looked over his shoulder and raised his drink in her direction, his lips twisted in derision. "Fake rancher boyfriend will be present for duty."

Then he downed it, savoring it in his mouth for long moments before swallowing like it might be his last. Like he was going to his death tomorrow instead of a freaking *feast*.

Cooked by someone else.

"I'm going to hit the shower," he said, moving away from the cabinet and not glancing in her direction.

Suzanne watched him go, striding through the archway and disappearing from sight. She shook her head. He was damn lucky she wasn't one of those bunny boilers, or Zoom would be in a pot on the stove right about now.

• • •

Grady felt lower than a snake's belly in a wagon rut the next morning when he strode toward the cabin at just past eleven. He had been avoiding Suzanne the past three days, staying late in the barn tinkering with shit and doing unnecessary maintenance, but he hadn't meant to be late this morning. He'd told her he'd be home in time for them to be at Winona's by eleven and he'd meant it.

He'd agreed to play a role and today was center stage. And he knew how much Christmas—this hokey, ridiculous Christmas—meant to Suzanne. Plus, Cora and Burl were going to be there.

But there'd been a situation with one of the bulls, and he'd had to get the vet. Goddamn it. This was just the reality of being a rancher. Rain, hail, shine. *Blizzard*.

And yes, fucking Christmas.

He noticed her parents' car was gone and breathed a sigh of relief. At least they'd gone on ahead without him and he could put off having to face Suzanne for a little while longer.

Yeah…*no such luck*.

He opened the cabin door to find her waiting for him. "And a Merry Christmas to you, too, Joshua," she said, folding her arms, obviously angry.

But it was the disappointment lurking in her eyes that was hardest to take.

He held up his hands in a placatory manner as he drew closer. "I'm sorry. I didn't—"

She sliced a hand though the air. "I don't care for your lame-ass excuses," she said, her voice low and tight, her jaw clenched. "Just go and get ready. They're expecting us."

Grady contemplated explaining but screw it. This was what he wanted, right? To push Suzanne away? He'd already let her far too close.

"Here." She picked up a folded long-sleeve T-shirt that was sitting on the back of the couch. "Put this on. I gave it to you for Christmas. You're welcome."

Crossing to where she stood, he took the shirt, holding it up to inspect it. It was red with the word *Ho* emblazoned in white across the front and the number 1 just above it and to the left like it was a chemical symbol. He shook his head. "Ho one? Seriously?"

She unfolded her arms to reveal she was Ho two. "It matches mine," she said, her voice steely. "We thought they were cute. Because we're *that* couple."

Yep. She was *pissed*. Grady's hands tightened on the shirt. None of this was his doing, damn it. He wasn't the one behind this ridiculous plan.

"My parents are wearing Ho three and Ho four. *My parents*, Grady."

Grady shook his head at the shirt. It was a fucking travesty. "This should be against the law."

"Your objection is duly noted. Now, can you please just put it on? I'm sorry I'm all out of paint-ings. Unless—" Her breath suddenly hitched and her expression morphed from spitfire angry to heart-wrenchingly anxious, her hand sliding to her throat as her teeth worried her bottom lip.

"No." Grady shook his head quickly, shoving the shirt under his arm as he took a step closer to assure her.

Christ…he knew he'd been a mean son of a bitch these last few days. It had been deliberate. Because the fact that he hadn't wanted to leave Suzanne the other morning had terrified him. He'd never *not* wanted to leave. But *she* was leaving. And it was just as well. She wasn't cut out for this kind of existence. The fact she was standing here pissed at him about having her Christmas morning ruined was a classic reason why.

She didn't understand the ranching way of life because she belonged in the city with its buildings and its galleries and its art. He was just helping to cement that in case thirty-six hours of mind-blowing sex was giving her any ideas to the contrary.

Giving *him* any ideas to the contrary.

"I know how much that portrait means to you. I would *never* take that from you."

Their gazes met, and her eyes searched his for a beat or two as if she was desperate for assurance. "Thank you."

Grady nodded. "I'll get changed. Give me ten."

• • •

Half an hour later, after a long, silent drive, they were pulling up in the parking lot behind the boardinghouse. Suzanne was used to Grady's silences and frankly, right now, it suited her just fine. She was way too busy grappling with the mixed signals to talk to him anyway.

Damn the man to hell. He'd been so surly and noncommunicative these last few days, and then he went and did a 360 turn, showing remarkable sensitivity and…kindness in his assurance he had no intention of using his portrait as a bargaining chip. She'd wanted to smack him upside the head all morning as the clock had ticked by without him and she'd had to act her ass off playing the deliriously happy Christmas girlfriend in front of her parents. Pretending not only was it all fine, *just fine*, that he wasn't there because *ranchers didn't get days off* but insisting how heartbroken Grady would be if they didn't all wear to Winona's the T-shirts he'd picked out for them.

Yes, she'd promised him she'd do all the heavy lifting in this fake relationship scenario she'd foisted upon him, but she hadn't expected it to be this damn hard.

But by the time he'd walked through the cabin door, she'd worked herself up into the kind of muted rage that husbands and boyfriend all around the world knew meant *trouble*. And then he'd taken the wind right out of her sails by rushing to put her mind at ease about the portrait.

Just when she'd thought he was irredeemable, he'd been compassionate.

But *why* was the question. She wasn't obtuse — she knew he'd been deliberately trying to put her at arm's length these past few days. But if that was the case, insisting on her handing over that last painting would have well and truly accomplished his goal.

Hell, it'd have set it in cement.

Because there was no way she'd have given it up. That painting was hers, and Grady was going to have to drag it out of her cold, dead hands if he wanted it. But he hadn't taken that step. So maybe that meant something? Hence the mixed signals...

Did he want her or not want her? Did he want to push her away or draw her closer? And what in the hell did *she* want?

The streets of Credence were deserted, the thud of the pickup door closing echoing around the quiet streets. "We have to go around front," he said as he placed his hat on his head and pulled down the brim. "There's no back entrance."

Suzanne nodded, pulling on her green knit hat as she mentally prepared for more fake relationship acting. To her surprise, Grady waited for her to join him around his side of the vehicle. She was even more surprised when he fell into step beside her as they headed for the front.

More mixed signals or just Grady also getting into his fake relationship space?

The sounds of their boots were dull on the pavement as they walked down the lane between the boardinghouse and the next block of shops. Suzanne's arm occasionally brushed the brick wall beside her as she hunched into her puffy red coat, trying to give him some space on the narrow sidewalk. Neither of them was walking very fast, and Grady's gait seemed to get stiffer and stiffer the closer they drew to the main street.

It was ironic, and probably some kind of divine punishment for her lies, that Suzanne was getting the Christmas she'd always wanted and now didn't want at all. Not with Grady so freaking tense.

God... Was it really *that* hard to spend time in her company?

"Do you think it might be possible to pretend that you actually like me for the next few hours?" she asked huskily, her footsteps slowing even further. "I know public displays of affection are out, but we're supposed to be a couple. Seriously, is it that hard, Grady?"

It wasn't like he'd had any problems with *private* displays of affection.

He stopped abruptly, and she did, too, risking a look at his tight face, their gazes locking as he stared at her, his mouth a grim slash. "Possible?" His voice went high and actually cracked. He swore under his breath, taking a step closer, forcing Suzanne to take one back, her ass bumping against the brick. "My problem is that I like you too damn much." Then he slid a hand onto her cheek, leaned in, and kissed her.

His lips were cold, and his nose was cold, but the kiss was hot and thorough. And it didn't seem to matter that he spent the last three days ignoring her and acting like he hated her but apparently actually liked her—Suzanne welcomed the press of his body. She clung to his shoulders, savoring the taste of his toothpaste and the deep rumble of his groan and the delicious invasion of his tongue.

Her pulse trembled; the air in her lungs went thick as soup and her blood surged hot and viscous as arousal flushed through her pelvis.

On a ragged groan, he ended the kiss, but he didn't pull away, just stayed close, pressing his forehead to hers as they both caught their breath. "It's not hard," he muttered. "I'm sorry. I know I've been…"

Horrible? Awful? Dreadful? Completely freaking

confusing? Giving her whiplash…?

"Difficult. These past days. I don't want to hurt—"

Suzanne placed her fingers against his lips. As much as she wanted to hear whatever Grady had to say, they couldn't have this conversation here, in an *alleyway* on their way to a Christmas lunch where everyone but his aunt and uncle and the hostess thought they were playing hide-the-salami every night. "Let's do this later, okay?"

He looked like he wanted to argue but stopped himself with a brisk nod and a smile that was more pained than happy. But when he slowly eased away, his gloved hand reached for her gloved hand hanging loose by her side and gave it a squeeze, which was still confusing but somehow helped.

She expected Grady to release her hand, but he didn't, and they walked to the end of the alley, side by side, hand in hand, their arms brushing. A little glow of hope found oxygen inside Suzanne's chest. She didn't know if it meant anything at all, but who'd have thought something as simple and innocuous as a handhold could evoke such optimism?

They rounded the corner to find the park across the road from the boardinghouse a hive of activity. The day was clear and sunny, with two inches of snow having fallen overnight, leaving a good covering of powder. Several snowmen in varying stages of construction stood sentinel at the front of the park, obviously abandoned in preference to the full-scale snowball fight going on behind them.

There was laughter and running and people darting among trees and behind playground equipment and the dull thud of snow as it found its target. It looked like everyone who'd been invited to lunch was in on the action. She didn't know them all, but she spotted a non-uniformed Arlo and Della, who was apparently his sister, and Tucker from Jack's. There was also Drew who she'd met last week. Molly and Marley were proving very accurate, as was Wyatt Carter, despite the handicap of balancing five-year-old Henry on his shoulders.

A pregnant Jenny was sitting it out, smiling at the antics of her husband and son as she chatted to Cora on a bench near the swings. Even her parents were enjoying the action from another bench. Suddenly Burl spotted them from across the street.

"Grady!" he bellowed, and everyone in the park stopped what they were doing to greet the new-comers. Grady dropped her hand like it'd just bitten him.

And the little flame of hope sputtered and died.

CHAPTER TWENTY-TWO

Suzanne's heart felt like a boulder in her chest as she crossed the wide road to the park. Grady stayed close, but his hands were shoved in his coat pockets, and there might as well have been an interstate between them after his obvious attempt to distance himself.

"Watch out, Grady," Burl called from behind a tree as their feet crunched onto the snowy ground and Grady laughed and easily ducked the snowball before scooping snow up and heading in his uncle's direction, which signaled a general resumption of the battle.

Suzanne headed for the bench where her parents were sitting, although not without Winona's snowball hitting her square in the back. "Bull's-eye," Winona shouted.

Suzanne laughed but wasn't in the mood to retaliate. She slid onto the seat next to her mother, pleased for the thermal layer beneath her jeans to stop her from literally freezing her ass off. "Okay, Dad. You're relieved. You go play—I'll sit with Mom."

Her father shot her a rueful smile. "It's fine," he dismissed.

"Dad. I know you're dying to join in the fun." One thing Albie St. Michelle liked was a good snowball fight. Suzanne had spent hours in snowy battle with him in Central Park over the years.

"Go on, darling," her mom said, giving her father's knee a squeeze. "I'm fine."

"If you insist," he said with a grin and a kiss to his wife's cheek that seemed more brotherly than husbandly, which would have bothered Suzanne more had she not had her own relationship—such as it was—to dwell on.

They sat for five minutes watching the shenanigans and laughing as the snowballs flew left, right, and center, some finding their marks but most missing by a mile. Suzanne was amazed a stray snowball hadn't hit them. "Behind you, Albie," her mom called out, and her father ducked, avoiding the missile.

"Thank you, darling," he called before slinking behind a tree with a handful of snow.

"How are things going with Dad?"

Simone nodded thoughtfully. "Good, I think. I've not been sketching the last few nights, and last night we decided we should make an effort to get away from New York whenever I finish a commission, to just be *us*."

"That's great, Mom."

It wasn't a red-hot makeup story—the chaste cheek kiss had underscored that—but at least her parents were talking about a future and how to work on their relationship, which was something. And at least it was some small justification for the lies and inconvenience of the elaborate scheme Suzanne had cooked up.

"Yes, I think we—" Her mother's sentence was interrupted by the splat of a snowball into her back. She gasped. *"Omigod."* Leaping up, she shook off the offending item, her face a picture of disapproval. "Albie," she yelled, swiveling around to find her father a few feet away, trying very hard not to laugh. *"Albie."* She glared. "That is not funny."

Her father didn't look remotely repentant, and Suzanne bit her lip, also trying very hard not to laugh. "What are you going to do about it?" he taunted.

Her mom's eyebrows shot up her forehead, higher than Suzanne would have thought anatomically possible. "You think I *won't* throw a snowball at you?"

He shrugged, playing it so perfectly cool that Suzanne almost applauded. "Talk's cheap."

Her mother turned her attention to Suzanne. "Excuse me, darling. I've got a little business with your father."

Suzanne jumped up. "I'll help. Let's get him."

In the next ten minutes, Albie landed another eight snowballs, but he'd also worn five. They were all laughing as her mother called a truce in the middle of the park. "That was fun," Simone admitted, the surprise in her voice genuine.

"You want to know what's more fun?" Albie asked.

"What?"

He slid a grin sideways at Suzanne before planting a hand firmly in the center of his wife's chest. "Snow angels," he said and pushed.

Simone grabbed for him as she went down, but he stepped out of reach and she landed on her back, her arms and legs flailing, her puffy coat a dark-green slash against the fresh powdery snow.

"Albie."

He chuckled and said, "Yes, darling?"

"Help me up! This instant. It's *freezing* and my beanie is going to be soaked."

Albie just shook his head. "Not until after you make a snow angel." Then he fell backward into the snow beside her, scissoring his arms and legs.

Her mother rolled her eyes, then turned them on Suzanne, holding out her hand. "Darling?"

But Suzanne also shook her head. "Not until you've made a snow angel, Mom," she repeated, and she, too, fell backward in the snow on the other side of her mother and proceeded to make her angel.

"You'll both be sorry you didn't help when I catch my death," she said waspishly.

Then her father reached his hand across to hers and stroked it down her cheek. "Live a little, darling."

Her mother sighed but clearly knew when she was beat, performing the very unfamiliar actions with total aplomb—like she'd been doing it every damn day of her life. "Now what?" she said as her limbs came to a halt.

Albie laughed and hauled himself up from the ground, so did Suzanne, and, between them, they pulled Simone St. Michelle, world-famous *artiste*, onto her feet.

"Look, Simone," her father said, gazing down at the three angels side by side, their wings touching. "Just look how beautiful they are all white and pure and fresh and new. Like a chain of paper dolls. Look how they're as individual as the snowflakes that make them up and how the light shimmers on the wings like they're actually fluttering. It's breathtaking. If that isn't art, then I don't know what is."

Simone looked—actually looked. She inspected each impression, stopping at the foot, then around to the head. She was using her critical eye, the one Suzanne had fallen foul of so many times. "You're right, Albie," she said eventually, her voice quiet. "They are quite beautiful." She glanced at her husband and smiled. "I can see how they could be classified as art."

Maybe this revelation had come about because it was *angels*—her mother's latest creative obsession—but it was still a major breakthrough.

Albie smiled back and held out his hand to her mother, and Suzanne felt tears prick at her eyes.

"Okay," Winona called, her big voice booming across the park, breaking into the intimate moment. "Let's go eat."

Everyone was in good spirits when they arrived back at the boardinghouse. The large living area had been decorated—tastefully—with tinsel and garland, and the real tree scented the room with a fresh piney aroma. Two tables had been pushed together to make one long one and decorated with pine cones and red candles. The heating was working well throughout, and everyone had shed their outside layers at the door.

The fire had burned low in the massive fireplace, and Grady was given the job of getting it roaring again. "You're an outdoors man. You know about logs and trees and stuff, right?" Winona asked.

He cocked an eyebrow. "I know how to burn them, sure."

"Perfect." She smiled. "Now, who wants eggnog?"

A general chorus of affirmatives followed, and Suzanne took on the role of glass filling as classy Christmas carols played and people flitted about, either socializing or helping in the kitchen to get the meal served.

Winona held out her glass for seconds. "Being hostess is thirsty work," she said with a grin.

Suzanne smiled. "You love it."

"I do." Winona laughed, and it was so damn happy, it made Suzanne want to cry, which was all kinds of screwed up. Winona's eyes narrowed suddenly. "Are you okay?"

"Not really."

She moved closer. "What happened?" she asked, her voice dropping.

"I went and fell in love with Joshua Grady."

"Ah." Winona patted her shoulder. "Yeah."

Suzanne frowned. "What do you mean, *yeah*?"

"Babe, I write love stories for a living. I have good antennae for these things."

What? "A heads-up might have been nice."

Winona patted her on the shoulder again. "What are you going to do?"

Suzanne glanced over at the fire, where Grady was standing along with Drew, Arlo, and Burl. They seemed to be doing all the talking, but he looked comfortable in their company. "I have no idea."

"Poor baby." The pat became a gentle squeeze. "Let's talk—tomorrow, okay? It's too hard now."

"Yeah." Suzanne nodded. "Thanks."

"Here." Winona reached for a wrapped present from a small pile sitting farther along the bench. "This is for you."

Suzanne smiled as she took the small boxlike gift, excited to see what gimmicky present Winona had bought her this year. Tearing off the paper, she opened the box to find a snow globe. Not one of those elegant, classy ones sitting on a wooden stand that played music. No, it was a tacky plastic dome-shaped one found in abundance in tourist shops all over the world. Inside were three miniature Greek statues, women with long flowing robes barely covering their ample bosoms and laurel wreaths in their hair.

The white plastic bordering on the outside proclaimed them to be Calliope, Clio, and Erato. Three of the nine Greek muses. Suzanne laughed, shaking it to watch the snow fall before clutching it to her chest and hugging her friend. It was cheesy and awful and perfect.

So perfect.

"I love it, thank you." Pulling out of the embrace, she quickly grabbed her gift she'd left on the table when she'd entered the room. "Your turn," she said, handing it over.

Winona gave an excited little shimmy as she, too, tore open the packaging to reveal the bag of dicks. "Oh my god," she said before dissolving into a fit of the giggles.

Suzanne laughed, too. "You like?"

"I *love*." Winona grinned. "I'm going to put one on every plate. Can't wait to see the look on Officer

Uptight's face."

Suzanne laughed. "Maybe we should keep it PG. You know, for the five-year-old?"

"We'll tell him it's a rocket ship," Winona said with a smile on her face and a dismissive swish of her hand. Her gaze shifted to something over Suzanne's shoulder and she called, "Hey, you two… mistletoe." She pointed at the bunch hanging in the doorway between the long hallway and the living room.

Suzanne turned to find her parents—Ho three and Ho four, who had been god knew where all this time—standing in the doorway, everyone watching them expectantly. Without missing a beat, her father wrapped his arm around her mother's waist, dipped her backward, and dropped a lingering smacker on her lips.

"Well, well," Winona said quietly to Suzanne as the room cheered. "Looks like your work here is done."

Suzanne blinked at her parents *still* kissing. Yeah. Mission accomplished. For her parents anyway.

Lunch was served and everyone ate till they were stuffed full. Some, like Burl, beyond that point, claiming he was going to pop if he ate another thing as he stuffed one more bean from the casserole into his mouth. Cora rolled her eyes.

After lunch, Winona made everyone play silly old-fashioned English parlor games she'd been researching for her latest book. Everything from the minister's cat to musical chairs to wink murder that were all a hoot before they moved on to a massive game of charades—men versus women— that got very competitive.

Suzanne was impressed Grady was joining in and even appeared to be enjoying himself. Maybe he was just playing the role of over-the-top Christmas guy she'd forced upon him and he was silently counting down the minutes, but he seemed to get along with the other men present. He hadn't suggested they leave. Not yet anyway.

At four in the afternoon, they had a special visitor who came bearing pies. Annie was welcomed with open arms even as everyone protested they were too full to eat anything more. They managed somehow, though, and not a single crumb was left when Annie left an hour later.

"That's it," Burl said, pushing his empty bowl away. "I'm never going to eat again."

"From your lips to God's ears, Burl Grady," Cora quipped, and everyone laughed.

"Okay," Winona said. "Let's—"

"Oh god, no, please," Arlo interrupted. "Spare us another one of those awful parlor games."

"Hey." Della whacked her brother on the arm. "Speak for yourself."

"Thank you, Della," Winona said, smiling sweetly at her. "But what I was going to say"—she shot death rays at Arlo—"was I think it's time to go around the table and tell one another what we're thankful for today. I know it's not Thanksgiving, but Christmas is a time for reflection, too, and we're so lucky to have full bellies and a warm house and clothes on our backs when so many don't."

"Hear, hear," Burl said.

"Good." Winona beamed. "Why don't you start first, Burl?"

Burl turned to his wife. "Cora, you go first, sweetheart."

"I'm thankful for Suzanne," she said, her eyes twinkling with mischief. "We look forward to spending many more Christmases with her."

Grady went very still beside her as Suzanne's cheeks heated. She knew Cora was aware of the real situation between Grady and herself, but it seemed like she wasn't above meddling, either.

"Me too," Burl chipped in. "Suzanne's been like a breath of fresh air at the ranch."

There was a general murmur of consent around the table, but Grady said nothing, his jaw tight, his smile not reaching his eyes. He obviously hated how Burl and Cora had built up their hopes despite his warnings.

They went around the table next, the relative newcomers, including Della, naming different aspects of their new town they were grateful for. Little Henry was unanimous in his decision—his new daddy was the best Christmas present ever, followed closely by his baby sister inside his mommy's tummy.

"Rocket ship cookies," Drew said with a smile.

Simone didn't hesitate when it came around to her. "Angels," she said, followed quickly by Albie saying, "Snow angels," and then smiling at his wife like they were eighteen again.

Then it was Grady's turn. "What about you,

Grady? And you can't say Suzanne," Winona ordered.

Suzanne felt like all eyes were on *her* as Grady considered his answer. She held her breath as she smiled at him with something she hoped looked like adoration and not some weird kind of facial palsy. "Tacky Christmas T-shirts, of course," he said after a considered pause, which got some laughs.

"Your turn, babe," Winona said, her voice soft, her eyes gentle as she delivered an encouraging squeeze to Suzanne's thigh.

Suzanne glanced at Grady, his expression carefully neutral. *Blizzards*. That's what she wanted to say. But given how much destruction they could wreak, she didn't think anybody but Grady would understand. Her gaze fell to the table, landing on the snow globe sitting there all garish and awful next to her empty bowl. "Muses," she said, deliberately not looking at Grady as she picked it up and shook it, causing a flurry of snow. "I'm grateful for muses."

"Good answer," Winona said with another squeeze to Suzanne's leg, and somewhere inside Suzanne, her muse preened.

"What about you?" Drew asked Winona. "You're the last one."

Their hostess grinned, raising her glass above her head. "Eggnog," she said, then toasted them all. "Merry Christmas, everyone."

• • •

It was seven before Grady stopped the pickup outside the back door to the cabin. Suzanne's parents had already disembarked from their vehicle and had barely stopped to say good night before disappearing into the cottage. No money for guessing why they were in such a hurry.

Looked like that had all ended well, at least.

"You're not coming in?' Suzanne asked when Grady kept the engine running.

"In a bit. I've got to check on a bull."

She quirked an eyebrow at him, her expression disbelieving. "Really?"

"Yes," Grady said, his voice steely, his gaze on hers. "It's why I was late this morning. I had to get the vet in and now *yes*, I'm sorry, but I've got to check on the animal."

"Oh…crap, sorry. Of course you have to deal with a sick animal. Why didn't you say anything this morning, for god's sake?"

Because keeping her at arm's length was easier when she was pissed at him than when her eyes were all sympathetic and her mouth was all soft and kissable. Grady shrugged. "We were in a hurry."

For a moment, Grady thought she was going to push back against his excuse, but then she nodded and glanced away, reaching for her seat belt and unclicking it. "I'll see you later."

On impulse, he grabbed her hand as she opened the door and turned away. "It's just in the yards behind the barn, so it shouldn't take me long. Let's talk when I get in." She glanced over her shoulder, her gaze settling on their hands. Grady admired how they fit together before remembering how he'd dropped that very hand like a hot coal this afternoon when he'd realized everyone's eyes were on them. It had been purely reactionary—muscle memory from years of rigid control over how he acted in public. But he'd sensed her stiffen, felt her withdrawal, and he knew he'd hurt her.

Which wasn't what he'd wanted. He just wanted things to get back to normal around here, damn it.

"Okay," she murmured, her hand slipping out of his as she slid out of the pickup and shut the door. He wondered with a sudden thump to his solar plexus if she'd slip out of his life as easily.

Grady was back within the hour. Suzanne was sitting on the couch reading but obviously waiting for him as she sprang to her feet. Part of him had hoped she'd given up and gone to bed and they could just avoid this conversation altogether even though he'd suggested it. He'd even contemplated lingering in the barn, but he'd never been a coward, and he wasn't about to start now.

She'd changed into those plaid pajamas he knew he was going to be dreaming about for a very long time, and he felt conspicuous in his Ho one Henley after he'd shrugged out of his coat.

"Is the bull okay?"

"Yep. Much improved."

"Oh…that's good."

"It is." He strode to Zoom's tank, the need to be active suddenly a driving force. "Should be able to join the rest of the herd in a couple of days." Grady felt her gaze right between his shoulder blades as he pushed the tank lid back a little. "Hey, Zoom," he greeted. "Hungry, little guy? Of course you are." He opened the container of turtle pellets. "You're always hungry; you should be way too fat for your shell, buster."

Grady tossed in the usual amount and watched as Zoom proceeded to snap them up.

"Are you still in love with her?"

The question dropped like a huge boulder into a still pond, and everything seemed to stop for a beat or two—all sound and thought and action—before a tsunami of ripples buffeted his body. Grady turned, his heart beating slowly and forcefully. "What?"

She looked surprised but stoic. Like she couldn't quite believe she'd asked the question, but now that it was out, she wasn't retracting. "Are you still in love with her?" she repeated.

"With Bethany?"

"Yes." Suzanne rolled her eyes. "Bethany."

God…where had *that* come from? "Because… of Zoom? I don't understand… Turtles live for a long time. Should I have…given him away or something?"

"No, of course not. I just mean…" She faltered like she couldn't really articulate what she meant now or where the question had come from. "According to Cora, there's been nobody else *since* Bethany. In *seventeen* years. So…you must still be in love with her, right?"

"Yes."

It was an automatic answer to a question he hadn't been asked or thought to ask himself for a long time. *Of course* he still loved Bethany. She was his first crush. His first girlfriend. His first kiss, his first…*everything*. And she'd been sweet and lovely and smart and funny, and it had been so fucking unfair that she'd been taken from this world when she'd had so much to offer.

Of course he still loved Bethany.

But…that wasn't the question Suzanne had asked. She'd asked if he was still *in* love with Bethany. And, Grady realized, as he stood in front of this woman who had driven him crazy for three weeks that he wasn't. He wasn't *in* love with Bethany anymore.

And that he hadn't been for a very long time. That somewhere along the way in the intervening years, time had done what time usually did—it had healed. Bethany…his parents…it still ached to think of what he lost, but it wasn't a big black-and-purple bruise anymore or even a yellowed, fading one. It was a scar. Like the one from the shrapnel. A reminder of the pain and injury but fully healed.

He just hadn't realized.

Or maybe he had and that had scared the bejesus out of him, so he'd doubled down on all those old feelings, hoarding them close, like a kid with candy, because it gave him a shield and a reason to keep away from people and situations that could wound.

Like falling in love again.

But then Suzanne had landed in his life like a fucking one-woman SEAL team and blown that all to hell. He swallowed. Jesus Christ…

Yes, he still loved Bethany. And he always would in the way that a first love *does* claim a piece of a heart. But God help him, he was *in love* with Suzanne St. Michelle.

Fuck. A blaring red warning light *whop-whop-whopped* in his head.

When had that happened? *When?* A sick feeling of dread sank to the bottom of his stomach as he realized it didn't matter when, that what mattered was that it happened at all. And what he was going to do about it. Because he'd already loved and lost once—there was no way he was ever traveling that road again.

"I will always love Bethany," he said, his pulse loud in his ears. He'd been pushing Suzanne away since the day after the blizzard. Now he needed to shove.

"What?" She gave a brittle kind of half laugh. "There's never going to be any room for anyone else? Sounds lonely."

"Being alone and being lonely aren't the same thing." Grady knew that too well. He'd not felt lonely these past three years on the ranch, although he had a bad feeling that was going to change. Thanks to Little Miss Chatty.

"Maybe. But everyone needs love, Grady."

He shook his head. "Not me." He *couldn't* go there again.

"You love Burl. And Cora."

"Yeah." He nodded. "I do."

And that only made his point. Thinking about how much he loved his aunt and uncle was gut-wrenching. Neither of them was getting any younger, and at some point, they were going to leave him, too.

Damn it, he hadn't asked to be taken in and loved by them. Why had the universe sent them in his direction? Why had it sent Suzy? Hadn't it fucked with him enough?

She took a step toward him. "What if I didn't return to New York?"

"What?" An instant leap of panic caused Grady to take a step back. *"Why?"* Clearly the universe *hadn't* fucked with him enough.

"I think I want to stay and paint here. Make Credence my home."

"You *think*?" No. Absolutely not. It was going to be hard enough shoring up his heart and turning his back knowing she was in New York. If she was here in Credence?

No. Just no.

"I know." She nodded with conviction. "It's the right thing creatively. I feel it."

A clash of questions roared around like a NASCAR rally inside Grady's head, all battling to be heard—a lot of them too big and too scary. So he chose something easier. "Where would you stay?"

A harsh half laugh slipped from her mouth. "Don't worry, Grady, I won't set up a tent in your front field. I think I'll buy land out by the lake, near Winona."

Grady frowned. The lake was a forty-minute ride from the ranch. But still way too close for his liking. Hell, New York wasn't far enough. Who was he kidding? *Australia* would be too close.

"You don't approve?"

Taking a breath, reining in his pulse and the desperation that was riding him, Grady chose his words carefully. Time to be smart. Strategic. Be military. If he stomped around in his boots demanding she leave Colorado and never come back, it could backfire. He hadn't forgotten how riled up Suzy could get. But if he was cool and reasoned, if he appealed to her intellectually rather than emotionally, maybe she'd see sense.

"Look…I know it's none of my business, and I can see it's probably a good move for your painting. For your…muse. And it's a free country. I can't *stop* you from living here."

Her lips twisted. "But you don't *want* me here."

Grady swallowed. He *did* want her here. But what he *wanted* didn't matter. Having Suzy in Credence wasn't what was *best* for him, and that's what mattered. Clearing his voice and expression of any emotion, he said, "No. I don't."

"Why?"

Her earnest demand was like a knife to Grady's heart as she wrapped her arms around her middle and searched his face.

"If you don't care about me, why do you care where I live?"

"Because I think that I might be part of the reason you want to move here, even if you're not prepared to admit it yet and, if that's the case, I'm trying to save you a whole lot of time and effort. I'm a lost cause, Suzy."

That there was the truth. It didn't matter if he loved her or not. He was paralyzed by the grief of his past. Powerless to move forward by the long reach of its pain. He may have healed from the intensity of loss, but he could never forget how devastating it was to lose someone.

Too devastating to risk it again.

"God, Grady…" She took a step toward him. "It doesn't have to be that way."

"You don't get it," he said, raising his voice as a wave of emotion rose in his chest at her naiveté. He was fighting for his emotional life here, damn it. "I *like* it that way." Why couldn't she just leave it be? "Now, if you can put your hand on your heart and tell me that there's *no* part of you holding out a chance for us, then welcome to Credence and have a great life. But if you can't, then please, I'm *begging* you—" He laid his hand on his heart because he didn't know what he'd do if she stayed, and he didn't even want to go there. "Don't bother. Go back to New York. Do your art. Sign your paintings. Find a New York guy. Have New York babies."

Fuck… The thought that she'd find a New York guy was like a knife to his guts, but just because he'd chosen to be alone didn't mean she should. Hell, it would be a *travesty*.

She, at least, should be happy.

But that thought right now *burned*, and he had to leave, get out of her company before he undid all the hard yards he'd just walked. "Please," he said, his gaze imploring her as his hand slid from his chest and he turned and walked out of the room.

• • •

Suzanne didn't sleep a wink, tossing and turning, making excuses in her head, listing reasons to stay. For her art and her muse. And because she was a grown-ass woman and she could live wherever she wanted. But it was no use. She knew Grady was right.

She could tell herself as much as she wanted that she was here for her art, but there would always be some blinking light of hope inside her that one day Joshua Grady would just wake up and decide he couldn't live without her. And eventually, it would drive her crazy. So as much as she felt that staying was the best decision for her painting, Suzanne chose to protect her heart instead.

And that meant leaving.

She made that decision at 4:34 a.m. and lay awake counting down the minutes until Grady left. She heard footsteps in the hallway just before six and listened to the noises of Grady getting ready for his day for the last time, refusing to cry. Half an hour later, the door opened, then clicked shut, and Suzanne got out of bed.

She spent the next two hours packing, getting everything ready to stow in the van, refusing to let herself think emotionally, forcing herself to be practical.

Including leaving the portrait of Grady behind in her room.

Prior to last night, she'd have laughed at the suggestion of leaving without it. But now…

The thought of taking it away from this place where it was created was inconceivable. Like the man himself, it belonged here, not in New York. It was her gift to him—given freely this time.

Not traded, not used as a bargaining chip.

Maybe he could stop her from staying, stop her

from trying to reach him, but he couldn't stop her from loving him and hopefully, one day, he'd be able to see that love right there in his portrait.

Fixing a note to the corner, Suzanne took an unsteady breath and turned her back on it, forcing her legs out of the room.

She had to go tell her parents they were leaving.

CHAPTER TWENTY-THREE

They ended up at the boardinghouse because Suzanne hadn't thought that far ahead—leaving had been her priority. Plus, she'd wanted to say goodbye to Winona. But with snow still being a problem in the eastern states, driving wasn't that safe, particularly in her Scooby van, which was borderline roadworthy in the best of conditions. And flights out of Denver for her parents were impossible at the moment because of Christmas and the backlog of canceled flights the airlines were still dealing with due to the blizzard. The earliest they could book was for the twenty-ninth.

Winona persuaded them to stay at the boardinghouse. She had a comfy sofa in her room where Suzanne could sleep, and Marley and Molly were happy to move into one room temporarily for Albie and Simone to have a bed. Suzanne went along with the plan because she was too mentally exhausted and heartsick to do anything other than stare into space a lot—and because there was a part of her that felt while she was still in Credence, there was still hope.

Which made her the worst kind of fool.

It took two days for Suzanne to talk to her parents. To confess all. They'd given her space, so had Winona, but she knew they wanted to help, wanted to understand, and she owed them the truth. About *everything*. So in front of the fire on the second night with a glass of red wine in hand and Winona there, too, she fessed up.

About her muse returning. About the paintings she'd done of Grady and him discovering them. About how she'd lied about Grady because she hadn't wanted to go home for Christmas.

"I'm sorry," she said to her parents as her dad frowned and her mom covered her mouth with her hand, obviously surprised at the information. "I just didn't want to spend another Christmas with a coat hanger tree and one lonely blue bulb."

Her mother patted her knee, and Suzanne continued, but she still felt bad about the admission. *And* how the lie had gotten out of hand, apologizing to her parents for not being honest and walking it back. She told them all about bribing Grady, *who hated Christmas*, to help her. About the Hokiest Christmas Ever plan.

"You just seemed so sad on the phone, Mom. About you and Dad. And your marriage. So I just came up with this ridiculous idea of pushing you together because I was sure you'd fall in love again if you spent time together."

"Well, you were right about that," Albie said, smiling at Simone.

Suzanne smiled, too, before continuing, telling her sorry story about the lines blurring and falling in love with Grady. About the blizzard. And the portrait she'd painted. And Bethany. And how she'd decided to move to Credence and become an artist in her own right, but she couldn't bear to face Grady's rejection every day, so she was going home.

Everything. She left nothing out.

Well…she didn't go into any of the *intimate* details, but everything else, talking almost nonstop for an hour.

"Oh, darling." Simone put an arm around her daughter's shoulders and pulled her in until Suzanne's head was resting in the crook of her neck. "You did that for us?"

"I didn't mean for it to get so out of hand, but I wanted to help," Suzanne admitted.

"It's our fault," her mother said. "If you hadn't felt like you needed to escape to *eastern Colorado* to get the kind of Christmas you wanted, this would never have happened."

Maybe. But it was pointless making a chicken-or-the-egg argument now. And it was no excuse for letting things get so out of hand. Suzanne wasn't going to compound her stupidity by trying to excuse it or find a scapegoat. She was an adult who had dug this hole all by herself.

"Have you told Grady how you feel?" Winona asked.

Suzanne shook her head. "No." She hadn't been able to utter the words in the face of his determination to push her away. She'd held off from baring all, needing to keep something back, to protect the thing that was most precious to her heart. Telling him she wanted to stay and being rejected had been hard. Having her *love* similarly rejected would have been devastating.

Having her hand dropped like a hot potato on Christmas Day had been bad enough.

"I kind of wore my heart on my sleeve, though.

I don't think it would have been that difficult for him to read between the lines."

"Oh, babe. Men can be surprisingly dumb when it comes to reading between the lines."

There was silence for a beat or two as everyone contemplated the lick of flames in the fireplace. "Are you sure he's not in love with you?" Simone asked out of the blue.

Suzanne pulled out of her mother's embrace and looked at her. "What?"

"I honestly thought you shacking up in Colorado with a rancher was some kind of joke until that first day we met him and he kissed you hello. He seemed *really* into you."

"That was acting, Mom."

"Was it? Because there was a definite spark between the two of you. Even your father remarked about it later when we were alone."

Oh, there'd been sparks all right. From the beginning. But sexual attraction wasn't love. She could find that in the arms of plenty of men. Love was rare.

Albie nodded. "The man could barely keep his hands off you."

"And look what he did for you," her mother added. "You tell us that Grady's supposedly this closed-off kinda guy, yet he helped you. He tolerated his house being wrapped in tinsel and lights and all kinds of Christmas crap that should never see the light of day, and he lied for you and carried on with a charade he didn't agree with and put up with your parents in his cottage. He didn't do that for us—he did it for you."

Suzanne shook her head. "He did it for the paintings."

"I don't know," her father said. "He's a big guy. Seems to me he could just have taken them from you if he wanted them that badly."

"It's against the law to steal, Dad."

"Maybe. Or maybe he knew how much they meant to you."

Suzanne thought her parents were reading far too much into the situation. Which was very sweet, but ultimately it didn't really matter because Grady had gotten them all off her one way or another anyway.

"And then there's other things as well," Simone continued. "I don't think I've ever seen you as happy as you have been these past couple of weeks, darling. You can be a little on the serious side, but you've been laughing and smiling all the time and just...reveling in the Christmas madness you created all around you. And you've been painting again. Original work. Because of him. That's marvelous. I can't wait to see it."

Suzanne snorted, thinking about Grady's head painted on a cherub. "I'm not sure you'd say that if you saw it."

"Well, as I'm coming to understand, art is in the eye of the beholder." Simone reached her hand out to Albie, and he smiled. "I'm also coming to understand that if you love someone, you should tell them. You should tell them and show them every day. And you should definitely fight for it."

"Speaking as the resident *luurve* expert," Winona said, "I concur. You should fight for love."

"Oh god." Suzanne shook her head. Were none of them listening to her? "He doesn't love me." He loved Bethany.

"Babe…" Winona squeezed Suzanne's thigh. "Just because he can't or *won't* say the words doesn't mean he doesn't love you."

Suzanne looked into Winona's earnest eyes. She wanted to believe that so much. But even if it was true, if Grady was determined not to act on his feelings because he was still clinging to his love for Bethany or he was just too broken, then wasn't it all just moot?

She'd never met a more stubborn man.

"Maybe he just needs some time and space to realize what he's turning his back on?" Winona suggested.

"Winona's right," her father said. "Maybe you should stick around, give him some time to miss you, then turn up on his doorstep and tell him you love him. Going back to New York is like admitting defeat when you haven't even pulled out your big guns yet."

The advice made good sense, but they didn't know Joshua Grady's resolve like she did. "He's ex-military, Dad. He can outgun me any day. And the only ammunition I really had is gone. Probably on a bonfire as we speak."

"You mean the paintings?" Winona clarified.

The thought of them being destroyed was an ache in her chest. "Yeah."

"Okay. Well…that's perfect." She put down her wineglass and sat forward, glancing sideways at Suzanne, a grin on her face. "Paint more."

"What?"

"If that's your ammunition, if that's what it takes to make him take notice, then paint more."

Suzanne stared at her friend. "What? No." She couldn't go down that road again. Could she?

"Yes. And put them up in public somewhere. Knowing how private Grady is, he'll hate that. Make him come and get them. Make him come to you."

"Annie's," Suzanne said without even thinking. "I threatened to do that once."

Winona snapped her fingers. "Yes! That's perfect. She wants paintings for the diner. And you're looking for somewhere to hang yours."

Suzanne looked at all three of them. "I couldn't." She couldn't do that to him again—could she?

"Why not?" her mother asked, also sitting forward now.

"It might work," her father agreed.

"It might not," Suzanne said.

What if he didn't even care enough to come and take a look? Although Winona was right. He did hate being the subject of public speculation so it *might* just work. And damn if the idea wasn't starting to grow on her.

It would be easy enough. She could paint Joshua Grady drunk, blindfolded, and with one hand tied behind her back. She knew every plane, dip, and freckle on his body.

"I guess I could just…paint more." It seemed so simple. Too simple. But maybe it *would* work. Maybe leaving Credence *was* admitting defeat, and why was she giving up so damn easily without putting everything on the table first?

God knew her muse was already buzzing at the prospect.

"Hell yeah you could," Winona agreed.

Suzanne stood, her heart rate picking up as the now-familiar flow of creative energy pulsed like a life force from the tips of her toes to the top of her head. "I could even start now."

Her mother also stood. "I can prep canvases."

Albie stood. "I'll grab your stuff out of the van."

"And I'll keep your glass and belly full and remind you to shower once a day," Winona offered.

Suzanne felt excited and jittery and like bursting into tears all at once. She had no idea if any of this was going to make a dent in Grady's armor whatsoever, but she was fired up enough to give it one more try. "Thank you," she whispered as she gathered her three coconspirators in for a group hug. "Thank you for the pep talk."

She just hoped it worked.

• • •

Reminiscent of her first days in Credence, Suzanne painted for three days solid. The sun shined and the snow melted outside and her parents canceled their flights and moved out to a hotel on the interstate they would never normally be caught dead in, so they could stay on and help. She produced nine portraits of Grady in all his many-splendored forms—the surly rancher, the reluctant nephew, the reclusive loner, the generous lover.

They were less detailed and half the size of the others and also he was dressed because this wasn't an exercise in trying to embarrass him—it was a proclamation. Suzanne, wearing her heart on her sleeve and proclaiming her love for Joshua Grady to everyone in Credence.

He'd wanted to keep their fake relationship a secret from the town because he hadn't wanted to be the subject of gossip or pity when she'd gone back to New York and, three weeks ago, that had been fair enough. But things had changed. She'd fallen in love with him, and *she* didn't want to keep that quiet. She wanted the whole damn world to know.

And it started with these paintings.

Every expression she'd seen flit across Grady's face was there. His pain and his anguish. His steely concentration and his frustrating recalcitrance. His amusement. His desire. The gentleness in his eyes when he'd assured her about the portrait, the muted grief she'd seen when he'd talked about his parents, and his torment as he'd admitted his love for his aunt and uncle. The tilt of his mouth when he was relaxed in sleep and his intensity just before he kissed her.

Her love was right there for all to see, just as it was in the nude portrait she'd painted during the blizzard except, this time, she was aware she was doing it and she laid it on *thick*.

She also painted some landscapes as alive and vital as the portraits.

The outside of Annie's. The boardinghouse. The old red barn on Harkins Street. The park where they'd had a snowball fight on Christmas Day. Suzanne had caught the play of winter light on cold ground, a sunbeam shining in a bead of liquid hanging from a frozen cobweb and the glisten of frost on anemic grass. She'd captured the peel of paint, the well-worn furrows in a railing, the echo of children's laughter in snowy footprints.

And she signed all of them.

Annie was throwing a New Year's Eve event and *Suzy* was the special guest—her first informal *gallery* showing and the landscapes were going to be auctioned, the proceeds going to the old folks' home.

Burl had assured her Grady would come to the event, but she wasn't so sure. He was probably immune by now to portraits of himself, and while he might cringe at being the center of attention, she didn't think that trumped his desire to never see her again.

Unless, of course, Winona's plan worked and the idea of her painting more portraits of him made him mad as hell and he stormed in and ripped them all down. He would have done exactly that four weeks ago, and frankly, she'd prefer that to the way he'd shut her out a week ago.

Spinning around the makeshift gallery, taking in all her paintings, Suzanne felt sick with doubt and worry. God…why had she let her mom and dad and Winona talk her into this?

What if Grady didn't come? Hell…what if he did?

• • •

At four o'clock in the afternoon on New Year's Eve, Grady was sitting on an Adirondack chair on his front porch amid a mountain of tinsel, garland, and an absolute tangle of Christmas lights no one was ever going to be able to undo. He'd tossed the Christmas tree, complete with all the awful baubles, over the railing of the porch like a fucking great Scottish caber. It leaned drunkenly half on said railing, half across the bottom of the stairs.

He'd been ignoring all Suzy's Christmas shit in the cabin for days now, but he'd come home in an absolutely foul mood to an empty, screamingly quiet cabin. No terrible chipmunk carols playing, no cooking aromas, no welcoming smile. And the decorations had been like a red flag to a bull. Wasn't it bad enough that she was in his every waking thought and all his sleeping ones? Did he have to be reminded of her everywhere he *looked*, too?

He'd torn them all down in a frenzy an hour ago. He felt much better. The bourbon was helping with that, too.

The sound of an engine drifted to him on the chilly afternoon air, and he flicked his gaze to the drive to see Burl's vehicle approaching. Perfect. *Just perfect.* His uncle pulled up in front of the porch a minute later and climbed out of the car, his eyebrows raised as he stepped around the tree to mount the stairs, then skirted Mount Christmas to get to the other Adirondack chair.

Picking up the mostly deflated giant Santa Claus slumped in the seat, he tossed it on top of the pile, where it promptly slid down and face-planted on the floorboards. "We have a tornado I don't know about?"

Assuming the question was rhetorical, Grady didn't bother to answer.

"What's going on, son?"

Grady took a mouthful of his drink, staring straight ahead out over the field. "Nuthin'."

"Sure is quiet out here without Suzanne flitting around."

Gripping his tumbler, Grady said, "Just the way I like it."

"Uh-huh." Burl looked at the mess on the porch. "I can see that." He stood. "Mind if I fix myself a drink?"

Grady shrugged. "Be my guest."

Burl was gone for less than a minute. He returned with the bottle and a tumbler. And the portrait that had been propped against the kitchen bench after he'd removed it from her room, the note still attached. Grady groaned internally as Burl placed it against the balustrades and studied it for a while.

"That's you?"

Grady didn't look. "Uh-huh."

"She paint it?"

"Uh-huh."

"It's a little…too much information for me."

"Me too," Grady said. Having his uncle staring at his junk was not one of the more comfortable moments they'd shared.

"Note says it's a gift."

Grady knew exactly what the note said. He'd read it about a hundred times.

Dear Grady,
Please accept this as a gift.
It belongs here with you. I hope one day you see what I see when I look at it.
Suzy.

The fact that she'd left early and while he was gone hadn't been terribly surprising. He'd welcomed it. The fact that she hadn't taken the portrait had been shocking. He knew how much it meant to her—or at least he'd thought he'd known. Her first original artwork.

But she'd just…left it behind. So how much had it really meant?

A part of him had reconciled when he'd come home to the empty cabin that at least she'd have something of him with her in New York. And then he'd found the portrait in her room, and it had felt like a kick to the nuts.

"You want to talk about it?"

Grady would rather redecorate the cabin for Easter than talk with Burl about this ache in his chest as wide and desolate as the field he was staring at. "Nope."

"Son, you know from old, bottling things up doesn't work."

"Answer's still no."

"Okay," Burl said cheerfully, making his way to the top step and sitting down. "I'll go first."

"Burl."

"I think you're in love with Suzanne St. Michelle."

Grady shut his eyes as Burl dragged the giant fucking elephant in the room right into the light.

No shit, Sherlock. But he didn't *want* to love Suzy. He didn't want to love *anybody*. And when she'd left, he told himself he was relieved. That he could get on with his life. That it was for the best.

It was just that...everything was so fucking *quiet.*

"You want me to go again?" Burl asked, breaking into Grady's silence. "Okay. I think you're running scared because you're in love with her. Because in seventeen years you've not let a single person get too close to you—including Cora and me—and you don't know what to do because despite your best efforts to keep her out, she's snuck in anyway. How am I doin'?"

"Bite me, Burl," Grady growled.

His uncle laughed, and Grady remembered how it had always been Burl, not Cora, who'd been able to distill Grady's emotions. He was really fucking irritating like that.

"It doesn't matter," Grady finally said, his heart weighing a ton in his chest.

"What doesn't?"

"Loving her." Although this knot of feelings inside him didn't feel like love. Like the fresh, first love he'd felt for Bethany. It was twisted and messy. And so fucking deep, he doubted he'd ever find the bottom of it.

"Oh yeah. How you figure that?"

"She's not cut out for this kind of life. She's a New Yorker. It was one of the first damn things she said to me. She's used to art galleries and a pizza place on every corner. She doesn't understand ranch life. She sleeps late and paints all night. She waits up for me and gets mad if I don't answer a text. She doesn't realize a ranch is twenty-four-seven, *including* Christmas. That it takes over your life."

"Well, sure." Burl shrugged. "It'd be a learning curve. But that should be her decision, don't you think? Cora worked in a lab in Denver when I first met her. You think she knew anything about ranching?"

Grady blinked. "She did?" He knew his aunt was from near Denver, but he'd always assumed she'd come off the land.

"Yup." Burl nodded. "And you and I both know, son, you could put on more hands or hire a foreman to cut your workload significantly. The ranch taking over your life is your choice, Grady, and a dumb one at that."

Burl had been beating this drum for the last three years, but it really needled today. "I've known her for less than a month," Grady said, irritation making him short.

"I proposed to Cora after three days."

Grady rolled his eyes. "She said no."

"Yeah." Burl chuckled. "She made me sweat it out for a few more months."

Having heard the Cora and Burl courting story more times than he cared to remember, another retelling was about more than he could stand right now.

"She's in love with you, you know."

Grady's heart thumped hard in his chest. "Did she tell you that?" Because she'd left the portrait, and if she loved him, she *wouldn't* have left the portrait. He knew that as surely as he knew all this Christmas crap around him was going to cause a helluva toxic cloud over Credence when he set it all on fire.

Burl pointed two fingers at his head. "I have *eyes*."

There was so much certainty in his uncle's voice, it gave Grady pause. But even if it was true, it didn't change the facts. Loving someone left you vulnerable. "I can't… I just…"

"What, Grady?" Burl said, searching his nephew's face in earnest. "*What?* Talk to me."

"Don't you ever think about Aunt Cora dying? About how *gutting*"—Grady blinked back the hot burn of tears and cleared the tightness in his throat—"that's going to be?"

"Oh…Grady." His uncle shook his head. "Of course. But if she'd been taken from me after just one day of loving her, it would have been worth every second." Burl put his glass down on the step. "Look, son, the damage is already done. You're *already* in love with her. It's not going to stop or go away just because you don't want to be. The decision now is whether you get to be happy for as long as it lasts or be miserable forever because you're too scared to take a risk. And, son…surely it's time to stop being miserable?"

Grady knew his uncle was speaking sense. He *did* love Suzanne. It was there right alongside his love for Cora and Burl. And the ranch. Glowing and hopeful.

But terrifying also.

Burl pushed to his feet and tipped his chin at

the painting. "You going to hang that?"

"Nope." It was too damn painful to look at.

"Well, if you're just going to shut it away somewhere, you might as well donate it for other people to appreciate."

Grady snorted. "Thanks. I think I'll keep my junk to myself. Besides, where in the hell would I donate it around here?"

"To Annie's. She's got quite the collection of you now. At least two on every wall. You're clothed in all of them, so a nude might raise an eyebrow or two, but—"

"Wait." Grady frowned. "What do you mean she's got quite the collection of me?"

"Didn't you know? Suzanne's been painting up a storm. They're not all of you; there's some landscapes as well."

Grady's brain felt like it had been switched to slow mo. *Suzanne was still in town?* "Why?" he asked, his head in a spin.

"Annie wanted art for her walls, and they thought they could turn the diner into a gallery of sorts for a fund-raiser tonight for the old folks' home. They're going to auction off the landscapes. Reckon most of the town will be there. Annie's even got one of those sparkly confetti canon thingies for midnight."

"No." Grady shook his head. "I mean, why did she stay?" And why hadn't his uncle said so earlier?

Burl shrugged. "I don't think she was ready to leave yet." He looked at his nephew pointedly. "You should come tonight. Cora and I will be there."

"Ah…nope." Go to Annie's, where his face was on every wall? Where everyone would be staring at him in stereo? And talking about *why*? Only his worst nightmare.

He may be in love with Suzanne, but he wasn't going to put that on display in front of the whole damn town. Not when he wasn't sure she loved him back. Burl might think she did, but the portrait against the balustrades—the one that meant so much to her and she'd left behind—said otherwise.

"Well…" Burl walked down to the next step. "If you change your mind, you know where we'll be."

Grady nodded. "Night, Burl."

His uncle made a detour around the tree at the bottom of the steps and was in his pickup and gone in less than a minute, leaving Grady alone with dozens of clashing thoughts and his portrait staring back at him.

Grady managed to distract himself for a few hours with office work before heading to his bedroom to take a shower. Flicking the light on, it spotlighted the portrait he'd placed on his bed earlier. Despite himself, he wandered over to it, gazing down at it again. Reading the note for what felt like the hundredth time.

I hope one day you see what I see when I look at it.

What did she see that he didn't? *What?*

And then, suddenly, as if a portal had opened to another world—he saw it. Maybe it was the way the light was shining directly down, or maybe he was looking at it through a different lens now than when he'd first laid eyes on the portrait.

But he saw it. All of it.

She'd depicted so much that he'd missed. His pain. His suffering. His *healing*. Sure, he looked well laid, but that was just part of it. She'd captured his love for her, right there in his face. Love he hadn't even been aware of at that point. And even more than that, there was *her love for him*, so obvious in every brushstroke, every nuance of his expression. She'd endowed the portrait with her feelings for him, and now that he could see it, the painting practically glowed with love.

She loved him. Suzanne St. Michelle loved him. And that's why she'd left the portrait. She was telling him through her art what she hadn't been able to tell him to his face because he'd been so fucking implacable.

Grady sat on the bed as a rush of emotion almost took his knees out from under him. Burl was right; loving Suzanne wasn't going to stop or go away because it hurt him too much to contemplate. And ignoring it, choosing to have nothing to do with her, wasn't going to shield him from the deep abyss of grief if, god forbid, something terrible did happen to her. He was in love with her, and it was going to hurt to lose her whether he was *with* her or not.

So he had a choice to make. Be happy with her, make a life with her for however long they might have together. Or be alone and miserable.

And fucking *word* it was time to stop being miserable.

Grady stood, his lungs suddenly too big for his

chest. He had to go to Annie's and hope like hell he hadn't ruined any chance he had with Suzanne. Yes, even if that meant doing it in front of the whole damn town. In fact, it was probably better if he did. Public spectacles weren't his thing, but the town was going to know soon enough, so they might as well hear it straight from the horse's mouth.

Although horse's ass was probably a more apt description.

Grady's brain scrambled as he headed for his bedroom door and briskly walked through the cabin, grabbing the keys off the hook, his heart pumping in anticipation and terror. He stalled as he reached the back door, a sudden thought stopping him in his tracks.

He'd screwed up big-time—pushing her away like that. So he had to make it up to her big-time. Prove that he meant what he said, and for that he needed the portrait. And a dumb Christmas sweater.

• • •

By nine o'clock, Suzanne had given up hope of Grady walking through the diner door. She'd gone through all the emotions, from nervous, to relieved, to really freaking pissed. And now she was just sad that he hadn't even cared enough to come and see her first-ever exhibition. Burl was still optimistic, but Suzanne wasn't. Grady was an early to bed, early to rise kinda guy.

Even on New Year's Eve.

So she put her disappointment and her *what the*

hell next planning aside to think about another time. She was wearing a dress and heels and the diner was packed—standing room only—and everybody wanted to talk to her. They loved her work. And not just the Grady paintings, although she did get a lot of questions about her choice of subject. They loved the landscapes, too, and so many people had asked her if she took commissions. Suzanne knew she could set up in Credence as an artist tomorrow and not starve.

Sure, she wouldn't be able to charge anywhere near the prices she could charge for her forgeries, but she could work on both, and the more she chatted and mingled with the locals, the more convinced she was to make the move Grady had talked her out of.

And he could just deal with it.

"What do you say about Ray and me here, posing for a portrait?" Bob Downey said as he and Ray sidled up to Suzanne. He put his arm around Ray's shoulder, and they both adopted blank, distant expressions worthy of Mt. Rushmore.

"Very distinguished," Suzanne said with a laugh.

"Suzy!"

Suzanne startled as a deep, familiar voice cut through the chatter of the diner. *Grady?* Her pulse spiked.

"Suzy!"

She turned in the direction his voice seemed to be coming from, although she couldn't see him through the bodies. But suddenly, as if by magic, the crowd parted, and he was striding toward her in jeans and that elf sweater he'd sworn he'd never wear in public. Not even for a blow job. His long legs ate up the space between them, his gaze intense, his face as implacable as ever. She had no idea if he was angry or not, but even in that ridiculous elf sweater, she couldn't take her eyes off him.

He was carrying a large canvas in his hands. *The portrait?*

"Grady?"

Her pulse was hammering at her temples as her eyes darted all around at the spectators agog with the unfolding drama. For a guy who hated gossip and being the center of attention, he was attracting an awful lot. Was he going to yell at her in front of everyone? These people who already knew how much she loved him because it was in every single damn painting of him on Annie's walls.

And why did he have the portrait?

He addressed Annie, who was standing on Suzanne's right. "Annie. I'd like to make a donation to the gallery, please."

And then he turned the canvas around to reveal his reclined naked form, as breathtakingly alive with her love today as it had been the day she'd painted it. Hot tears pricked at the backs of Suzanne's eyes and needled her nose. A well of emotion in her throat threatened to choke off her air supply.

No one in the diner reacted at first. It took a beat or two for them to realize what they were seeing. Then everyone talked at once.

A guy at the back called out, "Hey, Grady, how

much did you pay her to embellish that?" And someone else, a woman, said, "I'll give you a hundred bucks." Another woman said, "I'll give you two."

Suzanne stepped forward, ignoring the impromptu auction going on around them—this painting was *not* for sale. "What are you doing?" she hissed, keeping her voice low, not that there was much worry they'd be overheard with all the noise.

"I saw it," he said, his hand slipping onto her arm and pulling her closer. "What you saw. In the portrait."

A pulse tap-danced at Suzanne's temple, her heart thudding the fandango. *He had?* "What did you see?"

"You love me."

Suzanne's legs went wobbly as a surge of relief washed through them, making her feel lighter than she had in weeks.

"I see it in all these other paintings, too," he said as he looked around the walls.

"Yeah. Sorry about that," she said, depressingly aware of how inconvenient it was for him. "I know that's not what you want."

"Don't be sorry. I'm absolutely terrified to admit that I'm in love with you, too."

Suzanne's pulse skipped a beat. *He loved her?* But he was still in love with Bethany. She looked around; the spectators had started to quiet and pretty soon would be hanging on their every word. "How about we go into the kitchen or something? For some privacy?"

"No." He looked around at all the faces watching him and shook his head. "I want everyone to hear this."

"You do?" Suzanne's gaze darted to Burl, who shrugged but seemed pretty damn happy anyway. So did Cora.

"Yes." He grabbed both her hands and held them clasped between their bodies. "I've been too caught up in my pride and my desire not to be pitied to realize that these people"—he gestured around him—"love me and would do anything for me. That they've been rooting for me to be healed and happy since I came to Credence seventeen years ago, and this declaration is as much for them as for you." He took a breath. "If that's okay?"

Suzanne nodded, also catching a breath as the crowd all seemed to lean in simultaneously.

"I screwed up. I told you to go, that there was no hope for me. I pushed you away, and I shouldn't have. *I screwed up*. I love you, and I'm sorry it took me so long to realize it. I thought I was too damaged to love again when what I've actually been terrified of is *living* again. But not anymore. I *want* to live. I want to live and laugh and be happy again, and I want to do it with you."

He took a breath, and Suzanne let out the one she'd been holding. *He loved her?* Her foolish heart leaped at those three little words from a man who wasn't used to saying them. But she didn't dare let it fly.

"I thought you were still in love with Bethany?"

"No." He shook his head. "I will always love Bethany. She's part of the story of my life, and she will always have a place in my heart. Just as my mom and dad will always have a place there, too. But I'm not *in* love with her, and I haven't been for a very long time. It was just easier to hold on to what *was* to stop myself from reaching for what could *be*."

Suzanne heard a couple of female sighs from the crowd and, if it had been happening to someone else, she might have even laughed at their melodrama. But it was happening to *her*.

"And that's you," he continued, giving her hands a gentle squeeze. "I'm *in* love with you. You crashed into my life and turned it upside down and inside out and my cabin, hell, *my life* is so damn quiet without you. Nothing's the same, and I don't want it to be, either."

Suzanne drew in a shaky breath. Grady loved her. He *loved* her. It was there in his words and shining in those pale-green eyes she'd come to know so well. She smiled. "For a man who doesn't say much, you sure know how to put words together."

The crowd laughed, and Grady finally cracked a smile. "I practiced all the way over."

There was more laughter, and Suzanne eased up on the tight reins holding her heart in check.

"Suzy." Grady's face went all serious again. "Will you come and live with me on the ranch? I know it's a huge ask to take you away from the city and all your friends and your colleagues and it might not be an easy transition, but I promise—"

Suzanne threw herself into Grady's arms, cutting him off abruptly. She'd heard enough. "Yes," she said. "I love you, Joshua Grady. A thousand times yes."

And she kissed him, twining her arms around his neck and going up on her tiptoes, much to the delight of the cheering crowd. Kissed him until someone called, "Get a room, you two," and they reluctantly parted.

"How soon can you move in?" he murmured when they finally pulled apart. "Do you need some time to be sure?"

Suzanne looked at the clock above the entrance. Two and a half hours till midnight. "How about next year?" she said with a smile.

He laughed. "I think I can wait that long."

Then, out of nowhere, people started to gasp and look up, and Suzanne and Grady looked up, too, as a blizzard of metallic confetti drifted down all around them. The kind of blizzard it was okay to be standing in and the perfect sparkly way to be starting the first day of the rest of their lives.

EPILOGUE

Four p.m., December 24th the following year…

Suzanne hooked a candy-cane earring into the hole in her ear as she made her way through the archway and into the living room. Grady was fiddling with the tree, and she totally checked out her husband's ass in his Wranglers as she crossed to him.

Husband. It had been two months, and she still loved the way it sounded.

"What are you doing?" she asked as she drew even.

He grinned at her. "These came yesterday." He held up a red bauble attached to a short plastic chain. Sitting on the bauble was a small vampy-looking doll dressed in a tiny white crop bra, panties, and brown boots straddling the chain.

Suzanne pressed her lips together, trying not to laugh, pretending to be scandalized. "Oh no… Joshua Grady, that's awful."

"I know, right?" He waggled his eyebrows. "There are green ones as well."

She laughed then, her heart full as she looked around the cabin that was, if possible, an even bigger Christmas train crash than last year because, this year, Grady was fully involved. They'd had so much fun trying to find the gaudiest Christmas ornaments, but wrecking ball baubles took the cake.

Grady had outdone himself, and Suzanne had never been happier. The fire was on, the tree lights were twinkling, and there were delicious smells coming from the oven.

It was perfect. Or was about to be anyway.

"When are Simone and Albie getting here?"

"They should be here in the next half an hour."

This was her parents' third visit to Credence, having come for the wedding two months ago. And they were staying for just over a week so her mother could judge the ice-sculpture contest again, which was scheduled for New Year's Day.

"Burl and Cora should be here about then, too."

All six of them were sitting down to a huge Christmas Eve dinner together.

Grady stood back to admire the tree, slinging an arm around Suzanne's waist. "You should see the present I got you. It's totally going to win Christmas."

Suzanne smiled. She knew without a doubt that honor would be going to her, but she was happy to indulge him for a while. "Well, come on, then." She dug him in the ribs. "Where is it?"

They said they'd exchange one gift before the night's festivities began, and Suzanne was beside herself with excitement. Letting her go, Grady loped over to the table and grabbed the wrapped gift off the end, ferrying it back in several easy strides.

"Here you go."

Suzanne took it and ripped the paper off eagerly to reveal a truly tacky Christmas sweater. She laughed as she unfolded it to reveal a red V-necked sweater, trimmed with faux fur, two green hands spread over where her breasts would sit, and the slogan *feel the joy* printed beneath.

"Am I right, or am I right? Winning Christmas or what?"

"Very classy." Suzanne laughed. "I love it. But you haven't seen mine yet."

He wiggled his fingers at her. "Hand it over, then, woman."

Suzanne grinned and grabbed the box off the side table next to the couch. She'd packaged it in a shirt box so it wouldn't be immediately obvious to Grady.

Like her, he, too, ripped open the wrapping, then whipped the lid off the box to find another Christmas sweater folded carefully in tissue paper. It was green with a white stylized dinosaur on the front, its triangular body making a Christmas tree, the star on its head and the lights wrapped around its tail. The slogan said *Tree Rex*.

It was funny and cute rather than tacky. But it was still winning Christmas.

Grady grabbed it out of the tissue paper to hold it up. He frowned when there seemed to be a significant amount of it missing. "You wash this first, honey? I think it shrunk." He laughed as he held it up to his chest. "Don't think I could get this over my head."

Suzanne looped her hand through his arm. "That's because it's not meant to go over *your* head, Joshua."

He glanced down at her, and she smiled at him. He smiled back before returning his attention to the sweater. Watching realization dawn like a sunrise over his face would be something Suzanne would never, *ever* forget.

His gaze flicked to hers. "Is this… Does this mean…?"

Grinning like a loon, Suzanne nodded. "Merry Christmas, Joshua. You're going to be a daddy."

"I'm going to be a daddy?" he asked, his face running the gamut of emotions from incredulous to disbelieving to pure and utter joy.

"Yup," she said.

Grady whooped, dropping the sweater to pick her up and spin her around and around and around. Suzanne laughed and hung on until he set her back on her feet again.

"You *definitely* win Christmas," he said.

Suzanne sighed. As long as he was by her side, she'd always win Christmas.

ACKNOWLEDGMENTS

Unlike the hero of this book, I love Christmas! The tinsel, the carols, the tree, the lights. So it was super fun to give my surly rancher a big, fat, OTT Christmas with every wonderfully kitschy thing I could find on the internet thrown into the pot! I hope you enjoyed the sweaters, dominatrix Barbie and the cat baubles as much as I did putting them down on the page.

My thanks as always go to the team at Entangled Publishing who do all their magic behind the scenes to get a book from a Word document into a state where people can buy it in whatever form. Thanks to Curtis Svehlak who collates everything I need and gives it to me in one succinct place exactly when I need it. To Riki Cleveland and Holly Bryant-Simpson who hold my hand through the publicity stuff, which I suck at—really, I do. And thanks to Melanie Smith who pays me—you totally rock!

Special thanks to Stacy Abrams for the copy editing—sorry about the commas, the which's, and the choking thing. And extra special thanks to my editor, Liz Pelletier, who is my biggest cheerleader, who believes in me and seems to know the exact moment my ego needs stroking. I totally forgive her for sending gratuitous drinking pictures of her *and my best friend Leah* who, through freakish coincidence, ended up on the same Alaskan cruise together, while I was slaving over a hot keyboard, in *Australia*, finishing this book.

I forgive Leah, too.

Two last thank-yous. Firstly, to Naima Simone who told me all about melting butter on top of pecan pie to make it a whole other level of yummy. One day you and I, Naima, will have to eat pie together. And secondly to Janeen Wagner Phillips who provided the name Zoom for Grady's turtle. Turtle lovers unite!

The Truth About Cowboys

by Lisa Renee Jones

I had my life figured out.

Engaged to a successful man.

About to make partner at my firm.

Bought a high-rise apartment in downtown Denver.

And then, poof, it's all gone. Now, like in some cheesy romantic comedy, my car has broken down in the pouring rain on my way to "find myself" in The Middle of Nowhere, Texas. Cue hot guy coming to my rescue and changing my tire. This is the part where we flirt and have a meet-cute, right? That's how it works in romance novels, and I should know—after all, I'm coming to Texas to write my own cowboy romance. But nope. This sexy cowboy lights into me about not being prepared for the country roads and how inappropriate my high-heeled boots are.

Little did I know, Jason Jenks would tilt my world into a new dimension with his sinful smirk and his bad attitude. Every time I turn around, he's there to reluctantly save the day. And every time, I think there may be something to that spark we ignite. But there's a reason the majority of country songs are about broken hearts. The closer I get to this man, the closer I get to learning the truth about cowboys.

How to Lose a Guy in 10 Days *meets*
Accidentally on Purpose *by Jill Shalvis in this*
head-over-heels romantic comedy.

the aussie next door

by USA TODAY bestselling author
Stefanie London

American Angie Donovan has never wanted much. When
you grow up getting bounced from foster home to foster
home, you learn not to become attached to anything,
anyone, or any place. But it only took her two days to fall
in love with Australia. With her visa clock ticking, surely
she can fall in love with an Australian—and get hitched—
in two months. Especially if he's as hot and funny as her
next-door neighbor…

Jace Walters has never wanted much—except a bathroom
he didn't have to share. The last cookie all to himself. And
solitude. But when you grow up in a family of seven, you
can kiss those things goodbye. He's *finally* living alone and
working on his syndicated comic strip in privacy. Sure, his
American neighbor is distractingly sexy and annoyingly
nosy, but she'll be gone in a few months…

Except now she's determined to find her perfect match by
checking out every eligible male in the town, and her
choices are even more distracting. So why does it suddenly
feel like he—and his obnoxious tight-knit family, and even
these two wayward dogs—could be exactly what she
needs?

She's just one of the guys…until she's not in USA
Today *bestselling author Cindi Madsen's unique take
on weddings, small towns, and friends falling in love.*

Just One of the Groomsmen

by Cindi Madsen

Addison Murphy is the funny friend, the girl you grab a
beer with—the girl voted most likely to start her own
sweatshirt line. And now that one of her best guy friends is
getting married, she'll add "groomsman" to that list, too.
She'll get through this wedding if it's the last thing she does.
Just don't ask her to dive for any bouquet.

When Tucker Crawford returns to his small hometown, he
expects to see the same old people, feel comfort in the same
old things. He certainly doesn't expect to see the nice pair of
bare legs sticking out from under the hood of a broken-down
car. Certainly doesn't expect to feel his heart beat faster
when he realizes they belong to one of his best friends.

If he convinces Addie to give him a chance, they could be
electric…or their break-up could split their tight-knit
group in two.

Hiding the way he feels from the guys through bachelor
parties, cake tastings, and rehearsals is one thing. But just
asTucker realizes that Addie truly could be the perfect
woman for him—he was just too stupid to realize it—now
she's leaving to follow her own dreams. He's going to need
to do a lot of compromising if he's going to convince her to
take a shot at forever with him—on her terms this time.

AMARA
an imprint of Entangled Publishing LLC